MISS DELIGHTFUL

MISCHIEF IN MAYFAIR BOOK THREE

GRACE BURROWES

DEDICATION

To those who speak out

CHAPTER ONE

"That is a baby." Alasdhair MacKay stood back lest the woman holding the infant knock him flat as she sailed over the threshold into his foyer.

"Indeed, Major MacKay. How astute you are."

"*Former* major." Alasdhair closed the door because the day was chilly and babies were fragile. Also because this situation needed no witnesses among the nosy neighbors. "And who might you be?"

He turned his signature commanding-officer glower on the woman and allowed his burr to deepen to the consistency of a growl. He did not so much as glance at the wee child in her arms.

"Miss Dorcas Delancey." She dipped a curtsey, baby and all. "This good fellow appears to be your son, so I will leave him with you—"

"He is not my son." Of that Alasdhair was emphatically sure.

She turned serious gray-green eyes from Alasdhair to the baby and back again. "Perhaps not your legitimate son, but there is a certain—"

"That child is not my son, and you and I have not been introduced, Miss Delancey." Alasdhair would recall an introduction to such a woman. She wore propriety like a Sunday cloak and could probably deliver whole sermons on mankind's fallenness.

She was no classic beauty, from eyes that were neither slate nor emerald, to hair that aspired to auburn but stopped just past dark brown. Her features were elegant, though any emotion in them was held in check by an air of brisk detachment.

She would be difficult to shock, and even harder to impress.

As was Alasdhair, did she but know it.

"You recall your activities from well over a year ago?" she asked. "The child is a good six months or thereabouts. He's beginning to teethe, you see, and that is a good thing. The landlady heard him yelling and realized his mama was not with him. He was having rather a bad time of it."

A coldness assailed Alasdhair, the same coldness that had come over him in battle. His body would function with heightened efficiency, his mind would leap along paths of strategy and intuition, while his heart turned to granite.

But there was no battle here. No enemy. Only this demurely dressed female with her drawing-room English and earnest gaze, along with that... that bundle of trouble.

"I am sorry for the lad's misfortune, but he is not my son."

"He is still your responsibility." She unfurled the word *responsibility* like a pristine banner of righteous certainty. "Melanie Fairchild named you as his guardian, and as she is no longer extant, and her will is quite clear, that makes you—"

"*What?*" The coldness had never made Alasdhair light-headed before. "I saw her just last week. She was in excellent health." She'd been quiet when last Alasdhair had called on her, perhaps tired. Only that. "She cannot be dead."

"I am sorry," Miss Delancey said. "You cared for her."

"Of course I cared for her." Alasdhair cared for them all, fool that he was. "She had come so far, against such odds. She had a cousin or auntie who was helping her, though the rest of her family is a worthless pack of pious hypocrites. She doted on that baby, went on and on about him."

What a smart lad he was, how merry, what a good sleeper. Melanie had rhapsodized about one tiny infant and foreseen a great future for him, despite his mother's scandalous circumstances.

"I apologize for being the bearer of sad tidings, Major, but you will have young John here to console you."

"No, I will not."

The baby gurgled, a happy sound accompanied by a tiny fist flailing in the direction of Miss Delancey's not-quite-dainty nose.

"Might we continue this discussion somewhere warmer, Major MacKay?"

"Plain MacKay will do." Manners required that Alasdhair take the lady's burden from her, but he could not. "This way."

He led her through a town house that was more of a roofed campsite than a dwelling. London was not his home, God be thanked, but he bided here in cold weather and had cousins here. No siblings in Town, and certainly not a son.

"My study," Alasdhair said, opening the door reluctantly. "My guest parlor is unheated." Equally important, the guest parlor had windows visible from the street, and the draperies on those windows were tied back, the better to display Alasdhair's social life to any passerby.

Fortunately, he had no social life.

Based on the lady's merino wool cloak, matching blue gloves, and nacre buttons, she was one of those women who thrived on going from friend to friend, collecting gossip. She would expect a tea tray. Where were her chaperone, lady's maid, and footmen, for that matter?

"It's half day," Alasdhair went on, "which is why you find me answering my own front door and without help in the kitchen."

"You will need a wet nurse," Miss Delancey said, taking a place in the middle of Alasdhair's favorite napping sofa. "I'll have Mrs. Sidmouth send along the baby's dresses and whatnot, and those will tide you over for a time. He's taking some cereal, but he wasn't yet weaned."

Alasdhair remained on his feet, pacing the length of the carpet. "Miss Delancey, I care not which society for the oppression of beggars you represent, but I must observe that your hearing appears deficient. I cannot take in that baby. I am a bachelor. I have no staff to care for a child. I have no wish to care for a child."

Not quite accurate. Alasdhair would save them all if he could, and their mothers, but he had no *ability* to care for a child.

"Has anybody seen to Melanie's final arrangements?" He could not bear the thought of her lying in a pauper's grave, nobody to mourn her, nobody to leave a single flower.

"Please do sit, Mr. MacKay. You have had a shock."

Why were women such as Miss Delancey always telling others what to do? "How did she die?"

Miss Delancey adjusted the blanket swaddling the baby. "She surrendered herself to the embrace of Father Thames. No inquest has been held because we have no body. A woman fitting Melanie's description made her way to the Strand Bridge last night, and Melanie's best bonnet and slippers washed up on the morning tide."

The proper name for that newly opened bridge was Waterloo Bridge, an irony when many of the women who chose to die there were war widows. Alasdhair perched a hip against the battered desk. He'd have a word with the river police and see what the mud larks had to say.

First, he had to get this woman, *and that baby*, out of his house. She would see to the lad, come fire, flood, famine, or frost fair.

"Send the boy to his mother's family," he said. "They can pretend, as all the best families do, that he's the offspring of a widowed cousin in Scotland with too many mouths to feed. Make him into a badge of virtue for the very Christians who all but threw him to the lions."

One do-gooder spinster relation had taken pity on the child.

Melanie had never mentioned her by name, but the pittance that auntie or cousin had regularly sent along had been enough that Melanie had been able to cease selling her favors. Alasdhair had made sure of that.

"With you named as legal guardian, Major, Melanie's family would have no authority to raise the child."

"I will cheerfully give my permission for them to do just that."

"Are you ever truly cheerful, Mr. MacKay?"

Miss Delancey tucked the child against the corner of the sofa, banking pillows around him. Swaddled in his blanket, the baby could hardly crawl off across the cushions, but still, the lady took precautions.

Did the lad even know how to crawl?

"I will be very cheerful," Alasdhair said, "when I contemplate this boy growing up in the bosom of his nearest and dearest. I am a stranger to him. No relation at all. I have no children and don't expect I will ever be so blessed. Take him away, Miss Delancey, and I wish you best of luck with him."

The words hurt, like telling a wounded man he was bound for the surgeon's tent. A boy barely shaving was to lose a limb, if not his life, and all Alasdhair had been able to do was stop by to offer a nip from his flask and prayer that the soldier would survive the day.

"Melanie chose you to raise him, Mr. MacKay. You had best reconcile yourself to that honor." The woman rose, and though she was not tall, she carried herself with dignity. She undid the frogs of her cloak and draped it over the sofa.

Her figure was a trifle on the lush side, somewhat at variance with that ruthlessly reserved expression.

To be a plain creature of mature years in a society that valued beauty, youth, and malice equally was a tribulation, a battlefield of sorts. She'd chosen aloof dignity and virtuous meddling as her weapons. An interesting combination.

She inspected the framed copy of the dispatch mentioning the *notable gallantry* of Major Alasdhair MacKay and Major Dylan

Powell. From there, she moved to a landscape of the River Tweed, and Alasdhair realized he was being lectured with silence.

"I am no relation to that child, Miss Delancey, but I suspect you are."

She smiled, a sweet, astonishingly impish curve of her lips. "I am indeed an exponent of that tribe of pious hypocrites who turned their backs on Melanie. She and I were cousins. We grew up together, and when she ran off with her handsome soldier, I knew exactly what her fate would be. We lost touch for a few years, and then she wrote to me. I thanked God for that."

"Why not take in the boy now?"

The lady folded her arms. Perhaps in deference to her cousin's passing, she was attired in a blue so dark as to qualify as mourning, or nearly so.

"What do you think his fate would be, with my father angling for a bishopric and my great-uncle already in possession of one? Do you suppose John would be permitted to dine with us at table? Would he be made to say the grace and quote all the nasty proverbs and passages about ungrateful children, Jezebels, and Magdalens? I can assure you that would be the least of the miseries to befall him, and heaven help the boy if he's given to running in the house, yelling, or talking back. He would be bread-and-watered at public school to within an inch of his sanity—for his own good, of course."

"Nobody consigns babies to bread and water."

Miss Delancey regarded Alasdhair steadily, and his insides went squirmy.

"Babies cry, Mr. MacKay, a lot. They make messes and drool and refuse to sleep when it's dark outside. Babies cannot tell us what hurts or frightens them. They can only squall and whimper or go off their feed. If they are lucky, they grow up. Don't delude yourself that I would be free to intercede much on John's behalf as he matures."

Miss Delancey stalked over to Alasdhair, her bootheels rapping against the carpet. "If you cannot take in this child, then arrange for him to be fostered someplace safe. Not one of those dreadful baby farms, not the foundling homes. Take responsibility for him, or you are wishing upon the boy a fate no child should endure. Melanie asked this of you, and I demand it."

Alasdhair's paternal great-uncle had been an old-style Lowland Methodist. Three-hour sermons had been nothing in his congregation, and grace could go on for half an hour when the old man was in good form.

The squirmy feeling acquired the dimensions of resignation. Defeat was imminent, retreat a certainty.

"You may leave him with me for now," Alasdhair said, "but use your charitable connections to find a proper home for him. Your father's household might not be appropriate for an illegitimate child, but a soldier's bachelor quarters aren't much better."

Her smile returned, a benevolence so palpable and good-hearted that basking and wallowing came to mind.

"I knew Melanie's faith in you was justified. I will return tomorrow morning with a wet nurse if I can find one. John can make do with warm, thin porridge until morning, though you will also need a supply of clean clouts."

Alasdhair eyed the bundle waving chubby fists at nothing in particular. "Why will I need a supply of clouts? He's only one boy."

Miss Delancey's smile acquired a hint of mischievous. "Use your nose, sir. It's a very fine nose, and I'm sure you will deduce the situation soon enough. I will see myself out. Until tomorrow."

She shook out her cloak and swept it around her shoulders with a graceful flourish, then marched for the door. She had a good, sturdy march, typical of the inveterate crusader.

Those thoughts hummed along at the periphery of Alasdhair's mind, while the reality of the child's presence occupied the center of his mental stage. The front door closed, and the ticking clock on the mantel exactly matched the cadence of Alasdhair's thumping heart.

"You and me, lad," he said, "for the nonce. Only for the nonce." His brisk tone apparently did not fool the child, who regarded him with owlish caution. "The lady has gone, and we're to make do on short rations until she comes back. I'm MacKay."

How was the boy to learn to speak if nobody talked to him? Alasdhair came to within two feet of the sofa and bent to take up the child.

He straightened, assailed by a spectacularly foul miasma. "That woman. That woman ambushed me. That infernal woman *ambushed* me."

The baby flailed his fists and tried to kick against his blankets. His little face squinched up, and Alasdhair had no choice but to lift him off the sofa.

"I will court-martial her," Alasdhair muttered, trying to cradle the infant securely, but not too closely. "I will have her drummed out of the regiment. I will strip her of rank and see her reduced to private. Put me on latrine duty, will she?"

He kept up a similar patter—the boy seemed to enjoy it—until they reached the laundry. Alasdhair set the baby among a basket of folded towels and took a knife to the first clean length of linen he found.

"THAT IS a *table napkin* unless I miss my guess." Dorcas peered at the cloth tied about John's little waist. The linen was edged with white-work embroidery on one side, though the makeshift nappy drooped around John's belly.

"You see before you the remains of a table runner," Mr. MacKay said. "I seldom entertain, and needs must. The boy enjoys healthy digestion."

The boy had reached the indignant phase of hunger. "Timmens, you will please take Master John to the kitchen. He has missed you."

Timmens pressed a kiss to the baby's crown. "I've missed him too. Come along, poppet. Time for your breakfast."

Mr. MacKay watched the wet nurse depart, though his expression gave away nothing. Not relief, not worry, not gratitude for a problem solved. Melanie had spoken highly of him in her last letter, but then, Melanie's judgment when it came to the male of the species was suspect.

"That is John's regular wet nurse?" he asked.

"She is. Her baby was a chrisom-child. Poor thing expired in less than a fortnight. Melanie tended to John herself for the first few months, but she claimed her stores were inadequate. According to Melanie's landlady, Timmens was stopping by first thing in the day and at bedtime, and Melanie was making do with milk porridge otherwise.

"You'll want proper nappies for John," Dorcas went on, perching on the edge of Mr. MacKay's lumpy sofa. "A half dozen or so cloths per day. He'll need a cradle, too. I gather he was sharing Melanie's cot, and that cannot have been an ideal arrangement."

"You'd begrudge the lad his mother's warmth to cuddle up to?"

"Of course not, but a child can fall out of the bed onto the cold, hard floor, Mr. MacKay. Then too, an exhausted mother needs her sleep." This knowledge was theoretical, of course, as most of Dorcas's knowledge of children was.

Mr. MacKay prowled around behind the desk, but did not take a seat. This meant Dorcas had to look up at him from her perch on the sofa, and farther up than usual. She was surprised to conclude that he could have been attractive, had he exerted himself to show a little charm.

The major was not handsome in the fashionable sense, though. His physiognomy was the rough draft of a sermon on masculine pulchritude. Dark hair in need of a trim, enough height to be imposing. His most striking feature was a pair of brilliant blue eyes, the same shade as the infant John's but devoid of innocence. A weary soldier's eyes, looking out on the world in stoic anticipation of the next battle, or looking inward on memories of combats won and lost.

He was broad-shouldered and muscular, and much as his physique lacked refinement, his brow, nose, and jaw were sculpted with an eye for durability rather than beauty. He would age into craggy distinction, and in a fight, he would be tireless and without mercy.

Despite that daunting conclusion, Dorcas would rather John grow up under Alasdhair MacKay's protection than in a household of her family's choosing.

"He has a cradle," Mr. MacKay said, scowling at the bucolic landscape over the mantel. "I made it for him and delivered it myself. Not fancy, but sufficient for the purpose."

"You made a cradle?"

"I spent some summers with an auntie as a lad, and her husband was a master carpenter. A cradle is a good project for a boy learning the trade. The result can be plain, fancy, or in-between. Designed to rock, to sit level, to do either. If I'd had more time, I might have prettied it up a bit, but Melanie wasn't sure exactly when the baby would come."

Dorcas hated, hated, hated to think of Melanie anticipating a birth alone, uncertain, and without family. That Mr. MacKay had not only provided a cradle, but also made it with his own hands meant much.

"You are certain he's not your son?"

His gaze acquired a glacial quality. "I do not take advantage of ladies fallen on hard times, Miss Delancey."

Dorcas rose rather than be glowered down at. "Very little taking advantage was involved. Melanie was a willing participant in her own sorry fate, Mr. MacKay. I warned her that her gallant officer would abandon her. I knew with the inevitability of original sin that she was authoring her own ruin, but she would not be dissuaded. Her father hasn't spoken her name since the day she left except to cite her as a bad example."

Dorcas's papa, to his credit, mentioned Melanie kindly on rare occasion, even prayerfully, but never in front of company.

"So Melanie loved the wrong person," Mr. MacKay said. "Many a woman has done likewise. So has many a man."

Had *he* loved the wrong person? The question was irrelevant, a pesky distraction from whatever point Dorcas had been meaning to make.

"My cousin is dead, Mr. MacKay. She was a good-hearted, merry, mischievous girl, then a disgraced woman, and now she's d-dead." *Oh, pinfeathers. Not now. Please not a bout of the weeps now.*

The tears had been threatening at intervals since Dorcas had received the note yesterday morning. She'd fought them off, ignored them, and refused to acknowledge the grief that drove them. John had to be tended to and Melanie's affairs put in order, all without arousing Papa's notice.

Mr. MacKay brandished a lawn handkerchief with purple flowers embroidered along the edges. "Melanie is at peace," he said, stepping closer. "She is no longer anybody's handy bad example, no longer suffering. We will see to John, as she wished us to, and you can ensure the boy knows your happy memories of his mother."

His voice, so laden with command and confidence, had become an instrument of consolation. From burr to purr, and the shift wasn't so much one of volume, though he was speaking softly, as it was intonation. Grooms knew how to speak to horses like this, to soothe and reassure even while the words themselves might be prosaic.

Dorcas meant to snatch the handkerchief from Mr. MacKay's hand, but she missed, and instead, her fingers closed on his wrist. He came near enough to touch the fine linen to her cheek, and then she was leaning against him, wailing more loudly than John when his belly was empty and his teeth were hurting.

Mr. MacKay's arm settled around Dorcas's shoulders, and though it meant the complete surrender of her dignity, she yielded to the tears and let herself be held.

The comfort Mr. MacKay offered now was all the more substantial for being silent. He stroked Dorcas's back and stood, as solid and unyielding as a granite tor, while she mourned a cousin who should not have died, much less so miserably. Guilt limned her grief, as did a fortifying bolt of rage.

Rage at Melanie, for all her stupid choices, and at Uncle Simon, for trying to pray and exhort high spirits out of a girl who'd been meant for smiles and laughter rather than dour piety. Rage at a society that insisted women be raised in ignorance and judged without mercy when their lack of wisdom resulted in a mis-step.

"I'm sorry," Dorcas said as an after-shudder passed through her. "I am not usually prone to histrionics." She stepped back and dabbed at her cheeks with the handkerchief. The fragrance wasn't exactly lavender, maybe lavender and sage? No… heather. The sachets in Mr. MacKay's wardrobe and clothes press were apparently scented with heather.

"You have lost a cousin and dear friend from childhood," he said, holding out a silver flask. "When our hearts are broken, we ignore the sorrow at our peril. Have a nip."

The note of command had returned with that last suggestion. A note of challenge too. Dorcas heeded the challenge, in part because Mr. MacKay was trying to be helpful and in part because, outside of a sickroom tonic, she'd never been permitted strong spirits.

The flask was warm and embossed with a crest, a sprig of some herb or other. Dorcas took a cautious sip, while Mr. MacKay moved away. A whiff of honey and oak was followed by cool fire trailing down her gullet. The fire muted into a glow, and the glow developed soft edges that rippled out from her middle.

"That is pleasant. Thank you." She passed the flask back rather than try another sip.

Mr. MacKay returned the container to an inside pocket. "I mean to have a word with the river police, and I will speak with the landlady as well."

"About?"

"Melanie was in good spirits," he said. "She was taking in mending, watching another bairn in the evenings, getting by. She had her own healthy little boy underfoot and a few friends. She had much to be proud of and no reason to take her own life."

Dorcas folded up the handkerchief and put it on the blotter, though she was not nearly as composed as her steady hands might have suggested. "My father would say Melanie had much to be ashamed of."

"Then," Mr. MacKay replied, "meaning no disrespect to you, Miss Delancey, your father is an idiot. He probably thinks all females should be born apologizing for an error Eve made millennia ago. Adam raised his boys so the one killed the other, but we don't hear anybody blethering on about that spectacular failure of fatherhood, do we? Adam didn't keep a proper eye on his missus either, but again, he's not taken to task for that, is he?"

These blasphemies were so outlandish that Dorcas did not dignify them with a rebuttal. "Please do not think to cause a scandal, Mr. MacKay. Women regularly throw themselves off London's bridges."

That observation, while sadly true, was also a betrayal of Melanie. Another betrayal.

"Your late cousin is not *women*," Mr. MacKay retorted, "and Melanie had overcome much. She did not do herself an injury when she was abandoned by her dashing swain. She did not do herself an injury when she realized she was with child. She did not do herself an injury by trying to rid herself of that child, and she would not leave wee John all alone in the world with only the likes of me standing between him and your family."

Dorcas could not see that there was anything particularly wrong with *the likes* of Alasdhair MacKay. "I insist that you allow Melanie to rest in peace, sir. Poking your nose into a tragedy won't make it any less of a tragedy."

He nudged the pretty landscape over the mantel a quarter inch higher at one corner, then nudged it back to its original position.

"You can come with me to call on Melanie's landlady, or you can go back to memorizing Scripture, or whatever you spend your time on. I intend to find out what happened to John's cradle, at the very least."

He left off admiring the landscape and arched a dark brow at Dorcas.

That single gesture issued another challenge—a dare, even. "I'm coming with you," she said. "I'm coming with you to ensure you don't cause unnecessary bother to Mrs. Sidmouth or start the wrong sort of talk. Melanie's memory must not be burdened with further scandal."

He opened the door and gestured Dorcas through, something pugnacious about his courtesy. She preceded him to the foyer, head held high, but inside, her emotions were rioting.

Melanie had reestablished contact with Dorcas, who had been all too happy to offer what aid she could. Melanie had been doing honest work. She had no longer been attached to *that man*. She had clearly loved her son, and in Mr. MacKay, she'd apparently had an ally, if not a friend.

And Mr. MacKay was asking valid questions.

But oh, the upheaval and drama. If Papa found out Dorcas had been in touch with Melanie, if he learned of the circumstances of Melanie's death, if he learned about John... Papa no longer shouted, but his silent reproaches and muttered snippets of Scripture were worse than any tirade.

"You must promise me discretion, Mr. MacKay."

He settled Dorcas's cloak around her shoulders. "If I find out Melanie's death was at all suspicious, then the only thing I can promise you is one hell of an uproar, and I do keep my promises, Miss Delancey."

Of that, Dorcas had no doubt. No doubt whatsoever.

CHAPTER TWO

Women came in two varieties.

The first was above Alasdhair's touch, a category that included ladies from English families with any means. Between his chronically serious nature, his unprepossessing looks, and his Scottish antecedents, he had little to offer such ladies.

And they had nothing to offer him. In the second category were females deserving of his concern.

All women deserved his respect, but not all merited his concern. He'd been concerned for Melanie. He was concerned for old Mrs. Bootle, who lived next door. He was concerned for the Covent Garden streetwalkers and for the flower seller on the corner. He was concerned for many women, but Dorcas Delancey did not fit in any of the categories that would merit his concern.

He usually liked a quiet woman. Miss Delancey, since leaving his house, had said not one word, and he did not like that at all.

He was at ease with women who grumbled, lamenting the chilly weather, the gray skies, the detestable coal smoke that turned houses, gloves, bonnets, and coach horses sooty in the space of a few hours.

Miss Delancey hadn't uttered a single complaint in his hearing, and he wished she would.

He preferred women who were pragmatic. Until Miss Delancey had shed a few tears, she might as well have been delivering a load of potatoes as surrendering her wee cousin into the arms of a stranger. Pragmatic in the extreme.

But she had wept. She had wept genuinely, noisily, heat coming off her as she'd yielded utterly to grief. She had wept, and just as quickly as the storm had descended, she'd regained her composure.

Women learned to do that when they followed a marching army to war.

"Where are you taking me?" she asked as Alasdhair turned down an alley.

"To Mrs. Sidmouth's boardinghouse."

"This is an *alley*, Mr. MacKay." Miss Delancey came to a halt and gave the alley the sort of look an artillery mule generally reserved for flooded river crossings.

"Indeed, it is an alley, and as alleys are wont to do, it runs between streets, thus saving us time and travel."

She glanced around at a neighborhood that qualified as decent, but not fancy. Affordable, in other words.

"I cannot be seen to dodge down an alley with you. Bad enough I have accepted your escort on short notice. You are no relation to me, and no family friend of long standing, that I should entrust my welfare to you."

"I am an officer," Alasdhair began, only for her to wave a hand at him.

"Amery Beauclerk was an officer. He ruined my cousin."

Logic in a female was a vexatious quality. "I am a gentleman."

"Meaning you do not work to earn your bread and thus have more idle hours in which to get up to mischief."

Some emotion was trying to gain Alasdhair's notice, which was of no moment when he had a task to fulfill. "Idleness might be true of your English gentlemen, but I am a Scot, and indolence is foreign to our nature. You agreed to accompany me, Miss Delancey, and the longer we stand here spatting like a pair of fishmongers, the more likely you are to cause that talk you seem so wary of."

Finely arched brows twitched lower. "Alleys are dark and noisome."

She sounded as if she were reading the stitchery on a sampler. "Have you ever been in an alley?"

"Of course I have."

"Meaning you cross from your papa's garden to his mews. Come along, and I will introduce you to the wicked pleasures to be had in London's better alleys."

He winged his arm, a courtesy he'd not thought to offer previously. She coiled her hand at his elbow, her fingers lighter than winter sunshine on his sleeve.

"Some alleys are foul," Alasdhair said. "You are right about that, but this is not a foul neighborhood. This is where shopkeepers retire and old sea captains finally get to enjoy some time with their grandchildren. These alleys are as tidy and pleasant as the local citizenry. The birds love the alleys, and thus the cats do as well."

"And the rats," Miss Delancey said, peering around as her grip on Alasdhair's arm tightened. "Do they love alleys?"

"They love all of London, from what I can see." The figurative rats as well as the literal ones. "That's a sparrow hawk up in that maple. A female, given her size and splendid plumage. She's the better hunter, and she'll keep the rats from sight as long as she's up there."

"The female is larger?"

"And takes down the bigger prey. Unfortunately, she'll scare off the redwings, fieldfares, and robins who probably call this alley home."

"What do the other birds find to eat this time of year?"

What did the children scavenging London's alleys find to eat as winter descended? What fare did the streetwalkers and beggars subsist on?

"They manage. An apple core will delight a flock of thrushes for a morning. Rowan and cotoneaster feed them through the winter. The robins in particular go where the food is in winter, rather than defending a territory. That all changes when it's time to build a nest."

The winter wind had swept the cobbles bare of leaves, though the alley bore the pleasant scent of horses and hay.

"How do you know so much about birds?" Miss Delancey asked.

"I owe my life to birds. In Spain, we used birdcalls as signals between patrols and pickets. Whether the recruits hailed from Scotland, Wales, Ireland, or England, the lads knew their birdsongs. The French never cracked that code, for some reason, and thus I survived."

"Was the war very bad?" Miss Delancey asked.

Not a question anybody had put to Alasdhair previously. He gave some thought to his answer, because for Miss Delancey of the earnest gray-green eyes, only a thoughtful answer would do.

"Yes, it was awful. Imagine a pretty, sunny plain, perfect for grazing or growing fodder. Then imagine that every few yards, lying in that lush grass, is a man or a boy either killed in battle or longing for death. You can hear the flies from hundreds of yards away, see them like a miasma darkening the sky, and the stench..."

He fell silent. Be she above his touch, worthy of his concern, or neither, Miss Delancey did not deserve this recitation.

"I'm sorry," she said. "If we are consigning our men and boys to hell, we ought to at least make certain they've committed some mortal sin other than patriotism first."

"Not patriotism, Miss Delancey. Most of the enlisted men simply wanted to eat. In Scotland, the entire weaving industry was cut down by the power looms, and all those weavers' sons still needed to eat. So we made them killers and sent them to Spain, and the factory owners were left in peace."

Unlike in England, where the Luddites and machine breakers had wrought terrible mischief.

"Would you do it again?" Miss Delancey asked as they

approached the next street. "Would you serve again, knowing what you know now?"

"I served with two cousins," Alasdhair said. "The best of men, and they both came home safe and sound. There were some good memories." Dylan Powell and Orion Goddard were more than cousins and fellow officers, more than Alasdhair's brothers, even. Goddard had recently acquired a wife, though, a curious development.

"You dodge my question," Miss Delancey said. "You have not decided if the sacrifices our soldiers made was worth the gain."

"What gain, Miss Delancey? Hundreds of thousands of casualties on both sides, hungry women and children, and ruined land, and all so France has the same family on the throne they started with twenty years ago. For whom or what is that a victory?"

He expected her to have a handy retort. Women like Dorcas Delancey always had handy retorts. They spouted platitudes about God's will, the rights of Englishmen, and other drivel straight from the choruses of *Rule Britannia*.

"One cannot simply set aside regrets and wrong turns, can one?" Miss Delancey asked as the sparrow hawk winged away to some more promising alley. "What's done is done, and all the apologies and recriminations in the world cannot undo the harm we've caused or suffered."

What could Miss Delancey have to regret so bitterly that she spoke as one well acquainted with wrong turns?

"We arrive to our destination," Alasdhair said, nodding at the house across from the alley's entrance. "Mrs. Sidmouth's establishment."

Miss Delancey glanced behind them, down the alley. "That really is a shortcut, isn't it?"

"I would not lead you astray, miss."

She gave him the sort of skeptical perusal she'd turned on the alley, but said nothing.

As Alasdhair escorted her across the street, he realized that the problem with Miss Delancey was that she was both above his touch—Englishwoman, clearly from means, proper family, et cetera—and a woman who piqued his concern. She was too quiet, too noticing, and too stoic for a preacher's pampered daughter.

She was a problem, in other words.

Another problem.

~

"SHOULDN'T YOU HAVE A COMPANION?" Mr. MacKay asked as he rapped on Mrs. Sidmouth's door. "A few footmen trailing respectfully in your wake?"

"I am too old to have a companion. Papa took the coach today, and thus I am also free of coachies, grooms, footmen, and other bothers."

"You can't be seen on my arm, but you're permitted to jaunt about Town on your own? Not the done thing, Miss Delancey."

Well, no. It wasn't, for most young women, though Dorcas was fast parting from even a fiction of youth. "I am careful. I am also nine-and-twenty years old, the lady of my father's house, and firmly on the shelf. When I go shopping, when I pay calls, when I attend services, I observe the proprieties. When I am about my charitable endeavors, I am usually in the company of my fellow committeewomen. If they cannot accompany me, then the shield of righteous virtue is my escort."

He rapped on the door. "You sneak out of camp."

"I do not sneak, sir."

"You sneak," he retorted, "and because you have perfected the demeanor of a meddling do-gooder, your deviousness goes undetected."

"I *am* a meddling do-gooder."

He looked her over, his inspection dispassionate. "Which causes claim the honor of your allegiance?"

"Fallen women."

"I knew it." He rapped again on the door, hard enough to rouse the watch. "You bundle them into Magdalen houses, where they are worked to death under circumstances that would horrify most graduates of Newgate. Once a week, your victims are permitted to sing in church, but only behind a screen, lest the very sight of them contaminate the souls of their betters. Bleating hypocrites, the lot of you."

"I am not a hypocrite." Not in the sense he meant. "I do not advocate condemning such women to Magdalen houses."

"You give them a ticket to Dublin instead? I hear that's where the anti-begging societies are shipping our poor lately."

"Of course I don't give them—"

The door opened, revealing a pockmarked young maid with flushed cheeks and a dingy mobcap.

"Mrs. Sidmouth is off t' market, and we've only the one room to let. If you… Oh, it's you, MacKay. Wot yer want?"

"Let us in, Sally. This is Melanie's cousin, and we've come to collect the last of her effects."

The maid stepped back. "Not much to collect, sir. Mrs. Sidmouth will want ye to write out a list of what ye took so there's no bother later. She's canny like that. How's the boy?"

"He's with me," Mr. MacKay replied. "Appears to be thriving."

The maid grinned. "Ye'll teach him yer Rabbie Burns songs and have him swillin' whisky in no time. I suppose I can let ye into Melanie's room. Been a couple people come by to see it, but Mrs. Sidmouth didn't care for neither of 'em. They poked around a lot, though it's just a room, iddn't it?"

She chattered about the tribulation of three flights of stairs, her auntie's chilblains, and the threat of snow as she led Dorcas and Mr. MacKay up to Melanie's room. The chamber itself was chilly and dim. Neither the fire in the grate nor any candles had been lit.

The bed was a pathetic little cot, the wardrobe missing half its doors. The spindle-backed chair near the window had no cushion, and the hearth rug was threadbare and coming unraveled. Everything was painfully neat, which made the lack of any comforts all the more pitiful.

"Where is her rocking chair?" Mr. MacKay asked. "I bought her a rocking chair."

"And it were beautiful," the maid said. "I took a turn in it, before she sold it. That chair never made it up the first flight of stairs, Mr. MacKay. A man came by and give her coin fer it."

Dorcas opened the wardrobe door. "And her blue wool shawl?" Dorcas had knit it herself, using her smallest needles and the softest wool she could find. "I made John a blanket to match as well."

The maid edged toward the door. "I wouldn't know, ma'am. I'd best be about me duties. It's laundry day. Shoulda been Monday, but the laundresses had to do up all the linen at some grand house having a winter ball, which I never heard of such a thing before. We're all at sixes and sevens."

"Sally, where's John's cradle?" MacKay had not raised his voice, but the maid came to a halt two feet shy of the door.

"Sold."

"Did Melanie sell it?"

"Aye, to the same man."

MacKay peered out the window, which was grimy with coal smoke. "Describe him."

"Pleasant to look at, but shifty eyes. Sandy hair, mustache, middlin' tall, middlin' decent. Mrs. Sidmouth didn't like him, but then, she don't like nobody, 'cept you, of course, Major."

Dorcas closed the wardrobe's only door, a pathetic gesture in the direction of Melanie's privacy. The poor woman hadn't possessed half a wardrobe's worth of apparel. Closing the single door thus hid her entire store of clothing from view.

"Why does Mrs. Sidmouth like Mr. MacKay?" Dorcas asked.

"He's handy," Sally replied with the eagerness of one preparing to wax eloquent. "The market pony sprung a shoe, and Mr. MacKay got it off him without laming the little bugger. The boiler weren't working in the laundry room, and he fixed that, and when the flues are stuck, or the window won't open, he knows exactly how to deal with 'em, but he don't bust nothin'. Mrs. Sidmouth hates it when the gentlemen boarders force the windows and locks and whatnot and break everything."

"A useful sort of man," Dorcas said.

"Most useful, and he could charm that baby, no matter how fretful the lad—"

"Sally." MacKay's tone was mild, and yet he conveyed a rebuke. "You are needed in the laundry, I believe."

"Aye. Filthy laundry doesn't do itself, does it?" She sketched a curtsey, sent an admiring glance in Mr. MacKay's direction, and withdrew.

"Tell me about the blue shawl," Mr. MacKay said. "When did you send it along?"

"September, when the nights became chilly. I'd already sent John's blanket, and the wool was such a pleasure to work with, so soft in my hands, that I decided to make the matching shawl. I sized it generously, to keep Melanie's knees warm, or to be used for extra bedding, but it's not in her wardrobe."

He peered under the bed, then opened and closed the drawers of a rickety bureau. "No shawl, no blanket. Maybe she kept them in the boarders' parlor."

"We need to inventory what's here first, don't we?"

"Mrs. Sidmouth send you Melanie's clothes and to blazes with the rest. No cradle, no rocker. I assumed those were up here in her room. Melanie and I always met in the parlor, and it never occurred to me..." He gazed around the dingy little chamber, his eyes bleak. "I should have checked. I should have asked Mrs. Sidmouth or Sally. I should have known something was amiss."

"I did not even meet with Melanie in the parlor. I communicated with her through the post and sent along packages and coin that way. When I came by yesterday to fetch the baby, Mrs. Sidmouth brought him out to my coach."

Mr. MacKay ran a hand over the top of the hard little chair. "Didn't want to get your hands dirty?"

Dorcas had vast experience curbing her temper. She could cajole entire committees of beldames, reason with bishops, and keep order among feuding domestics, but Alasdhair MacKay's question offended her past all bearing.

He could be a kind, decent man, apparently, though he was also snide, judgmental, and condescending. Then too, Melanie had sent John into his keeping rather than entrust the child to her own cousin.

Dorcas stalked over to him, standing between him and the door lest he think to take the usual male dodge of exiting the stage.

"I hinted, Mr. MacKay. Said in my notes that I would like to meet John. I offered to come by. I made express requests to renew in person the bond Melanie and I shared in our youth. She ignored me, she demurred, she pleaded fatigue or a sniffle or anything rather than allow me to see her circumstances firsthand. She was *ashamed*, and I hate that. She did not come to this pass all on her own, and yet, she alone was left to deal with the shame of it. The magnitude of that injustice defies description."

Mr. MacKay's expression was devoid of emotion. "Don't you dare cry again. I forbid it."

This close to his person, Dorcas caught a whiff of fresh, heathery fragrance. She patted his lapel when she wanted to slap him. "I don't cry when I'm furious, Mr. MacKay."

A curious moment ensued, in which Dorcas was unwilling to step back, as if in her very person, as unprepossessing as she was, she could compel some sort of accountability from this seasoned officer. She gave him the same baleful stare he'd turned on her. Flat, unflinching, cold...

A corner of his mouth tipped up. "I apologize, Miss Delancey. I have leaped to conclusions that are apparently in error. I beg your pardon for my mistake. Let's be going, shall we? I want to talk to Mrs. Sidmouth, and that means coming back another time."

He hadn't quite smiled. That little quirk of his lips had been fleeting and barely reached his eyes, but for a moment, he'd not been the austere soldier, but rather, the gallant officer.

"Don't try to cozen me," Dorcas said, marching for the door. "Don't flatter me, don't charm me, and do not, on your most feckless day, think to flirt with me. If I even suspect—"

He touched her arm as they passed into the dingy corridor. "If I flirt with you, Miss Delancey, you will not be left to suspect. You will know it, and if I go about the task properly, your reaction will be anything but a nervous scold."

"Now you flatter yourself."

He peered down at her. "I am an honest man, and I speak the honest truth. We can argue about that another day. We have a pawnshop to visit."

Good thought. Dorcas was too wroth with him to concede that aloud. Had he offered that little proclamation about his abilities as a flirt any time prior to the past five minutes, she would have been amused—also too polite to laugh in his face.

But she'd seen that hint of a smile, seen the fleeting warmth in his eyes and the crack in the armor he wore on life's battlefield. If Alasdhair MacKay ever did flirt with her, she'd be far too surprised—and pleased—to offer him any sort of scold in return.

Which was, of course, of absolutely no moment when they had a pawnshop to visit.

CHAPTER THREE

Pawnshops were a fact of London life, though Alasdhair hated them. They were toll booths on the low road to ruin, and nearly every woman forced to go on the stroll had paid her pence to them.

"Are we visiting any particular pawnshop?" Miss Delancey asked as she and Alasdhair returned to the walkway.

"The nearest one, which would be two streets over." He set off down the walkway, moderating his pace in deference to the lady. "The neighborhood improves to the south and west, but there's another pawnshop two streets north. They often mark the boundaries between the areas in decline and the ones considered decent."

"How do you know such things?"

"I make it my business to know. The taverns tell a tale as well. If the intersection nearest the tavern is clean by day, that means the patrons can afford to tip a barmaid and, a few moments later, tip the crossing sweeper too. If the intersection isn't as tidy, then the sweepers aren't getting their vails."

"What of the churches?" Miss Delancey asked. "What do they say about a neighborhood?"

Interesting question from a parson's daughter. "Not much. Some of our churches predate the Great Fire and are relics of a neighborhood's former glory. Others were rebuilt in a hurry after the fire and are more modest than the surrounds at present merit. I'm sure that for you an appraisal of the vicar would tell a tale, while I find them all... vicarly. Tell me of your charitable undertakings, Miss Delancey. Why fallen women?"

Of all causes she might espouse, why fallen women?

"Because if I leave their plight to the city fathers to resolve, nothing will change."

How determined she sounded. "You've been able to single-handedly shift the course of London's flesh trade? How did you effect this miracle without the newspapers trumpeting your success?"

Alasdhair was honestly curious, and also baiting her. When Miss Dorcas Delancey was angry, all the propriety fell away, leaving a firebrand in its place. She was, quite possibly, one of those women who delighted in her spinster state with the unrepentant glee of the happy bachelor.

Such women were rarities in Alasdhair's experience, and their combination of guile and ferocity intrigued him. They needed that ferocity in a society that rendered women invisible, save as they could be—or aspire to be—wives or mothers.

"The newspapers," Miss Delancey spat, "sell their vile drivel by making that flesh trade as lurid and sensational as possible. They celebrate adultery, scandal, ruin, and tragedy instead of fostering anything approaching an elevated or constructive dialogue. This city needs sewers, Mr. MacKay, but what do the newspapers have to say about it? Who will pay for these sewers? That is their sole contribution to the discussion."

The city did need sewers, desperately. What sort of minister's daughter brought *that* up?

"London is an old city. Reconstructing its drainage will be a huge undertaking."

"And waging war for most of the past century wasn't a huge undertaking? Packing our thieves and vagrants off to the Antipodes to colonize a wilderness isn't a huge undertaking? Fat George's endless extravagances aren't a huge undertaking? But we haven't the coin to build the sewers that would make our air breathable for John Bull?"

The average soldier was a fighter of necessity and a grumbler by inclination. Miss Delancey's tirade went from grumbling to debate. She recited facts. Britain had all the money in the world for expanding its empire, she was right about that. The revenue was on hand in part because Britain plundered one colony to extend its reach in another, and in part because the gentry and shopkeepers were taxed unmercifully.

But for the increasing masses of London poor, nothing was spent.

To encourage sloth or dependency in those not born to wealth would be *unkind*—and giving them clean air and safe water would be only the first step on that misguided—and expensive—road to coddling them.

"So why have you attached yourself to eradicating prostitution in the capital?"

"We will never eradicate prostitution, Mr. MacKay, here or anywhere else. Many enlightened thinkers don't believe we should try."

"Then what is your aim, Miss Delancey?" The answer mattered to him more than she knew.

She tromped along in silence as the shopfronts they passed went from genteel to worn.

"Those women should have a choice," she said, her tone weary. "Many of them don't. They have no trade, and if they did have a trade, their wages would belong to a father or husband. His wages aren't sufficient to feed the family, and thus she's expected to... She's required to..." Miss Delancey waved a gloved hand, the gesture both exasperated and eloquent.

They arrived at the pawnshop, the three balls hanging beneath its sign showing only flecks of gold paint. The shop had no name, the sign simply proclaiming, "Items bought, sold, and traded. J. Shroop, Prop." London had a thousand such shops, most of them relying as much on stolen inventory as on goods legitimately pawned.

"Keep a sharp eye," Alasdhair said. "You might see the shawl and blanket, or other items that belonged to Melanie. If you want me to redeem them, I will."

"I have coin, Mr. MacKay."

Alasdhair paused outside the pawnshop. "What you have is a bad temper, else you would never make such an imprudent announcement in such a location. I am angry, too, Miss Delancey, but we are here to gather information. Reforming all of London will have to wait."

She looked about, her gaze falling on a one-legged man sitting on the walkway on the sunny side of the street. A worn cap sat before him, while he stared straight ahead at passersby.

"I am angry. Mr. MacKay. Good of you to notice."

"I like that about you, and I like almost nobody. Let's get this over with." He held the door for her, and she swept into the dim little shop with all the dignity of Wellington reviewing the troops.

Alasdhair slipped in behind her and gave his eyes a moment to adjust to the gloom. The shop was barely heated, which was fortunate. The stench of mildew and dust was pervasive even in the cold.

Miss Delancey moved off down a row of goods. Furniture made up the foundation of the rows—sagging sofas, dented sideboards, bureaus missing drawers. Piled atop the furniture were sundries—a washbasin here, mismatched boot trees there, a stack of hats adorning a clothes press. The detritus of lives going in the wrong direction.

"Greetings," said a skinny young man with sandy hair. He stroked his mustache, which grew in luxuriant abundance over a too-hearty smile. "Looking for anything in particular?"

Miss Delancey shot Alasdhair a glance over the stack of hats. Smart woman. He excelled at leading initial charges.

"I am looking for a rocking chair," Alasdhair said, "and a cradle made to match it. These items were formerly in the possession of Miss Melanie Fairchild."

The fellow's smile took on a brittle quality. "What I have to sell is all on display, my friend. It appears your missus is interested in buying you a hat."

Miss Delancey set aside the high-crowned beaver she'd been inspecting. "I am interested in answers regarding the rocking chair and cradle. You will please provide them."

"I find," the proprietor said, his smile disappearing altogether, "that limiting my business to goods rather than questions and answers makes for healthier custom. If you'd like to purchase something, I am happy to quote you a price."

None of the prices were displayed, of course, the better to bilk every shopper of the maximum coin they appeared able to pay.

"I find," Alasdhair said quietly, "that when a young woman in good health dies under mysterious circumstances, and her most precious possessions have been given into the hands of the nearest swindler, that my fists develop a curious itch, Mr. Shroop."

"I find," Miss Delancey said, coming up on Alasdhair's right, "that a great impulse to discuss Miss Fairchild's situation with the authorities has come over me. You were seen by multiple witnesses accepting possession of her rocker and cradle, and my companion here can describe that cradle in detail, right down to the maker's mark on the underside. When did Miss Fairchild sell you these items, Mr. Shroop?"

Shroop remained behind the scarred counter, beneath which he'd doubtless secreted a knife or possibly a loaded gun.

"I took those items on consignment," Shroop said, "and it's not like you think."

"It never is," Alasdhair replied. "Enlighten us."

"I liked Melanie—Miss Fairchild. I wanted to get the best price for her."

Miss Delancey folded her arms. "Do go on."

"She needed money, worse than usual. She'd brought by some halfway nice things before. Clothes mostly, a Bible, a hat. But the furniture... Folk around here don't have the means to pay what that was worth. I put it in a shop down in Knightsbridge, where the nobs go to look for bargains."

"When?" Alasdhair asked.

"The rocker right around Michaelmas, and it sold within a fortnight. Got her a good price for it. She brought in the cradle just before Christmas. I hated to take it, but does a lad need coal or a cradle more?"

A lad needed both.

"And has the cradle sold?" Miss Delancey asked.

Had she used that arctic tone on new recruits, they would have been quaking in their uniforms.

"Not as yet, missus. It's only been a few weeks. Miss Fairchild was in here on Monday asking me about it."

Alasdhair kept his eyes on the man's hands. "Did you offer to make her a loan?"

Mr. Shroop swallowed. He stroked a finger over each side of his mustache, and his gaze flicked downward. "I'm not that sort of pawnbroker."

"I'm no sort of pawnbroker at all," Alasdhair said, "but if I find out you propositioned Melanie Fairchild when she'd entrusted goods to you for sale and that you withheld the money she was due so you'd have a better chance of getting under her skirts, I will rid London of your existence. Now, what is the name of this fine establishment in Knightsbridge?"

"Or," Miss Delancey said, "is it actually in Bloomsbury? Think very hard, Mr. Shroop, before you answer. I would not want to add your eternal soul to the list of the departed for whom I pray nightly."

Oh, she was good. Naughty schoolboys would swear eternal reform for her, and at the time they made those oaths, they would mean them.

"The shop's in St. James's," Shroop said. "Caters to gents looking to furnish second households, if you take my meaning. Good quality, not necessarily made-to-order. Marplewood's, just around the corner from the fencing school and Jackson's."

Around the corner, where a fellow's comings and goings would be a trifle more discreet, but only a trifle. Setting up a mistress was a rite of passage for young men of a certain ilk.

"And has the cradle sold?" Miss Delancey asked again, ever so pleasantly.

"As of Friday, it had not. I swear that."

Miss Delancey cast a gimlet eye over the dusty shop. "That is fortunate, because the cradle did not belong to Miss Fairchild. It belonged to her son, and she did not have the authority to surrender the cradle to you."

Bless the woman, she wielded a barrister's reasoning like a cudgel. Shroop glanced to Alasdhair, as if expecting masculine solidarity. Alasdhair gave him Uncle Whitlaw's best thee-art-bound-for-hell-laddie stare.

"But her son's just a..."

"Right," Miss Delancey said, "a baby. Now he's a motherless child. What else can you tell us about Miss Fairchild? Was she upset when she paid her call on Monday?"

"Not upset," Shroop said. "Melanie wasn't like that. She was sunny by nature, always looking for her situation to improve, but she was worried. She would usually stay to chat and at least pretend to be looking over the inventory, but she was in a hurry, and she came straight to the point. I thought she had to get back to the baby. Said he was cutting teeth."

That detail rendered an otherwise dodgy recitation trustworthy. "Miss Fairchild patronized your shop regularly?" Alasdhair asked.

"She'd come in with other women from time to time, but about four months ago, she started doing business with me. She's not a woman a man like me would forget."

What he meant was that Melanie had been pretty, with a lady's airs and graces. Motherhood without benefit of wedlock had befallen her nonetheless. She had been both desirable and—in the opinion of the Shroops of the world—available, albeit perhaps for a price.

"Recall her in your prayers," Miss Delancey said. "And her infant son as well. Shall we be going?"

Alasdhair considered grabbing Shroop by the lapels and administering some Elixir of Truth here among the orts and leavings of unfortunate lives.

But no. Not today. Not with a lady present. "We are off to St. James's," Alasdhair said. "Thank you for your assistance, Mr. Shroop."

Miss Delancey waited while Alasdhair held the door for her, then she took his arm as they crossed the street. "What an odious, disgraceful man."

"He fulfills a need."

"So does a privy, Mr. MacKay. Do you think he extorted favors from Melanie?"

So does a privy? "No. I'd have pummeled him to flinders otherwise."

"Good. You'd have spared me the trouble."

She marched on down the walkway, her stride more than matching Alasdhair's. He flipped the beggar a coin and kept his gaze on the foot traffic all around them.

Inside, though, he was trying very hard not to smile. Melanie's death was a tragedy and something of a mystery. The winter weather was growing downright nasty, and finding a situation for John weighed increasingly on Alasdhair's mind.

But the notion of Miss Delancey putting up her fives to teach Shroop a lesson... Alasdhair would like to see that, and his money would be on the lady.

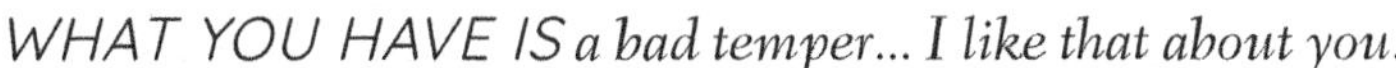

WHAT YOU HAVE IS *a bad temper... I like that about you.*

Dorcas had no idea where she was going, striding along at Mr. MacKay's side, but he knew. He knew the alleys and pawnshops, the crossing sweepers and taverns. He'd also known she was angry.

Dorcas had nearly forgotten that about herself, so ingrained had the habit of concealed ire become. Admirable reformist zeal, Papa called it, usually with a pained smile as he trotted off to have supper with this or that functionary from Lambeth Palace.

He would never become a bishop, and he would never reconcile himself to that fate.

"I am peckish," Mr. MacKay said. "Would you dare be seen breaking bread with me?"

He was peckish, while Dorcas was cold. "A cup of tea wouldn't go amiss." Or another nip from his flask... but no. That way lay disaster.

"If we turn left at the next crossing, we'll be one street away from a tea shop. They do a good job with sandwiches and baked goods."

Tea shops were a recent addition to the city's offerings, a genteel variation on the old coffeehouses, which had been primarily male domains.

"Do you have a map of the whole city in your head?"

"I am a former reconnaissance officer. When you grow up in the Scottish Borders, you learn to pay attention to landmarks and navigate by the stars."

He'd been *a spy*? Spying was held in low repute, and yet, Wellington had relied heavily on his intelligence officers.

"How did a former reconnaissance officer from the Scottish Borders make my cousin's acquaintance, Mr. MacKay?"

"Melanie and I met in the park. I was walking my horse, who'd picked up a stone. I'd got the stone out, but was muttering to him in my father's tongue about the inconvenience the mishap was causing me. Late for my next appointment, missing breakfast, that sort of thing. We passed Miss Fairchild sitting on a bench, and she greeted me in that same language, though 'good day, sir' was apparently the extent of her Gaelic."

Where would Melanie have learned even a Gaelic greeting? "You stopped to chat?" A gentleman might exchange a few pleasantries under such circumstances, but he would not presume upon the company of a lady to whom he hadn't been introduced.

Though a gentleman-spy probably had the knack of striking up conversations with strangers.

Mr. MacKay indicated they were to take a left turn, and the neighborhood improved.

"I am, like all good Scottish lads abroad, chronically homesick. I occasionally hear the Lallans Scottish from a drover down from the north, but Gaelic in much of London is a rarity. I tarried for a few moments, and when I saw Melanie again on the same bench two days later, we picked up the conversation. It became obvious that she could use a friend."

Obvious, because her own family had turned their backs on her. "Merely a friend?"

"First, what does it matter? She's dead, Miss Delancey, and her private affairs deserve our discretion. Second, yes. I was merely a friend."

Merely a friend. What would it be like to have this taciturn, ungenteel Scot as a friend? How did friendship between men and women work, if at all?

"Thank you for that," Dorcas said. "If Melanie never thanked you for your friendship, I'm thanking you on her behalf. I mean that. A good friend is a treasure for the heart."

"Friends can also lead us astray," Mr. MacKay said as they approached a shopfront that displayed racks of pretty tea cakes and fresh pastries in the window. "Heaven should bear a scent like this," he said, hand on the door latch. "Warm and rich and nourishing. I never smelled cinnamon as a boy. My first whiff was a revelation. I decided I would be a baker so I might inhale that fragrance all day long."

And yet, he wore the scent of heather on his person now. "You'd grow accustomed to it."

"One never grows accustomed to heaven or hell, Miss Delancey." He held the door for her. "The quieter tables are at the back."

"You are being polite, suggesting I need not be seen sitting with you by the window, which concerns me not at all. I am interested at present in warmth, Mr. MacKay, in a seat that spares me the cold drafts by the door."

The shop was half full, perhaps because the morning was half gone. Red-and-white-checked tablecloths lent the place a cheery air, and more baked goods were displayed at a glass-enclosed counter opposite the door. Pots of violets sat in the corners of the windowsills, and the warmth was a benediction.

"That table," Mr. MacKay said, nodding toward an unoccupied corner. "You would not be so cold if you left your bonnet at home and wore a scarf about your ears instead."

"You wear neither bonnet nor scarf, and yet, you seem indifferent to the elements."

"I am a plow horse. You are a Welsh pony by comparison. I cannot abide the stifling summers here in the south, while you probably delight in them."

"I've never been compared to livestock before," Dorcas said, stripping off her gloves and stuffing them into the pocket of her cloak. "I like the notion that I'm as sturdy as an equine, not some delicate creature in need of cosseting." He, of a certainty, did bring plow horses to mind. Powerful, robust, muscular...

She fumbled with the ribbons of her bonnet.

"Allow me." Mr. MacKay had her ribbons undone in a few deft tugs, his knuckles brushing warmth along the underside of her chin. "We all benefit from a bit of cosseting. You should try the hot chocolate here. They serve it with whipped cream and sprinkle it with cinnamon. For a bit extra, they'll stir in hazelnut liqueur to ward off the chill."

Friends can also lead us astray... Not that he was a friend. "You bought that treat for Melanie, didn't you?"

He hung Dorcas's bonnet on a peg among a row along the wall. "We came here before Christmas, with wee John. Sat at the window so he could watch all the passersby. If I'd known Melanie was planning to pawn his cradle..."

"I didn't know either. Did not even think to wonder if the baby had a cradle."

Mr. MacKay took the cloak from Dorcas's shoulders and hung it on another hook. "Guilt will destroy you, Miss Delancey. You tried to help, and that meant worlds to Melanie."

"Worlds," Dorcas replied, taking a seat at the table, "but not enough. To take her own life... She despaired, Mr. MacKay. Despite that beautiful healthy baby, despite a roof over her head, despite me, despite you, she despaired. That breaks my heart."

He hung his greatcoat over Dorcas's cloak and took the opposite seat. "Mine too. Breaking Shroop's head might have cheered us up a bit. Perhaps another time."

Dorcas could not tell if she was on the receiving end of some Scottish-soldier-plow-horse humor, or a true reflection of Mr. MacKay's thoughts. No twinkle in his eye, no hint of a smile, and yet... he had a sense of humor that lurked like a sea creature beneath the waves. A ripple on the water, a fin breaking the surface, only to disappear as if imagined.

Mr. MacKay gestured to a youth with an apron tied about his middle.

The waiter approached. "Major, ma'am. Sandwiches and cakes, same as usual?"

"The lady might be interested in your hot chocolate, Silas."

Silas brushed overly long dark hair from his eyes. "It's a right treat, ma'am. I whip the cream myself, and we can serve it with cinnamon or nutmeg or both, though the nutmeg is dear."

"Have the nutmeg," MacKay said. "Be bold."

"Cinnamon, please," Dorcas said, rather than accede to MacKay's temptation. "I'll try the nutmeg another time."

"Major, same for you?"

"Tea, lad, and some tucker. Be off with you."

Silas bustled away, still grinning. The boy clearly knew and liked MacKay, and MacKay had some fondness for the boy too.

"I will investigate the pawnshop in St. James's," Dorcas said. "I had better find your cradle among its offerings, or a receipt for its recent sale."

"You will not inspect any pawnshops in St. James's without me," Mr. MacKay said. "And you should not go at all."

"I am not a former soldier," Dorcas said, favoring him with a warning smile. "I do not take orders well, Mr. MacKay."

"My guess is you don't take orders at all, excepting perhaps from the Almighty, but women frequent St. James's without escort at their peril."

"I am not *women,* though I appreciate your concern. I am known for my indifference to the strictures of propriety when about my charitable activities, though I take the occasional unconventional step only in the interests of good causes. I am labeled eccentric, crusading, or simply bothersome, rather than scandalous. I spent a few nights in jail last autumn, for example."

"You were arrested?"

"Nothing so exciting. I was investigating. I wrote an article about the experience for the *Charitable Circular*. Everybody mutters that my father ought to take me in hand, but polite society would never accuse me of seeking untoward notice from idlers in the windows of the gentlemen's clubs. The gossips would dismiss my folly as more odd behavior from Thomas Delancey's headstrong daughter, nothing more."

"And the gossips didn't read your article either, did they?"

"They complimented me on my zeal. I hate that word when it's used to mean foolishness."

"So why not give up, Miss Delancey? Find some nice young clergyman with good prospects and excellent family. Become the helpmeet whose demure devotion recommends him for advancement more strongly than his most brilliant sermons. Set his feet on the path to a bishopric and spare yourself the nights in jail and the committee meetings."

Of the two, the committee meetings were the worse penance. "Mrs. Fry has eight or nine children, at least. She hasn't given up her charitable work with the female prisoners at Newgate, and the place is much better for it."

"But she has a banker husband and the Quaker community behind her. What backing do you have?"

Dorcas ought to resent his questions, but she was too pleased to find herself in the midst of an honest discussion. "When you went out on those reconnaissance missions, making forays by dark of night into enemy territory, what backing did you have, Mr. MacKay?"

The bell at the door tinkled merrily as more patrons arrived.

"The trouble with you," he said, leaning partway over the table, "is that you are both smart and confident of your convictions. If you were intelligent but lacking courage, or arrogant but dull-witted, society would have a much easier time with you. You flummox them, and they hide that by pretending to ignore you."

A reconnaissance officer was perceptive by nature, though Dorcas was unnerved at the accuracy of Mr. MacKay's assessment—also a little pleased.

"Is this more of your backhanded flattery, Mr. MacKay?"

"No. It's an explanation for why you worry me. When you flummox the wrong people long enough, they stop pointing and whispering and go on the offensive."

Rather than argue his point—which was valid—Dorcas ate her share of good sandwiches and unremarkable but pretty tea cakes. Mr. MacKay consumed his portion with the steady focus of a hungry man. His manners were refined, though he didn't bother with small talk while he ate.

Dorcas felt as if she'd been given a reprieve, a few minutes in a neutral corner to regain her wind.

He was *concerned* for her.

Nobody was concerned for her, and she preferred it that way. Papa tolerated her eccentricities because she was useful to him and because she never crossed the lines that mattered. She could not afford to.

But Alasdhair MacKay saw her. Saw that she was angry, that she took risks, that she might someday fall from grace—publicly. What else would he see if Dorcas gave him the opportunity for further reconnaissance missions?

What would she learn about him? "Did Melanie proposition you?"

He set down his mug of tea slowly. "And if she had? Am I so awful a specimen as all that, Miss Delancey?"

He was not awful. He was, in his way, impressive, also unpredictable. Smart and confident, to use his words.

"I don't care if you're a royal duke with a private fortune. My cousin should not have been reduced to trolling for custom in the park."

"Drink your chocolate. It's best consumed hot."

"I want to know, Mr. MacKay. I need to know."

"She was working up to it. I turned the conversation in a different direction. I did not see her in the park after that. I'll have a look around that pawnshop and let you know what I find."

"I'm coming with you."

He dusted his hands over his plate and patted his lips with his table napkin. "No, you are not. I will call upon you, Miss Delancey, at the day and time of your choosing, and I will make a full report like the reconnaissance officer I am. You fear I will simply drift away, relieved that the managing Miss Delancey cannot vex me further. That is the price you pay for being difficult. People avoid you. Or perhaps that's the reason you are difficult in the first place—to keep them from coming near?"

"For a man who never wore a collar, you excel at delivering sermons, Mr. MacKay."

"I carried a gun into battle instead. Turned me up all philosophical. I also have an unaccountable fondness for difficult people, perhaps because I am one. If I say I will call upon you, I will call upon you, if for no other reason than I expect you to help me find a situation for John. Trust me, Miss Delancey. I *will* call upon you."

He spoke softly, and maybe another woman would have heard menace in that rumbling burr, but to Dorcas, he sounded utterly sincere. Stating immutable facts.

She did not trust anybody, much less any man. That she was tempted to trust Alasdhair MacKay could become a problem.

Not that she would permit herself such folly.

CHAPTER FOUR

Was a call truly social if the motivation for making it was to discuss a young woman's death?

Alasdhair debated that question as he rapped smartly on Rev. Thomas Delancey's front door. Delancey was vicar to a genteel parish that hugged the fringes of old money to the west and new money to the north, while commercial districts lay conveniently close by to the south.

A good place to shepherd a flock, judging by the flagstone walkway swept free of mud, the freshly painted wrought-iron porch railing, and the vicarage's abundance of spotless windows.

"Good day, sir." A housekeeper in cap and apron had opened the door. "Welcome, and do come in from the cold, though if you're here to call upon the vicar, I'm afraid he's out."

She was cheerful about her sentry duty, though *out* might well mean Delancey was in his study, trying to fashion the week's sermon.

"I'm here to call upon Miss Delancey," Alasdhair said, passing over a card. "She should be expecting me."

The housekeeper's smile vanished, suggesting that either the wrong sort of man called on Dorcas Delancey, or that men never called upon her at all.

"I'll see if Miss Delancey is at home. The guest parlor is this way."

The guest parlor was intended to tastefully impress. Lathe-turned wooden candlesticks graced the mantels, and tall beeswax tapers arrowed toward a twelve-foot ceiling. The gilt was kept to a minimum—tracery on sunbeams frescoed among the ceiling's celestial clouds, flourishes on the corner moldings.

The scene overhead involved two stone tablets held by some old bearded fellow whose gout looked to be troubling him. Not a bare breast or fat, half-clad cherub to be seen.

The carpet was Axminster, the drapes velvet, both emphasizing a lush raspberry hue. The mantels on the opposing fireplaces were rose marble, their carvings limited to the capitals and pediments of the pilasters. The walls boasted two landscapes, both rural scenes featuring a venerable village spire reaching for the cerulean English sky.

Only one fire was lit, though the second was laid, probably for later in the day, when callers were more likely.

The balance between luxury and austerity was perfect, exactly befitting the household of a vicar of a prosperous metropolitan congregation. Of Dorcas Delancey, Alasdhair could see nothing—not in the embroidered chair covers (cabbage roses, of course), not in the porcelain shepherdess and her adoring lambs on the sideboard.

And that was probably the point. Dorcas Delancey, like any good spy, excelled at concealment in plain sight. That quality intrigued Alasdhair more than it should. Most young women developed the opposite skill—the ability to attract notice without seeming to work at it.

The lady herself appeared in the doorway, frowning, as was her habit. Alasdhair was also intrigued by the question of what might make her smile.

"Master of Abercaldy?" She brandished his card. "What does that mean?"

"It means my father is a Lord of Parliament, in the Scottish tradition, and I am his heir. Papa inherited the title through an auntie, who held it for all of fifteen days prior to expiring. The role amounts to presiding at some annual village affairs and keeping a lot of books."

Paying out an exorbitant amount quarterly in pensions made up the rest of the job. Alasdhair had chosen to use the calling card that included his honorific, knowing that the card might eventually find its way into Thomas Delancey's hands.

"A Lord of Parliament is like an English baron?"

"An English baron without the right to sit in Parliament per se—or the obligation." The Scots sent a delegation to Parliament, and Alasdhair hoped to never be among their number.

She gave his card one last scowl, then tucked it into a pocket. He'd surprised her, having expectations slightly above a mere former officer's, and Dorcas Delancey clearly did not like surprises.

"We can sit here and swill tea, Mr. MacKay, or walk in the garden. My preference is the garden, despite the chill."

"So is mine. I feel as if a pair of stone tablets are about to drop upon my head if I utter even a polite falsehood."

She cast her eye upon the ceiling. "If prevarications and falsehoods had that effect, the Commandments would have fallen from the ceiling long ago. I'll fetch my cloak."

She reappeared a few minutes later in the same dark blue wool cloak she'd worn the previous day, but—interestingly—she'd wrapped a plain gray scarf about her neck and eschewed a bonnet.

"The garden is small," she said, "but the walls keep away the worst of the wind and hold some of the sun's warmth. I have yet to venture forth today and would enjoy some fresh air."

She wanted privacy. Alasdhair had not raised the topics of Melanie or wee John, and Miss Delancey hadn't either. That suggested she did not confide in her staff or consider them allies.

"This is your idea of a small garden?" Alasdhair asked as they emerged onto a wide terrace. The enclosed area was a half acre at least, with crushed-shell walkways running along square beds framed with low privet borders. A stone-lined water feature ran the length of the garden's center, the surface a glaze of cloudy ice dotted with dead oak leaves.

"In summer, when all the greenery is blooming, it feels smaller. I come out here to think and walk the paths around the flower beds by the hour."

A lioness pacing her cage came to mind, or a stall-bound pony weaving before her open half door. Neither image flattered the lady.

Alasdhair offered his arm, and Miss Delancey took it after a slight hesitation. He descended the steps with her, mindful—as she doubtless was—that they could be observed from the house.

"May I speak freely, Miss Delancey?"

"Permission granted, Mr. MacKay." Her pace was slower here than it had been on London's streets, her voice less clipped. Perhaps she, too, was tired.

"We still have no body," Alasdhair said. "I dropped around to the river police, made inquiries of the mud larks, and asked questions among the watermen. Melanie's mortal remains have yet to wash ashore, and they might never be recovered."

"Because of the tides?"

"Yes."

"And because dead bodies have value," Miss Delancey said. "In life, Melanie had no value to anybody. In death, the resurrectionists can sell her remains to the medical students."

"She might well have been carried out to sea. Speculation will merit you nothing but nightmares."

"A soldier learns that, doesn't he? He learns to leave the battle on the battlefield."

She would make that connection. "He tries to. Speaking of battles, John is not a good sleeper." The nurserymaid had phrased it thus. Alasdhair's version of the situation involved profanity in several languages.

"Hence the fatigue in your eyes. Is John well?"

"Quite. Timmens says teething children are simply wakeful. He wasn't hungry, he wasn't in need of fresh linen, he was simply..."

"Missing his mother?"

Alasdhair hadn't wanted to say those words. "Perhaps. He likes lullabies."

"You sang to him?"

"Either I sang to the lad, or nobody for three streets in all directions would have had any peace. He'll soon know every marching song and camp ballad ever sung by Wellington's army." To say nothing of Burns's vast catalog of laments.

Miss Delancey stopped at the foot of the garden, her gaze on the dirty ice in the little artificial canal. "And his cradle?"

"He slept in it last night, such as he slept at all. Shroop spoke the truth—it hadn't sold, so I redeemed it."

"With your fists?"

"You sound hopeful, Miss Delancey."

"I would like to use my fists on somebody, Mr. MacKay. My cousin should not have died as she did, and the fact of her death troubles me more by the day."

"If you were a soldier, you could march off your dismals. You could turn your attention to the next battle, to moving camp, or to regimental gossip. If the grief gets to be too much, you must find a distraction, Miss Delancey. I suspect you are good at distractions." If she had been a soldier, she could also drink, brawl, or swive away her dismals. Alas, neither she—nor Alasdhair—were soldiers.

"Let's sit, shall we, Mr. MacKay?"

The bench she'd chosen was in a square of taller privet hedges that offered protection from the vicarage's curious eyes. A birdbath sat in the center of the square, the bowl filled with more dirty ice.

"I come here to think," Miss Delancey said as Alasdhair took the place beside her, "but I don't know what to think of Melanie's death. Papa says we must trust in the Lord, but what sort of God... What sort of Christian turns a blind eye to a new mother in desperate straits?"

"What sort of king musters up his farm boys and apprentices and makes killers of them? What sort of emperor marches a half million men to Moscow with winter coming on, only to lose them by the hundreds of thousands to disease, starvation, battle, and cold?"

The bitter breeze pushed dead leaves along the walkway, and a lone raven landed on the edge of the birdbath. It cocked its head at Alasdhair, bright dark eyes suggesting otherworldly intelligence. Alasdhair expected the bird to speak—some ravens did—but the creature instead flapped away into the leaden sky.

Miss Delancey shivered. "You are not cheering me up, Mr. MacKay."

He turned on the bench to rearrange her scarf, which she'd tossed about her neck as an adornment. Alasdhair unwrapped the wool, then wound it over her ears and hair and about her neck and chin so her face and head were mostly swaddled, and her cheeks and mouth were covered.

"You are very presuming, sir."

"You are welcome. How soon can you find a place for John? Another night like last night… I am nearly dead on my feet. I'd just doze off, and he'd start up again, which I can assure you is worse than simply keeping watch all night."

"John is where he should be. He is where Melanie wanted him to be, and if you think to cheer me up by offering me a good scrap, please choose another topic."

He'd thought to do exactly that. "Very well. Explain to me, Miss Delancey, why a woman intent on ending her life by jumping from a bridge wears her best slippers and bonnet?"

"Because she wants to be a pretty corpse?"

"Think, Dorcas. Think about walking the distance to the Strand Bridge, in bitter weather, at night. Think about the wind on the river, colder than charity in hell. You walk everywhere, because you are poor, and you know the feel of London's cobbles through the thin soles of your only decent pair of boots. *Think.*"

She sat up, brows knit. "I would for no amount of coin subject myself to that march wearing only my good slippers. I could not. My feet would freeze, and even were I in the pit of despair, I would need for my feet to get me to the bridge. I would not wear my good bonnet on a walk after dark for which I'd want few witnesses. I would wear whatever was cheap and warm and hope my bonnet was sold to provide for my son. And yet, the only evidence we have of Melanie's passing is her best pair of slippers and her good bonnet. She was seen making her way to the bridge, but nobody saw her jump, did they?"

Alasdhair had walked half the length of London before he'd been able to connect what few facts he had with any logical conclusions.

"The mud larks told me they almost never find both shoes at the same time," Alasdhair said, recalling earnest, grimy little faces. "They find only one or one at a time, but the shoes and bonnet were barely damp and all in a heap in the tidal mud." Manna from heaven to those little scavengers, and it had been one of them—a wraith of a girl—who'd pointed out the strangeness of tromping to the bridge in slippers despite streets abundantly cursed with ice and mud.

Alasdhair had rewarded her and her cohorts with every coin in his pockets.

"We must find somebody who saw Melanie jump, Mr. MacKay."

No, *we* must not. "Melanie might not have jumped, or she might have simply waited for a moment when the bridge was deserted. Suicides commit both a crime and a sin when they end their lives. Who wants witnesses to those transgressions when death by misadventure is possible if the death is simply unexplained?"

Miss Delancey got to her feet with considerably more energy than she'd shown thus far. "I can understand, far more than you know, why a fallen woman would want a fresh start. Why she'd want a clean break with the past. This theory makes sense, given Melanie's situation. If she's alive, then she pawned everything of value, made a trustworthy plan for John, and put period to an existence that didn't work out. I cannot approve of her abandoning her baby, but I can understand her motives."

Alasdhair rose as well. "And she might well be dead, Miss Delancey."

"We will find somebody who saw her jump, then. I knew something was amiss with this whole situation. I knew it."

"Where are you off to?"

"Come along." She took a firm hold of Alasdhair's sleeve. "If Melanie's everyday boots and bonnet are not among her effects, then we will have further evidence that your theory has merit, because she's likely wearing them."

"It's not my theory." Though Miss Delancey's suggestion made sense.

"I could hug you, Mr. MacKay. I could just throw my arms about you and squeeze the stuffing out of you."

Interesting, and somewhat alarming, notion. "Stop," Alasdhair said. "Please stop for one moment."

She paused on the path. "Do not lecture me about misplaced hope, or the Lord's will, or—what are you doing?"

He gently unwound the scarf so her face was once again revealed.

"Mr. MacKay?"

"Never mind." Her eyes had been so full of joy, so luminous, but no smile curved her lips. He wrapped her up in the scarf again, taking extra care to tuck the ends beneath her chin. "Wouldn't want you to take a chill."

She hauled him along the walkway. "Into the house with us. I set my maid to sorting Melanie's effects, though we'll launder the lot before we donate it, of course." She chattered on, about quilts and charities and Melanie having been more clever than people realized, while Alasdhair pondered a question.

Miss Delancey appeared to have life organized exactly as she pleased. She was the de facto lady of her father's very comfortable house. She flouted convention in the interests of her charitable undertakings and did so with virtuous impunity. The matchmakers saw her as no threat, the bachelors saw her as no prize, and she liked it that way.

Why would a woman who'd gone to great trouble to fashion that life have such empathy for a cousin who'd desperately needed a fresh start?

BUSYNESS, the most effective camouflage known to womankind, was driving Dorcas barmy. She'd met with the flower committee to hear them bemoan the difficulty of adorning the church with blooms in midwinter. She had heard the same lament every winter for the past ten years and offered the same sympathy and solutions.

Silk bouquets, for pity's sake.

A hint to the wealthier parishioners that some hothouse loans would be appreciated. Mrs. Oldbach would doubtless be delighted to send along some winter heath or hellebore. If she was feeling particularly generous, she'd show off her camellias.

Another option was an expenditure from parish funds for a tastefully understated bouquet from Mr. Prebish's shop, with a note of thanks for his ecclesiastical discount.

At the mention of an expenditure, the ladies looked as if Dorcas had offered to get out a volume of naughty prints. Half horrified, half fascinated, and more than half willing to be convinced. The ritual was as familiar to Dorcas as the children's Christmas play. Mr. Prebish saw some extra business—nobody wanted the job of asking Mrs. Oldbach for anything—and two pots of tea were consumed for no useful reason.

Dorcas had endured a call from the choir director, an earnest young fellow who believed the key of F major to be a *tonic* for the nerves—*pardon the pun, Miss Delancey*—while B-flat minor was a sure road to derangement. His culprit of choice the previous week had been E minor. Rag-mannered and shrill, that was E minor. *Mark me on this, Miss Delancey.*

She had paid a call on Mr. Bothey, hearing his stories of the war in America for the three-hundred-and-forty-seventh time.

And amid all this activity, no further word had come from Mr. MacKay regarding Melanie's death, John's situation, or the price of primroses in January. Busyness could hide Dorcas's worry, though worry had become a dragon prowling in her mind.

And because she was worried, Dorcas bundled up—scarf and straw hat rather than a bonnet—and set off without benefit of the housekeeper's companionship.

She was safe enough traveling the length of four streets in broad daylight, provided she dressed plainly—worn heels were a must—and spent no time gawking at shop windows. A woman inclined to browse shop windows was a woman with leisure time and—very likely—disposable coin. A woman whose boots were never down at the heel was a woman who never had to budget carefully.

Amazing, what an education a few nights in the women's jails could provide.

Dorcas approached Mr. MacKay's door, and only then did she admit that perhaps a very small part of her motivation for this call was simply to see the man himself. He'd been tired when last they'd met. His blue eyes had been shadowed, his manner a trifle less guarded.

He'd *touched* her. Taken it upon himself to *adjust* her scarf, such that she was swaddled in soft wool. He'd presumed to the extent of fleeting brushes of his fingers against her cheek and chin. How could a man have warm hands when out of doors on such a bleak day?

And then she'd threatened to hug him, heaven help her, because he'd seen what Dorcas had not: There was hope. There was hope for Melanie, and there was hope that she'd been motivated by something more daring and courageous than despair. Dorcas had found no boots among Melanie's effects, but then, Mrs. Sidmouth's maid might well have helped herself to a sturdy footwear.

"Good day, miss."

A fellow in a dark suit opened the door to Major MacKay's home.

He was young to be a butler, though a former officer's household wasn't a Mayfair mansion. He was also blond when, for some reason, Dorcas associated either baldness, gray hair, or, at the very least, dark hair with butlers.

"Please do come in."

She slipped inside without sparing a glance for who might see her calling alone on an unmarried man. She had traveled past the bounds of Papa's parish, and if anybody asked, she was seeing to the welfare of a foundling.

Prevarications and falsehoods, camouflage and disguises. This was her life. Perhaps it was the life any woman who aspired to propriety had to live.

"Miss Dorcas Delancey," she said, passing over a card, "come to call on Major MacKay."

"I haven't lit the fire in the parlor, miss, though I can remedy my oversight. Callers are a rarity. The major might be some time coming down, or rather, might not be home."

The fellow colored to the tips of his ears, while Dorcas passed over her hat and scarf. "Another busy night?"

"Timmens says it won't last, that the boy has had a shock, and he's teething. The major has the knack of calming him. Says all recruits need time to adjust to life in uniform. I certainly did."

"You served under the major?" Dorcas offered him her commiserating, confidential smile, the one she used in the churchyard on young bachelors, new parents, and poor relations forced to accept the charity of a parishioner's household.

"I were his batman, and you could not have asked for a better officer, miss. I recall once when we were on a forced march..."

The butler's gaze went to the stairs, though Dorcas hadn't heard footsteps. Mr. MacKay stood on the landing, no coat, cuffs turned back, hair disheveled, and a day's growth of beard giving him a piratical air.

"Miss Delancey. Good day. Henderson, that will be all."

Henderson bowed and withdrew.

"To what do I owe the invasion?" Mr. MacKay said, holding out a hand. "Your cloak, please, for I am well aware you will not quit the premises willingly until you see for yourself that John has created pandemonium where a tranquil household used to be."

Fatigue, or perhaps hours of singing lullabies, had dropped Mr. MacKay's voice from baritone to bass.

"Did you miss your beauty sleep again, Mr. MacKay?"

He undid the frogs of her cloak. "What day is it? What month is it? No wonder old George went mad. He and his darling queen had fifteen children. I can no longer reliably count to fifteen, though that is about fourteen and three-quarters too many offspring for my feeble brain to grasp. Why Charlotte did not commit regicide is a mystery for the ages."

"You are adorable when you babble."

He drew off her cloak. "That's something, I suppose. Always good to learn new skills. Adorability has eluded me thus far. Come along. The despot is all smiles as he anoints himself with porridge and flings toys about his domain."

As happy as Dorcas was to follow Mr. MacKay up to the nursery, she also wanted to linger and inspect. His house was every bit as clean as the vicarage, though it lacked appointments. No bucolic landscapes or battle scenes were framed on the walls.

The sideboard in the entryway held no venerable wooden tray full of keys, correspondence, the odd penknife, or stray pair of spurs. The landing was devoid of a philosopher's bust or even a bowl of dried flowers. The windowsills held no pretty little sketches or struggling ferns.

Perhaps Scottish thrift was at work in this lack of personal touches, or perhaps this serviceable domicile was a reflection of Mr. MacKay's soul. Lived in, but planed down to essentials, ripe for abandonment on short notice.

"I did not think the boy should be banished to the eaves," Mr. MacKay said. "He has the guest room two doors down from my quarters, or he and Timmens do. Henderson is in love with Timmens, but she—wise lady—has avoided his advances. Henderson was in love with the cook's helper from next door last week. If you spend enough nights pacing the nursery floor, you learn an impressive store of secrets."

"Rather like spending a night in jail."

"I would not know, though not for lack of trying." He showed Dorcas into a room full of warmth and sunshine, though the unique smell of Baby in Residence was also evident. "His Highness is receiving. Timmens, I believe you know Miss Delancey. Don't get up lest the fiend resume howling."

Timmens sat in a rocking chair, nursing the baby, though she'd arranged a shawl over her shoulder and over the baby. Modesty was preserved, not that Mr. MacKay seemed at all unsettled to have come upon wet nurse and infant at such a moment.

"I will leave you, Miss Delancey, to admonish John regarding the proper deportment of babies in the middle of the night. I must repair my toilette before I rejoin you. That assumes I don't fall asleep facedown in my washbasin."

He assayed a bow and left, closing the door silently in his wake.

"That one's canny," Timmens said, adjusting her shawl. "Knew to close the door quietly, lest the lad notice. Young John is canny too."

Dorcas took a seat in the reading chair near the window. "Does John thrive?" He appeared to be the picture of cherubic health, nestled against his nurse. The sight provoked an odd blend of annoyance and longing, so Dorcas rose and commenced tidying.

"John is adjusting," Timmens said. "My ma claimed that any change—washing the blankets, moving the crib, forgetting to close the curtains—could set some babies off. John has lost his ma, lost his home, lost his everything, and he's cutting new teeth. He'll settle, or Mr. MacKay will know the reason why."

Clearly, Mr. MacKay had an admirer. "He's good with the baby?"

"He's magic. Has the touch, or the voice. Never lets on that he's tired or hungry or out of patience. A man like that..." Timmens paused for the business of switching John to the other breast.

Dorcas smoothed quilts, she straightened blankets. She folded up little dresses and arranged a trio of small stuffed bears on the windowsill.

"Where did these come from?"

"Mr. MacKay raided a toy shop. We have two rattles, a proper baby spoon for our little mouth, three storybooks, and he ordered booties and caps too. John will want for nothing."

Save his mother's love? Dorcas sat on the bed, which was a true bed, not a cot. The cradle in the corner was lovely and large enough to keep John comfortable for months yet. And Mr. MacKay thought to uproot the boy all over again to send him off to some foster family in the shires?

"You are attached to that baby, aren't you?" Dorcas asked.

"Hard not to be, what with losing my little Enoch. Named him for a prophet, more fool me." She fussed the baby, who made odd slurping noises. "I know what you're thinking, Miss Delancey, and you're not wrong."

Dorcas wasn't thinking. She was in the grip of emotions that refused to be named, but left her uncomfortable and restless. Mr. MacKay had already procured *baby things*. He'd known to do that—which was important—but had he made any further inquiries regarding Melanie's death?

Her disappearance, rather?

"What am I thinking?" Dorcas asked, shaking a rattle in the shape of a jester's pole. A coral teether protruded from one end—coral was traditionally thought to ward off illness and enchantment—and the rattle and its bells were silver, a metal that brought the moon's protection in darkness. The whistle fashioned into the silver doubtless worked, for the rattle appeared to be new.

"You are thinking that I'd best watch myself with Mr. MacKay," Timmens said. "He'd never trespass, but a man like that..."

Like that? A man who bought a new rattle and three stuffed bears for a boy he intended to hand over to the care of strangers? A man who knew how to tuck up a scarf so a lady was finally warm? A man who urged that lady to choose the more exotic spice for her hot chocolate?

"What about a man like that?"

"He can have all he likes from the females, because he don't go about waving his sword. That's irresistible. He's not a pizzle with some arrogance and good tailoring attached. To gain his bed, you'd have to gain his trust. I like that. Mr. MacKay is a gentleman. He don't clean up as good as some, but he don't presume, and he sings to a cranky baby."

"A hungry baby, apparently."

"The second breast always takes longer. The milk makes him drowsy. Would you like to burp him?"

How Dorcas yearned simply to hold the child. "I wouldn't want to introduce another element of novelty to his routine."

Timmens rearranged her shawl and slanted Dorcas a look. "And once he burps, we know what happens next, don't we? I do not envy the laundresses all the work this boy makes for them. Child makes a stink to revive the departed, he does. Always happens when they start on the porridge."

"I'll leave you to John's many talents, but if you need anything, Timmens, for yourself or the boy, please send word to me at St. Mildred's vicarage on Holderness Street."

"Won't be needin' nothing, miss, except a good night's sleep."

Dorcas let herself out of the nursery, moved two doors up the corridor, and entered without knocking.

CHAPTER FIVE

One moment, Alasdhair's mind had been filled with the lyrics of a ballad about a jolly border reiver, the next he was reaching for his sword and grabbing only empty air.

"At ease, Mr. MacKay." Dorcas Delancey stood beside his bed, looking all too pleased to have found him resting his eyes. "You did, indeed, fall asleep."

"I got my boots and stockings off and fell onto the mattress," he said, peering at his bare feet. "What happened next defeats my powers of recollection. If you will excuse me, I will make myself presentable, and we can guzzle tea and lament the dismal weather."

Alasdhair knew he should be mortified to find her in his bedroom, to know she'd seen his bare feet and hairy calves. He should be leaping from the mattress to cover his exposed flesh and apologizing to her in midair, except that, first, she had invaded his sanctum sanctorum, the place where a man had every right to display his naked flesh.

Second, Miss Delancey did not seem mortified, quite the contrary. She seemed happy to inspect his bedroom *and* his person.

Third, he had *never* been exhausted like this.

"The next time we want to defeat the French," he said, "we should first make sure they all have large families. They will be too tired to put up a decent fight, and we'll take Paris in a fortnight."

Miss Delancey's eyes danced at that profundity, though her humor was a subtle thing. "War doesn't toughen a man sufficiently for the rigors of the nursery?"

Pride alone had Alasdhair shoving up to recline against his pillows. The only time a fellow was permitted to lie about like a spent salmon was after he'd pleased a willing partner.

"War is mostly marching and learning to endure boredom. You tromp along in the middle of a train of men and wagons that stretches for five miles. You spot a copse of aspens leafing out and tell yourself, 'I will march that far.' When you get to the aspens, you see a farmhouse a quarter mile up the road, and you think, 'I will march that far.' Your mind drifts, your body gets into a rhythm. Your mates troop along beside you, somebody starts up a song. The time passes."

Miss Delancey gathered up his boots and set them beside his wardrobe, then began collecting articles of discarded clothing. She retrieved his jacket from the back of his reading chair, his wrinkled cravat from the privacy screen where three others hung, starched and ready for wearing.

"You paint a very different picture of war from the stirring dispatches and fashionable paintings of battle scenes."

"I am gaining a very different picture of child-rearing. I knew babies were a lot of work, but that one wee lad... My mind cannot drift when I'm walking the floor with a colicky infant. I attend him. Has his crying changed? Is he trying to convey a pain in his belly, or did he dislike the brandy Timmens rubbed on his gums? Then he dozes off, I doze off, and fifteen seconds later—I vow to you, it's seconds, not minutes—he's whimpering again. My body is ramfeelzed, my mind is flogged to flinders."

Miss Delancey's next objective was to tidy up his vanity, which was already tidy enough. Alasdhair was by nature organized, and that his bedroom had gone a bit the other direction was a temporary aberration. Such was Miss Delancey's innate decorum that seeing her in his bedroom evoked no prurient imaginings. She was that proper, that far above the melee.

Rather like Wellington on the battlefields.

And yet, Alasdhair liked watching her handle his brush and hand mirror, liked seeing her sniff at his scent bottle. A woman's hands were fascinating, capable of creativity, competence, and—surely Alasdhair's mind had turned to porridge—tenderness.

"Nonetheless," Miss Delancey said, aligning his slippers side by side on the hearth, "if Timmens burst in here, calling for you to come to the nursery on the instant, you'd take off at a run."

"At a hobble." Alasdhair made it to the side of the bed, though the change in position left him a trifle swoony. He hadn't been this far gone since he'd collapsed at Lisbon. "That child has aged me thirty years in three nights."

"He's having a difficult time," Miss Delancey replied, gaze upon Alasdhair's privacy screen, which was a japanned scene of grazing horses and towering mountains. "And this is precisely why you must not think to uproot John yet again for some time."

Alasdhair rose from the bed and caught sight of himself in the cheval mirror. He was wrinkled from brow to breeches, his hair would put Medusa to the blush, his cheeks were dark with day-old beard.

"I look like a reiver after a bad raid. You should be terrified at the sight of me."

"I did not toss all propriety aside by coming into your personal demesne to discuss your questionable appearance, Mr. MacKay. My concern is John's future. Promise me you will not send him off to some village family in the next fortnight. Not while he's so upset."

Alasdhair stood, which occasioned more weavy-wavy sensations, just as if he'd finished a straight week of forced marches.

The key to his salvation popped into his mind like a revelation: "I need to eat." And he needed coffee. Stout, nearly bitter, with a dollop of cream and a dash of honey. A whole pot of serious coffee for a man in extremis. He was supposed to meet Goddard and Powell at the club for an early luncheon, and the morning was already well advanced.

"You need to listen to me." Miss Delancey smoothed the quilts on the bed and rearranged Alasdhair's pillows into a neat, symmetrical stack.

"I cannot think, much less listen, in my present state, Miss Delancey, and you must not be capable of much rational thought either, or you would never be closeted with me in my bedroom when I am half undressed."

She swatted at the pillows. "You are prevaricating, Mr. MacKay. That child's welfare is more important than your delicate sensibilities. If I had meekly awaited you in your chilly parlor, you would be wrapped in the arms of Morpheus, while I wasted an hour waiting for you to recall you have a guest."

"For your information, Lord Justice Miss Delancey, I was not asleep. I was resting my eyes." Alasdhair had been beyond merely sleeping and heading for the territory of complete, restorative oblivion. Now that he was out of bed, he needed to head for... clean clothing?

Shaving was out of the question until he'd found some sustenance to steady his hands.

Miss Delancey held a round velvet pillow before her middle, like a shield. "My nickname is Miss Delightful. If you intend to ridicule me, I will thank you not to go venturing off into new insults."

Alasdhair sauntered over to her, a saunter being all he could manage. "But you are delightful, Miss Delancey. Delightfully tart, delightfully articulate, delightfully intelligent. Delightfully fierce. You are delightful in many regards."

He'd hoped to make her smile. Why had that become an objective? Instead, her gaze clouded with what appeared to be bewilderment.

"You seek to distract me with false flattery. I want your promise that John will remain under this roof for at least the next two weeks.

We must think of his wellbeing before all else, Mr. MacKay, and Melanie entrusted him into your keeping."

Dorcas Delancey did not smell tart and articulate. She smelled of a thousand flowers, of soft breezes, and gentle sunshine. She smelled of lazy summer days and murmured endearments.

That baby has reived my bloody wits. "You have ambushed me in the one place where I should be safe from all attackers." Strategic brilliance on her part. "You have pressed your advantage when I am weak and wan. You have shown no mercy when I am famished and muddled. Napoleon should rejoice that he did not meet you before he went a-plundering across Europe."

"I am not trying to wrest an empire from a tyrant, Mr. MacKay. I am trying to secure peace and safety for one tiny baby for a mere two weeks."

The last, stumbling, mumbling part of Alasdhair's mind that could still claim a spark of reason sensed what Miss Delancey was up to. This was not an ambush, a skirmish, or even a minor battle. This was how she intended to win the war. She'd chosen her moment with a cunning that earned his admiration, even as she upended his rest, his privacy, and his thinking mind.

Two weeks of sleepless nights would turn into two years, then twenty. Twenty years of fretting, of not knowing what to do or how to help the lad. Twenty years of awkward discussions, of not setting a good enough example, of not having the right answers to all the worst questions.

"He needs a family, Miss Delancey. My empire consists of my tyrannical self and my horse, and his loyalty is to his oats."

Alasdhair's voice had taken on that faraway, across-the-glen quality that presaged falling out of the saddle, except he wasn't in the saddle.

"Mr. MacKay, are you well?"

"Exhausted, famished. I don't do so verra weel when famished." And there was the burr, as furry and unapologetic as a Highland wildcat. "I need a wee sittie-doon."

"Promise me John can stay, and cease your dramatics."

"Aye, the lad can stay." Alasdhair heard himself say the words as if they'd been spoken across a loch at dewfall. Water did strange things to sound.

And then he pitched headlong into Miss Delancey, and all was sweet, fragrant, curvaceous oblivion.

~

"I STRUGGLE," Thomas Delancey said, passing over another hymnal that would no longer meet the standards appropriate to St. Mildred's congregation. "I struggle nigh constantly, in my heart."

Isaiah Mornebeth set the worn book on a growing stack. "How could any struggle befall you, Thomas? You have more moral and spiritual clarity than any man I know."

They had taken on this task of sorting hymnals in the sacristy of St. Mildred's, a space small enough to be kept warm by a lit hearth and braziers. The lavender sachets stored with the vestments and the cedar-lined wardrobes also gave the room a pleasant scent.

A confessional sort of space, and Mornebeth had always been easy to talk to, as Thomas imagined the truly holy were easy to talk to.

"Appearing resolute before the flock is part of the job," Thomas replied, "and they are a good flock, for the most part. They pay their tithes, they show up for services, they tolerate Dorcas's little projects and committees."

The next three hymnals would all last at least another year. "But is this why the Lord called me?" Thomas went on. "Is it merely ambition that draws me to a more challenging post?"

Thomas hated to use the word *ambition* aloud, and he would not speak even to Mornebeth of a bishopric. A pious man could have ambitions for others—that they kept to the path of righteousness, that their talents were appreciated, that they observed the Commandments...

But could that pious man have ambitions for himself?

"To yearn to use one's abilities in service to the fullest extent of one's capabilities is not ambition," Mornebeth replied. "That is the essence of a vocation."

Thomas started on the next stack of hymnals. "You are such a comfort, Mornebeth. Always so sensible."

Isaiah Mornebeth was at least twenty years Thomas's junior, but he had the settled air of an older man, always had. He was a sweet, calm, good-humored, kindly fellow, and a favorite of the archbishop's inner circle.

Mornebeth embodied that passage from Matthew about being as wise as a serpent and as harmless as a dove. He was also wellborn—his mother's uncle had been an earl—and his blond good looks would age well.

He was ideally poised to rise to the very top of the church hierarchy and had precisely the humble temperament that ensured nobody would envy him his successes.

"Speaking of sensible comforts," Mornebeth said, "how is your dear Dorcas?"

The day took on a bit more of winter's gloom. "She thrives in the execution of her duties, as always. I could not ask for a more conscientious daughter."

Though Thomas could, and regularly did, ask the Almighty for a less obstreperous daughter. Dorcas had the best intentions, but her methods... *nights in jail*? As if she were some reforming Quaker biddy? Thomas hadn't learned of that undertaking until he'd seen Dorcas's article in the *Charitable Circular*. She'd used a pen name, thank the merciful intercessors, but her tone, her utter confidence in her convictions, had been plain to read.

"Tell me, Thomas, is Dorcas's devotion to you what has prevented her from marrying some lucky fellow?" Mornebeth bound up the stacks of discarded hymnals with twine.

They would go to a poorer parish for another several years' use. Dorcas had set up a fund five years ago to cover the cost of replacing hymnals and purchasing music for the organist and choir. She'd seen that a small, regular offering allowed the congregants who cared for music to make a greater contribution than if they'd been given only an annual drive to respond to.

"Isaiah, I confess I do not know why Dorcas is so unnatural in her proclivities. I adored her dear mama. Dorcas saw in our union what a happy marriage looks like. I pray that my daughter finds a suitable fellow, but I no longer dare urge her in that direction. Until she does marry, I do not feel I can take on another wife myself, and that, I fear, hampers my chances of making a greater contribution."

Of earning a bishopric. A post at Lambeth. Even a post on the staff of the Archbishop of York would be a step forward. Isaiah had spent five years in the north and made all sorts of connections during his time away from London.

Now he was poised for a stint at Lambeth itself, renewing old acquaintances and making new acquaintances. That was how a man of ability and dedication should go forward with his calling. Not this trudging about in the same parish circle like a mill horse, Sunday after Sunday.

"Dorcas is a strong-willed female," Isaiah said. "They are in a particular quandary, knowing their proper place to be one of submission and meekness and yet having much to give if properly guided. She needs a special man to provide that guidance."

Thomas started on the last stack. "I honestly do not know what she needs. She could run the vicarage blindfolded, her committees execute their duties without drama, and she makes all the proper calls and the charitable ones too. She has dedication, I'll give her that, but she lacks..."

Dorcas exercised discretion. She bent the rules only in the interests of her causes and was respected for her convictions. Her personal decorum was never wanting—far from it—and she attended to the purely social duties conscientiously.

"She lacks humility, perhaps?" Mornebeth said. "I would never accuse Dorcas of pride in the sense of vanity, but she is quite assured about her objectives, isn't she? She hasn't failed often enough or publicly enough, hasn't endured the sort of significant embarrassment that would temper her self-assurance."

Two more hymnals were found wanting. "You have the gift of delicacy, Isaiah. I have wondered if Dorcas isn't lonely and if all of her odd flights and outspoken articles aren't some backhanded attempt at gaining notice. I appreciate her. I tell her regularly what a help she is to me, but a father's words are pale consolation compared to the esteem of a husband and family."

Plainer than that Thomas could not be. Dorcas would do well—very, very well—to gain Isaiah Mornebeth's notice. He was a rising star in the Church and well connected in polite society. The right wife would all but assure him of stellar success.

Dorcas was perhaps a dozen years younger than Mornebeth, at which nobody would bat an eye. Her older, wiser husband could curb her misguided ways as Thomas had been unable to.

And then perhaps, Thomas himself could look about for a suitable helpmeet.

"Invite me to dinner," Isaiah said. "Let it be a surprise, and I will exert myself to charm our Dorcas. I truly missed her when I was in the north. Even as a girl, she argued morality as enthusiastically as any cleric, and she has ever been a handsome woman."

Dorcas was plain, alas. She didn't bother over her appearance as a lady ought, though she was always appropriately attired at supper. She was also unfailingly polite to Mornebeth, though Thomas had the sense that kind, practical Dorcas had never cared for Mornebeth.

Which made no sense at all. Perhaps that was simply more of her backwardness, of which she had an abundance. She would turn up her nose at the very fellow best suited to make her into a proper, loving wife.

"I'll consult with my calendar," Thomas said, "and you may expect an invitation shortly." He'd consult with Mrs. Benton, his cook-housekeeper, and she would determine when it was convenient to entertain.

"St. Olaf's will consider this quite a windfall," Isaiah said, surveying the bound stacks of used hymnals. "They will be making a much more joyful noise, thanks to your generosity, Thomas. You can be sure I will remark your kindness at the palace. We ought to institute sister-parish relationships throughout London and even between rural and metropolitan churches. A village boy should have friends in Town when he comes seeking workl."

"I made precisely the same observation to Dorcas the other evening." Or had Dorcas been the one expounding on the greater potential of her sister-parish concept? She did tend to expound, if left unchecked.

"You are a man of superior insight, Thomas, and of vision. Vision is rare in a parish cleric, and I intend to do all in my power to see that you are recognized for it. Are we to take these offerings to St. Olaf's now?"

"Gracious heavens, in this weather? Dorcas will see to the delivery, and you and I will enjoy a hot meal at my club. You must tell me all about your sojourn in the north and how you are finding the palace upon your return."

Isaiah smiled, a sweet, wistful smile that made him look like a choirboy, though choirboys tended to be a naughty lot.

"Not much to tell, Thomas. Sheep and scenery, never enough funds to do the Lord's work, and more tea and shortbread than one man should have to endure."

"Then it's steak and a good claret for us, my friend. Dorcas is off somewhere fussing over a foundling, and she will not miss me at luncheon."

To be seen sharing a meal with Mornebeth would be a small victory and also a pleasure. Mornebeth deserved that courtesy at least, for calling on an old friend and for offering to put in a good word for Thomas at Lambeth.

That cheering thought almost made up for the misery of having to walk four streets to the club on this dreary, chilly day.

CHAPTER SIX

Dorcas and Mr. MacKay toppled to the floor in an odd progression of dance steps. First, he careened into her, and his size was sufficient that, for a moment, she was pinned beneath him against the edge of the bed.

He was absolute dead weight and plenty of it, but she tried to prevent him from crumpling to the floor. Her efforts were unsuccessful, and he subsided to the carpet beside the bed like a kite caught in a downdraft.

He twitched once on the carpet, then curled onto his side. "Nighty-night, love," he murmured. "Dream of me."

Dorcas hopped off the bed and stood over him. "Mr. MacKay?"

A gentle snore was her reply.

"Major?"

His foot twitched.

He was not drunk, of that Dorcas was certain. She was equally certain that rousing him would be unkind, if not impossible. She tucked a pillow under his head—his hair was much softer than it looked—and draped a quilt over him. The bedroom had no bell-pull, so she went out into the corridor and called down the steps.

"Henderson! Mr. MacKay has need of you." The instant she'd raised the alarm, she regretted it. John might be napping, and he, too, would need to catch up on his rest.

Two men appeared at the foot of the steps. Both tall, dark-haired, a little weathered, and looking quite concerned.

"Is MacKay in difficulties?" The fellow on the right asked in accents that suggested Welsh antecedents.

"I don't know," Dorcas replied. "He's fast asleep on the floor. One moment, he was nattering on about his horse's loyalty. The next, he said he needed to sit down, except he did not sit. He more or less collapsed."

Both men were grinning as they came up the steps. "MacSwoon rides again, does he?" The larger fellow was English and wore an eye patch. "MacKay goes a bit short of tucker and keels right over. Has a right temper when he's hungry too. Can hold his drink like a stevedore, but doesn't dare skip a meal."

Dorcas led them back to Mr. MacKay's suite, though she was leery of allowing two large, unserious men into Mr. MacKay's bedroom when his dignity was imperiled.

"He has been going very short of sleep lately," Dorcas said. "I am Miss Dorcas Delancey, and I came by to discuss a charitable matter with Mr. MacKay. Who might you gentlemen be?"

They were apparently too delighted to contemplate their friend's collapse to introduce themselves.

The Welshman paused outside Mr. MacKay's door. "Dylan Powell, at your service. This wretch is Colonel Sir Orion Goddard, and we are cousins to the patient. Served with him in Spain too. Let's have a look, shall we?"

Either one of these men could have flipped Dorcas over his shoulder, but she stood her ground anyway. A point needed to be made.

"Mr. MacKay does not need your ridicule," she said. "He hasn't had a decent night's sleep for much of the past week." And his days had likely been taken up asking difficult questions of mud larks, river police, and beggars when he wasn't shopping for stuffed bears or tiny silver spoons.

"He can usually manage without sleep," Sir Orion said. "It's the empty belly that lays him low. He simply cannot abide hunger as most others can. He could fight like a demon when the moment called for it, but the instant we ceased battle, he had to eat or he'd keel over."

"The Scots are a delicate race at heart," the Welshman—Mr. Powell—said. "All growl and howl when the whisky is upon 'em, but poetical and retiring by nature."

Sir Orion hit his companion on the arm, probably for trying to make a play on the word *retiring*.

Dorcas allowed them into the sitting room and preceded them into the bedroom. Mr. MacKay had not moved. He lay on the rug, one bare foot sticking out from under the quilt.

"The poor wee lad," Mr. Powell said. "Shot right out of the saddle, didn't even make it to the bed." Mr. Powell brushed Mr. MacKay's hair back with a gentle hand. "MacKay, you worthless slug. Time to get up. We're marching for Valencia today."

He'd nearly shouted, and Mr. MacKay's only response was a sigh.

Sir Orion knelt on the rug. "MacKay, on your feet! Parade inspection in fifteen minutes!"

Another sigh.

"Stop amusing yourselves," Dorcas said, turning down the covers. "Get him onto the bed, please, and loosen whatever needs loosening so he can rest comfortably."

"He is resting comfortably." Sir Orion covered Mr. MacKay's exposed foot with the quilt. "He will nap here for about twenty or thirty minutes, then wake up ravenous, though he might not realize he's ravenous. My wife claims some people are like birds. They must eat constantly in small amounts, or they grow muddled, tire easily, and become snappish. MacKay is such a one, rather famously in some circles."

"Goddard's wife is a chef," Mr. Powell said. "Our Ann is also a paragon among women, for she took on the thankless business of being married to Goddard, didn't she? There's no accounting for the fortitude of women."

Dorcas did not care if Sir Orion was married to the Queen of Brobdingnag. "Mr. MacKay will rest more comfortably in his bed. Please get him off the floor."

The men exchanged the look of fellows humoring an upset female, though Dorcas wasn't even beginning to approach *upset*. One man grasped Mr. MacKay under the arms, the other took his feet, and they half lifted, half slung him onto the bed.

"If you would please tell him we came by to collect him," Mr. Powell said, "we'll await him at the Aurora Club. He'll need to eat before he leaves the house, mind, or we'll be scraping him off the walkway. Food first, *before* coffee. Tell him to take his time and not to bother shaving. We've seen him looking much worse."

Sir Orion took his friend by the arm. "We'll wish you good day, Miss Delancey, and you have our thanks for your concern regarding MacKay." He bowed correctly, smacked Powell, who bowed as well, and then they were out the door.

Dorcas folded the covers over Mr. MacKay, who'd again rolled to his side. She shook out and folded the quilt from the floor and tossed the pillow into the reading chair. When Henderson showed himself, she ordered a tray for Mr. MacKay and a pot of coffee, and then she peeked behind the privacy screen.

Everything was orderly and neat, from the razor strop, shaving brush, and straight blade to the hard-milled soap in a flowered ceramic dish. Two plain white towels were draped over the washstand's rail, and a mirror hung high enough to reflect only what lay north of Dorcas's eyebrows.

Most curious were a dozen sketches of serious, dark-eyed children, all of whom looked to be less than ten years of age. Orphans. Dorcas knew the look, knew the caution and banked bewilderment in their gazes.

A noise from the bed had her withdrawing from what she ought not to have seen.

Mr. MacKay had switched sides, but not roused. Dorcas took the reading chair when she should have left Mr. MacKay to slumber on in solitude.

She was merely resting her eyes when an annoyed burr roused her.

"Have they gone? I know Powell and Goddard were here, or did I dream that?"

"They have traveled on to the Aurora Club, where they await you, though you are not to hurry to join them. A tray is on the way, and I forbid you to leave the house until you eat something."

Mr. MacKay nuzzled his pillow. "I love it when you give me orders."

Was he still half asleep? "I do not love it when a grown man in otherwise apparent good health collapses in a heap at my feet. I don't care for that at all."

"Every woman should have a grown man collapsing in a heap at her feet from time to time. Keeps us grown men humble."

"Mr. MacKay, you frightened me." Dorcas hadn't meant to say that. Hadn't allowed herself to think it, but if anything happened to Mr. MacKay, where would that leave John? How would she investigate Melanie's disappearance?

He sat up, scrubbed a hand across his face, and swung his feet over the side of the bed. "If I frightened you, then we're even, because you for damned sure intimidate the hell out of me. You are fearless, woman, and I apologize for my language, but profanity is another indication that I need to eat."

"I am not fearless." Far from it.

"Then you bluff exceedingly well. I suppose I ought to shave, and I refuse to do that with you glaring daggers at me."

"Your friends said you weren't to bother, that they've seen you looking far worse."

Mr. MacKay sighed and looked around the room as if he

expected those friends to pop out of his wardrobe. "What else did they say?"

"Not much. That you needed to eat very regularly, or you got into difficulties. They weren't worried."

"They were worried. They are my nannies, those two. They carried extra rations at all times..." Mr. MacKay rose, stretched, and gazed down at Dorcas. "I did not mean to frighten you, but that's part of the nature of the beast. I don't realize I need to eat, and then I get too muzzy-headed to think through the situation. I always come right, so please don't fret. My cousins admonished me not to shave, because when I'm peckish, my hands shake too badly to manage a razor. I could always shoot straight, though."

"I can shave you. I have shaved my father from time to time, when he's ill, or once when he sprained his wrist. I will be careful."

"One suspects you are always careful. Has the fiend gone to sleep?"

He thought of the boy even now. "I don't know. The nursery is quiet, and thus I gather John enjoys a full belly." Dorcas *was* always careful, because she had to be. The offer to shave Mr. MacKay was not one a careful woman would have made. Charitable, perhaps, but not careful. "Shall I shave you?"

"I'll be fine once I eat something. My thanks for your concern."

Henderson arrived with a tray of sandwiches and a ceramic carafe swaddled in a thick linen towel. Dorcas poured out, the coffee aromatic and strong.

"You are to eat before you swill the whole pot." What about this man tempted her to be so, so imperious?

He saluted with his cup. "A sip to revive the dying. You want to leave me some privacy, but you are worried, Dorcas Delancey, because you think I will try to back out of my promise to house John here for the next fortnight."

She resorted to making the bed, the only bit of busyness available. "I am more concerned that you forgot you made such a promise. You were half swooning at the time."

"And yet, you badgered me into an admission. I admire your tenacity." Mr. MacKay consumed a sandwich and poured a second cup of coffee, this time adding cream and honey.

"Swoony men should not be held to account for their delirious declarations."

"I do not swoon," he said. "I grow light-headed. I become vertiginous. I am prone to syncope—a French doctor patching up British troops taught me that one—and presyncope, but I do not swoon. Perish the thought."

Dorcas went to the wardrobe and began laying out a suit of morning clothes. "You *fell* upon me. I could not stop you from collapsing. You must promise me to leave the nursery to Timmens tonight. She can sing as well as the next person, while you cannot... lactate."

"My dear Miss Delancey, you are blushing."

I am not your dear. Wasn't anybody's dear. "Have another sandwich."

He did, this one disappearing more slowly. "Now, I can tell I'm hungry, but this will hold me for the present." He rose and surveyed the outfit Dorcas had chosen.

"I would not have paired that mulberry waistcoat with a blue morning coat."

"Too showy? A touch of gold—cravat pin, sleeve buttons, watch chain—will pick up the gold embroidery in the waistcoat. You must have a care with your appearance to reassure your cousins that you are back on your mettle."

He stood improperly close, but then, what was propriety when she'd offered to shave him? When she'd seen him snoring on the floor? When she'd badgered him—his word—into keeping John here for the next two weeks?

"*You* put me back on my mettle," he said, "and I state only the surprising truth."

Dorcas moved away, for she was blushing again. "Then I am no longer needed here. If you have any news to impart regarding

Melanie's situation, please call on me at the vicarage, and keep me informed regarding John's wellbeing."

She wanted distance between herself and Mr. MacKay, or that's what she *should* want. What Dorcas truly wanted shocked her.

To touch his hair again.

To see him without his shirt.

To watch the transformation from bearded ruffian to clean-shaven *Master of Abercaldy* and former officer.

To ensure that he did not again grow peckish because he was too worried about a teething baby.

Perhaps she was the one grown light-headed and unsteady.

Mr. MacKay escorted her as far as the bedroom door. "I will keep John for the next fortnight, and I will not part with the lad until I'm certain he'll be well cared for. If possible, I'll send Timmens along with him, and I make you a solemn vow, Dorcas Delancey, that he will never want for anything."

His gaze was serious, more serious than usual.

"I should not have carped at you," Dorcas said. "That's why they call me Miss Delightful—because I am *not* delightful. I am tiresome and difficult." She made that confession while staring at the bare flesh of Mr. MacKay's throat. She was tempted to collapse against him, to give him the weight of all her disappointments, and forget for a time who she was and where the line lay between propriety and folly.

He really had given her a bad turn.

"You are delightful," he murmured very near her ear. "I keep my promises, Dorcas, and I do not lie. You are maddening, brilliant, determined, and as persistent as a seagull at a picnic, also entirely delightful. That boy is lucky to have a champion such as you."

Something warm and soft brushed Dorcas's cheek. *His lips.* Mr. MacKay moved behind the privacy screen with its intriguing collection of portraits.

She had just been kissed by Alasdhair MacKay, *and she had enjoyed it.* On that startling revelation, Dorcas slipped out the door.

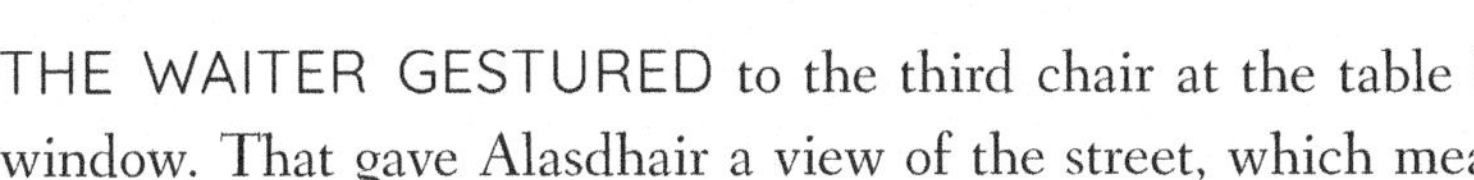

THE WAITER GESTURED to the third chair at the table by the window. That gave Alasdhair a view of the street, which meant his back was to the club's dining room.

Not ideal, but such was the penance the last to arrive should serve.

"Don't start," Alasdhair said.

"Haven't said a word," Dylan Powell replied mildly, while Goddard simply smirked at his ale. Since marrying the former Miss Ann Pearson—Miss Delectable to those who'd consumed her cooking—Goddard was much given to smirking and smiling.

About damned time too. "I'd prefer a private parlor," Alasdhair said to the hovering waiter, "if any are available."

"Of course, Major. Allow me a moment to consult with Monsieur Lavellais. I'm sure he has a private dining room available."

Lavellais was part magician, as every good *maître de maison* should be, and part mystery. He was invariably cheerful and unassailably discreet, most especially discreet about his own past. He lived at the club, and Alasdhair suspected he had an ownership interest in it.

More than once, Lavellais had directed that a cheese board be sent to Alasdhair's table before the waiter had even taken orders. Perhaps Goddard and Powell had told tales out of school, but Lavellais was also that perceptive about the club's members.

"If you don't want us interrogating you," Goddard said, "then you'd be better off in the main dining room."

"You will interrogate me anyway, and half of the club's members will be entertained by the spectacle. I'm not in the mood to oblige them."

Powell took a considering sip of his ale. "Did you at least eat, MacKay? A bear coming out of hibernation has more manners than you do on an empty belly."

"She made me eat." Made him eat, made him take in the boy, made him trouble over his appearance... The behaviors of a meddling bedamned female, and yet, from Dorcas Delancey, all of those feminine imperatives felt more like fussing than meddling.

And fussing from her was a consummation devoutly to be treasured.

Lavellais appeared, looking as dapper and pleasant as always. "Gentlemen, greetings. Will the blue salon suit? We lack fresh flowers this early in the day, but perhaps good company can compensate for the absence of such a small touch?"

Powell and Goddard collected their drinks and rose. "The blue salon will suit," Goddard said. "Thank you, Lavellais."

Lavellais escorted them up a flight of carpeted stairs and down a corridor. The faint aroma of pipe tobacco wafted from the cardroom, which was likely still being aired from the previous night's play.

A footman was lighting the fire in the blue salon and a waiter setting out cutlery as Alasdhair entered. Lavellais occupied himself with the decanters on the sideboard until the other staff had withdrawn.

"Nobody reserved this parlor for the midday meal," Lavellais said. "You will be undisturbed while you solve the problems of the world." He bowed cordially—Lavellais was never in a hurry—and left, doubtless intent on seeing to some other small dilemma elsewhere.

"Before you go," Alasdhair said, "is the girl working out? You can speak freely before my cousins."

Lavellais smiled beatifically. "Miss Beulah knows little of the kitchen, Major, but she knows a lot about hard work and about being cheerful. She will do quite well."

"Keep her away from the strong spirits if you can, and she should manage adequately."

Lavellais nodded. "An admonition many would do well to heed." He slipped out the door on silent feet, and Goddard passed Alasdhair a scant finger of brandy.

"Miss Beulah?" Goddard asked, pouring another for Powell and one for himself. "Would that be the former Mademoiselle Belle, late of Covent Garden at unsavory hours?"

"She's expecting a child," Alasdhair said. "She wanted out. Half of Lavellais's kitchen staff is female, and he employs charwomen too." Several, like Lavellais himself, of apparent African descent. "You are both dying to know what Miss Dorcas Delancey was doing in my bedroom."

Both Powell and Goddard were largish, dark-haired, and battle-worn. As a result of an intimate encounter with an exploding powder magazine, Goddard often wore an eye patch. Powell was a preacher's son with a wide and well-hidden streak of devilment, a hallmark of preachers' sons, according to him. He had soulful blue eyes, a dazzlingly warm and rare smile, and an absolutely lethal temper.

Alasdhair loved these men dearly. He did not love that they worried about him and that the worry took the form of nosy questions and awkward silences.

"Miss Delancey is the daughter of Thomas Delancey, vicar of St. Mildred's," Powell said. "Her reputation for virtuous works nearly equals your own reputation for foul humors. She has the unfortunate nickname of Miss Delightful in polite circles, because she tends to wax eloquent about all the undelightful realities of life in our fair metropolis."

"It's not my metropolis," Alasdhair said as a waiter brought in a cheese board and set it on the table.

"I'll claim Paris before I'll accept the blame for London," Goddard said, peering at the offerings. "Annie does a much better job with a cheese board. Makes it into a sort of still life, so all the colors are like art."

Goddard's Annie, a prodigious talent in the kitchen, had turned Goddard's life into a work of art, gilded with smiles and smug innuendo.

"Powell, how is it you know of Miss Delancey?" Alasdhair asked, taking up a slice of toast adorned with melted brie.

"My sisters," Powell replied. "I keep telling you, they know all.

They see all. They hear all. They also occasionally come to London. Though we are a tribe of Dissenters, clergy are ever cordial toward one another. Vicar Delancey enjoys a very comfortable post at St. Mildred's and is invited to some of the lesser entertainments to make up the numbers. His daughter serves as his hostess, and though she is applauded for taking an interest in the less fortunate, she's also ridiculed for going about it with more genuine purpose than is deemed strictly necessary."

"She's resented for it," Alasdhair said, taking another bite of cheese and toast. How many *days* had it been since he'd had a proper meal? That little snack with Miss Delancey did not count. "Do either of you know anything about a Miss Melanie Fairchild?"

"Not again, MacKay," Powell said, taking a seat at the table. "London is home to thousands of prostitutes, and half of those are women too ashamed to return to their families in the shires. You cannot save them all."

"Your figures are off. Most of the women providing favors for coin are simply supplementing wages too meager to live on. They have occupations, they have families. Many are married and would rather not work the streets ever again. If we paid the ladies better wages—or allowed married women to keep their wages rather than force them turn every groat over to a husband who squanders his coin—we'd have a lot less vice. Instead, we harangue the women about morality, while male greed and lustfulness are the real problems."

"Tell us about Miss Delancey," Goddard said, taking the chair nearest the hearth. By tacit agreement, Alasdhair and Powell left that chair to Goddard, who also had a bad hip as a result of his military frolics.

"I hardly know Miss Delancey." Not quite true. Alasdhair knew Dorcas was brave, principled, softhearted, and fierce. He knew she was kind, that she smelled of every good thing in the flower garden, and that something drove her to be so protective of those she cared for.

"She was *in your bedroom,*" Powell mused, "and you hardly know her, though by reputation, she'd only venture into such a location to save a lost soul. What in the hell are you up to now, MacKay?"

"I am apparently in the business of raising a baby," Alasdhair said. "A business I am ill-suited to on my best day." A gratifying silence greeted that announcement. Alasdhair had left both Powell and Goddard speechless, which surely qualified as a minor miracle.

"You are raising a baby," Goddard said slowly, "and you've enticed Miss Delightful herself into your bedroom. Have you run mad, MacKay?"

"No enticing necessary," Alasdhair said, slicing himself off a bite of cheddar and wrapping it around a piece of apple. "She invaded. A novel approach, but it has a certain charm."

Powell and Goddard exchanged a look of genuine concern, while Alasdhair was feeling better than he had in ages. He had learned something else about Miss Delancey: She was lonely. She was weary of fighting all her battles as a single combatant, and Alasdhair knew exactly how that felt.

"Stop gaping, you two. Miss Melanie Fairchild apparently took her own life a short time ago by jumping from the Strand Bridge in the dead of night. Her child is now in my keeping, and Miss Delancey is related to the boy. She and I have questions about Miss Fairchild's passing, and I have been investigating."

"We could argue all afternoon and not talk you out of further involvement in such a mess," Goddard said, "so tell us the rest of it, and leave out nothing."

"Especially not the part about being ambushed by Miss Delightful."

Alasdhair gave them what facts he had, and passed up the opportunity to argue with Powell. Dorcas was delightful, though Alasdhair was apparently the only man with sense enough to see that.

CHAPTER SEVEN

Dorcas occupied herself drafting an article on the plight of London's prostitutes. She had alluded delicately to "the problem" in articles about prison reform, poor laws, Corn Laws, labor reform, and female education, but she'd veered around the twin institutions of marriage and prostitution.

Three days of jotting down thesis statements and supporting facts, three evenings of trying to revise jottings into coherent prose, had left Dorcas feeling housebound and restless. The article would be worthy, thought-provoking, and easily ignored. Not so easily ignored was the memory of Alasdhair MacKay toppling onto her and his weight pressing her against the bed.

Even harder to ignore was his sweet, respectful kiss to her cheek and his insistence that she was delightful. Maddening, brilliant, persistent, and utterly delightful. He'd heaped that praise upon her with the gravity he claimed so effortlessly and then punctuated his decree with that lovely little kiss.

Kisses could be lovely. Dorcas had known that in a theoretical sense. She'd known in a very real sense that they could also be horrid. The garden called to her as the place to ponder that conundrum and to recall the feel of adept male fingers wrapping her in warmth and consideration.

"Going for a turn out back in this weather?" Papa asked.

Dorcas tucked a scarf around her neck. "Fresh air is good for us, and there's a breeze from the north today." Meaning London's winter miasma of coal smoke was for once blown away almost as quickly as it accumulated. "I've been meaning to raise a difficult topic with you, and walking in the garden sometimes helps me organize my thoughts."

She'd put off this discussion for more than a week, too busy fretting about John and trying to ignore the memory of Mr. MacKay's lips softly pressed to her cheek.

"No more nights in jail, Dorcas. You're lucky you did not come down with jail fever. Lucky you did not spread contagion to my whole congregation. I forbid any more such outings, for your own good and because I have my reputation to consider."

The congregation was his, not *ours*. The reputation worth guarding was his. Papa was a good man, better than most, but he was plagued by a human need for public recognition and respect, which church work merited rarely and begrudgingly.

And he missed Michael. Dorcas's brother, also a clergyman, had been able to challenge Papa and cheer him up as Dorcas never could.

"The difficult topic is not another night in jail," Dorcas said. "Mrs. Fry has that initiative well in hand. The difficult topic is Cousin Melanie."

Papa had been a bit more cheerful lately, a bit less inclined to lament Michael's posting to Northumbria, a bit less grumbly. He looked to be preparing a spectacular grumble at the mention of Melanie's name.

"I pray for your cousin," he began. Not for *his niece*, but for *Dorcas's cousin*. "I pray for her earnestly and regularly, but she brought upon herself the sort of ruin that can destroy an entire family's standing. If her peccadilloes had not taken place beyond the watchful eye of London's gossips, you would find her behavior redounding to your own discredit."

How quickly and harshly Papa judged. How confidently he condemned.

"I am sorry to tell you, Papa, that she is thought to have jumped from the Strand Bridge more than a week past. She left behind a small son, John, and I've seen to the charitable distribution of her effects."

Papa's brows twitched as he looked past Dorcas's shoulder to the frozen garden beyond the door to the terrace.

"Melanie took her own life?"

At least he sounded sad rather than relieved. "Apparently so. Some of her effects were recovered by the mud larks, though as far as I know, nobody saw her jump."

"Well, that's something."

Something that could protect the family from having to deal with the repercussions of the "rash and melancholy act" so frequently decried in the same newspapers that turned private despair into headlines shouted from the street corners.

"Without a body, no one is inclined to hold an inquest. She made provisions for her son, and the child appears to be thriving. I don't see the gossips getting wind of the situation."

"A small mercy that," Papa said, aiming his Vicar Delancey Understands smile at her. "He works in mysterious ways, does He not? We can hope that Melanie is at peace now."

Papa wanted peace, for himself, for his almighty reputation. Dorcas wanted the peace and solitude of the garden.

"You don't intend to ask me about Captain Beauclerk?" she asked.

Papa's smile vanished. "I will ask you not to speak his name. Shame upon him for despoiling a young girl like that. Melanie chose to run off with him, but he enticed her as surely as the serpent enticed Eve."

And yet, nobody blamed the serpent for his slithery, mendacious nature. "As far as I know," Dorcas said, "Beauclerk is still in Canada. I doubt he's even aware of the child's existence."

"And you intend to tell him? Dorcas, why must you stir up mischief in situations that are already troubling enough? A father has neither rights nor responsibilities to an illegitimate child unless he chooses to take an interest. Beauclerk could have mustered out, he could have taken up a trade and made an honest woman of your cousin, but he did not. Let us put this topic behind us, a sad chapter come to a tragic close. I have more pleasant news to discuss."

Fine, then, Dorcas would not trouble Papa's handsome head with the fact that Melanie might well be alive and desperately in need of help. She might be alive and kicking her heels in Paris. Wherever she was, whatever had driven her to a desperate ruse, Dorcas wished her cousin safety and joy.

Dorcas arranged the scarf about her ears, chin, and cheeks, as Mr. MacKay had. "What's your news, Papa?"

"We're to have a guest for supper tomorrow night." He made this announcement as if Mrs. Benton should be pleased to have her plans upended at what—for the kitchen—was the last minute. "A special guest."

Retired bishops were special guests, and they all seemed to appreciate a free meal and a captive audience. Dorcas enjoyed most of them, in moderation, provided they were not too prone to leering at her or patting her shoulder.

"I will tell Mrs. Benton to set an extra place," she said, "and I will make it a point to review the wine selections. The everyday will not do for a special guest."

"This fellow isn't particular," Papa said, taking on the air of a small boy with a delightful secret. "He's humble and handsome and..." Papa paused to assay his signature twinkling eyes, "He likes you."

Heaven defend me from lonely choir directors. "I'm sure the meal will be very pleasant." Dorcas put her hand on the door latch, needing the sanctuary of the garden more than ever if she was to endure hearing the rascally key of E minor disparaged over the soup.

"Right you are. I was supposed to keep the guest's identity a secret—he hoped to surprise you—but you will want to practice your party piece at the pianoforte and spare a little extra time for your coiffure. I daresay in the circumstances, you'll also want to pick out a pretty frock to wear for this guest."

Dorcas never wasted time primping. Her objective was to escape notice, not invite it. Humility was a virtue and camouflage a necessity. She mustered a smile because Papa was so pleased with his secret and so obviously dying to tell her who the special guest was.

"Don't keep me in suspense, Papa. I have little enough occasion to trouble over my appearance. Who could possibly merit such singular effort?"

"Our guest is to be none other than our own dear Isaiah Mornebeth. He's done such a capital job with his responsibilities in the north that he's been posted to Lambeth itself. One of his very first calls upon returning to London was upon his old friend at St. Mildred's, and, my dear..." Papa beamed as if he were watching the parish children rehearse the Easter play. "Mornebeth asked specifically to be remembered to you. Enjoy your outing."

Papa rocked up on his toes so great was his glee, then strode off, probably to sort through topics of conversation that would impress the eligible and much respected Mr. Mornebeth.

When the door to Papa's study had closed, Dorcas stumbled into the garden. She made it past the hedges surrounding the birdbath before she fell to her knees and was sick upon the snow-dusted grass.

"I OWED YOU A PROGRESS REPORT," Alasdhair said.

He'd also simply wanted to see Miss Delancey again, to bask in the delight of her prickly, difficult, darling presence. "I suspect you would come see John daily, except that you don't want to grow attached to him, nor do you want to insult me by implying that Timmens and I cannot manage adequately without your supervision."

Alasdhair had once again been received in the vicarage's celestial parlor of propriety, though this afternoon, both hearths had been lit, and a bouquet of pink camellias graced the low table. The windowsill was adorned with a pot of blooming violets, and a lace runner had been added to the mantel.

Dare he hope those touches were for him?

"I have never raised a child, Mr. MacKay. Timmens's experience eclipses yours and mine combined, and we must trust her expertise and dedication."

"Hers and Henderson's. He's the second-oldest of nine. Henderson has more to learn as a butler, but what he doesn't know about infant ailments isn't worth knowing."

Miss Delancey hadn't invited Alasdhair to sit, and she wasn't by nature rude. Determined, bold, outspoken... but not rude. She stood over by the window as if half tempted to leap out of it.

"I notice," Alasdhair said, "you do not correct me when I say you are avoiding an attachment to the child." He was certainly trying not to become entangled in gummy smiles and trusting sighs.

"John is my cousin's by-blow, Mr. MacKay. In the normal course, I would be forbidden any attachment to him at all."

Miss Delancey smoothed her skirts, a gesture Alasdhair would have called nervous in another woman. She was decked out in a spectacularly drab gray ensemble that was clearly intended to hide the perfection of her form. Her coiffure was a severe chignon, not an elegant little curl or clever braid to be seen. Alasdhair, lucky, tormented sod, had known fleeting instants of proximity to that perfect form, had touched the dark, silky abundance of her hair.

"You are plainspoken," he said, "but not impolite, and your observation regarding John is very nearly rude. Is something amiss?"

She half turned to rearrange the pot of violets so it sat squarely in the late afternoon sunbeam. "I am quite well, thank you. I assume John thrives too?"

"Last night, he permitted me six hours of uninterrupted sleep. I woke today prepared to wrestle titans and subdue dragons. Instead, I made some inquiries at Horse Guards."

She crossed to the mantel, shifting a vase holding a single camellia bloom six inches to the left. "This has to do with Melanie."

When she set the vase down, it apparently caught in a wrinkle of the lace runner and nearly tipped. Miss Delancey's hand got splashed before Alasdhair could right the vase.

He passed her his handkerchief. "Shall we take a turn in the garden, Miss Delancey?"

She dabbed at her hand. "I'd like that. I am not myself today. We're to have company for dinner, a guest my father expects me to charm and flatter."

"Keep it," Alasdhair said, holding the parlor door for her when she would have returned his linen. "Any man expecting flattery from you had best also be alert for flying swine."

She passed through the door, her dignity in full sail. "I am a gifted flatterer. I flattered Mrs. Oldbach into providing flowers until Lent begins. I flattered our choir director into adding a children's chorus to the Easter program. I flatter my father..."

She trailed off as she reached the foyer and took a cloak down from a peg. Alasdhair appropriated the cloak from her and draped it across her shoulders.

"You flatter those who could never mistake your overtures for flirtation. Why is this dinner guest different?" He wrapped his own scarf around her neck, cheek, and ears, careful not to disturb her Mother Superior coiffure. The MacKay plaid, a lighter blue and green than the Black Watch, went well with her coloring.

"This guest is not different, or he should not be different," she said, helping Alasdhair into his greatcoat.

He'd donned proper morning attire for this call, needing very much to prove to Miss Delancey that he'd regained his competence with a razor, brush, and comb.

"We entertain frequently at the vicarage," Miss Delancey went on, leading Alasdhair to the back hallway. "That's part of the job with a parish such as St. Mildred's, and my father is particularly conscientious about socializing with his fellow clerics. He is keenly mindful of church politics and does his best to navigate those waters carefully."

Alasdhair was glad to get back outside, glad to enjoy the afternoon's last rays of sunshine. The air might be frigid, but the light was lovely, and the days—thank Zeus—were growing ever so slightly longer.

"Your father curries the favor of his superior officers." Alasdhair offered his arm and expected at least a glower for his presumption. Miss Delancey instead curled her gloved fingers around his elbow.

"I should argue with you. Papa aspires to a greater calling than St. Mildred's, and just as polite society has rituals for who dances with whom, the Church has its protocols too. Curates are to be regularly invited to Sunday suppers, as are deans, bishops, subdeans, missionaries—provided they don't beg for money at the table—and widows of same."

The Church and the military got on well, oddly enough, considering one organization should have been about faith, hope, and charity, and the other was about violence, murder, and conquest—or defense of the realm, to use the preferred euphemism. They were both large hierarchies much concerned with power and influence.

Alasdhair had never realized that a parish vicar might have a lot in common with an ambitious officer.

"Your father expects to flatter his way up the ladder of holiness? Is your independence to be sacrificed to his ambitions? Has he already chosen your prospective husband from among the ranks of bishops' nephews and godsons?"

Miss Delancey half dragged him down the terrace steps. "Tell me about your visit to Horse Guards."

So there was bad news—Papa was scheming—and good news:

Miss Delancey disapproved of her father's choice. Alasdhair considered those developments as he and Miss Delancey made a circuit around the bordered beds and reached the privacy of the birdbath.

"I asked at Horse Guards after Melanie's... after the man she eloped with, Captain Amery Beauclerk. His regiment shipped out for Canada after the fall of Paris and missed the whole debacle of the Hundred Days and Waterloo. He was back in London on leave more than a year ago, but nobody knows much besides that. Did Melanie indicate if John was baptized?"

"He was," Miss Delancey said. "Melanie assured me of that by letter, though she did not tell me which parish. Might we sit for a moment?"

A fine idea. Alasdhair took the place beside Miss Delancey on the bench and retreated into silence. She was upset about her father's grand plans, but Alasdhair derived backhanded comfort from the realization that whatever was bothering her, his presuming little peck on her cheek apparently hadn't signified.

At all.

"I'm glad you came to call," she said. "I am not at my best, and you remind me that larger issues demand my attention. I will endure supper as I have endured many other suppers."

She sounded grimly determined, not cheerfully, obstreperously, or pleasantly determined. "You are afraid of this guest." That any man should intimidate Dorcas Delancey was an abomination against nature.

"He took advantage of my brother, and I will never forgive him for that. Papa doesn't know the details, and Michael has since been dispatched to an obscure congregation in Northumbria. Papa expects the same man who nearly ruined Michael to boost Papa up that ladder of holiness you refer to. This varlet could easily knock that ladder over when Papa reaches the highest rungs. If I were ever to hate, I would hate the one man my father is determined to flatter."

Hate? Dorcas Delancey *hated* somebody? "He's a churchman?"

She nodded, and something daunted and wary about her posture alarmed Alasdhair. This holy scoundrel had betrayed Dorcas's trust somehow and could still threaten the aspirations of her menfolk.

"Go ahead and hate him, Dorcas, particularly if that's the only alternative to hating yourself. You did not lead your brother astray, you did not take advantage of a foolish young man, you are not spouting churchly platitudes while weaving a web of deceit and extortion. Your brother's malefactor deserves your contempt."

She peered at Alasdhair, and he had the sense that now, a quarter hour after he'd bowed his greeting to her, she was actually noticing his presence. "You speak from experience."

What to tell her when she had troubles enough of her own? "Some officers are described as leading from the rear, shouting orders to the men they send charging directly into enemy fire, while they themselves remain safely out of bullet range. Wellington was emphatically not such an officer. He was inhumanly cavalier about his own safety and inhumanly lucky. He earned the ferocious loyalty of the common soldier as a result."

"You would lead the charge too," she said. "You would never allow others to expose themselves to danger while you sat back and observed their struggles."

Whoever this pious reprobate was, Alasdhair certainly hated him. "I am no saint, Dorcas Delancey. Far from it. Come see John tomorrow and tell me how supper went. Perhaps you can spike your enemy's soup with a physic, and he'll have to cut the evening short."

The last five minutes of the visit went well. The best part was not that Alasdhair made Dorcas laugh, a low, quiet little ripple of mirth. The best part was not even that she was looking quite fierce again when she saw him out the garden gate.

The best part was that after she'd shown him into the alley, she pressed a slow, warm kiss to his cheek, and whispered, "Thank you so much for calling," before disappearing back into her chilly garden.

~

ISAIAH MORNEBETH BOWED his good-nights to the Delanceys and congratulated himself on time well spent. He was so pleased with the evening that he allowed himself to linger over Dorcas's hand in parting. That little gesture of regard subtly flustered her, as Isaiah had hoped it would.

"I trust supper was enjoyable?" Uncle Zachariah asked when Isaiah stopped by the library for a nightcap. Uncle Zachariah wasn't truly an uncle, but rather, a connection of Grandmama's who'd once held some minor deanship at Canterbury. He was a generous host when a young man needed temporary lodgings, and he was an equally generous source of church gossip.

"Thomas Delancey is as skilled a conversationalist as any successful vicar must be," Isaiah replied, helping himself to an ample portion of brandy. "The evening was thoroughly enjoyable." Then too, Isaiah's decision to spend years shivering in the north had been vindicated.

More than vindicated. He'd left London, knowing himself to be too young for serious consideration for the higher church offices. He'd been aware as well that Dorcas was too upset over her brother's foolishness to consider a proposal of marriage. Isaiah had gone north, solemnly promising old Thomas that he'd keep an eye on Michael, and had even dropped in on the younger Delancey from time to time.

That had been great fun.

"Thomas never gives up," Uncle replied, pouring a drink for himself. "He will be eighty years old, delivering the same well-reasoned sermons in the same annual rotation, and still, he will long for more than a pastor's pulpit."

"We must commend his capacity for hope." Poor Thomas simply wasn't bright enough to navigate the intricacies of church politics. He took people at face value and—bless him—was ambivalent about his own plodding ambitions.

"You don't miss the Dales?" Uncle asked, tossing another scoop of coal onto the hearth. The library was not large—it needed to hold only theological treatises and philosophical tomes, after all—and thus it was warm. Whatever else was true about Uncle Zachariah, he'd prospered handsomely while heeding his calling.

"The Dales are pretty, but the winters last four years each, and one must learn to discuss sheep in excruciating detail. Shearing, lambing, the wool markets, foot rot. I was grateful for a chance to serve in the shires, and I am even more grateful to return to civilization."

"You did more than discuss sheep, my boy. Your grandmother kept an eye on you."

Isaiah saluted with his glass. "Grandmama taught me most of what I know of any use."

She advised setting ambitious objectives and taking the long view, the strategic view. Thus Isaiah had done the tedious work of ingratiating himself with the coteries around the Archbishop of York and in the various cathedral circles. He'd taken tea with all the right wealthy old beldames and stood up with all the daughters of the titled houses.

He'd been "caught" praying alone by every notably pious bishop, and he'd been seen to dutifully mail monthly letters home to his grandmother, though those letters had mostly reminded her to send along his quarterly allowance as soon as may be.

All the while, he'd hoped Dorcas, in some small way, had missed him. He'd hoped that, despite herself, she'd wondered how he was managing. He did not expect her to care for him—not yet, as she wasn't a woman to yield her allegiance easily—but he hoped that he'd occupied some peripheral corner of her mind. A memory, a regret, a wish, a puzzlement... something.

Clearly, he had. Clearly, she recalled their past dealings and speculated about future dealings. There was *interest*, however careful she was to pretend otherwise. Interest was a start, and if Isaiah was again patient and determined, Dorcas would eventually realize that they were perfect for each other.

"How did you find the estimable Miss Delightful?" Uncle asked, settling into a wing chair. He was a widower and apparently enjoyed his unattached status. He'd aged from handsome to distinguished, complete with a full head of snowy-white hair. If he and Grandmama did more than gossip and scheme together, Isaiah would not judge them for it.

"Miss Delancey remains quite unmarried, which I admit pleases me." Isaiah could find another candidate for the post of Mrs. Isaiah Mornebeth, but he *wanted* Dorcas. Had wanted her for years. She would be a fitting reward for his ambition and hard work, and she would come to accept that her freedom—also her frustrations—would soon be at an end.

"She's half the reason old Thomas will never rise above parish work," Uncle said, dragging a lap robe across his knees.

"Too headstrong and outspoken?"

"Headstrong, outspoken women who channel their boldness into haranguing Parliament and the public on behalf of the less fortunate are to be treasured. They spare their menfolk the necessity of taking on lost causes and dealing firsthand with the wretched masses. Miss Delancey's problem is that she's too valuable in her present post."

Isaiah took the opposite wing chair, which had been positioned to catch the fire's warmth. "Explain, please. From what I can see, if Dorcas Delancey is permitted to grow any more independent, she'll succumb to the sort of impulses that nearly ruined her brother and precipitated the downfall of her pretty cousin."

Dorcas had a wayward streak, and Isaiah intended that he be its sole beneficiary. She needed precisely the disciplined, loving guidance he would provide, because he alone knew how far she'd gone in service to her principles, even the misguided ones.

"Thomas is stuck at the parish level," Uncle said, "because Miss Delancey has made him into something of a pattern card for parish priests. He's established this sister-parish initiative, pairing wealthy parishes with poorer jurisdictions, and now he'd like to pair urban parishes with rural ones. The shepherds entrusted with larger church affairs love that sort of thing."

"So Thomas took credit for an idea Miss Delancey concocted." A good idea.

"One of an endless store. We're getting up a competition here in London next year, also Miss Delancey's idea. Each congregation that chooses to participate will come up with two improvement projects—turning a vacant lot into garden plots, distributing laying hens, sending boxes of necessities to new mothers. The nature of the projects is entirely up to the imaginations concocting them."

"A competition of do-goodism? Isn't that what most of Mayfair's charitable efforts are?"

"So young and such a cynic. Miss Delancey's scheme has another element. The first project is to be accomplished with only congregational resources—donations of supplies, labor, means, and so forth. A congregation with few material resources might be rich in ingenuity or labor, a congregation with a lot of means might not have much creativity to bring to bear on the challenge. The first project is most of what each contestant congregation is judged on."

"Who are the judges?"

"Chosen by lot from the rolls of the parishes that prefer not to attempt projects. Men and women."

"Fair enough, I suppose." If decent women were useful in any sphere beyond the domestic, it was the charitable. "What's the extra component?"

"The second project is a proposed undertaking and intended to be of greater scope than the first. The congregation that accomplishes the most impressive first-round task and proposes the most ingeniously charitable second-round task wins the funds to embark on that second project."

"And Miss Delancey came up with this scheme?"

"We all know it was her idea, but Thomas has done a good job of presenting and advocating for the plan. Churches all over London are looking a bit more spruce already, because the judging committee members will drop around unannounced to monitor progress on the various projects. Mark me on this, Isaiah, you will see tidier cemeteries, cleaner church steps, and less dust on the pews this spring because of Miss Delancey's notions."

Isaiah wrinkled his nose, torn between admiration—the notion was clever—and unease. The notion was *quite* clever, putting vanity and competitiveness to a constructive, Christian use. The Dorcas he'd known years ago hadn't aspired to cleverness, and he much preferred her that way.

He took a sip of his drink and adopted a thoughtful, troubled expression. "Is that outward display of housekeeping where our parishioners ought to direct their energies? Does that not encourage pride on a congregational scale?"

Uncle was quiet for a moment, then rose and folded his lap robe over the back of the chair. "You are so intelligent, Mornebeth—the apple of your grandmother's eye—and yet, you lack wisdom. The objective is not to encourage congregational vanity, though where is the harm in taking pride in one's house of worship? I'm not talking about popish excesses. I'm talking about a fresh altar cloth, clean windows, a few posies... The touches the poorest congregation can aspire to."

Isaiah swirled his drink and downed the rest of it. Good brandy should not go to waste. "No harm in that, I suppose."

"How gracious of you." Uncle set his unfinished drink on the sideboard. "The more subtle objective is to encourage people to see their churches and neighborhoods with new eyes, to look about for what can be improved, for who or what has been neglected. To inspire them to take responsibility for the edifice where they gather and for the community it represents."

This was sounding perilously like a sermon, and Isaiah's evening had gone too well to be blighted with one of Uncle's perorations.

"You want the folk to rally 'round the old kirk, is that it?"

"And to rally 'round *each other*, Isaiah. To work together for the common weal. To shift from weekly spectators at divine services to members in a community of substance. To visit across parishes and see how the neighboring community fares. That is the genius of Miss Delancey's idea. The charitable projects are all to the good, but she has devised a way to strengthen the Christian purpose within our congregations at the same time. And this is just her latest suggestion. She's working on a plan for children's choirs to put on charitable benefits as a sort of competition as well, and... her ideas are endless."

Uncle took up an elegant brass candlesnuffer. "Thomas will never be permitted to abandon a post where he's an instrument of such unparalleled good. Because the ideas come through him, a lowly vicar, the other vicars are more inclined to accept them, as they'd never accept such schemes if the bishopric had concocted them. Miss Delancey has a genius for parish organization, and that genius must be allowed to flourish."

Dorcas's notions were halfway to outlandish, which only proved to Isaiah that she was urgently in need of the right husband.

"Surely you don't approve of her visiting women's jails?"

Uncle's gaze took on that pitying quality the old aimed at the young whom they in truth envied. "Betsy Fry's little prison stunts gain notice because her Quaker connections are also *banking* connections. Where she aims the light of charitable reform, money follows, and the reform happens without Parliament lifting a beringed finger. She has organized schools within the prisons she visits, workshops for making blankets, and more. Dorcas Delancey sought to emulate that success. If you had half a brain in your handsome head, you'd see the credibility to be gained by such tactics. Credibility matters, Isaiah. Your grandmother taught you that."

"Grandmama taught me that a good night's sleep matters too," Isaiah said, rising, empty glass in hand. "I am in truth quite pleased to hear you extol Miss Delancey's abilities. I have long been impressed with her many virtues and hope to become better acquainted with her now that I'm back in London."

"Your grandmother will be pleased to hear it. Have you had any luck finding lodging in Southwark?"

"A few strong possibilities. I should be out of your hair in another fortnight or so." Unbeknownst to Uncle, Isaiah had taken rooms in a modest boardinghouse back in December. He did use those quarters from time to time when he wanted a bit of privacy. Uncle's establishment was far more commodious, and the old boy was a font of useful knowledge.

Nonetheless, Uncle's picture of the estimable Miss Delancey was missing a few parts that only Isaiah had seen.

The lovely Dorcas had a temper, for example. One she was learning to govern, however imperfectly. She also had the sweetest little scar on the inside of her right wrist from where a cat had swiped at her in childhood. Must have been quite the scratch.

"Miss Delancey will not suffer foolishness from you, Isaiah," Uncle said, using the snuffer on the candles on the mantel and sideboard. "She has turned down a few offers over the years."

Of course she had, from spotty boys and doddering widowers, the perennial proposers. "I'll be patient. I excel at patience."

"You excel at singing your own praises," Uncle said as the scent of candle smoke filled the library. "Much like your darling grandmama. I'll bid you good night and wish you good luck with Miss Delancey. She's sent better men than you packing, so mind you go about the business with some humility."

Isaiah offered his signature beamish-young-sprig smile, though humility had no place in his plans. "Thank you for the warning, Uncle."

Uncle Zachariah shuffled off to dream whatever dreams old men dreamed—of regular bowels and warm quilts, perhaps—while Isaiah poured himself another generous portion of brandy and took the seat Uncle had vacated. A darkened library was a good place to think, and the situation with Dorcas wanted some pondering.

That she was appreciated in church circles was all to the good, because the benefit of accepting Isaiah's suit would be that much more apparent to her. If she became difficult, he could destroy her father, her brother, and her, too, though he certainly did not want to.

"The business wants guile and boldness both." A drive in the park would serve. Deceptively unassuming, and yet, if Isaiah simply showed up at the vicarage on the next sunny day, he'd also have the element of surprise. Dorcas would hesitate, but she would not refuse.

She'd never been able to refuse him anything, and—could a marriage have a stronger foundation?—she never would be able to either.

Marriage to Dorcas Delancey would be *such* fun. One might almost say the prospect was *delightful.*

CHAPTER EIGHT

The day after supper with Isaiah Mornebeth, Dorcas woke to one of nature's little jokes. The same sky that had offered mostly snow, sleet, clouds, and coal smoke arched bright and blue overhead for the second day in a row. The breeze that had been biting and remorseless for weeks was gone, and some misguided bird was chirping away in the garden.

The air was far from warm, and not exactly soft, but it was fresher than usual and contributed to Dorcas's sense of hope.

Mornebeth had comported himself at supper exactly as if he were the devout, dedicated churchman he wanted the world to think he was. He never once alluded to Michael's problems, never once hinted that his discretion regarding the whole, miserable business had lapsed.

Perhaps he even felt some shame for his part in that debacle—as well he should.

A lot of shame.

"You are going out?" Papa asked as Dorcas wrapped Mr. MacKay's scarf about her neck. "Too fine a day to spend inside, I suppose."

"I'm paying a call on the household where Melanie's son bides."

Dorcas offered that admission, prepared to defend it if need be. She had given up rebelling out of sheer contrariness, but she would not allow Papa to stop her from calling on Major MacKay.

Papa removed his glasses and used a handkerchief to polish them. "The lad is healthy?"

"At present, yes. Melanie took good care of him, as best she was able."

He held up his spectacles to the light. "I recognized her handwriting, you know."

Papa was the beloved, unchanging lodestar of Dorcas's existence. Not the cleverest of men, too concerned with the opinions of those who hadn't earned his respect, but he was good-hearted and hard-working. He was her papa, and she would do anything to protect him.

She could not, however, protect him against the slight stoop that had crept into his posture, or the fact that he now needed spectacles throughout the day, rather than only for reading by candlelight.

"You recognized Melanie's handwriting?"

"She started writing to you last year. I assumed you wrote back and probably sent along a bank note or two. Half hoped you would, sparing me the conundrum. She has—had—a way of flourishing her capital letters that some governess or other told her was pretty."

"You knew we were corresponding, and you said nothing?"

Papa put his spectacles on and tucked his handkerchief away. "You think I am too much the sermonizing old windbag, Dorcas. Too cerebral in my calling, too rigid in my morals. I am inclined to spend half a morning looking for all the biblical references to donkeys when instead I ought to be calling on our poorer parishioners. I know I am something of a cross for you to bear."

Never that. Never, ever that. "Your sermon on Balaam's ass was quite thought-provoking." Though Papa had given it only the once, thank heavens. That a donkey could see an avenging angel before its rider did and thus save the rider's life had inspired Papa to draw all manner of peculiar analogies.

Though Dorcas had enjoyed that sermon more than most of Papa's learned exegeses.

"I cared very much for your cousin," Papa said, "but I care for you more. You are my only daughter, the best of what I have left of your mother. Association between you and Melanie was a risk to you, but I chose to turn a blind eye because I trust your discretion."

He could trust Dorcas's discretion now, though that, unfortunately, hadn't always been the case. "I'm sorry I deceived you, Papa. I did not want to choose between my duty to Melanie and my respect for you."

"So you took the whole matter upon yourself, as you so often do, and shielded me from difficult choices."

He looked away, and the winter sunshine streaming through the window aged him. His eyes, usually such a genial blue, were troubled and sad.

"I can't help but feel," he went on, "that I have failed you and Michael as a parent, just as I've failed to distinguish myself in my calling. I want to see you happily settled, Dorcas, not tiptoeing around your old papa's delicate sensibilities and church politics. I will leave you with a competence, and you will always have a home under Michael's roof, but that's not..." He rubbed a hand across his brow. "I digress. I digress with alarming frequency these days."

"You have much on your plate." Was he growing more vague? More easily preoccupied?

"Not so much that I missed your strategy with Mornebeth last night. You played the part of the demure mouse, but I doubt your ruse was effective. He's a clever chap, Dorcas, and his star is on the rise."

Not this again. "Mr. Mornebeth was a pleasant guest, and I'm glad you enjoyed his company." She pulled on her gloves and gathered up a parasol that she carried mostly for self-defense. Another lesson learned in jail.

"Mornebeth enjoyed *your* company," Papa said. "He always has. He saw past that dreadful gray frock and your governess coiffure to the intelligence and integrity that shine so brightly through your disguises. Isaiah is poised to soar, Dorcas, and you could soar with him."

"No." She'd spoken more harshly than the moment called for. "I mean, did you notice how he had to mention the name of every viscountess and bishop in Yorkshire? How the names of his grandmother's titled friends found a way into a conversation about Lenten traditions?"

Papa smiled, a hint of his usual good cheer back in evidence. "He did lay it on a bit thick, didn't he? A puerile tactic for impressing a lady. A wife would gently correct that tendency."

Alasdhair MacKay had impressed Dorcas by staying up all night with a colicky baby, by pressing for answers regarding Melanie's disappearance, by sitting with Dorcas quietly in a frigid garden. He would never attempt to aggrandize himself by trumpeting the names of illustrious associates. He'd admitted to being in line for some sort of title only when Dorcas had questioned him about his calling card.

"I will not marry a man that much in need of correction, Papa. Isaiah Mornebeth should aspire to humility, not claim he's but a humble parson while wedging mention of peers and heiresses into every other sentence."

Papa's smile was wistful. "You are as smart as your mama, and she would be proud of you, Dorcas."

Are you proud of me? She did not dare ask, and she did not deserve his praise in any case. "I intend to keep a fond eye on young John, Papa. My conscience must have it so. He's family, and he's a mere baby, in the care of people who are no relation to him at all."

"Good people?" Papa asked, gaze on the plaid scarf about Dorcas's neck.

"Very good."

"Then I will leave the matter in your competent hands, but if the boy should want for anything..."

"Yes?" John would want for nothing, not lullabies, not stuffed bears, not bedtime stories or abundant affection. Mr. MacKay would see to it.

"We are his family, as you say, and a little discreet assistance here and there would be no bother. Perhaps if Melanie had been able to turn to us for help sooner..."

"Perhaps if Melanie had not been so determined to run off with her officer in the first place, Papa. Don't torment yourself."

"So sensible." Papa patted her shoulder and wandered off toward his study.

Dorcas watched him go, both saddened by the exchange and encouraged. Papa was aging. The years left to him in any professional capacity were trickling away, and he'd labored conscientiously in the church's vineyards for decades. The contribution he'd made didn't seem adequate in his own eyes, and that was wrong.

But his attitude toward John put compassion—albeit discreet compassion—over appearances, and that counted for a lot.

"Papa?" She wanted to call him back, to once again be a girl wrapped in the security of a paternal embrace that sheltered her from all perils.

He paused at his study door, hand on the latch. "Daughter?"

"I love you."

"And, I you." He shuffled through the doorway and gave her a little wave. "Until supper."

"THE THING TO DO," Alasdhair muttered, "is ask the lady what she thinks of kisses to the cheek and all they signify." Not for anything would Alasdhair welcome a return to the battlefield, but a discussion of romantic sentiments struck him as nearly as daunting.

"Bah." This was John's response to most of Alasdhair's maunderings. "Bah-buh-buh-bah."

"Thank you for that learned reply," Alasdhair said, taking the boy for another circuit around the desk. Timmens was napping, bless her, and Alasdhair was… fretting?

"Pondering," he said, pressing a kiss to John's downy crown. "Pondering the proper course with a very proper lady."

Though not too proper. Dorcas had a sense of humor, she had a temper. She had above all an independent and formidable intellect, as well as an unerring moral compass.

"She will not let me falter where you are concerned," Alasdhair said, making a rude noise with his lips against the top of John's head.

John chortled and bounced in Alasdhair's arms.

"Like that, do you?" Alasdhair did it again, though he knew the result could be an entire morning spent making the boy laugh and smile. "We fellows are uncomplicated creatures, aren't we?"

And yet, the subject of kisses with Dorcas would be complicated, by honesty and by the fact that if Dorcas wanted nothing more to do with Alasdhair and his kisses, there was an end to some dreams.

"I had stopped dreaming," Alasdhair told the boy quietly. "Stopped hoping. Hope must be the greatest torment the damned suffer. You put it aside, or lose your wits."

Except Alasdhair was not damned. He lifted John high before him. "You might be that tall someday, young John. A braw, bonnie laddie with your mother's gorgeous blue eyes and your cousin Dorcas's quick mind. The ladies will besiege you, and I will say, as all the elders say, 'I knew him when he was in leading strings.'"

He cuddled John to his chest, already wanting fortification against the day when the boy went out into the world, leaving home, possibly going to war.

"Go for the Church," Alasdhair said. "You can do a lot of good in the Church, and your most powerful weapons will be kindness and courage. No firearms, no artillery that can rip a man in two."

"The Church has its artillery."

That voice… that crisp, clipped, confident voice. Alasdhair was in serious trouble when even the sound of Dorcas's voice made his heart lighter, but how long had she been standing in the doorway, and how much had she heard?

"Miss Delancey, a pleasure to see that you survived supper with the serpent. John was assisting me with estate matters."

"Was he really?" She swished into the room, her dress a becoming blue ensemble that brought out the unusual verdigris color of her eyes. "I'd advise him to become a steward long before I'd send him to the Church, Mr. MacKay. The godly excel at vexing one another. I assume Timmens is enjoying a cup of tea in the kitchen?"

"A nap. John wakes her up at least once a night, usually twice. He prefers the breast to his porridge, though Timmens says that will all change on the day and at the time of the boy's choosing. Would you like to hold him?"

When Dorcas Delancey was in the grip of strong emotion, she tended to look as if she was puzzling over a conundrum. She regarded John with exactly that expression now.

"He appears quite comfortable with you," she said. "Henderson offered to bring up tea. I declined."

No tea, no cuddles with the baby, but when last they'd parted, she had kissed Alasdhair's cheek. "Tell me about the serpent."

"Mr. Mornebeth was on his best behavior."

Mornebeth. Alasdhair had a name, and if he had to waltz with all of Powell's sisters nightly for the entire spring Season, he'd soon know more than just a name about the man.

"His good behavior worries you?"

She took the seat behind Alasdhair's desk—of course. "When the French left off skirmishing, when they packed up camp and disappeared into the night, did you conclude they were about to surrender?"

"Just the opposite. Shall I accost this Mornebeth person in a dark alley, Miss Delancey? I would bring reinforcements if necessary. My cousins excel at pugilism, thanks in no small part to my helpful tutelage."

She rearranged the quills in his standish such that all three tilted in the same direction. She moved the pounce pot so it sat equidistant from the standish and the wax jack. She reached for Alasdhair's stack of correspondence, probably intending to sort it by date, but stopped herself.

He hoped she was trying not to smile.

"You will teach John to defend himself."

They had both, somehow, made the leap from John biding with Alasdhair for a fortnight, to John having become a fixture in the household.

"His papa is an ocean away, and for all we know, Captain Beauclerk might remain in the New World for years. His mother is missing at best, and I am entrusted with his care. He'll have a home with me as long as he needs one."

"Thank you."

"You are trying to dodge a discussion of Mr. Mournful."

Timmens's arrival spared Miss Delancey from having to reply. "So you've off with the lad again, Major. Greetings, Miss Delancey. These two wander the premises when my back is turned, exploring the great, wide world. I found them in the kitchen last evening, playing fling-the-porridge. John should be a champion at horseshoes thanks to Mr. MacKay's early instruction."

"Mr. MacKay is apparently generous with his many forms of expertise."

"He is," Timmens said, plucking the boy from Alasdhair's arms. "And God be thanked for that, or a poor nursemaid would never get any sleep. Come along, young man. Major MacKay has better things to do than entertain my favorite tyrant."

She dipped a curtsey, John in her arms, and bustled off.

"I adore a managing woman," Alasdhair said. "Life is so much simpler when a lady of purpose takes matters in hand."

"And yet," Miss Delancey said, "I don't envy the woman who attempts to manage you. Is that your sword hanging over the hearth?"

"Aye. A reproach and a reminder. My cousins and I display our swords by agreement. We were at our club one dark and dismal night, and some other former officers were telling tales before the fire. They regaled one another with recollections of a certain siege and the ensuing battle, the scene of my worst nightmares. To hear those fellows, you'd have thought it was all a grand lark. My cousins had to haul me from the place by force, lest I correct a narrative as false as it was self-serving."

"You were angry?"

"Murderously so. Goddard and Powell promised me they would keep their swords in plain sight to remind them of the truth of war, the violence and injustice of it. What the Spanish went through, thanks to the competing ambitions of the French and the British, was beyond horrific. To hear savagery and rapine reduced to 'jolly good fun'... Suffice it to say, I owe my cousins for putting distance between me and the gallows."

Miss Delancey rose. "Some of us lack the strength to deal in truth, Mr. MacKay. We create fabrications in defense of our sanity. A little self-delusion can spare us an inundation of sorrow and remorse."

"Does self-delusion figure into your dealings with the serpent, Miss Delancey?" Had she been sweet on Mornebeth once upon a time? If so, and the fool had let her go, he was a very stupid serpent.

She moved away from the desk to study the portrait of Alasdhair's grandparents. They were decked out in the clan plaid, their expressions deceptively genial for a pair of aging rogues.

"My self-castigation has more to do with Melanie. I knew she and Beauclerk were growing too close. He was a penniless squire's penniless son, a charmer. I appreciate charm, particularly subtle charm, and aspire to it myself on occasion, but his attentions bore an ardency that boded ill."

Must work on my subtle charm. "You blame yourself for their elopement?"

She peered at the artist's signature. "This is a Nasmyth."

And *that* was another dodge. "My grandparents approved of his liberal politics, and say what you will about him, he's an exceptionally bright man. Grandmama in particular took an interest in his career, seeing him as an emblem of modern Scotland. That woman was a force of nature. She could tell you in excruciating detail about every spat between the MacKays and Sutherlands, who among the ancestors scarpered for Denmark when Cromwell razed our castle, and why Great-Uncle George was no sort of Jacobite."

Dorcas looked from the painting to Alasdhair, who was lounging with a hip propped on a corner of the desk. "You have her eyes. I will think of them as force-of-nature eyes."

A silence bloomed, while Alasdhair reeled from a genuine compliment freely given. He'd adored his granny, and his last memory of her was a tearful farewell when Papa had bought him his colors.

"Why are you looking at me like that?" Miss Delancey asked, gaze firmly back on the painting. "Your grandparents made a very handsome couple."

"I'm looking at you this way because I want to kiss you—properly, or improperly, depending on your definitions—and that is complicated."

He braced himself for a tart little set-down, a cool rejoinder that would leave him in no doubt as to the futility of his aspirations.

"Why complicated? Most men simply steal a kiss and congratulate themselves on their successful thievery. I have presumed somewhat on your person, too, a casual gesture between cordial acquaintances."

"We're not friends? You've seen me insensate on the bedroom floor, a bedroom you invited yourself into, I might add, and we're not friends?"

He remained perched against the desk when he wanted to interpose himself between her and the portrait and force her to meet his gaze. Except he would never force a woman to do anything, least of all this woman.

"We are... something," Miss Delancey said. "I like you."

"And that bothers you?"

She nodded.

"Good. I like you, too, and that bothers me as well, but in a lovely sort of way. Would you like to meet my horse?" Alasdhair sought to leave this house, where Timmens could intrude at any moment, and Henderson might blunder along with a bucket of coal, or some nosy cousin was bound to drop by at the exact wrong moment.

Miss Delancey slanted him a fleeting glance. "Meet your horse? The one who's loyal to his oats?"

"They are all loyal to their oats, but it's as pretty an afternoon as winter offers, and I usually look in on Charlie at some point every day. Bonnie Prince Charlie, to his new acquaintances."

"You named him for royalty?"

"I named him for a lost cause, which he certainly is." And for Grandmama Charlotte and all her causes.

Miss Delancey scooted around the desk and made for the door. "Will you kiss me in the stable, Mr. MacKay?"

"My cordial acquaintances call me Alasdhair. And as much as I want to kiss you, I want to first ensure that you grasp that I am not a Captain Beauclerk, though once upon a time, I could have been."

She waited by the door until Alasdhair opened it for her. "Once upon a time," she said, "I was a sweet and trusting girl. I have parted ways with that girl, and I have no intention of regaling you with a recounting of her fate."

The serpent—Saint Mornebeth—figured in that tale. Alasdhair knew that much without Dorcas having to admit it. "Then I will explain about me and kisses, and you will render judgment as you see fit."

She paused on the threshold, spearing Alasdhair with a glower. "You will explain what it means to be bothered in a lovely sort of way?"

"Yes." Given a chance, he'd do better than explain. He'd show her precisely what it meant, but only if she allowed him to, which, given what he had to tell her, she really should not.

THE SIGHT of Alasdhair MacKay and baby John charming each other had stolen Dorcas's breath—stolen her heart too. Mr. MacKay had been confiding in the boy. An infant could not grasp the import of specific words, though he could sense when he was being cherished.

Your most powerful weapons will be kindness and courage.

I adore a managing woman.

I like you, too, and that bothers me... in a lovely sort of way.

Alasdhair MacKay deserved cherishing, and what a relief to be able to admit that about any adult male.

"This is your noble steed?" Dorcas beheld a big, roman-nosed bay. "Hello, Your Highness."

Charlie wuffled and craned his neck over his half door.

"He's a shameless flirt. For a bite of carrot, he will sing you odes with his soulful brown eyes, and for an apple, he will promise you his firstborn, though, mind you, the poor lad's a gelding." Mr. MacKay passed Dorcas a carrot, which she broke in half.

"Tell me about kisses, Mr. MacKay, and about being bothered."

The horse crunched his treat into oblivion and wiggled his lips in Dorcas's direction.

"Horse, you are not helping my cause," Mr. MacKay said, scratching the beast's chin. "I saw her first, and she likes me better."

Dorcas fed the horse the rest of the carrot. "I like you. I don't like many people, and especially not many men."

"Neither do I. Come along with me, and I'll show you a secret." He took Dorcas by the hand, and she wished she wasn't wearing gloves. "The saddles and whatnot are stored in here." He opened a plank door and ushered Dorcas into a cozy space redolent of leather and oats. The room had a pair of windows—latched in defense of the winter cold—and a little parlor stove, as well as a cushioned settle and sagging wing chair.

"Henderson and Oldham spend the milder evenings out here,

dicing with the other grooms and domestics, lamenting the state of the world. Oldham was my groom, though I shared him with Powell for much of the campaign. He bides mostly with Powell, but when I come to London, my cousins send Oldham to spy on me."

Halfway through this explanation, Dorcas spied a pile of toweling in the corner of the floor near the stove. Upon that toweling was a calico cat, and curled next to her were three kittens.

"Kittens at this time of year?" One orange, one black, one orange and black.

"My secret treasure. Come spring, there won't be a mouse left standing. Diana and her offspring will see to that."

"Diana the huntress."

"The enchantress, to hear the neighborhood tomcats opine on the matter. Sit with me."

As badly as Dorcas longed to hold John, as much as she wanted to press kisses to his russet curls and cuddle him close, the kittens tugged at her heart nearly as much. Alasdhair MacKay *treasured* kittens, maybe half in jest, but only half.

"Will you be back in Scotland come spring, Mr. MacKay?"

"I might." He took the seat on the high-backed settle and patted the place beside him. Dorcas lowered herself to the cushion, though the seat was narrow and afforded no room for a proper distance between her and Mr. MacKay.

Not that she wanted such a distance.

"I will explain why I winter in London," Mr. MacKay said, "and a few other matters too. I was soldier, a good enough officer, as officers go. Looked after my men, obeyed all but the patently stupid orders, of which there were a few. My cousins and I weren't part of the inner circle. We have little wealth, only minor standing, and our driving ambition was to survive the hostilities without disgracing ourselves."

Dorcas's own ambitions in a nutshell. "Did you disgrace yourself?"

"Yes. Abominably." He scrubbed a hand over his face.

"Abysmally. Sometimes, you disgrace yourself by failing to act, failing to speak up. The disgrace is private and thus all the more corrosive."

He spoke in eternal verities, and yet, Dorcas could respond. "Sometimes, speaking up is futile." Worse than futile. "Speaking up can cause hurt and misery for no good reason."

"A gentleman has a duty to speak up, especially when the exercise is futile. What do you know of the Siege of Ciudad Rodrigo, Miss Delancey?"

Dorcas thought back to the years before Waterloo. "Britain was successful. Wellington's artillery opened two breaches in the walls, and the French could not adequately defend them both. The entire French siege train fell into our hands and occasioned quite the celebration by the victorious troops."

How the newspapers had crowed, and how anxiously the citizenry had scanned the casualty lists.

"Not a celebration, Dorcas, a riot. Compared to what followed, that was an easy victory. A few hundred lives lost on both sides, but our rank and file didn't realize how much worse it could have been. They sacked the town, though the Spanish were our allies, and it was hours before order was restored."

"One heard rumors." But rumors only. Military misconduct would never have been permitted to reach the ears of the British public. They had sacrificed much to finance a war that had dragged on for nearly two decades, and many had been against the Peninsular campaign altogether.

"You heard rumors," Mr. MacKay replied, "but the reality was the stuff of nightmares."

The orange kitten rose, stretched and arched, then tottered away from the mama. So tiny and so sweet.

"Tell me of your nightmares."

"Ciudad Rodrigo was in January. By March, we were besieging Badajoz, and that... The damned rain would not let up, we couldn't get our cannon forward, the French were picking us off like so many nesting partridges, and Soult was breathing down our necks. When battle was finally joined, we lost thousands of good men in just a few hours. Wellington, who has seen many a battle, wept at the carnage."

"A victory though," Dorcas said. "A costly victory."

"Badajoz made the aftermath in Ciudad Rodrigo look like a speech-day romp. Many soldiers were flogged for misconduct, but nobody was hanged. We were left instead to pickle our souls in the shame of a victorious army turned into a mob of demons."

None of this had been in the papers. "The soldiers misbehaved?"

"For three days, we looted, raped, killed, and drank without limit. Hundreds of civilians died—and they were our allies. Rank and file shot the officers they'd fought beside the day before, and if I am ever consigned to hell, I will regard it a mercy provided I'm not forced to relive those experiences."

"But you do relive them." Dorcas had her own version of hell, and it was never far from her thoughts.

"Time helps," he said softly, "but I don't want to forget what can happen to good men when they are pushed too far. Had circumstances been different, I might have been among those too drunk to govern my behaviors."

"What happened?"

"I remained sober, thank the Deity. I walked the streets, a loaded gun in my hand, and more than once, that weapon was all that stood between me and St. Peter. The world as I knew it was inebriated with evil."

This recounting was clearly important to Mr. MacKay, a confidence, and not at all what Dorcas had been expecting to hear when she'd agreed to make Charlie's acquaintance.

"Go on."

The kitten attacked the toe of Mr. MacKay's boot. Such a fierce little ball of fluff.

"I came upon my commanding officer, a newly promoted lieutenant colonel. His papa was a viscount, he'd been mentioned in the dispatches, and yet, he was one of those cowards who lead from the rear. The men were wary of him. Left to his own devices, he'd send them into stupid situations for the sake of his own advancement. Still, I thought him inexperienced and vain, not truly wicked. I got along with him because I had to."

"Because he could have had you flogged for a loose button."

"Officers weren't usually flogged, but we were held to account in other ways."

The kitten pounced and retreated, then pounced again. Mr. MacKay watched this assault and remained unmoving.

"Lieutenant Colonel Dunacre was with a woman," Mr. MacKay said, his voice taking on a distant quality, "a young woman. They were in the courtyard of a home that had to have been among the better residences in the town. Most of the families who could had left before the battle, but some stayed, much to their sorrow. The lieutenant colonel was clearly intent upon revelry with the young lady."

MacKay's calm made this recounting all the more dreadful. "What was the woman intent upon?"

"At the time, I told myself that only the prostitutes would have remained in a besieged garrison town, that the young woman did not appear to be objecting. She had some English and kept urging Dunacre toward the stable, which I assumed was a gesture in the direction of privacy. I did not want to see my commanding officer at less than his best. When I should have asked more questions, should have taken the lady aside and assured myself of her willingness, I did not."

"Would Dunacre have allowed you to intervene?"

"That's not the point, Dorcas. The woman was a civilian, a noncombatant who'd just seen her entire town destroyed and very likely lost loved ones in the battle. Dunacre should have left her in peace. In the midst of a riot, he was choosing the side of mayhem and rapine, when he should have been helping to restore order. I ignored his ignominious behavior and went about my own business."

And how Alasdhair's voice wielded the lash of contempt for that choice now. He picked up the kitten, who commenced batting at his chin.

"If there's more, Alasdhair, you can tell me." Though what he'd told Dorcas so far was bad enough. "I've been to jail, you know. The stories I heard there broke my heart. Women having to make terrible choices, to endure terrible consequences. My own troubles faded to annoyances in the face of what I heard, and I am no longer so easily shocked." Dorcas had regained her soul during those nights in jail, an utterly unexpected place to find redemption.

Alasdhair gently scratched the kitten's shoulders, which resulted in a gentle purring. "That young woman was a mother. She'd been leading Dunacre away from the house in which her two small children were hiding. She hanged herself later that day, and the next time I saw her, she was laid out on the cobbles, those children standing dry-eyed and helpless beside her body. Dunacre, by contrast, was bragging about the pretty bit of Spanish lace he'd enjoyed most of the afternoon with. I nearly blew out my own brains, but I still had duties to attend to, men to look after. Taking my own life would have served no purpose and upset my cousins. There was a war to win, and too many lives had already been lost..."

It's not your fault would be no comfort. Viewed from a certain honorable perspective, this tragedy within tragedies might have been prevented—if Alasdhair had acted differently—or it might have ended with Alasdhair laid out on the cobbles.

"I am glad you did not blow out your brains, Mr. MacKay. Exceedingly glad."

The kitten snuggled against his chest, while the mother cat watched from across the room.

"I wasn't glad, not for a long time. I took the children to the church, because the fine soldiers of His Majesty's army certainly hadn't a thought for the town's orphans. Dorcas, the nuns were sheltering dozens of children. Boys, girls, all ages... The little ones looking after the littler ones. Their parents were gone, killed in a war the Spanish had tried desperately to avert. More than a few were orphaned when a mother despoiled by drunken soldiers could not endure the shame of her ill treatment. I have never been so disgusted to be a man or a soldier and never felt more helpless."

Dorcas took off her gloves and possessed herself of Mr. MacKay's free hand. "I felt that way in jail. Surrounded by injustice and despair, unable to change any of it. We lock children up with their mothers and consider that an act of compassion, though we incarcerate those children amid disease, bad rations, and regular violence. We leave those children—some of them little more than infants—sitting on the dock when their mothers are transported. I think of them when Papa wants me to temper my articles. Instead, I sharpen my words."

"And I adore you for that," Mr. MacKay said. "I adore you for your rapier-sharp words."

Dorcas had never been adored before, had never met a man whose adoration would have mattered to her.

"What did you do, back in Spain?"

"I talked to the nun who admitted me to the church. Babbled, more like. We sat among the children, under the olive trees, and that old woman with the weight of the world on her shoulders listened to me. She pointed out that I could atone for any harm I had done. I could send along some coin for the children. I could intervene with the next officer bent on enjoying himself at the expense of innocents. I could pay attention to the instincts that warn a man when his fellows are about to behave evilly. I was not powerless in the face of evil. I could *do better* and hopefully even do some good. She never once used the typical language of piety. She simply told me to make what amends I could."

Dorcas allowed herself, ever so slightly, to lean against Mr. MacKay's arm. "And you have been atoning ever since."

"I come to London in winter and keep an eye out for the streetwalkers. They suffer badly in the colder months. No custom to be had, Town half empty of those who can afford to pay for their pleasures. I've sent a few children to Goddard for a meal and a safe place to sleep, but the ladies are my concern. I also made a decision in that churchyard, Dorcas, that I would be a gelding, so to speak, until I had spent as many winters in London as I had spent soldiering in Spain."

"You took a vow of chastity?" Again, not what she'd expected to hear on this visit with Charlie.

"Nothing so noble as a vow. I made a decision to temporarily put aside an aspect of life that had grown too complicated. That decision afforded me relief, and it was the right choice at the time."

"You became a spinster, which can be a relief." A haven, a form of camouflage that the world would never understand.

"I became a spinster, but I have also served out the term of my indenture to self-restraint, though I remain bound by my memories."

The mother cat rose to sit on her haunches, and Mr. MacKay gently set the kitten on the floor. The little creature returned to his mama, and she commenced licking his head.

What an extraordinary tale Mr. MacKay had told. What an extraordinary man he was. "How are you bound by your memories?"

"Though I have served out my winters of self-restraint, I am still unwilling—perhaps unable—to pursue recreationally that which most men of means regard as harmless frolicking."

He was being delicate, which he did surprisingly well. "You do not kiss me merely to flirt?"

"Such a bright woman. You make a difficult conversation as easy as it could possibly be. I would never trifle with a lady's regard or with her good name. I kiss you because you bother me in the best possible way and because I hope that when you kiss me back, you are not trifling with me either. And if you are trifling with me, I must ask you to desist."

Dorcas eased the rest of her weight against his side. This conversation was part confession, part declaration, and entirely right. This was precisely how two people ought to embark on becoming a whole greater than the sum of the parts.

With honesty and trust, with words that could be painful, but were intended honorably.

"Say something, Dorcas. I am not in the habit of discussing my past, but with you, the topic had to be broached."

Dorcas did not discuss her past either. "I will respect your confidences, Alasdhair MacKay, and I respect you."

His brows knit. "Does that mean no more kisses?"

"Quite the contrary."

The mama cat curled up with her offspring again, and Alasdhair's arm came around Dorcas's shoulders. "That's all right, then."

CHAPTER NINE

Alasdhair and his cousins often spoke of the lessons learned at war. Powell swore he'd never again take for granted a letter or scold from his sisters, that simply hearing them rip up at him in their native Welsh tongue was now a joy.

Goddard had become devoted to the French vineyards he'd inherited from his mother's family. He was convinced that fine French vintages, and champagne in particular, were a way to knit together English conviviality with what was best about France and her traditions.

Alasdhair had learned the bitterness of regret, of wishing he'd been a better man, and the determination to become that better man. He'd learned that change might come to some people in a revelatory moment, but for him, change had been a slow, uncertain process. A man who'd once proclaimed himself born to carouse could now rejoice to sit beside a woman in silence and let the peace of a chilly stable fill his heart.

"I have regrets too," Dorcas said. "Nothing so terrible as what you've endured. Nobody died, nobody was orphaned. No towns were razed. I've nonetheless had to make my peace with situations where all of my choices led to sorrow."

Sorrow was more bearable than dishonor. Alasdhair had learned that too. "Have you forgiven yourself?"

She rested her head against his shoulder. "For the most part. Tell me about Scotland."

Right. Enough about the war. Finally, enough about the war. "Scotland is more beautiful than you can imagine, Dorcas. The light is purer, the water sweeter, the breeze fresher than anything England has to offer. My family delights in hard work and in each other. We are full of song and naughty jokes, and our whisky is as fierce as our winters."

"You make whisky?"

"Everybody back home makes whisky, but the MacKays have blazed a trail of mercantile daring. Now we actually pay the tithe to the exciseman so we can export our whisky. *Uisge beatha* is not a drink for gentlemen in their drawing rooms, but there's demand for it in the taverns and a few of the lesser clubs. The drovers in particular are fond of our brew. Would you like to try a nip?"

He withdrew his flask and passed it over.

"You are daring me?" She'd sampled from his flask before, but to offer the libation now was more than a friendly gesture to distract a woman from her upset.

"I'm inviting you to enjoy the MacKay family's pride and joy, or one of them. I count myself as another, and you're welcome to sample me too." Though simply sitting with his arm around Dorcas's shoulders and her soft weight against his side was a delight beyond words.

She uncorked the flask and tipped it to her lips. "I could grow to enjoy your family's pride and joy. The warmth is impressive, Mr. MacKay."

Alasdhair. Please call me Alasdhair. "So are your kisses."

"I've only kissed you the once." She corked the flask and returned it to him. "Barely a kiss, at that."

Alasdhair needed for her to make the next overture, not only because he was out of practice and still somewhat at sea—a recitation of ancient history had not been among his plans for the day—but also because a woman might say one thing and mean something else entirely.

Come with me to the stable might mean *Please, don't murder my children.*

Powell's sisters berated him for racketing about London, but what they really meant was *we miss you, we love you, we worry for you.*

I respect you from Dorcas could well mean something other than *I would like to tear your clothes off this instant and spend the rest of my life with you.*

Though a man could hope.

She studied the toes of her boots. "I am not in the habit of kissing anybody. I nuzzle my cat."

"Lucky cat. Would you perhaps like to nuzzle me, Dorcas?"

She nodded. Just that, but her nod was firm. She knew what she wanted, though perhaps not how to embark on its pursuit. Alasdhair rose and offered her his hand.

"I desperately long for your nuzzling," he said, helping her to her feet. "I dream of your voice, full of light and confidence, and the sound of it wraps around my heart. I recall the brush of your lips against my cheek, and everything inside me turns to yearning." *Kiss me, please. For the love of all that's dear, kiss me.*

He kept hold of her hand, lest she march off to flirt with his horse again.

"You think I am delightful." She slid her palm up his arm to rest her fingers at his nape. "You are daft, Mr. MacKay."

"I am yours."

She pressed her lips to his, gently and sweetly.

He held still, buffeted by tenderness and desire, determined that the initiative remain hers. "More, please." He'd beg if she wanted him to beg.

Dorcas tried a brush of mouth upon mouth, then settled in for a taste of him. By the stealthiest of increments, she rested her weight against him, until she was enfolded in his embrace, and he was kissing her back. The joy was too profound to be rushed, the relief even greater. A homecoming for the soul, a wonderment Alasdhair had never thought to experience.

When Dorcas kissed him, the pleasure wasn't merely of the body, but also of the heart. She respected him. She *respected* him, and how he had needed to hear those words and not known it.

"I like kissing you," she said, resting her cheek against his chest. "I wasn't sure I would, but you don't plunder and strut. You listen with your kisses."

Alasdhair had no earthly idea what she was going on about. "I can plunder, if you tell me that's what you want of me."

She recommenced kissing him and proved that she was capable of plundering too. Also of making off with his wits and inspiring a certain masculine appendage to stand at attention.

"You desire me," she said, peering up at him.

"I delight in desiring you and hope you want me as well."

Dorcas eased away, and despite all temptation to the contrary, Alasdhair let her go. He would always let her go.

"I know where kittens come from, Alasdhair MacKay. Don't think a preacher's daughter is permitted to remain ignorant at my great age. I know precisely the path Melanie trod to become a mother. Kissing isn't the end of it."

"Kissing is only the beginning, but we'll not tread that path unless you decide I am who and what you desire. The choice is yours, and no amount of kissing or tippling or petting my *horse* changes that."

She stroked his lapel. "You are so fierce. Melanie was right to entrust John to you."

High praise, also a wee bit of a dodge. "You are safe with me, Dorcas. I realize the words are meaningless, but I offer them to you as a pledge nonetheless. I am the last man who will coerce, threaten, or inveigle you into anything about which you are reluctant. I will charm you, though, to the extent of my modest capabilities, and you are free to charm me as well."

She regarded the cat and kittens, all heaped together for yet another family nap. "My charm is the kind that winkles flower donations out of dowagers or encourages the choir director to take on a program for the children. The other kind of charm..."

"Yes?"

"I have never aspired to it, but with you..."

"With me?"

"You think I am delightful. Perhaps I can be charming in your direction as well. The mind boggles to contemplate such notions, and I am growing a bit chilly. Shall we return to the house?"

The stable wasn't *that* chilly, and Alasdhair was learning just how much passion Dorcas Delancey kept trussed up behind her starch and manners. "Do you truly want to return to the house, Dorcas?"

"No, but I want to savor this encounter, to marvel that a man of substance and honor is attracted to me. I should aspire to regain my bearings, but I have clung to my bearings for years, afraid any misstep would lead to ruin, when in fact..."

She came to him and wrapped him in a hug. "I have been lost, Alasdhair MacKay, and you know how that feels. I never thought to find, or to be found by, such a one as you."

His arms came around her, and he rested his cheek against her temple. "You think I'm delightful?"

"And that is an understatement."

He wallowed in the pleasure of Dorcas's embrace, of her words, of her trust. She was right. The world had changed for them both in the past hour, and the situation wanted savoring and considering. No need to rush, no need to panic. Dorcas Delancey was not a woman of mercurial temperament or flighty notions.

And if Alasdhair was very, very patient, and very, very lucky, then someday, Dorcas would explain to him how she'd landed in a situation where all of her choices had led to sorrow.

~

DORCAS WALKED HOME with Alasdhair MacKay at her side, the experience feeling novel, though he'd performed that courtesy previously.

As a younger woman, she'd observed the proprieties, never setting foot outside the vicarage without Papa or Michael, or at least the housekeeper and a footman, to scare away brigands and footpads. If she'd ventured into the slums, she'd done so among a well-guarded committee of the charitably inclined.

Then Michael had proved he was incapable of keeping himself from harm's way, much less protecting Dorcas. The church work had taken up more and more of her time, Isaiah Mornebeth had made a pest of himself, and the habit of venturing forth alone had taken hold.

Papa had objected, but he'd seen the futility of spending all of his days jaunting about calling on new mothers, ailing elders, or the parish's shopkeepers. His objections had faded to grumbling and, in the past year or so, to patient resignation.

When Dorcas ambled along beside Alasdhair, his scarf tucked around her neck, people *noticed*. She was no longer an anonymous female, neither shopgirl nor matron, hurrying down the walkway on some domestic errand. She was an escorted lady, with a brawny Scotsman guarding her from all perils.

You are safe with me. He could not know—and Dorcas must never allow him to learn—why that assurance was worth more to her than all the flowery speeches or graceful waltzes in Mayfair. He could not know that his little conversations with John had melted her heart. That his kindnesses to Melanie had won her admiration.

"What does the rest of your day hold?" Alasdhair asked as they approached the tea shop.

"The midwinter fellowship meal is next Sunday. I must confirm who is bringing what dishes, who will look after the younger children so the parents can sit and enjoy some adult conversation for a change, and who will assist with cleanup."

"You don't aspire to planning formal dinners or musicales?"

"Aspire? To organize a meal for a mere thirty people is no work at all, sir."

"Speaking of meals... I am a tad peckish and, more significantly, willing to resort to any subterfuge to spend another half hour with you. Might we stop for a snack?"

He did not manage well on an empty belly, according to his cousins. Dorcas liked knowing that. "A cup of chocolate would suit, and it's not subterfuge if you announce it on the very street."

"Stratagem, then." He held the door for her, and she preceded him to the same quiet table they'd taken before. Would this become *their* table? Couples created routines and rituals like that, not that Dorcas considered that she and Alasdhair were a couple—yet.

Though they were *something*. They had kissed, they had *discussed* kissing, and he had confided his wartime memories to her.

"When you finish organizing the fellowship melee, what will occupy your time?" he asked.

"It can become a melee, if the children are allowed too many trips to the dessert table and Mrs. Davenport gets to bickering with her nephew. I have thank-you notes to write, to a parishioner who donated flowers this month and to another who always gives the church a generous discount on floral arrangements."

Alasdhair unwrapped the scarf from Dorcas's neck and hung up her cloak for her, then held her chair. Small courtesies, but she'd learned to manage without them for the most part.

Until it was time to be the proper lady again, in which case, she slipped into that role for an evening or an afternoon. The waiter came around to take their order, and Dorcas asked for both nutmeg and cinnamon to go with the whipped cream on her hot chocolate.

"Celebrating something, Miss Delancey?" Alasdhair wasn't smiling, but those blue eyes of his were quietly dancing.

"The approach of spring. I can feel it in the air. We are not done with the annual penance referred to as winter, but spring approaches nonetheless." Spring approached in the person of Alasdhair MacKay, after a long, dreary winter.

The food arrived, and as Alasdhair tucked into his sandwiches, Dorcas took a spoonful of sweetened whipped cream dusted with spices.

"This is heavenly... This is... I don't know when I've enjoyed a treat more."

"Do you enjoy the church work?"

With anybody else, she would have trotted out some little platitude about finding joy in service, but this was Alasdhair MacKay, who'd become a self-declared male spinster rather than brush awful memories aside with drink and worse.

"I have learned to be patient," Dorcas said. "To do what I can when I can. I *enjoyed* the nights I spent in jail, I'll have you know. I asked those women what assistance they would find useful, and it wasn't prayer, I can tell you that. I had the ladies equipped with slates and books. Sent along a crate of myths, fables, and children's stories hidden beneath a few tattered copies of *The Book of Common Prayer*. The literate women took on the teaching of those without letters. It gave them something to do and improved their chances in life."

Alasdhair started on his second sandwich. "And you did not stop there."

"Mrs. Fry's scheme, making quilts, is ingenious. Anybody can learn to sew a straight seam, and every household has scraps of fabric to donate. Fashions change, figures change, projects are put aside as children grow too quickly. The material is readily available, the expertise minimal to get started. The ladies learn to work together, and some of the designs they create are magnificent. That matters so much, to know that you can make something beautiful and useful, that you can add to the world's joys with the labor of your hands."

"These sandwiches add significantly to my joy. My brain knows I must eat every few hours, but the same brain grows very forgetful as those hours pass by. Goddard and Powell knew to feed me when I started babbling in my native tongue. I am only as smart as my last meal, according to them. If your calling is prison reform, why not delegate the more tedious church work?"

Because I need it for the camouflage it provides. "I am the vicar's daughter, and unless Papa remarries, which he shows no signs of doing, I am the logical party to deal with the orts and leavings of running a congregation."

Alasdhair had consumed his sandwiches with a businesslike dispatch, and Dorcas had enjoyed watching him do even that.

There was no camouflaging the joy she took in his presence, or the wonder his esteem engendered. *You are safe with me.* She was more than safe, she was cherished. He showed her that in the way he tucked the ends of his scarf around her neck, in the sauntering pace he set as they strolled the walkway. By his own admission, he was in no hurry to part from her, and that was both daunting and lovely.

"You have ambitions beyond keeping peace at fellowship meals," Alasdhair said. "You want to write fiery treatises on behalf of those illiterate women, remonstrate with society regarding the care of our mendicants, and exhort Parliament on the need to keep children out of the factories."

She did. As badly as Papa wanted his bishopric, Dorcas wanted London to be a more hospitable and humane city. "While you are concerned with fallen women."

Alasdhair helped himself to a piece of shortbread from the plate in the center of the table. "Most of them aren't fallen in any moral sense. They have regular jobs, they might be married, they look after their grannies and say their prayers every night. They simply aren't paid enough coin to keep body and soul together. The law, in its wisdom, has made a life on the stroll safe from prosecution."

"And society, in its foolishness, has made that life perilous in other regards."

"Precisely. Many a client refuses to pay, others are abusive. Disease is a constant risk, as is childbed. It's a desperate life for the streetwalker, and as the children come along, one that sinks her only more quickly into poverty. This is not a cheerful conversation. My cousins would despair of me for raising the topic with you, but in their way, they share your zeal for change."

"You did not bring up this topic. I did." Something that would not have happened with Papa or even Michael. "I want us to be able to discuss such matters, Mr. MacKay. More of society as a whole should be discussing such matters. They need discussing."

His gaze grew bashful as he chose a second piece of shortbread. "You said *us*. A lovely little word."

And his burr had acquired a lovely little softness about the edges. Dorcas imagined that burr as a whisper in the darkness, a murmur near her ear, and the ease and pleasure with which those thoughts scampered through her mind took her aback.

She had expected to grow into contented middle age, eventually shifting from Papa's household to Michael's, leaving a trail of modest good works and carefully worded articles in her wake. A meaningful life, a life to be grateful for.

But Alasdhair MacKay valued her for more than her ability to organize a fellowship meal or wheedle flowers from people who could easily afford to donate them. Then too, there was John... Dorcas's heart ached to be more than a distant cousin to him, to do more for the boy than she'd been able to do for his mother.

But most miraculous of all, Dorcas yearned to be closer to Alasdhair MacKay and longed for that closeness to encompass the physical as well as the intellectual and emotional. She had thought herself beyond desire, thought that aspect of life lost to her for all time.

What a stunning pleasure to be so wrong. "'Us' is merely a word, Mr. MacKay."

"Not when it refers to thee and me, Dorcas Delancey. 'Us' is the embodiment of all things dear and delightful. Would you like another cup of chocolate?"

"I could not possibly. One is almost too rich a pleasure."

"Then you've not been enjoying the right pleasures." Though his tone was admonishing, he winked at her, tucked a piece of shortbread into his pocket, and rose. "I'll see you home now, and should your dear papa be on hand, an introduction would be appreciated—if you're comfortable with that?"

Papa would be polite, also puzzled. Alasdhair MacKay was not a Mayfair dandy, not a churchman, possibly not even Church of Scotland. He consorted with game girls, grew testy when hungry, and named his horse for the Young Pretender.

But he was a good man, ferociously honorable, and more genuinely respectful of women as a gender than was any bishop Dorcas had met—and she had met many. She was pondering the nature of respect as she and Alasdhair rounded the corner onto her street. A red-wheeled curricle tooled by, matched grays in the traces...

And Isaiah Mornebeth at the ribbons.

"Fancy equipage," Alasdhair said, "but then, it's a pretty day, and the toffs must display their finery."

Mornebeth hadn't so much as glanced Dorcas's way—he'd not expect her to have an escort, would he?—but her cup of chocolate soured in her belly. Mornebeth had no reason to be on Holderness Street other than to call on Papa—or her.

Dorcas resumed breathing when the matched grays trotted around the corner.

The introduction of Alasdhair to Papa went smoothly, as Dorcas had known it would. Papa did not bring up John's circumstances, though he had to grasp that Alasdhair had taken in a member of the Delancey extended family. Dorcas was hanging up her cloak and scarf—it was *her* scarf now, thank you very much—when Papa peered out the window at Alasdhair's retreating form.

"They grow them big up north, your mother always said."

"I suppose the Scots come in all sizes. Mr. MacKay is a gentleman. His father is some sort of minor Scottish lord."

"Impoverished, no doubt. The Scots have not had an easy time of it." Papa's gaze shifted from the street to Dorcas, but she had long ago learned to evade paternal scrutiny.

"I must put the finishing touches on the fellowship meal plans," she said. "You will be glad to know that John thrives in Mr. MacKay's care."

"I am glad to know that, though I wasn't about to ask the man directly. Will you be calling on MacKay again, Dorcas?"

"Yes." And he would be calling on her, and if all went well... Dorcas cut off that thought before she was grinning like a fool in her own foyer. He had bowed over her hand with exquisite politesse while squeezing her fingers ever so gently.

Papa pretended to sort through the afternoon mail. "You might be interested to know that Isaiah Mornebeth stopped by on the spur of the moment. He'd been squiring his grandmother about and wanted to take her grays for a turn in the park. He thought you might enjoy driving out with him."

Dorcas's good mood, her *hopeful* mood, evaporated into a miasma of resentment and worry. "He should have sent a note around. I don't exactly idle away my hours, Papa."

"Don't be churlish. Mornebeth wanted to surprise you."

He had wanted to ambush her. If Dorcas knew one thing about Isaiah Mornebeth, it was that she was not safe with him and never had been. She forgot that lesson at her peril.

"If he calls again, Papa, I am not at home to him."

"You are letting this MacKay fellow turn your head? That's not like you, Dorcas."

"My lack of regard for Mr. Mornebeth has nothing to do with Mr. MacKay. I know you value your friendship with Isaiah, but I have my reasons for keeping my distance."

More than that, she dared not say.

Papa's regard grew pensive. "Be careful, Dorcas. Isaiah Mornebeth is a man of substance and influence. He is playing his cards shrewdly and could do much to benefit this family."

The truth begged to be spoken. Mornebeth was a serpent, as Mr. MacKay had said, but Papa could not see that. He would believe every lie to come out of Mornebeth's mouth, and the occasional self-serving truth too.

"I will be careful, Papa, and I will be civil and even cordial to Mr. Mornebeth, but allowing him to develop aspirations in my direction would be unkind."

Papa let her have the last word, though Dorcas felt no sense of victory. The day's glorious developments had been overshadowed by Mornebeth's sneak attack, and having been frustrated in his aims once, he'd come around again.

Mornebeth was nothing if not as determined and as devious as the devil.

"HIS NAME IS RICHARD SCOTT," Dylan Powell said, keeping up a brisk pace as the western sky turned infernal shades of red and gray. "He will answer only to Scotty, though he hails from Yorkshire. Has an obsession with keeping his fingernails clean, which you will not remark upon."

"Former infantry?" Alasdhair asked. The majority of Dylan's old soldiers were former infantry. The cavalry had been mostly from the wealthier ranks of Society, and the artillery had been the smallest division of Wellington's army.

"Scotty was artillery, though his hearing seems to have escaped unscathed. His brother is nearly deaf. They work occasionally for the night-soil men."

"Hence Scotty's obsession with keeping his hands clean. What of the brother?"

"Bertrand likes the quiet of the night. He can hear some, but manages more easily when sounds are isolated rather than charging at him en masse. His favorite thing to do is to listen to organists practicing in the evening. Says he can feel the music even when he can't hear it."

Powell was devoted to his former soldiers—even to knowing such an odd detail about a part-time night-soil man—though Alasdhair could not see that they much appreciated Powell's concern. But then, that wasn't the point. The point was that Alasdhair, Powell, Goddard... anybody fighting on the Peninsula could have come home without an eye or an arm, his family scattered to the winds by misfortune he'd not been on hand to weather with them.

"What exactly did Scotty see?" Alasdhair asked.

"I don't know. I put out the word that you were looking for information relating to Miss Fairchild's disappearance from the vicinity of the Strand Bridge. Scotty and Bertrand were abroad that night, and they allowed as how they would like to discuss the situation with you. You have something of a reputation in low places."

That was not good news to a man recently embarked on a courtship—or a something-ship—with a prominent preacher's daughter. "What sort of reputation?"

Powell paused at a street corner to let a wagon full of steaming manure pass. As the sun set over London, the nature of both foot traffic and wheeled conveyances changed. The open curricles and phaetons of the fashionable disappeared, replaced by stout closed coaches and utilitarian wagons.

As dawn approached, the farm carts and fish wagons bound for the markets would increase in number, unloading edible produce to take on the sort of cargo perfuming the night air so pungently.

"You have a reputation for gallantry, of all things," Powell said. "You ran off some drunken tulip who was pestering the game girls by Covent Garden around Yuletide. You are known to provide coach fare back to the village for any of the streetwalkers who ask you for it. You brought the midwife to some female in extremis and helped see the child safely into the world. That you never sample the wares on offer makes you fascinating to the ladies, and what fascinates them must be discussed."

"The tulip was a prancing arsewipe with a bad temper and no honor. The women were afraid of him, and he wouldn't take no for an answer." The tulip, doubtless already conversant with the languages of the fan, parasol, and glove, had been a very quick study with the language of the fist too. Since Alasdhair had treated him to a short demonstration of Scottish pugilism, the tulip had found someplace else to bloom.

"Liked to beat them, did he?"

"He liked to lock them in and terrorize them. Bad enough we consign streetwalkers to starvation, the elements, and disease. They should not have to put up with outright brutality."

"I hate London." Powell, who was for the most part obnoxiously even-tempered, sounded uncharacteristically despairing. "The whole place is a swamp of misery, but for the lucky and the few. We have poverty in Wales, dire, desperate poverty, but we don't regard it as anything other than bad fortune, a situation to be endured and pitied. Here... bad luck is God's way of saying everybody else can piss on you while pretending to pray for you."

"Go back to Wales. I can stand this place in part because I spend much of the year at home."

"You'd miss me," Powell said, smacking Alasdhair on the arm as they approached a seedy little tavern doing business as the Cat Among the Pigeons.

"I would, actually. With Goddard lost to wedded bliss, we see less of him."

"Drop 'round The Coventry Club," Powell said, leading the way into the dim common of the tavern. "Goddard is in his element taking that place in hand, and the buffet Ann puts out will make you swoon."

"Persistent hunger makes me swoon."

Powell nodded to a pair of old men playing chess in the snug. "Have you eaten lately?"

"A substantial snack before going out." Had Powell asked his question even a fortnight ago, Alasdhair would have fashioned a reply intended to insult in the same superficial manner the question itself did, except that Powell meant no insult. He meant to keep Alasdhair on his feet, as he had done many a time in Spain.

Two weeks ago, Alasdhair would not have suggested that Powell go back to Wales, would not have suggested that Powell muster out and return to his peacetime haunts.

Two weeks ago, Alasdhair had not kissed Dorcas Delancey, nor put into her hands the whole of his sad and sorry past, only to hear that she respected his efforts to atone for a tragic wrong.

Powell ambled over to a pair of older fellows sitting side by side on a settle against the wall. The table before them also had two chairs, though the occupants of those chairs would have to sit with their backs to the common. Powell extended a hand.

"Scotty, Bertie. I believe you know MacKay."

They went through the usual greeting ritual of soldiers: who had served with what regiments and under which commanders and seen action in which battles. Powell ordered another round of winter ale and some sustenance.

The food—a cold collation of ham and cheese served with a loaf of warm bread and a pot of mustard—was half gone before Scotty exchanged a look with his brother. They were a good-sized pair, prematurely stooped, their lank hair going salt-and-pepper, though they might well be a few years shy of forty. Their attire was on the shabby side of serviceable, and their features were weathered. Bertie's expression had a sweetness Scotty's visage lacked.

"Nights are quieter than days in t' Auld Smoke," Scotty said, his Yorkshire accent thickening. "But there's plenty mischief afoot after dark. We were down by t' Strand Bridge at a place called t' Dove's Nest, and Scotty had to step into t' ginnel for a piss, as the boghouse were unavailable-like."

Ginnel—a northern word for the narrow channel between two buildings. A dark and usually foul place.

"Can't 'old me ale," Bertie said, smiling slightly and gesturing with his tankard.

"I don't let Bertie out on his own at night if I can help it. Thou thinkst to bide a moment in the shadows to heed nature's call, and thou gets a knife in t' gut and a pair of angel's wings for thy trouble.

Bertie can't hear t' scrape of a footpad's boot on t' cobbles. He sees better in darkness than I ever will, but he don't hear fer shite."

Bertie smiled vaguely through this recitation, while the barmaid sent Powell a tacit invitation that was quite clear.

"Go on," Alasdhair said. "Anything you recall, anything out of the ordinary that niggles at your memory, could be helpful."

"I've seen some jump," Scotty said. "Mostly men. They knows to leap as the tide goes out, when the currents are strong and deadly. T' bridges make currents worse, and t' Strand Bridge is on a bend in t' river, which disturbs t' currents even more. Won't stand like them old bridges have. T' river will have t' last word."

Alasdhair did not want to discuss bridge design. "Did you see Miss Fairchild jump?"

"I saw yer lass," Scotty said quietly. "Did not see her jump. We know her. She used to try her luck on t' street from time to time, but she hadn't t' knack for it. T' other girls tried to show her how to get on, but it's not t' life she was raised to."

"A good girl," Bertie said, nodding vigorously. "A good, sweet girl."

Not a girl at all. A woman grown, a mother, and very likely a suicide. "So what did you see?"

"She walked right past us," Scotty said, "not that we was exactly in t' middle of t' street. She marched right onto t' bridge. Beastly damned cold on t' bridges in winter. The wind cuts right through ye like so many bayonets."

Nor did Alasdhair want to think of bayonets, if at all possible. "What was she wearing?"

"Cloak, hat, scarf, gloves. Odd t'ing was, she had a bonnet under one arm and carried a bundle as well. Who packs a bag to jump off a bridge?"

Who indeed? "Did she jump?"

"Bertie and me had finished tendin' to business, and I was for gettin' out t' cold, but Bertie kept an eye on Miss Fairchild."

"She were moving quick," Bertie said, "on account of t' cold, maybe."

Or because she dreaded to lose her nerve? "Then what happened?"

"We'd turned to get back to t' Dove," Scottie said, "when I heard a splash. Sound travels on water, and that was not a fish leaping nor a frog hopping. It were a splash."

"Then she did jump?"

Scotty shook his head. "I hear for me and Bertie both, and I've seen other jumpers. It weren't that kind of splash. 'Twasn't heavy enow, if ye take my meaning. A good-sized woman in a winter cloak jumping from that height... It's a long fall, MacKay, and though ye might not think it, a hard landing when a body hits the water. The river police claim most of the jumpers don't survive that drop."

"Bad business," Bertie said, taking the last of the ham from the platter. "Turrible bad business. I thought maybe she tossed her babe into t' river, but she wouldn't do that unless 'twere dead."

"The child is thriving and well cared for. You think she threw her bundle or bonnet into the river?"

Bertie and Scotty exchanged a look before Scotty tore the last strip of cheese in half and shared it with his brother.

"Bertie thinks she kept walking, off to the Lambeth side of t' river, but I can't see as well as he can, especially at night, and Bertie has a soft heart for the ladies. He wouldn't want to think a woman jumped to her death while we simply stood by buttoning our breeches."

"She were walkin' quick-like," Bertie said again. "Too damned cold to tarry. Scotty and me didn't tarry neither."

Powell signaled for another platter. "You say she did not jump?"

Bertie touched a finger to his ear. "Wot's 'at, guv?"

"Miss Fairchild did not jump?"

Bertie sat back. "I can't be sure. Even late at night, there's foot traffic on t' bridges, but I hope that were her striding off to the South Bank. It looked like her walk."

The Southwark area was a cheaper place to bide than London

itself, also a better place to hide from friends and family if a woman was bent on hiding.

"If you recall anything else," Alasdhair said, "please let Powell know, and he can find me. This has been very helpful."

"Ask t' ladies," Scotty said. "They hear things, they see things, they know things."

Much as Powell's sisters did. "An excellent suggestion. Gentlemen, thanks for your time. Here's to an early spring."

They drank to that, and to Wellington's health, and, less enthusiastically, to *t' auld mad bugger* King George. By the time Alasdhair and Powell left them to their second platter, they were debating the strategy of some skirmish outside Salamanca, which, in their informed opinion, had turned the entire tide of the war.

"That conversation raised more questions than it answered," Powell said as he and Alasdhair walked in the direction of London's more genteel neighborhoods. Lamplighters were shuffling from one lamppost to the next, and only three cabbies were lined up at the nearest hackney stand. The horses, blanketed against the cold, breathed plumes of white into the chilly night air. "Shall we take a cab, MacKay?"

"I'd rather walk."

"You'd rather keep a lookout for your game girls. How much longer will you beat your head against the sheer stone walls of London's appetite for vice?"

"Until I forget Badajoz."

"We will none of us ever forget Badajoz, but you might at least tell me and Goddard why it haunts you so."

To recount that horror to his cousins had been previously unthinkable, a private shame and a personal sorrow. "Someday, I might. Suffice it to say, Dunacre disgraced his uniform as badly as many others."

"Another reason to be grateful that Dunacre fell at Waterloo."

Alasdhair was grateful for the darkness and grateful beyond

words for his cousins. "Did you kill him? You are a dead shot, Powell, and he was a blight upon the earth and your commanding officer."

"You are the sharpshooter among us. A bullet killed him, and he died a hero's death, which was more than he deserved. How's the boy getting on?"

Alasdhair was grateful for the blatant change of subject too. "Wee John is thriving. I know now why Goddard is so concerned with his urchins."

"They eat prodigiously, which makes Ann happy. Ergo, Goddard is happy."

"Children change everything, Powell. They stand your world on its head, and that's exactly as it should be."

Powell, who generally had a rejoinder for everything, remained silent, but Alasdhair knew exactly what he was thinking: If Melanie Fairchild was alive, how could she have simply walked away from her own son, the child for whom she'd eschewed a life on the stroll, and begun the long, nearly impossible struggle back to respectability?

CHAPTER TEN

Isaiah's quarry hadn't changed much in all the years he'd been up north. Her figure was still matronly, her eyes still kind, though the hair visible beneath her poke bonnet had more gray. She moved from stall to stall with a brisk efficiency that had nothing to do with the nip in the morning air.

A woman serving as cook-housekeeper in a busy vicarage could not afford to dither over the choice of watercress or cabbages. Isaiah left off flirting with the flower girl and chose a bunch of unopened daffodil buds, probably stolen from some sheltered churchyard.

He flipped the girl a coin, aiming far enough from her boot that she had to scrabble for it, then donned his signature genial-bachelor smile and approached the greengrocer's stall.

"It's Mrs. Benton, isn't it?" He touched a finger to his hat brim and bowed, being sure to hold the flowers in plain sight. "Isaiah Mornebeth. Years ago, I used to racket about with Michael Delancey. Your cooking figures fondly in my memories."

"Mr. Mornebeth!" The old girl's smile would have lit up Piccadilly. "Of course I recall you. What a pair of rascals you were.

Vicar said you'd returned to London, and I believe you dined at the vicarage earlier this week."

"The roast was superb. No wonder Thomas is such a happy man, when he sits down to meals like that regularly. Might I carry your basket? I've made my purchase and would enjoy your company if you don't mind the bother of an escort."

She passed over her market basket, which was heavier than it looked. "Very gracious of you, sir. What did you think of my apple walnut torte?"

"Madam, if I did not know you to be devoted to the Delanceys, I would steal you away simply to have that recipe."

She beamed at him. "You are shameless, Mr. Mornebeth, though you are also right: I am devoted to the Delanceys. You could not ask for a better family to work for. Vicar toils without ceasing for the good of his congregation, and Miss Delancey is a paragon of organization and charitable inclinations. She's not boastful about it, but she is much respected in the parish. *Much* respected."

Miss Delancey was also going completely to waste. "Might I walk you back to the vicarage?"

"I must pick up some carrots." Mrs. Benton moved along at a slower pace than she'd set earlier. "I prefer the brightest orange, but not too large. Carrots grow tough with age, and the flavor suffers with excessive size."

"I never knew that." Nor did Isaiah care about rubbishing carrots. "Are you responsible for all the cooking at the vicarage, or does Miss Delancey take a hand in running the kitchen?"

Mrs. Benton slanted him a look. "If you are trying to be subtle, young man, you are failing utterly."

Isaiah would not see thirty again—thank God—and he was not trying to be subtle. "You've found me out, Mrs. Benton. I suspect divine providence has guided me to this encounter with you, because I am concerned for Miss Delancey. It would never have occurred to me to seek your counsel, but here you are, and even I can grasp the wisdom of sharing my worries with you."

Isaiah had spoken in his best churchman-ese, in half-prayerful roundaboutation. Mrs. Benton had obviously learned to translate the same dialect.

"You want to court Miss Delancey." She examined a bunch of carrots and apparently found them wanting, for she embarked on an inspection of another half-dozen bunches.

Isaiah waited with saintly patience until she'd concluded her transaction, then added the chosen carrots to the basket.

"Miss Delancey never used to be a solemn girl," he said. "She's grown positively dour with the passing years. Why is that?"

"She was livelier before Master Michael went up north, but that was ages ago, Mr. Mornebeth, and even lively girls eventually settle down. You want to know if she's pining for a reluctant suitor or waiting for some fellow's fortunes to come right."

Isaiah let a silence build while he and Mrs. Benton left the bustle of the market behind. "I am apparently to have no secrets from you, am I?"

"The Delanceys are as close to family as I have, sir. You trifle with Miss Delancey, and you will have me to answer to."

Such a foe—a cook-housekeeper growing long in the tooth, one who prided herself on choosing the best carrots. *Archangels defend me.*

"Trifling is the furthest thing from my mind, though I must ask another question. Does the vicar grasp what an ally he has in you?" Such an inquiry required a delicate touch—reluctant to pry or give offense, motivated by only the highest principles. "Churchmen, being occupied with lofty spiritual matters, can sometimes miss the earthly realities deserving of immediate notice."

Mrs. Benton stepped around a puddle on the walkway. "Vicar is much occupied with his duties, and he has a devoted daughter to keep him company. I will not stand for criticism of either father or daughter, Mr. Mornebeth."

Loyalty to an employer was such a useful failing.

"I mean no criticism of either when I suggest, in a purely theoretical sense, that if Miss Delancey were to meet a man worthy of her esteem, then her father might more easily appreciate another lady in his household who has contributed much to his happiness for years on end."

A titled lord usually would not marry his housekeeper, but among the humbler folk, practical unions were the norm. Thomas Delancey likely had no designs whatsoever on Mrs. Benton, but Mrs. Benton clearly was carrying the torch of matrimonial regard for her employer.

Too bad for her, but very convenient for Isaiah.

"He does dote on his Dorcas," Mrs. Benton said. "She is very mindful of her papa's standing, too, for all she has her crusades. I can tell you she's not walking out with any young man at present. She's too busy, for one thing, and she doesn't suffer fools, for another."

"Are all men in love fools?"

"When a man loves a woman, Mr. Mornebeth, he hands her the ability to make a fool of him, and that requires far more courage of him than strutting about the clubs or prattling from the pulpit. Are you offering that power to Miss Delancey?"

Only an idiot would surrender his dignity to a woman. Isaiah was not an idiot. "My esteem for her eclipses the regard I have harbored for any other young lady, Mrs. Benton. My grandmother has introduced me to half the belles in Mayfair. They haven't a patch on Miss Delancey for intelligence, purpose, or a firm grasp of what a life in the Church requires of a man."

Or for temper. Dorcas did have that lovely, simmering temper, and her dear brother had strayed so very far from strict propriety all those years ago—as had Dorcas.

"Vicar thinks well of you," Mrs. Benton said, a trifle grudgingly. "But then, he thinks well of most people."

"I'm sure he thinks well of your roasts and of your delicious apple walnut torte too."

"That is precisely the sort of balderdash that will get you nowhere with Miss Delancey, Mr. Mornebeth. Talk to her of the plight of mothers in jail or children in factories. Speak to her of the Corn Laws, and she will think more highly of you."

Isaiah's grandmother owned thousands of arable acres. She thus tended to favor keeping the price of grain high, as did most of the gentry and aristocracy. As heir to those acres—something Isaiah did not bruit about *much*—and as a devoted grandson, he shared her opinions. Besides, if England were suddenly bereft of its starving paupers, the Church would have much less relevance, and then where would society be?

"I am happy to discuss Corn Laws by the hour if you think such a topic will raise me in Miss Delancey's esteem."

"She makes up her own mind, Mr. Mornebeth, but Master Michael considered you a friend, and Vicar has always liked you. That will mean much to Miss Delancey."

They turned onto the vicarage's street, and Isaiah stopped at the corner. "I will part from you here, though I thank you for bearing me company. When next I am blessed with an invitation to dine with the Delanceys, I will be sure to extol the virtues of the meal as pointedly as possible. Even a godly man can overlook the treasure under his own roof, Mrs. Benton."

She clearly liked that observation. "Then I will hope you are a frequent guest, Mr. Mornebeth. Who are the flowers for?"

"When they open, they will be for Miss Delancey, unless you think that's too forward of me? Thanks for a pleasant meal and all?"

"Give them a day or two in a sunny window. I'm sure they will look splendid and be appreciated." She bobbed a curtsey and turned for the vicarage.

Isaiah tipped his hat and turned back the way he'd come, lest he be seen fraternizing with the housekeeper. She'd been admirably protective of her employer, not entirely vulnerable to flattery, and not entirely immune to it either. A productive sortie, and one that confirmed that Dorcas Delancey was both unencumbered with competition for her hand and careful of her reputation with the congregants.

All to the good. All very much to the good.

THOUGH FRIGID TEMPERATURES returned to London, spring had come early to Dorcas's heart. Her days were developing a pattern that included an early call on John—and on Alasdhair MacKay—and then a pleasant walk home with Mr. MacKay by way of the tea shop.

The joy of small indulgences—a cup of chocolate, a kiss to the cheek, an embrace that demanded nothing—had slipped from her grasp, or perhaps she'd pushed such joys away. Remorse was the thief of contentment. That Alasdhair should be the one to return those joys to her was unexpected and wonderful.

"If I were to bring John around to call at the vicarage, would your father object?" Alasdhair asked after demolishing his customary two-sandwich snack.

"Is it wise to take a child out into the elements at this time of year?"

He sat back. "You are avoiding the question, my dear. If I chose a milder day and bundled John up, he'd enjoy the outing. Timmens and Henderson would enjoy the respite even more. Mamas take their babies to market, to divine services, to the shop. The lad's up on all fours now, and soon he'll be crawling. The world awaits the pleasure of his exploration."

Michael had had that sort of confidence as a young man, that sort of optimism. All the world had awaited the pleasure of his exploration, more's the pity.

"I will ask Papa." The conversation would be difficult.

Alasdhair patted her hand. "Family is the ultimate challenge. If I must begin my campaign by calling upon you without John, then I will start up the hill that way. Your father strikes me as a reasonable man of genuine convictions, and John should know his family."

Convictions, yes, but did Papa also have the courage to acknowledge Melanie's by-blow under the vicarage's very roof?

Dorcas could only hope so. "Speaking of family, you've had no further word regarding Melanie's disappearance?"

Alasdhair selected a piece of shortbread. He typically ate one and slipped another into his pocket and probably didn't even realize he'd formed that habit.

"Nary a word. Goddard's juvenile minions are listening at the dockside keyholes, and Powell's former soldiers are on the alert, but if Melanie has decamped for Southwark or left London altogether, she might as well be a ghost."

"I hope she's a happy ghost, wherever she is." Though how could she be when parted from her only child? "Perhaps before you bring John around, you should come to dinner at the vicarage."

Alasdhair took Dorcas's hand. "I know you love your papa, Dorcas. You must not fret that I'll make an issue of the boy. He's a mere baby. There is time for old wounds to heal and for memories of his mother's scandal to fade. But he will never be more dear or lovable than he is now, and your father won't live forever. If a lad cannot count on family, then who does he have in this life?"

"Fortunately, John has you."

"And if something happens to me, my cousins will intervene on John's behalf, but I want you to have the raising of him. I'll be making an amendment to my will to that effect."

Spring brought flowers, beautiful days, and sunshine. It also brought hay fever, flies, and mud. "I have never raised a child, never borne a child. For me to take over John's upbringing... I pray it doesn't come to that."

"I intend to offer you marriage, Dorcas Delancey." Alasdhair rubbed his thumb across her bare wrist. "Accommodate yourself to that notion right now. You can refuse me, put me through my paces, break my heart, or have your way with me before making up your mind, but my objective is to secure your hand in marriage."

"You are quite clear on this objective of yours." And Dorcas was all manner of pleased with his declaration—also unnerved. "We haven't known each other long."

"Most courtships in polite society are short, lest the happy couple be caught anticipating their vows once too often. I hope we do anticipate our vows, by the way. If you'd rather trot me out to all the church socials and tool around the park with me of an afternoon, I will cheerfully squire you about. I'm the considerate sort of lover, and you deserve to be lavishly doted upon."

"You will cease making scandalous pronouncements in public, Mr. MacKay." Scandalous, delightful pronouncements.

"I'm not making pronouncements, I'm making promises. Besides, the shop is all but empty, and nobody overheard me. I have a care for your dignity, Dorcas, as well as my own."

Alasdhair used her name occasionally, just often enough that every time Dorcas heard him speak it, she felt the urge to preen.

"I'd best be getting home," she said. "The grounds committee is meeting after luncheon, and I'm expected to take the minutes."

"You'll run the meeting, take on half the assignments, and make every committee member think their suggestion was the most brilliant offering of the day. Do you ever consider how much you could accomplish if you weren't your father's unpaid curate, sexton, verger, and deacon? How many more articles you could write, how many more prison schools you could start?"

Dorcas eased her hand from his grip. "Yes, as a matter of fact, I do think about that. I want to write a series of pamphlets, about women and poverty. I want to write sketches for the newspapers, about the mendicants we dismiss as lazy and sly. I have ideas..."

And Alasdhair MacKay would listen to those ideas, refine them, and help her realize them. More than his kisses, more than his audacious courting plans, Dorcas was enthralled by his ability to *see her*. To Alasdhair MacKay, she was not only the dutiful daughter and resident spinster at the vicarage, she was also a person in her own right, with a unique and valuable contribution to make.

"If your evening is taken up composing meeting minutes," he said, "your reformist ideas are less likely to see the light of day. Then too, if Thomas Delancey were forced to take his own meeting notes, he might be less preoccupied with the blandishments of a bishopric and more interested in his own congregation."

"Papa is very interested in his congregation." He was also prone to spending hours in his study working on sermons while Dorcas called on his parishioners. She had not considered those calls to be a disservice to her father's happiness.

Alasdhair stood and extended a hand. "I'm sure he's utterly devoted to his congregation."

"I could smack you." Dorcas took his hand and rose. "You have a way of piquing my ire, then dancing away. Of firing conversational mortars over my parapets and then looking about with an innocent expression. Your parents doubtless despaired of you regularly."

"That's where having younger siblings came in handy." He draped her cloak around her shoulders and did up the frogs. "My brother Finn won highest honors for parental despair. He's a good man, brave and loyal, but in his youth, he was much given to impulse. Dashing and bold. You know the sort."

Michael had been prone to impulsive foolishness. "Always getting into scrapes and expecting other people to either forgive the misstep or smooth it all over. Is he married, your brother?"

"Finn's a widower. Not as prone to recklessness anymore, and damned if we don't miss the old Finn. He made the rest of us look steady by comparison."

Alasdhair settled Dorcas's bonnet on her head and did up the ribbons. "I wish we were married now, Dorcas," he went on. "We'd toddle back to the house and, if the mood struck us, toddle right on up to the bedroom for a wee marital interlude. Then you would write your fiery tracts, I would answer all three of my father's letters about the business. In the afternoon, I'd sally forth to peddle Papa's whisky, and you would meet with your reforming ladies. We might have another marital interlude before supper, and we would definitely spend some time with our wee John."

The life he sketched was breathtakingly intimate, also happy and full of meaning. Not grim, lonely, and frustrating.

"You are flirting with me, in your usual outrageous fashion."

He paid the bill and escorted her onto the walkway. "I am dreaming with you and of you. You are a prudent woman, and you are entitled to make up your own mind about my suit on your own excruciatingly deliberate schedule. I mean to call on your father next week, Dorcas. That is not a warning, that is another promise."

Dorcas was mostly reassured by that promise. Alasdhair MacKay would never willingly break his word.

"Are you prepared for me to refuse your proposal?" She was asking for form's sake and also to fortify herself against his version of charm.

"If you break my heart, I will bow politely, apologize for having misconstrued the situation, and stay drunk for a week. I will confide my sorrow to John and Charlie, and my cousins will drop around from time to time to nettle me about my blue devils, because they love me, of course. Why would you refuse me, Dorcas?"

Alasdhair asked the question quietly as they ambled along the walkway.

"I don't know, but that is my prerogative. Did you mean what you said about anticipating the vows?"

"Aye. With my whole heart and a few other parts of my anatomy."

Dorcas had the most extraordinary conversations with him. They argued, they challenged one another, they teased each other. They debated everything from the Acts of Union, which had obliterated Scotland's national sovereignty, to expansion of the right to vote, to the poor laws.

And when Dorcas made a telling point, Alasdhair did not regard her as if she'd stumbled onto a lucky shot, like some village lad tossing balls to win the prize at a Bartholomew Fair booth.

He *listened* to her, and he rebutted her arguments without giving quarter or descending into insults about a woman's limited understanding or lack of worldly experience. Did he but know it, those moments when he cocked his head, raised his eyebrows, and marshalled his counterarguments were as gratifying to Dorcas as all the spicy cups of hot chocolate in London.

He bowed his farewell to her at the vicarage door, to all appearances the soul of gentlemanly manners—which he also was.

"I know what you're about." Dorcas also knew the porch's overhang shielded them from all but the most determined prying eyes. "You haven't kissed me today because you think to make me long for you. You need not bother. I already do long for you."

"And that perplexes you? I'm not hideous to look upon, Dorcas, and I will exert myself to the utmost to see to your—"

She bussed his cheek, not entirely to silence him. "We have matters to discuss, Mr. MacKay, matters to which I must devote some thought before I raise them with you. Your inherent honesty compels me to deal with you truthfully, and though I doubt I can match your brother Finn for recklessness, I, too, have disregarded prudence in my youth."

She could have tipped her chin down, such that her bonnet brim would have obscured her features from Alasdhair's view, but she aspired to be as brave and honest as he was. *Begin as you intend to go on*, Mama used to say.

And Dorcas did very much want to go on with Alasdhair MacKay.

"You had a beau, and you permitted him liberties. Did you give him your heart, Dorcas?"

That was not even close to the truth, but it was as close as Dorcas had planned to come. "Never. I was the typical preacher's daughter, headstrong, easily affronted by parental rules, and convinced of my own sophistication. I was a lackwitted young fool who might well have ended up in Melanie's situation."

Alasdhair paced to the edge of the porch, and for a harrowing moment, Dorcas thought he was leaving, just walking away, never to return. He took relations between men and women seriously, for all his references to marital interludes. A younger Dorcas had tried very hard to convince herself those same relations were of no moment. Sauce for the goose, and so forth and so on.

Except that a lady's virtue was not a roast fowl, to be dispatched between vegetable courses after a perfunctory grace.

"Say something," Dorcas muttered. "Or leave. I will understand if you leave." She might also stay drunk for a week, or at least have two glasses of cordial. "I hadn't meant to raise this issue without considerable forethought, but now that I have, I want your honest reaction."

He remained at the railing, his expression as remote and cool as any winter breeze.

CHAPTER ELEVEN

Some philandering Lothario had toyed with Dorcas's affections. That fact, which she tried to present as a stale crumb of ancient history, explained much to Alasdhair.

Her unrelenting reserve, which she wore like the clergy's high church vestments.

Her compassion for women suffering society's judgment.

Her guilt over Melanie's fall from propriety.

Alasdhair sat on the porch railing, to outward appearances calm—he hoped—though his cousins would have known that his explosions of temper were often heralded by a period of brooding quiet.

"Very well," Dorcas muttered. "Don't say anything. Silence can speak volumes. I wish you good day—"

"Haud yer wheesht, woman."

She remained by the door, hand on the latch, ready to make an exit from the conversation and from Alasdhair's life. He'd used his commanding-officer voice, and that had been the wrong choice.

"I will leave this place," he said, remaining seated by dint of sheer resolve, "and I will go directly to procure a special license. We should have the documents within the week. Your father can marry us. You have soldiered on alone long enough, Dorcas Delancey, and so have I. I don't care a donkey's damn that you were a little adventurous as a younger woman. God knows I was a roistering lout. I care very much that the experience still clouds your opinion of yourself."

"A special license?"

"Or we can have the banns cried. The how of it matters not, though those will be the longest three weeks of my life. What matters is that you put aside the notion that your earlier experiences could in any way diminish you in my eyes. My God, Dorcas, you know what lies in my past. The utter lapse of honor, the—"

"That was war."

"Which makes my failing all the more egregious. I was an officer, and I had seen the havoc soldiers could wreak in victory. You were innocent, likely overlooked by your only parent while your brother was fawned upon at every turn. You would never think to judge the women you see in the jails, but you have sentenced yourself to needless shame."

Her chin came up a gratifying half inch. "Not shame. I was, as you say, young and foolish. I regret my decision, and I did not think I could in good conscience allow you to pay me your addresses without... Why are we having this discussion all but on the street?"

Alasdhair rose, though he stayed a good two yards away from Dorcas. "Because inside this vicarage, you are not free to raise topics that trouble your saintly father. You cannot acknowledge that had he been a more competent parent, you might have been spared the fumblings of some rutting hound. Your dear Papa was too busy panting after a bishop's miter or parading his brilliant son around to guard you from the plundering troops."

That comment went too far, and yet, Alasdhair would not take the words back. No daughter of the vicarage, in the absence of a mother's guiding hand, could grasp the extent of her own vulnerability. Even with a mother, chaperones, and all the admonitions in the world, such a girl would be tempted to break the rules.

"You must not disparage Papa."

Alasdhair wanted to do more than disparage the old windbag. "Fine, I won't, but neither will I allow you to disparage yourself. You know how many of your father's parishioners are married in June and parents by December."

"Those couples are engaged, already committed to a shared lifetime..."

He took a step nearer. "Bollocks, Dorcas. Let us deal honestly with one another. Some of those couples were engaged, many were not until an engagement became necessary. Your father's parishioners might be genteel, but they aren't a collection of courtesy titles and pampered heiresses. They are flesh-and-blood humans with all the folly and glory attendant thereto."

She looked, of all things, like she wanted to argue the case for her own wickedness, which was nearly laughable, except that this was Dorcas, and this was probably the most important discussion of Alasdhair's life.

"You don't understand, Mr. MacKay."

"Alasdhair. We've shared my flask, *Dorcas*, and I hope to share much more than that with you. I understand *firsthand* that young people are exceedingly foolish and lusty and that you are worrying for nothing. I don't care if you were among the Regent's many conquests, or if you danced naked in the Carlton House fountains. I am not in love with the girl you were, though I doubtless would have been, given a chance. I am in love with the woman you are."

Alasdhair had eaten recently. He could not blame his tirade on a lack of sustenance, though a chilly porch was no place to make such a declaration.

He was horrified to see that his rash words had brought Dorcas near tears.

"You awful man," she muttered. "You outrageous, brave, heedless... I could thrash you." She instead pitched into him, her arms lashing around his waist. "You have no idea... not the first clue. Nobody took advantage of me, but I refuse to descend into debate. You are awful, abominable, horrid, and hopeless."

Never argue with a lady, particularly not when she was in the throes of what for her was doubtless a cataclysmic lapse in dignity. Alasdhair held Dorcas, wondering at the great upheaval shuddering through her. All this passion, buttoned and bonneted behind endless good works and meeting minutes.

The sooner he freed her from this vicarage, the sooner she could unleash her thunderbolts of reform on the unsuspecting and take the world by storm.

And take Alasdhair by storm too, of course. He was looking forward to that part very much.

He stroked her hair, searching idly in Gaelic for the state of bliss that came after *in love*. "Shall I get that special license, Dorcas?"

"You haven't even spoken with Papa yet."

Nor did Alasdhair need to. The vicar's daughter had been ordering her own affairs for years, all unbeknownst to her father. But Dorcas would appreciate the usual protocol, and Alasdhair had planned to observe it.

"I will beg a moment of his time tomorrow, then. When would suit?" The vicar would not know his daughter's schedule for the rest of the day, but Dorcas would be acquainted with every appointment and outing on her father's calendar for the next month.

The mulish light flickered across her features, then she used the end of the plaid scarf to dab at her eyes. "Right after the noon meal. Papa has no appointments in the early afternoon, and he relies on me to deal with any callers."

She did not look like a woman who'd all but agreed to become engaged. She looked forlorn and bewildered, and Alasdhair wanted to take her in his arms all over again.

"Dorcas, do you trust me?"

"Yes." A gratifyingly swift and certain answer.

"And I trust you. This is all moving too quickly for you, I suspect, but I have searched for years to find the woman my heart has yearned for. If I am not the man your heart has yearned for, then set me aside, and there's an end to it. You remain in control of this situation, though it might not feel that way at the moment."

He could hear his cousins berating him for that speech. Bad strategy to remind a woman she was always free to change her mind. But maybe not. Goddard hadn't married his Ann for anything less than true love, and Powell was cut from the same cloth. When he fell —and he would fall eventually—he'd fall hard and forever.

Dorcas gave Alasdhair a considering look, then patted his chest. "You are right. You have quite swept me off my feet, and the novelty of such an approach is disconcerting. Much to my consternation, the last thing I want to do is set you aside, *Alasdhair*."

She brushed a kiss to his cheek and slipped into the vicarage. She had perfected the art of the effective retreat, had Dorcas.

Alasdhair stood for a moment, staring dumbly at the closed door, then made his way back to the tea shop for a reprise of his snack. By the time he'd finished his second sandwich, he'd resolved in his mind that the morning had been a victory.

Dorcas had confided her worst regret to him, which was only fair when he'd imposed the same burden on her first.

She had called him Alasdhair, and on purpose.

She had not forbidden him to get a special license—very telling that, very encouraging.

She had permitted him to schedule a call upon her dear papa. More telling still.

She had flung the most endearing string of insults at him—awful, abominable, horrid, and so forth. She'd have to do better than that once they were married. He'd teach her some Gaelic, and she could doubtless brush up his Latin.

By the time Alasdhair had returned home, he was entirely pleased with the morning's events. Dorcas had also called him hopeless, but—finally, at last—that adjective no longer applied. And as long as he was married to his darling Dorcas, Alasdhair would never be hopeless again.

DORCAS FREQUENTLY LONGED for solitude at the vicarage and was just as frequently denied that boon.

After the discussion with Alasdhair—how she delighted to think of him thus—she stood behind the closed front door and contemplated the enormity—the wonderful, miraculous, heady enormity—of becoming his wife.

Possibly becoming his wife, for more challenges lay between her and that objective. Such ponderings called for several long, slow circuits of the garden, though meeting minutes would have to come first of course.

Dorcas was no stranger to joy. Every time a parishioner was safely delivered of a healthy baby, every time an engagement was announced, when Papa's sermon was especially well received, she was moved to happiness on behalf of those involved.

But to marry Alasdhair and leave the vicarage would mean more than joy, it would mean freedom of a magnitude Dorcas had not permitted herself to contemplate. Papa *had* doted on Michael, Papa *had not* seen the danger to a young daughter as clever as she was headstrong.

Not that the past was Papa's fault, of course.

"Oh, there you are." Mrs. Benton stood at the top of the steps that led down to the kitchen. "Did you have a nice outing, Miss Dorcas?"

"I did," Dorcas said, setting her bonnet on its customary hook. "How was the market?"

"The price of setting a table worthy of your father's household only increases, though some of that is simply the season. You were off to see to Miss Melanie's baby?"

Dorcas did not want to be interrogated now, did not want to fashion the careful, diplomatic answers that the topic called for. "Papa told you about that?"

"He's concerned for you, miss. Charitable works are one thing, but the child's antecedents are lamentably irregular, and the baby is apparently well provided for without your efforts." She held out her hands to take Dorcas's cloak. "Albeit the boy dwells in a bachelor household."

Dorcas moved away, tidying up the inevitable stack of morning mail. Mrs. Benton was a good soul. Her contribution to keeping the vicarage running was enormous, and yet, she'd never presumed to mother Dorcas, never shown an ambition to be more than a valued employee.

"Mr. MacKay is a former officer and heir to the Scottish equivalent of a barony." *And John won't be living in a bachelor household much longer, if all goes well.* "Mr. MacKay took a kindly interest in Melanie's situation despite her circumstances. I esteem a man who can set aside judgmental conventions where the welfare of a mother and child is at risk."

"So do I." Mrs. Benton used a handkerchief to dab at a smudge on the mirror over the sideboard. "Was Mr. MacKay troubling you, Dorcas? I could not hear what he was saying, but his tone was somewhat emphatic."

"We argue," Dorcas said, the admission surprising her. "I delight in arguing with him. He doesn't mince off into gentlemanly restraint owing to my inferior female intellect as soon as he senses that I'm about to checkmate his theories. He can admit that he's wrong."

Mrs. Benton moved on to straightening the cloaks, coats, parasols, and umbrellas on their various hooks. "You like that about him?"

Like was too pale a word for adoration mixed with relief and joy. Oh, to cut loose with logic, facts, learned citations, and persuasion... to demolish empty posturing and conveniently false equivalences...

"Major MacKay is easy to talk to, Mrs. Benton. He's told me about the war, about childhood pranks with his siblings, and when I prattle on about women in prison or the inane politics of the grounds committee, he listens to me."

Mrs. Benton's gaze traveled down the corridor toward Papa's study. "A man who listens well is a treasure. I have always regarded your father's patience as a listener quite highly."

Something wistful in her tone caught Dorcas's ear. What else about Papa did Mrs. Benton regard quite highly?

"I suppose for Papa it goes with the job."

"The grounds committee is a tribulation to you and the vicar both," Mrs. Benton said. "If you'd like, I can take the meeting minutes. I've baked an extra dozen hot cross buns in case Mr. Knorr and Mr. Crown come to verbal fisticuffs over flowerpots on the church steps again."

A battle royal, that discussion. Flowerpots, in the opinion of Mr. Knorr, were the devil's trap for the unwary, just waiting to trip the unsuspecting, also an exercise in vanity. Mr. Crown—brother-in-law to Mr. Prebish—returned fire with quotations about the lilies of the field and congregational pride.

All quite ridiculous.

"The issue isn't flowerpots," Dorcas said. "The issue is who will be promoted to the pastoral committee when Mr. Riley rotates off next year." Until Dorcas had established mandatory retirements for all committee members, the jockeying had been relentless.

"And the solution," Mrs. Benton said, "is to promote neither of them until they learn to behave with greater decorum, but will the vicar see the wisdom of that suggestion? You'd think they were a lot of schoolboys. I gather your Mr. MacKay is not a schoolboy."

"Far from it. He's a good man. Somewhat unconventional, but decent to his bones." Decent enough that Dorcas was actually, truly, honestly contemplating marriage with him. The heart boggled to consider such a possibility.

"You are a good woman," Mrs. Benton said, twitching at the folds of Papa's greatcoat. "I see how hard you work, Dorcas Delancey, and I believe another young man sees that too."

"Has our choir director come by extolling the virtues of F major again?"

"Mrs. Tritapoe has him in mind for her oldest. The young lady is quite musical, which is fortunate, because she has more hair than wit.

I refer to Mr. Isaiah Mornebeth. I ran into him at the market, and he was inquiring very pointedly about you."

All the joy, all the glee, trepidation, and wonder in Dorcas catapulted top over tail into dread. "Mr. Mornebeth?"

"Not as youthful as our choir master, nor as dashing as your Mr. MacKay, but still an impressive fellow."

"In his own mind, he's doubtless the catch of the Season." As soon as she muttered the words, Dorcas regretted them. Thomas Delancey's daughter would never disparage another churchman, much less a friend of her father and—ostensibly—of her brother.

"Mr. Mornebeth purchased flowers for you," Mr. Benton said. "Daffodils symbolize new beginnings, if I recall correctly."

"And chivalry." Neither meaning had any relevance where Isaiah Mornebeth was concerned. "Will I find these flowers in the library?"

"That's the curious part. He bought a bunch of unopened buds, which would make no sort of bouquet. He claimed they were thanks for a fine meal, but, Miss Dorcas, one delivers flowers the day after enjoying a fine meal, and one delivers a blooming bouquet. I found his choice odd."

Sinister, one might even say. "Perhaps he could not afford the opened flowers."

"I pay attention to prices, Miss Dorcas, and every bunch was priced the same. I know your father enjoys Mr. Mornebeth's company and that he's considered a rising star, comely, with a genuine calling, and from good family. That doesn't mean you must tolerate his overtures."

This display of support, at variance with Papa's guidance, was both surprising and welcome. "I cannot afford to offend him, Mrs. Benton." The admission disgusted Dorcas, as Isaiah Mornebeth disgusted her—now that she was permitted to be honest with herself. "I've told Papa I am not at home to Mr. Mornebeth, and I am telling you the same thing now."

"I understand."

"You do?"

Mrs. Benton paused at the top of the steps, her hand on the newel post. "I was married to a good man, Miss Dorcas. My Patrick wasn't given to flowery speeches, but I knew he loved me. He worked hard to keep a roof over our heads, never complained about my modest portion, and never berated me when I could not have children. That man said more with silence and genuine affection than all the flatterers and fawners have ever said with their flummery and flowers.

"Mr. Mornebeth," she went on, "is the sort of fellow who thinks himself cleverer than all the rest, special. Anointed by providence for lofty rewards, though he's getting too old for such hubris. He hides it well, but he's so busy planning his own canonization that he can't be bothered to notice the difference between apple walnut torte and pear tarts."

"You make splendid pear tarts." Had served them on the occasion of Mornebeth's supper at the vicarage, if Dorcas recalled correctly.

"I do—my mother's recipe—but Mr. Mornebeth was so intent on prying details of your situation from me that he forgot the first rule of flattery: Root your compliments in truth, or they are so many lies."

"I appreciate the warning, Mrs. Benton. I do not wish to create awkwardness with Mr. Mornebeth, and I have even less wish to encourage any ambitions he holds regarding my future."

"Then best of luck to your Scotsman, I say." She hugged Dorcas, an unprecedented display of affection, then bustled off for the stairs.

Dorcas felt as if she'd taken ship on a vessel caught up in successive storms. First, Alasdhair's ferocious declarations and insights, delivered with all the intensity and integrity he possessed. Dorcas hadn't told him the whole of her past, but she'd told him enough to have sent any other suitor packing.

Alasdhair MacKay had instead gone to arrange a special license.

Then this exchange with Mrs. Benton… Dorcas took herself out to the garden and perched on the stone bench beside the frozen birdbath. That Mrs. Benton could see through Isaiah's posturing was a vindication.

"I am not foolish to mistrust him." He'd never apologized for his bad behavior toward Dorcas, never expressed regret for his trespasses.

And he had trespassed. Egregiously. Admitting that was easier now. Breathing was easier now too. Dorcas had much to consider, much to sort out, but her perspective on the past had been given a healthy nudge in the direction of objectivity.

Dorcas was contemplating the wonder of Mrs. Benton's apparent tendresse for Papa when Papa himself came out into the garden, waving a piece of paper.

"Daughter, Daughter, I have the best news! Come inside, for we must make plans!"

A bishopric? Now? What else could put such a spring in Papa's step. "Tell me," Dorcas said, rising. "Tell me the great news, and then I have some news to share with you too." Papa did not deal well with surprises, and Alasdhair's call tomorrow would be surprising indeed.

Papa hadn't bothered to button his coat, nor had he donned a hat. "Michael is coming." He brandished the paper again. "Your dear brother is coming for a visit, and by heaven, Dorcas, if we had a fatted calf, that creature's days would be numbered. Michael is coming home for a good long visit, and I daresay if a post opens up closer to Town, he'll be applying for it."

"That is wonderful news, Papa. I'll have Mrs. Benton air out his room and see that your calendar is free of appointments while Michael is with us. And if you have another moment—"

"A post in Kent would be ideal," Papa went on. "Never hurts to be within hailing distance of Canterbury. The Kentish congregations tend to be well fixed, with plenty of titles. Surrey is also pleasant, and even Sussex or Berkshire would do. I am off to the club, my dear, and will likely not be home for dinner. Such news, such news..."

"But, Papa, if you could tarry for five minutes..." He went flapping and waving back toward the house, leaving Dorcas standing on the garden path. "Papa! When does Michael arrive?"

"Next week," he called over his shoulder, "weather permitting. I shall pray without ceasing for his safe arrival until that blessed day."

Papa disappeared back into the vicarage before Dorcas could tell him that Alasdhair MacKay intended to call tomorrow, much less why he'd be calling, or how Dorcas hoped Papa would receive him.

"IF YOU'VE COME ABOUT MONEY," Mr. Delancey began, folding his hands on the desk's leather blotter, "then I will disabuse you of the notion that the boy's family has much in the way of coin. We are comfortable, through the grace of God. We intend that the child want for nothing essential, but I will not tolerate repeated attempts at extortion. You are apparently his legal guardian, MacKay, and he is your responsibility."

The vicar's version of wrathful sternness might have convinced a recruit in his first week in uniform. Even a very young Dorcas would have paid her father's temper little mind. She had exaggerated Delancey's sternness when advocating for John, a tactic Alasdhair understood.

For Dorcas's sake, he allowed the insult in Delancey's words to pass. "The lad's name is John Fairchild, though I'd be pleased to see him travel under the MacKay banner if that's his preference. He's about so long, and his smile would light up your whole household."

Delancey cleared his throat. He scooted in his chair. "That the child thrives is, of course, an occasion for gratitude."

"I did not come here to discuss John with you," Alasdhair said, getting as comfortable as possible on a wee, creaky chair with lumpy cushions. The shelves of theological treatises added to the study's pontifical air, and a landscape of some gleaming cathedral reinforced the trappings of churchliness. The urge to burst forth into one of Rabbie Burns's more rollicking airs nagged at Alasdhair. "I am honored to have been entrusted with John's upbringing, and I had nothing but respect for his mother."

"*Nothing* but respect?" Delancey added a judgmental little sniff.

"Respect, admiration, and perhaps a smidgeon of pity. Melanie was abandoned by the man she eloped with, cut off by her family, and she hadn't an aptitude for either venery or industry, but she tried her heart out for that boy."

"And then committed the sin of ultimate selfishness by taking her own life. I pray for her soul nightly, Mr. MacKay, and I pray for the boy as well. Nonetheless, as the twig is bent, so grows the tree, and that baby is the fruit of a pair of very... Suffice it to say, he will struggle mightily against his parents' legacy."

"He'll struggle, particularly if you treat him as if he's some sort of blight on what appears to be a fairly humble escutcheon. Fortunately, Miss Delancey's charitable inclinations are genuine, and it's about her I've come to speak with you."

"About Dorcas? She is honestly not at home, Mr. MacKay. A parishioner was brought to childbed yesterday afternoon, and I have not seen my daughter since then. Her life is one of irreproachable good works, as her willingness to monitor John's progress doubtless proves."

Alasdhair was about to deliver a tongue-lashing worthy of his Campbell granny—*of course* Dorcas was beyond reproach—but Delancey had steepled his fingers and was tapping his two index fingertips together.

Thomas Delancey was nervous, more likely worried, perhaps even terrified. Alasdhair had come to announce a plan to take Dorcas away from the vicarage permanently. Delancey apparently sensed that his little castle of rectitude was imperiled.

And the vicar was right to be scared, because once Dorcas won free of this prison, she'd not come back to it.

"Dorcas doesn't permit herself to hold the boy," Alasdhair said. "She has to be that careful with her heart. If she holds him, she might not be able to let him go, because he is so trusting and so vulnerable. She cannot refuse aid to the vulnerable. I love that about her—love her soft heart and her ferocious convictions."

"You presume to call her Dorcas?" A note of bewilderment had slipped past Delancey's bluster.

"I hope one day soon to call her Mrs. MacKay."

Delancey's mouth worked, his brows twitched. The tapping of his fingertips picked up speed. "You seek to court *my Dorcas*?"

"She's not your Dorcas." Alasdhair spoke gently, for he'd no wish to antagonize his future father-in-law. "She's not my Dorcas either. She belongs to herself, and though I would much prefer to have your blessing, the lady has indicated that my addresses would be welcome. Her favor is what concerns me most."

"Then you misunderstood her." Delancey rose and paced to the window, hands behind his back. "As you say, Dorcas is very considerate of others' pride. She clearly has no notion how you have interpreted her loyalty to a deceased cousin's offspring. Such devotion is commendable, but look at the confusion her behavior has wrought. I am very sorry that you have misconstrued the situation, Mr. MacKay, but you'll not turn Dorcas into John's unpaid nanny and governess by virtue of taking her to wife."

Oh, the irony. Dorcas was the *unpaid* pastor of the congregation, while Delancey donned the church finery and delivered a weekly homily.

Alasdhair remained in the creaky little chair. "Allow me to disabuse *you* of some confusion, Mr. Delancey. My family traces its heritage back to the Bruce. We have three castles, counting only the ones commodiously appointed, and town houses in Glasgow and Edinburgh. Walter Scott is among my father's boon companions, and I have been presented at court. I am an Honorable, not that I bother with such nonsense. Married to me, Dorcas's children will also someday claim that courtesy, while she will be addressed as lady. I am happy to schedule an appointment for you with the family solicitors should you need the details of my situation."

Delancey had turned to face Alasdhair somewhere in the midst of this recitation. "You're Church of Scotland?" he asked, his earlier ire fading into chilly reserve.

"My father is Church of Scotland, but like many a Scottish

family, we have Dissenters among our ranks and even Catholics not too many generations back."

"But you are Church of Scotland now."

"My immediate family is. My own loyalty is to the Church of Basic Decency. Shall I have my solicitors prepare you a report?"

Some shift in perspective had come over Delancey as a result of learning that Alasdhair was no penniless former soldier.

Delancey considered him for what was doubtless meant to be an uncomfortable, silent moment. "Do that, MacKay," he said, "though in all candor, I must tell you that your prospects with Dorcas are slim. She has caught the eye of a colleague of mine, a churchman from a good family—good *English* family. He has known Dorcas much longer than you have. He grasps the nuances of her situation as you cannot. Dorcas might well like you and esteem you for taking in Melanie's by-blow, but she would never marry a man who'd drag her off to Scotland."

Alasdhair was tempted to inform Delancey that Dorcas despised Isaiah Mornebeth. That disclosure would shatter at least one wing of the castle of self-serving fancies in which Delancey dwelled, and Dorcas would feel bound by loyalty to sweep up the mess.

"We can agree that Dorcas is an eminently lovely young lady," Alasdhair said, "and that she should have her pick of marital options. If I win her hand, I hope our union will have your blessing."

To his credit, Delancey nodded. "My daughter's happiness matters to me, and she is nothing if not sensible. I will abide by her wishes in this matter, though I cannot admonish you strongly enough to anticipate disappointment, Mr. MacKay."

"I appreciate the warning, and I can see myself out." Alasdhair rose, glad to be quit of the lumpy chair, and made for the door.

"MacKay?"

"Sir?"

"You'll send the boy to Scotland to be raised?"

Out of sight, out of the eye of the gossips? "Is that a condition of your blessing upon the nuptials?"

"I doubt you have nuptials to look forward to, but no, that is not a condition. I am merely curious and concerned for the boy."

"His name is John, and because he is as a son to me now, he will bide for the most part with me, though he'll certainly become acquainted with my Scottish relatives. Where Dorcas and I make our home will largely depend on her wishes. Good day."

"I mean no insult to you, MacKay, and I do care about the child. I am well acquainted, though, with how the morally upright can treat those of questionable birth. Perhaps in Scotland, society is more tolerant, but here in London... John will face challenges."

"Then he will face them supported by me and every resource I command."

Alasdhair left the vicarage with a sense of having escaped an enemy garrison. Delancey doubtless did aspire to a godly life, but he also found virtuous excuses for every occasion when his striving fell short. Wishing John to Scotland, for example, was not expedient for Delancey's ambitions, but rather, a kindness to wee John.

Warning Alasdhair of competition for Dorcas's hand was not an effort to destroy his confidence, it was merely paternal fair play.

If Dorcas was Miss Delightful—and she was—then her father was Mr. Self-Delusion.

Alasdhair was debating whether to stop by the tea shop on his way home when a flash of dark green wool on the walkway ahead of him caught his eye. Many a lady wore a heavy cloak on such a nippy day, but this lady also wore a poke bonnet adorned with a single pheasant feather on the left side.

Alasdhair knew of only one woman who'd trimmed her everyday bonnet thus, and that lady was Melanie Fairchild. He quickened his pace, intent on taking a closer look, but when he turned the corner, the woman had vanished.

CHAPTER TWELVE

Dorcas drowsed before a roaring fire in Alasdhair's sitting room, her mind drifting over thoughts of hot chocolate, babies, and blooming heather. Scotland was said to be beautiful, and she had no idea which corner of Scotland Alasdhair called home.

A soft kiss grazed her cheek. "*Dùisg, a ghràidh.*"

The warmth of Alasdhair's burr curled around her heart as the heat of the fire had taken the chill from her body. "I dozed off," she said, straightening. "What did you say?"

"Wake up, my dear. How are mother and child?" He set a tea tray on the hassock before Dorcas's chair and took a seat on the raised hearth.

"They are well, thank heavens. The child waited until this morning to arrive, but Mrs. Bonner tends to have long labors. I wanted to let you know that I haven't had a chance to warn Papa that you intend to call, except I am apparently too late. Is that lemon cake?"

He passed over a fat slice. "From the tea shop. I could not enjoy my snack sitting all on my lonesome at the back table. Did Mrs. Bonner name the baby?"

"Mr. Bonner did. Alma, because her safe arrival lifted his spirits so. He cried, Alasdhair. Held that squalling little scrap of humanity and cried with no dignity whatsoever."

"You cried too," Alasdhair said, taking a bite of the lemon cake when Dorcas held it out to him. "Exhaustion can make us impossible or turn us up sweet and saintly. You've looked in on John?"

"He went down for a nap shortly after I arrived. Timmens says he had a lively night and will probably sleep a good two hours. She's off to see her sister, and Henderson has guard duty. You should have a sandwich. Lemon cake is not proper sustenance."

Alasdhair poured two cups of tea. "The sight of you, curled up in my reading chair, is the best nourishment. Your father tried to be difficult." He added a dash of honey and a dollop of cream to her tea, stirred it, and passed it over. The mug was heavy—no delicate porcelain—and its warmth felt good in Dorcas's hands.

"Papa does not like surprises." The tea, by contrast, was surprisingly good. Stronger than Dorcas was used to and smooth and rich rather than harsh.

"Your papa does not like the idea of you living in Scotland with me, though he's happy to consign John to some drafty old Highland castle. The vicar said if I could out-court the wondrous Mr. Mornebeth, he would tolerate me for a son-in-law."

"Papa did not say that."

Alasdhair took up a sandwich, gnawed off a bite, and chewed in silence.

Dorcas had dreamed of his kisses, of the feel of his hands on her back, the pleasure of his embrace. That was all quite lovely, but this cozy chat by the fire, the perfectly prepared cup of tea, the chance to report on a mother and child safely through their travail...

This is heaven. The thought popped into Dorcas's mind all of a piece, knitting together caring, kisses, and something more, something to do with what drew her to linger at Alasdhair's house even when he was absent from it.

"Your father," Alasdhair said, "dreads to lose you to holy matrimony. He might not admit it to himself, Dorcas, but he knows that you keep his congregation running smoothly. Mornebeth would put some claims on your time as a husband, but he wouldn't disappear with you to Scotland."

Dorcas cradled her mug in her hands as some of the glow of the moment faded. "I would just as soon never hear that man's name again."

Alasdhair finished his first sandwich, dusted his hands, and considered her. "Was Mornebeth the partner you chose for your foray into wicked rebellion, Dorcas?"

No accusation or disgust colored that question, merely curiosity. That Alasdhair would leap to such a conclusion was unnerving, though he was a man who thought much, observed carefully, and denied himself the comfort of willful blindness.

The urge to disclose the whole sordid truth nearly undid Dorcas, but the habit of dissembling was too ingrained and the trust she'd placed in Alasdhair too new. Time for truth later, when they were in that Highland castle, far, far from ugly memories and the man who'd precipitated them.

And yet, she could not lie outright, not to him. "And if he was?"

"Then I hope he was considerate, but I suspect—given your antipathy toward him—that he bungled matters badly. My first encounter was noteworthy for how poorly I acquitted myself. I shudder to recall the brevity of the interlude, but the lady, who was ten years my senior, said she was pleased with my youthful ardor—or graciously pretended she was."

The memory made him frown as he took up his second sandwich.

"The recollection is awkward?"

"Awkward, but also... dear. That randy, bumbling boy wanted so badly to become a man and had not the first inkling of what manhood entails. He tried his best, pathetic though that often was. My father, bless him, made sure I knew every detail of whisky-making, but was much less forthcoming regarding dealings with the ladies. I will try to ensure that John is better informed than I was. More tea?"

The question was so prosaic, and the topic so intimate, that Dorcas felt tears well again. Alasdhair already saw himself as a parent where John was concerned.

"This is why you resisted taking John in, isn't it? You know not only what manhood entails, but what honor entails. You will be a good father to John or no father at all."

He brushed a finger over her lips. "The things you say, my heart. I am not the lad's father, though your papa assumed I was. Does the vicar know of your past with your other suitor?"

"He must never know."

Another silence ensued, while all manner of arguments bubbled up from Dorcas's guilty conscience: Papa would be devastated to know what she'd done, he'd try not to blame her, Mornebeth would play the moment with exquisite skill, and the whole sordid mess would never die.

"You are tired," Alasdhair said, pouring her a second cup of tea, "and this is a difficult topic that need not be raised again." He fixed the second cup as he had the first—exactly how she liked it—and passed the mug over. "I have applied for a special license."

That announcement was cause for all manner of relief. "Have you?"

"I am poorer by five pounds and wealthier by an infinite abundance of hope. I will be notified by messenger when the documents are ready, and if you don't mind, I'd like my cousins to be present at the ceremony."

"You are very efficient, Mr. MacKay. I have not accepted your proposal."

He sipped his tea, and even that commonplace activity had Dorcas focusing on his mouth.

"Why haven't you, Dorcas? It occurred to me that we have not discussed money, and that is an oversight on my part."

"We need not discuss money."

"The hell we need not. Life is uncertain, and no wife of mine will be left to make shift when the MacKay resources can provide for her amply. I've written to my father, but he has been urging me to the altar since I turned one-and-twenty. I well know what my bride can anticipate in terms of settlements."

"Alasdhair, I'm sure the settlements will be very much in order. I meant no insult."

He set down his mug and regarded her with the sort of glower he'd affected on their first meeting. "If it's not the money, and it's not your Papa's blessing, then what holds you back, Dorcas? I'm in good health, I have all my teeth. My family isn't awful, except for Finn, and he can't help himself."

Alasdhair shifted from the hearth and knelt beside her chair. "I adore you. You know that, don't you? I'm not good with the pretty speeches, but you will always have my love and protection, Dorcas. I will honor my vows all my days, and—"

She kissed him and slipped an arm around his neck before her courage failed. "Before, you said you hoped that I was shown consideration..."

Alasdhair wrapped her close. "I did say that, I do hope that."

This much truth she would give him. "It was awful. It was... I threw up afterward, all three times. Mornebeth said I'd learn to enjoy it, but, Alasdhair... I am haunted. He did not hurt me. Physically, I felt almost nothing. Some awkwardness, some confusion that such a graceless business should garner so much interest. I stumbled around in a fog of dismay for months, wondering what on earth I'd done, and I very much worry that..."

Alasdhair spoke quietly. "That you won't enjoy marital intimacies?"

She nodded, grateful that he could not see the blush heating her face. "That there is something wrong with me, that I *cannot* enjoy them. That I have no animal spirits. That my punishment is an inability to enjoy that which I stole for my own purposes. I hardly know how to put into words the combination of worry, resentment, longing... Will you take me to bed? I want to get it over with."

She expected him to sit back, or worse, move away. To recall a pressing appointment at his club that required him to walk her home in the next quarter hour.

"Say something, Alasdhair."

He stroked her hair. "I'm thinking. What does honor require of me when you are in such a state? When you are in my arms, I could convince myself that a stiff prick has become the embodiment of chivalry rather than Beelzebub's magic wand. You are weary and beset. I have badgered you into disclosures you dreaded to make..."

"Do you want to take me to bed?" *Please say yes.*

"Of course I do, but that doesn't signify. I want you to be happy, Dorcas."

I don't know when I was last happy. Except that wasn't true. She was happy chatting with Alasdhair over a cup of tea. Happy watching him hold his one-sided conversations with John. Happy simply walking down the street at his side.

"I will marry you, Alasdhair. I esteem you greatly, I delight in your kisses, and I want to be your wife. I'm simply... wary of what awaits on our wedding night. I want that ordeal behind us."

He did sit back, but kept hold of her hands. "We will take each other to bed, Dorcas, and if you truly don't care for what happens there, you will tell me that we don't suit. You will not consign yourself to decades of intimacies that you don't enjoy. You will not exchange one form of captivity for another. Promise me that."

She wanted to argue. Marriage to Alasdhair could never be captivity, but life at the vicarage was certainly taking on the quality of an incarceration.

"I promise. Enough talk, Mr. MacKay. To bed with us."

NOBODY HAD SEEN fit to warn Alasdhair that Dorcas bided in his sitting room. He'd thus come upon her all unaware, his mind still offering up clever, learned retorts he should have fired at Thomas Delancey's paternal conceits.

Then Alasdhair had seen Dorcas, felled by exhaustion and curled up in his reading chair. Her peacefully slumbering form was the best argument he could have made for a permanent union with her: She *trusted* him. She trusted him enough to come and go from his home unescorted, trusted him enough to encourage his advances, trusted him enough to leave John in his care...

And trusted him enough to confide the details of her sorry initial foray into sexual intimacies. Mornebeth had chosen the worst possible manner in which to bungle, but in true Dorcas fashion, she'd not considered that her erstwhile lover might have failed her.

She, who excelled at recounting society's shortcomings, looked for the flaw within herself.

"I should shave," Alasdhair said, scrubbing a hand over his cheeks.

She marched past him toward the bedroom. "You shaved before calling at the vicarage. If you tarry behind the privacy screen, I might lose my nerve."

Alasdhair stopped her on the threshold by putting a hand to her shoulder. "Then lose your nerve. Tell me you've changed your mind, that you have decided to send me packing. The only request I make of you, Dorcas, is that you be honest with me and with yourself. I insist upon it."

She gazed up at him, expression unreadable. "Women are not generally encouraged to have opinions, much less to speak them."

"If a woman is not entitled to hold forth about her own bodily joys and woes, then she has been reduced to the status of an automaton, a device fashioned for the convenience of men and children. Is that how you think of yourself?"

Her hesitation was a blow to his heart. Him, she might trust, but herself? Damn Mornebeth, Vicar Delancey, and anybody else who had caused an eminently intelligent, kind, sensible, and dear woman to doubt herself.

"It's complicated," she said, moving into the bedroom.

"Then let me simplify it," Alasdhair said, coming up behind her and wrapping his arms around her waist. "I love you. You can tell me that your ears are ticklish."

"My ears are not ticklish."

Oh, but her dignity was. To Alasdhair's first outright declaration of love, Dorcas had no retort, and that pleased his enormously. "You *could* tell me if your ears *were* ticklish. I would desist from nuzzling your ears."

She stood quite straight in his arms. "Would you tease me about it? Bring it up as a private joke with your cousins?"

Mornebeth had done worse than bungle, he'd shown himself to be an utter buffoon. "My dearest heart, I might remark to my cousins that I cannot wait to become your husband, that I want a honey month of five years duration, but the particulars of your ears or toes or the way you sigh when I take you in my arms... Those belong to us alone. They are private. Sacred."

She let him have the smallest increment of her weight. "With you, I hope it can be. Will you see to my hooks?"

Hell yes. "Hold still."

She undid his cravat, and he assisted with her hooks, but they mostly undressed on separate sides of the bed. For Alasdhair, that was a sop to self-restraint. For Dorcas... maybe a chance to assess him in an undressed state? She folded her clothes tidily on the clothes press. Alasdhair hung his over the top of the privacy screen. He wanted to tackle her, and she likely wanted to leave.

By the time Alasdhair was wearing only his breeches, Dorcas stood in her shift and bare feet, looking chilly and uncertain.

He draped his dressing gown around her shoulders. "Borrow my toothpowder. I'll warm the sheets."

She scooted off behind the privacy screen, while Alasdhair filled the warmer with coals. Their first intimate encounter was off to a miserably unimpressive start. The issue was not one of skilled kisses or alluring caresses—he had no doubt whatsoever that he was adequate to those challenges—but of the mind and heart.

Taking a new lover always entailed mustering a dash of courage in hopes of a banquet of pleasure, but in Dorcas's case, the boot was on the other foot. She was marshaling her courage in anticipation of no pleasure whatsoever.

She gave her teeth what had to be the most thorough scrubbing in the history of teeth, while Alasdhair ran the warmer over the sheets twice. When she emerged from behind the privacy screen, his dressing gown was belted snugly at her waist, and her hair was still in its tidy coiffure.

"You'll want to climb under the covers while they're warm," Alasdhair said, ambling past her to the privacy screen. "I'll be along in a moment."

He heard the snick of the bedroom door lock as he tended to his ablutions. The bedcovers rustled, and he had the sense that he was in the very early stages of a long siege. There was no such thing as a good siege. The rank and file had hated sieges, coming as they did at a high cost in human life after a long and brutal struggle to breach the city walls.

Alasdhair hated sieges for more reasons than that. Better by far to win a battle outright with massed armies or, best of all, to prevail by strategy rather than bloodshed.

When he was as well washed and as sweet-smelling as soap and water could make him, he came around the screen and found Dorcas lying on the far side of the bed, covers pulled up to her chin. What strategy could possibly prevail against so much uncertainty and misgiving? Against all of those bad memories and all of that bewilderment?

Alasdhair was debating whether to peel out of his breeches when it occurred to him that he was viewing the whole situation the wrong way 'round.

"You have doubts," he said, unbuttoning his falls. "About yourself, about your entitlement to marital joy."

"About my *ability* to enjoy certain acts..." Dorcas fell silent as he tossed his breeches on top of her tidy stack on the clothes press.

He was only half aroused, a flannel soaked in frigid water having a calming effect on the humors.

"I have doubts too," Alasdhair said, making no move to climb under the covers when Dorcas was conducting such a thorough visual inspection of his person. "I have not been with a woman for years. For a long time, I had no desire for such intimacy, then indifference became a habit. With you..."

She ceased her brooding perusal of his parts, her gaze traveling over his belly and chest to fix on his face. "With me?"

"I might be too eager. I might disappoint you. I might think I've shown you a fine time only to find a polite farewell note awaiting me on the blotter in the study. I might inadvertently offend you or—God help me—cause you discomfort. I might fail you."

Alasdhair well knew how to please a woman, and his equipment was in roaringly good working order. Nevertheless, a recitation that had started off as a list of theoretical risks—*purely* theoretical risks—had become an admission of honest worries.

"You might fail *me*?" Dorcas asked, folding back the bedcovers. "Explain yourself."

He joined her on the mattress and snuggled up along her side. "I am haunted too, Dorcas. Not in the same manner you are, but by memories and doubts. I want only to acquit myself well in your eyes, even to impress you, but the possibility exists that I will fall flat, as it were, and earn your pity or contempt instead."

Dorcas bundled closer, her chemise bunched about her thighs. "It's complicated?"

"I don't want it to be. I want us to be two people who are smitten with one another and anticipating their vows, as smitten couples do. No sieges, no regrets, only rejoicing and gratitude. If we don't precisely blast open heaven's front door in the next hour, I hope we enjoy the view from the gates and give it another go the next time we're so inclined."

A small, tight knot in his gut eased to put that hope into words.

Marriage was a long-term undertaking, ideally, and becoming lovers was a joy to be savored.

"Rejoicing and gratitude," Dorcas said. "I like that. Also kisses. I do enjoy your kisses, Alasdhair." She pressed her lips to his chest. "You cannot know what glee it brings me that I enjoy your kisses, and I like kissing you too."

Well, yes, he could know. He of all men could know the wonder of reviving a pleasure that he'd put aside years ago out of moral necessity. The mechanics were the same now—lips, sighs, tastes, tongues—but the objective was not only physical pleasure, but also physical *loving*.

He offered Dorcas flowery phrases—in Gaelic—and she nuzzled his ears. The fire burned down, her chemise ended up at the foot of the bed, and she caressed him in places that had gone uncaressed for too long.

"Your touch is special," he said, mildly disconcerted that the words had come out in English. "You soothe and arouse at the same time."

Dorcas was wrapped along his side, her fingers brushing through the hair on his chest. "I am not soothed. I am relaxed, but also restless —inside."

Relaxed was good. *Restless inside* was very good. "Why not climb aboard and see where the restlessness takes us?"

"Climb aboard?" She propped herself up on an elbow. "I thought you did the climbing aboard."

Alasdhair added a lack of imagination to Mornebeth's many, many faults.

"If you are astride me, you control the particulars." Then too, if she was in the saddle, his hands were free to explore other particulars.

"Astride you. Women do this?"

"Dorcas, beloved of my heart, I don't care if Queen Charlotte is a regular exponent of certain procreative practices or has a confirmed disgust of others. If you and I choose to try a little experiment in this bed, that is nobody's business but ours. I do believe you like the notion of being in charge."

She was clearly intrigued and not about to admit it. "One sometimes had difficulty breathing with a grown man collapsed atop one."

Mornebeth was a complete, humping mongrel, a disgrace to the gender. "One absolutely delights to have a grown female sweetly expired on his chest."

"Does one?" Dorcas sat up, and though it took some clutching of the covers on her part and pretending not to gawk—much—on Alasdhair's, she threw a leg over him and cuddled up.

"This is cozy," she said. "I can feel your heartbeat."

While Alasdhair could feel the heat of Dorcas's sex hovering an inch from his cockstand.

INTIMACY WITH ALASDHAIR WAS EXHAUSTING, but sweet, too, as he'd said. Dorcas positively wallowed in the feel of his arms around her, the expanse of his chest beneath her, and the slight, steady percussion of his heartbeat. Try as she might not to make comparisons, the contrasts were so stark as to be undeniable.

Coupling with Isaiah had been a silent, furtive, *pushy* undertaking. He'd pushed himself at her, then into her. He'd been in a tearing hurry, and Dorcas had just wanted the whole business over with. She had not enjoyed it—of course she hadn't, she'd been thoroughly disgusted—despite his smug assumption to the contrary.

Alasdhair was a chatty lover, dragging into the conversational light of day his own misgivings—*mirabile dictu*, men *had* sexual misgivings, some men at least—and making suggestions as opposed to demands. With him, Dorcas could not become that silent, opinionless automaton he'd described. She instead had to direct her energies to taking charge of the situation.

Though that wasn't quite right either. To be in charge, one had to know how to go on.

"Do you spear me now?" She crouched up enough to peer at Alasdhair's face, glad they were making love in daylight. He was an honest man, but his eyes told the truths even his bold words danced around.

"Am I to tilt at the quintain, Dorcas?"

His hands glossed over the sides of her breasts, a slow, cherishing caress that turned her thoughts to soap bubbles. "Jousting analogies seem apt."

On the next pass, his thumbs grazed her nipples. The soap bubbles evaporated into a vast blue sky of sensation.

"You thrust..." she said, grasping for words of more than one syllable.

"I certainly can." Another pass of his magic thumbs, along with a whisper of warmth against her sex. "Or I can be subsumed into the maddeningly sweet heat of your luscious body."

The words—*sweet, luscious, maddening*—were not words anybody would use to describe Dorcas Delancey, but from Alasdhair they were believable. When he touched her like that, when his voice acquired that slight rasp, the fetters of propriety and regret fell away.

"Take me for your own, Dorcas. I yearn..." He bowed up to kiss her on that tender spot where her neck and shoulder joined. "I need, I dream, I burn..."

Between shivery kisses, Dorcas realized that Alasdhair also *waited*—for her. He was not intent on taking or even simply on giving, but rather, on *sharing*. The magnitude of that revelation gave her courage, and the way he moved beneath her made her desperate.

She caught him with her sex on a slow undulation of his hips.

He went still. "You are certain, my heart?"

"Beyond certain. You?"

He said something in Gaelic, then eased forward. Answer enough.

His patience was a mighty thing, but so was Dorcas's impatience. She wanted him, more of him, all of him, and the wanting became a clamoring, then a riot. Just when she would have told him to *go faster*, he shifted the angle of his hips and went *harder*.

Bodily pleasure welled, then became a torrent. Sensation transcended words and thoughts and crested higher still to obliterate Dorcas's separateness from her lover. She clung, she shook, she gloried and rejoiced, and when the wildfire faded to a sunset glow, she was afloat on a sea of wonder.

Alasdhair's hands moved on her back in slow, warm caresses, and tears threatened. *So cry*. The voice in Dorcas's head was confident and compassionate. *Cry if you need to*.

Alasdhair dabbed gently at her cheeks with the edge of a sheet and kissed her damp eyes, but mostly he held her. Their bodies remained joined, and the intimacy nearly provoked a fresh spate of tears.

"I'm not sad, Alasdhair MacKay."

"Maybe you are, sad for that younger woman, who put up with much and always suspected she'd been misled and cheated. I am certainly sad for her."

"Maybe it's like that." It was *exactly* like that. Misled, cheated, manipulated. "But I'm glad too, Alasdhair. Very glad."

"I did not fail you."

Dorcas was snuggled in his arms, though she could hear the faint smile in his tone—also the all but hidden question.

"You upheld the honor of the house of MacKay most impressively." He was upholding it still, rather than falling flat, to use his words. "I am... I have much to think about."

"If you are capable of thinking right now, then I am not done being impressive, Dorcas. Kiss me, please."

She did much more than kiss him, and when she fell asleep with Alasdhair spooned at her back, her last thought was that marriage to him would be absolutely, utterly, profoundly *delightful*.

CHAPTER THIRTEEN

"Are you pleased to have your grandson back among the civilized?" Zachariah Ingleby asked.

Lady Phoebe Mornebeth smiled at him over her tea cup, as she'd been smiling at him for decades. Once upon a time, smiles over tea had led to the occasional frolic, but then dear Zachariah had married.

Phoebe had scruples. A married lady trifled only with handsome bachelors, and only after her duty to her husband had been fulfilled. She did not poach on the preserves of other wives, unless they poached first, of course.

She set down her tea cup and chose a tea cake. "Having Isaiah back from the north is an occasion for unbounded joy, of course." A slight exaggeration. "His sojourn in the provinces has given him an air of thoughtful gravitas without costing him a young man's sense of genial bonhomie. I gather you have had enough of his company for now?"

Zachariah was that most wonderful of specimens, the wise man. He looked the part now that his hair was snow white and his bearing dignified, but he'd always had a sense of how to go on, of how to attain the objective with the least fuss.

He lacked ambition, though, or Phoebe might have married him when they'd both finished with mourning. And now... Now she was consumed with preventing Isaiah from making the worst errors the Mornebeth menfolk were prone to making.

"Isaiah is out most of the time," Zachariah said, "up to heaven knows what, because his duties at Lambeth don't start until next month. I have occasion to know that he has already found bachelor quarters near the palace, and yet, he continues to avail himself of my hospitality."

Phoebe sipped her tea. She'd taken to swilling gunpowder rather than the stout China black of earlier years. The black tea sat uneasily —or the adulterants used in it sat uneasily—while green tea was still enjoyable.

"What aren't you saying, Zachariah?"

He rose, and though he was no longer young, his posture as he paced across the parlor was still impressive. "Whatever else Isaiah learned in the north, he hasn't learned humility or even how to feign it. He talks to me as if I'm a dotard who cannot sort my own mail—much less his mail from my own correspondence—and with the hours he's keeping, I can assure you regular prayer is not much on his schedule."

"He's a bachelor and a Mornebeth, recently returned to London. There's a reason we have so few monks in England."

"Two reasons: Good King Hal needed to plunder the monasteries, and he also sought to set aside a wife who hadn't given him sons. Isaiah has been in Town long enough that the initial celebrations, as it were, should be concluded. Disease is everywhere, Phoebe, as are the gaming hells, the cockfights..."

"He's not likely to run into any bishops in those locations, and I've already decided that Isaiah must take a wife." The right wife, of course.

Zachariah resumed his seat with the air of a man whose rhetoric has failed to win over the congregation. "Matrimony with your grandson will be difficult, unless he marries a dull-witted saint."

"He cannot marry a dull-witted saint. When Isaiah is bored, he gets into mischief. He must marry a woman who's up to his weight in intelligence, who knows how to navigate church politics, and who will abet her husband's ambitions."

Zachariah poured himself a second cup of tea and topped up Phoebe's cup.

She did not care to have her tea topped up. The result was a little more heat, true, but the brew lost the proper balance between preferred sweetness and the richness of the added milk.

But Zachariah was trying to be considerate, and for that she had learned to appreciate him.

"If you seek such a mercenary lady for Isaiah's wife," he said, "then a pampered heiress won't serve. Perhaps a military bride?"

"Isaiah has no need of an heiress. I've seen to that. A general's daughter might do, but her connections would hardly add to Isaiah's sphere of influence."

"A bishop's daughter?"

That list was long—bishops tended to have large families—but woefully unimpressive. "The right bishop's daughter might serve well, but Isaiah's pride will not allow him to feel that his station is inferior to his bride's."

Zachariah saluted with his tea cup. "You inherit your diplomatic instincts from the late countess. The boy is vain and insecure, but thanks to you, he has means."

Mama had understood the need for coin as Papa had not. The previous generation of Mornebeths, due largely to a privateering great-uncle, had had coin. Phoebe's papa had been an earl, and the match with the Mornebeth heir had been declared successful.

The match *became* successful once Phoebe took over management of her husband's finances—along with management of him, their progeny, and the family properties. He'd been content to ride to hounds, impose on his mistresses, and collect art, while his younger brothers had climbed the clerical ranks, and Phoebe had flirted with handsome bachelors.

A successful match, by any measure. That she'd buried both of her sons as well as her husband didn't make it any less so.

"Isaiah is a good catch," Phoebe said, and that was true. He was by no means a great catch.

"Isaiah is arrogant, but then, I suppose I was, too, at his age."

"He wants a wife whose reputation will give him cause for pride and who will deliver him a proper dressing down in private when he needs one."

"Which will be frequently." Zachariah finished his tea and returned the cup and saucer to the tray. "I do not envy any young lady that challenge."

Phoebe realized with no little dismay that Zachariah found Isaiah's company *tedious*. Perhaps an old man's jealousy of the young accounted for that, because Isaiah was shrewd, charming, and good-humored, much as Zachariah had been at that age.

"You know Thomas Delancey?" she asked.

"Everybody knows old Tom. He's a fixture at St. Mildred's and uniformly well liked."

But not precisely respected, and Phoebe knew why. "He's nigh a decade your junior, Zachariah Ingleby, and he has a daughter, Dorcas."

Zachariah made a face as if the milk in his tea had soured. "Miss Delightful. She's something of a crusader."

"Precisely. Somebody needs to take the girl in hand and put all that zeal to a constructive use. Isaiah is perfect for her. She can attach herself to his career instead of trying to reform London's great unwashed. Isaiah needs a challenge, and Miss Delancey needs to concern herself with a family, rather than carping in the newspapers about her silly causes."

Zachariah rose again. He'd always had too much energy for a sedentary calling. "Dorcas Delancey is not a girl, Phoebe. She's on the shelf, or shortly will be, and her silly causes are exactly the sort of reform most sensible people support."

"Most people, who haven't a pot to piss in or a groat to their names. Most people, who will never have the vote and who grumble about paying their tithes. Her father has the right idea—advocate for generosity and tolerance at the individual level, appeal to the conscience, and leave the politicians to wrestle in the mud. Isaiah can teach her that." Phoebe could teach her that, given enough time.

"Isaiah will want a biddable wife," Zachariah said, tossing a half scoop of coal onto the hearth. "His habits make that plain enough."

Isaiah wasn't any naughtier than half the other young bucks swanning about Town on their quarterly allowances. Of that, Phoebe had no doubt. True, she'd received a few unsavory reports from her connections in Yorkshire—Isaiah was a Mornebeth male in his prime—but that had been the very reason for sending him north. He'd been enjoying the gaming hells and fleshpots of Mayfair a little too enthusiastically for a man of the cloth.

A lot too enthusiastically, if Phoebe's reporters had been accurate.

Yorkshire, owing to a paucity of both gambling establishments and houses of ill repute, had served as a place for Isaiah to while away a few years.

"I have reason to believe that Isaiah will be amenable to a match with Miss Delancey. If I am adroit—and I am—I can make him think the notion is his idea. His pride will do the rest. The lady is as good as wearing his ring."

Zachariah remained before the fire, poker in hand. "Phoebe, don't you ever tire of the machinations? Doesn't any part of you want to see Isaiah stand or fall on his own merits? He's not stupid, he's had a good education, and you see that he wants for nothing. Give him a chance to make his own way."

Men left to make their own way got up to wenching, warfare, and making bastards. "I cannot rehabilitate the nature of the male beast, Zachariah, but Isaiah is the best and brightest of the Mornebeth brood. I owe it to the family to support his advancement, and that means he must marry as I see fit." Isaiah was also her oldest grandchild and thus believed himself *entitled* to Phoebe's aid.

Except he wasn't. Her aid would come at a price, and that price would be marriage in the very near future to the wife of Phoebe's choosing.

"What of Miss Delancey? She's apparently content to support her father, to be the comfort of his old age. What of Tom Delancey when you snatch his daughter away? She's not simply a reformer, she's also exceedingly clever, and Tom's congregation thinks quite highly of her."

"While they murmur in their tents about how flagrantly improper she is. I have my spies, Zachariah, and Ophelia Oldbach knows her neighbors well."

"Ophelia Oldbach's approval has ever been a prize beyond reach. If she truly thought Miss Delancey in need of a sermon, she'd speak to the young woman herself. I urge you not to meddle, Phoebe. Inform Isaiah that a man employed by the archbishop has no need of a quarterly allowance from his grandmother. Warn him that he's no longer a young sprig who will be forgiven for indulging in high spirits. I would hate for his bad judgment to result in your disappointment."

"Come have another cup of tea," Phoebe said, favoring Zachariah with her most charming smile, because the moment had come for some cajolery. "Do you know what I treasure most about you, Zachariah?"

He set his poker aside and tried for a smile of his own, though the effort was tired. "You treasure me because I am the best whist partner you will ever have, and I usually tell you what you want to hear."

He was certainly falling short of that mark today. "You are lethal at whist because everybody is taken in by your charm."

The smile turned rueful. "Fat lot of good my charm does me with you."

"Pouting on a man of your years is undignified. I treasure you because you do not tell me what I want to hear when honesty matters most. I know Isaiah lacks humility, but so do I. I understand him, and with your aid, a great deal of patience, and some luck, I can pilot

Isaiah safely past the shoals of bachelordom. Now come have your tea, and tell me how the grandchildren go on."

That was Zachariah's cue to start spouting off about his brilliant brood—Phoebe could never keep them all straight—but he remained by the fire.

"I believe I will instead bid you adieu for the nonce, Phoebe dearest. The cold takes a toll on my dignified bones, and for the past three days, my steward's report has been silently reproaching me from the top of my pile of unread correspondence. Thank you as always for your excellent company. I will give your regards to the prodigy when next he deigns to afflict me with his company at breakfast."

Zachariah bowed over Phoebe's hand and withdrew to see himself out, as he'd long been doing in her household. Phoebe dumped her tea into the nearest potted fern and poured herself a fresh cup. As she stirred in a dash of sugar and a dollop of milk, it occurred to her that dear Zachariah would not be around forever.

Well, neither would she, and it was time Isaiah took Dorcas Delancey to wife. Thomas Delancey would support the match, and Miss Delightful would have nothing to say to it.

"SHE WANTS TO LEARN THE GAELIC," Alasdhair said, taking a sip of the finest libation the Aurora Club had to offer, meaning Goddard's own champagne. "And what Miss Dorcas Delancey sets out to do gets done and done right." The lady was soon to be Mrs. Dorcas MacKay, and didn't that just have the prettiest ring to it?

"Does she want to spend her life shivering away in your Highland rock pile?" Dylan Powell asked, propping his feet on a hassock. "Does she want to leave everything familiar and dear to have your brats between bouts of chilblains and lung fever?"

Goddard opened his eyes and shifted in his reading chair. "Even for you, Powell, that's a bit gloomy. Most women are happy to leave their father's house and set up their own domiciles."

Powell spared Goddard a glance. "Your Ann hasn't followed that path. She's advanced professionally at a time when most women would be giving up employment altogether."

"Giving up *paying* employment," Alasdhair said. Powell was in a taking about something, but then, he was in a taking nigh incessantly. "Have your sisters been nagging you to marry, lad? If it's the right woman, you'll gallop joyfully to your fate. Goddard will agree with me."

"Goddard," said the man himself, "does agree with you, but he also agrees with Powell. This engagement is precipitous, MacKay, and you know little of Miss Delancey besides what her late cousin told you."

Alasdhair knew that Dorcas was brave, principled, passionate, and honest. Her integrity shone forth like a city on a hill, or whatever that biblical passage said, and she had decided to gift Alasdhair with her entire future.

"She knows me," Alasdhair said. "Knows I am ruled by my tummy, knows I will never desert her or the boy. She knows I am honest and loyal and an excellent dancer."

Goddard guffawed. "That didn't take long, and her a preacher's daughter."

Powell's scowl had acquired a hint of bewilderment. "You got out the swords and hopped about in your kilt for her?"

Goddard sat up and scrubbed his hands over his eyes. "Would MacKay be ordering a bottle of my best champagne if he'd merely shown the lady his sword dance?"

"But MacKay's a monk," Powell said. "He took holy orders or something, and now he's letting this Puritan reformer lead him up the church aisle. What the hell is going on, MacKay?"

"You're *worried* about me?"

Powell smacked him on the arm. "There is no stupidity like Scottish stupidity, saving perhaps English stupidity. You were as drunk, swaggering, and lusty as the next officer until something happened at Badajoz. Then you stopped talking, you stopped drinking but for the occasional wee nip, you never again so much as sang your filthy pub songs after that. You began consorting with nuns and orphans, and when you mustered out, you developed the thankless habit of aiding streetwalkers."

"Now," Goddard said, taking up the narrative, "you are courting a woman who is the furthest thing from a streetwalker, and she has won your heart—or something—in a matter of a few short weeks. We are not worried, MacKay, we are *panicked.* We did not lug extra rations for you all across Spain to see you fall victim to the wiles of a scheming spinster."

"Dorcas is a schemer," Alasdhair said, touched at his cousins' concern, but not about to embarrass them with an expression of thanks. "I adore that about her. She will work tirelessly on behalf of others, flatter, reason, cajole, and plan, but she would never dissemble on her own behalf. She's an honest woman, and if she says she likes me, then I rejoice to believe her."

Rejoiced to *love* her, in every sense of the word.

Powell and Goddard were both looking at Alasdhair as if he'd just announced plans to wear his father's coronation robes on his next hack through Hyde Park.

"Cut line, you two." Alasdhair held his glass of champagne up to the firelight. "I told her about Spain."

Powell set aside his drink, though he'd finished his serving doubtless to be polite. The Welsh were a contradictory people. Full of manners while they called a man's sanity into question.

"What exactly was there to tell her about Spain, MacKay?" Powell asked with uncharacteristic gentleness.

Rejoicing faded into a familiar sadness, though regret had lost its bitter edge. "You are right that I had a bad time of it in Badajoz," Alasdhair said slowly. "Everybody did, and that's all we need to say about it. Will you two stand up with me when I speak my vows?"

A silent exchange took place between Powell and Goddard, while they apparently decided to permit Alasdhair to change the subject.

"You had best not speak those vows without us on hand," Goddard said. "Ann will prepare your wedding breakfast, which you will hold at the Coventry, if Miss Delancey is amenable. Consider it a wedding present."

"I'll lend you my housekeeper," Powell said. "She'll put your house to rights before you can inflict that ordeal on Miss Delancey."

"What's wrong with my house?"

Another look passed between Alasdhair's cousins, and he realized they had been having these silent exchanges ever since Badajoz. He simply hadn't noticed. Just as Goddard's eyesight and hearing had suffered during the war, so had Alasdhair's perceptions, but in a different way.

"Your house hasn't any..." Goddard waved a hand. "Touches of grace, small comforts, or displays of sentiment."

Oh, but it did. Behind Alasdhair's privacy screen, he had a dozen displays of sentiment, and Dorcas had seen those too. "Clutter, ye mean? Fripperies?"

"Something like that." Powell shoved the hassock away with a booted foot. "Miss Delancey will doubtless have a few ideas, and you will give her free rein, MacKay. Be generous with her pin money, and don't question what she does with it unless the larders are empty, and she's frequenting gaming hells."

"If she wants to frequent gaming hells, I'll happily take her around to a few. She will then draft the most scathing pamphlets imaginable on the glorification of games of chance. If she turns her sights on the Coventry, you had best prepare to move to France, Goddard."

"Will she do that?" Goddard's tone was curious rather than offended.

"No. Dorcas is more concerned with the truly destitute, with corruption in law enforcement, and with the injustices women face daily."

Powell rose and stretched. "She'll get on with my sisters famously."

"You say that," Goddard murmured, "as if my lady cousins might be planning to besiege London."

"Don't even think it. You are married, MacKay is hearing wedding bells, and I am the lone holdout defending the garrison of bachelor freedom. The last thing I need is the petticoat regiment descending upon my household to see me matched to the harridan of their choosing. I wish you the best, MacKay, but I am worried for you."

"Your honesty is, as ever, appreciated," Alasdhair said. "Goddard, anything to add to Powell's fretting?"

Goddard finished his champagne and set the glass aside. "What have you learned about Miss Delancey's late cousin?"

"Nothing since Powell and I interrogated his friends. No body has been found. Therefore, no inquest, nothing. It's as if Miss Fairchild vanished."

"People do," Powell said, a little wistfully. "People come to London expressly to vanish."

"People without your sisters, perhaps." Alasdhair rose, ready to get home and ensure John had gone down for the night without a fuss. "The odd thing is that twice now, I've been going about my business, simply walking along, and I've seen Melanie's ghost."

Powell peered at him. "Does your intended know you see ghosts?"

"He doesn't mean an actual ghost," Goddard said. "He means the mind plays tricks. When my parents died, I would swear I heard my father humming in his study, but he wasn't there. I thought I saw the flash of my mother's skirts in the garden, but in the next instant, the impression vanished. We want them to be alive, and grief sifts through memories to create that fiction for a fleeting moment."

"The old men," Powell said, "the veterans, say they dream of their fallen comrades, and it feels more real than waking life."

What did Powell dream of? Apparently not marriage. "The old soldiers and the urchins are all keeping an eye out for a woman matching her description," Alasdhair said, "but Father Thames doesn't always give up his dead, and perhaps that's for the best."

"Now you're a philosopher." Powell collected the empty glasses and put them on the sideboard. "I am simply a tired Welshman ready to seek my bed. Give me some warning before I'm to attend the nuptials, and I will do my best to be there. I would not miss one of Ann's wedding breakfasts for all the pub songs in St. Giles."

He sketched a bow and left, while Goddard stood with his backside to the fire. "He'll manage. His sisters will see to it."

"They are formidable."

"So is he," Goddard said. "Is this hasty engagement about the boy, MacKay?"

Alasdhair's engagement wasn't any hastier than many others, and besides, Dorcas hadn't set a date yet. Her brother was coming south for a visit, and that apparently had the vicarage in an uproar.

"A child needs parents, Goddard, and a bachelor guardian isn't an ideal substitute. Dorcas loves the bairn, but then, who wouldn't?"

Goddard moved away from the fire and shoved the hassock Powell had displaced back before its appointed chair.

"Will you ever tell us what really happened in Badajoz, MacKay?"

You don't need to know. You don't want to know. Mind your own business. Answers that would have served Alasdhair in the past.

"Perhaps." But not soon. Probably not ever. "Give my love to Ann."

Goddard offered a two-finger salute and left Alasdhair alone by the dwindling fire.

"I CONFESS," Isaiah said, "when Grandmother suggested I'd spent enough time in the north, I was pleased to heed her summons in part because I knew a return to London meant..."

He assayed a beamish smile at Thomas Delancey across the parson's venerable if somewhat cluttered desk.

"A chance to court Dorcas?" Delancey suggested.

"Precisely, sir. A chance to renew a warm friendship of old, with Dorcas and with her family."

Delancey was rubbing pounce into unsized paper, an exercise Isaiah would have thought within the housekeeper's purview, or Dorcas's. When he and Dorcas were married, she'd do as he told her, and without complaint. When she'd learned the habit of obedience, then he'd allow her small freedoms, provided she did not abuse his indulgent nature.

"Tell me specifically of your prospects, Mornebeth."

So they were to do the pretty. Very well. Isaiah excelled at doing the pretty. "I am my grandmother's heir, though I try not to mention that too frequently. First, I prefer to advance on my own merits. Second, the old dear is worth a pretty penny, and if I become seen as a good catch, I will be besieged. I already know which lady will make me the perfect wife, and I have no need to look further."

This little recitation was mostly balderdash. Isaiah would advance on his own merits, Uncle Zachariah's kind influence, Grandmama's gift for collecting tattle, or Dorcas's fine reputation for good works. The means mattered naught compared to the advancement.

Besides, Isaiah was a *splendid* catch. He was handsome, mannerly, as gainfully employed as a gentleman could be, neither too old nor too young, and as any sensible fellow knew to do, he kept his vices and virtues in separate compartments of his life.

Did Delancey want to count Isaiah's teeth, for pity's sake?

"A match between you and Dorcas would have my approval," Delancey said, setting aside his cloth and curving the paper to allow the sandarac to trickle back into the pounce pot. "You are well known to me and much respected in church circles. Your family is well situated, and I know Dorcas has had a chance to take your measure."

Isaiah kept his hopeful smile in place, though Dorcas had done *far* more than take his measure.

Delancey ran his fingertips over the paper. "I cannot, however, give you permission to court my daughter at this time."

Bloody bedamned hell. "My dear sir, neither the lady nor I are in the first blush of youth. What can possibly justify a delay of the courtship at this stage?" Isaiah tried to balance affront with courtesy, because Delancey needed to know that Dorcas's days as St. Mildred's ecclesiastical maid-of-all-work were numbered.

She would doubtless thank Isaiah for freeing her from the post of congregational charwoman. She was going utterly to waste at St. Mildred's, entertaining the spotty choir director when she could be planning dinner parties for the archbishop's staff.

Delancey ran his cloth over the paper one more time, then got out another sheet from the box at the corner of his desk and sprinkled it with sandarac.

"I say this kindly, Mornebeth: If you haven't the patience to wait a few weeks to begin your official courtship, then you haven't the patience for marriage. From what I hear, you have yet to find lodgings, yet to begin your duties at the palace, and I'm not sure where you're attending services these days."

The rubbishing old windbag was enjoying himself, enjoying the role of papa with a suitor at his mercy.

"I am escorting Grandmama to services until I'm established in Southwark. To be honest, I've put off leasing a house because I hoped I'd not be searching for bachelor quarters."

A small half-truth. Isaiah had not leased *a house*. He'd taken rooms, though. A bachelor needed the occasional private situation if he wasn't to expire of excessive good behavior.

"If you don't marry Dorcas, then Lady Phoebe will soon see you matched with another equally estimable young lady. Best lease a house, Mornebeth, and then your suit will be that much more attractive when you do commence the official courtship."

"I am to be permitted to court the lady soon?" Grandmama had been very clear that Isaiah's engagement to Dorcas was to be short and immediately commenced. That suited him famously, and it ought to suit Dorcas as well.

She was no longer young. That much had been the God's honest truth. She would also have awkward explanations to make on the wedding night if she married any man other than Isaiah.

Delancey commenced rubbing the sandarac into the paper in gentle, methodical circles that followed the typical path of the pen—from upper-left corner to bottom right.

A task for a halfwit.

"My permission truly matters little, Mornebeth. Dorcas has ever known her own mind, and your suit will stand or fall on its own merits. The issue is that Michael is coming to visit at long last, and Dorcas must be free to enjoy her brother's company. We haven't seen him for several years, and for you to hover about looking eligible at such a time won't flatter your cause."

Michael. Interesting.

Isaiah's immediate reaction was resentment—Michael had served his purpose years ago and deserved his banishment to the Dales—but perhaps having him on hand would encourage Dorcas to realize her good fortune that much sooner. Dorcas would do anything for her brother and father, after all.

"I see your point," Isaiah said. "I also note that you refer to an official courtship that cannot commence until the happy occasion of Michael's visit has concluded. What of an unofficial courtship?"

Delancey started again with his rubbing cloth in the upper-left corner of the paper. "I enjoy this exercise. I find it meditative, and I spare somebody else the effort while saving a coin or two by buying the unsized paper. Michael and Dorcas used to do this for me, and I feel closer to them when I do it."

"You'll miss her," Isaiah said, arranging his features in a sympathetic expression. "She will miss you, too, but we will be right across the river, and you will be a frequent guest at our table."

Delancey was good for that at least. Everybody liked him, he was a fine conversationalist, and Dorcas's image as the devoted daughter should not be entirely abandoned.

Delancey paused halfway down the page. "You are very confident of your success, Mornebeth, but Dorcas is not the girl you knew years ago. She is an independent spirit, much like her mother was. Marriage to you—to anybody—might not appeal to her. She's had other expressions of interest, you know."

The perennial proposers. No threat whatsoever. "Curates seeking to curry your favor? Dorcas deserves better than that."

Delancey looked up from his paper, and while his gaze wasn't hostile, neither was it friendly. A show of fatherly something or other. Sternness? Gravity? Isaiah's own father had passed to his reward when Isaiah had turned eleven. Isaiah had thus never acquainted himself with the lexicon of paternal facial expressions.

"And you think you are what Dorcas deserves?" Delancey asked, resuming his rubbing.

"I esteem her greatly, sir, and I will provide for her well."

"But does she love you?"

Who would have thought a high-church-ish vicar would turn up sentimental? But then, Delancey was a widower. Even Grandmama occasionally waxed wistful about her departed spouse. Grandpapa had been a hounds-and-horses, wenching-and-wagering old scallywag, but she'd seen something worth marrying in him.

"Love has many guises," Isaiah said. "If Dorcas is not in love with me now, I hope she can grow to love me after we speak our vows. She does not strike me as overly plagued with romantic fancies, one of her many fine qualities."

"She doesn't? Perhaps you're right. When Michael comes, you must join us again for dinner. He will certainly want to renew his acquaintance with you, particularly if you aspire to join the family."

Oh, raptures. Another boring roast with boring potatoes, indifferent wine, and endless church talk. "Then I have your permission in principle to court Dorcas when the time is right?"

Delancey set aside his rag and rose. "No, Mornebeth, you do not. I thought I was quite clear on that. You are to maintain the demeanor of a family friend until such time as Michael's visit ends, or he resolves to bide here in the south indefinitely. The approach of spring is always a busy time in any congregation, and Dorcas has much on her mind."

Delancey gestured toward the door, and Isaiah had no choice but to rise and be escorted from the study.

"Your ambitions will be better served by patience," Delancey went on. "Believe me. You must acquire the habit of cheerful forbearance if you hope to marry Dorcas. She dislikes surprises, cannot be ordered about, and will not be hurried. She's like me in that regard."

"I appreciate your counsel," Isaiah said when Delancey had handed him his hat at the front door. "I will school myself to appreciate the lady from the posture of friendship—for now."

Delancey opened the door. "My regards to your grandmother."

"Of course, and to Dorcas as well." Isaiah bowed and took his leave because he had been—literally—shown the door.

How odd. But then, Delancey doted on his only son, and if his comments could be taken at face value—they could, for Delancey had no guile whatsoever—then the old boy was enhancing Isaiah's chances of success.

Or thought he was. Dorcas would not refuse Isaiah's suit, just as she'd not refused his overtures all those years ago. She'd had no real choice then, and she would have no choice regarding her prospective spouse either.

The only question remaining was exactly how and when Isaiah would explain her situation to her.

CHAPTER FOURTEEN

"Tell me of your brother," Alasdhair said, ushering Dorcas onto the walkway.

Well, of course. Everybody wanted to know how Young Vicar Delancey went on, and probably always would.

"I have missed him," Dorcas said, tucking the plaid scarf up around her cheeks. She'd also been relieved to be parted from her only sibling. "Michael was the best of big brothers in many senses. When Papa was too bombastic, Michael would wink at me behind Papa's back. When Mama died, Michael began taking me to the subscription library every Tuesday. He wasn't the sort to tease me in public or hide my dolls."

"My sisters would have thrashed any brother who attempted either infraction. Powell's sisters would have pilloried such a brother." Alasdhair shifted his extra bag of sandwiches and shortbread to his left hand and offered his arm. He was walking Dorcas home from the tea shop, and then he'd repair to his club to tend to correspondence.

His house was undergoing a thorough cleaning, an occasion

which merited his absence, by decree of the staff and Powell's housekeeper.

"Powell's sisters bide in Wales?"

"Aye, for now. 'Formidable' is the closest English word to describe them. Female fortresses of determination, for all they are quite mannerly. When the lady cousins get together, we gents repair to the billiards room to pray."

"To get drunk?"

"We've outgrown that phase, though Powell, being of Dissenting stock, was never prone to excessive imbibing. Goddard, thanks to his French mama's influence, prefers a small portion of good-quality libation to inebriation. He owns vineyards, and his champagne will be the centerpiece of our wedding breakfast. Tell me more about Michael."

Alasdhair was prone to making passing references to the wedding ceremony, to the solicitors' efforts to draft the settlements, and other evidence of the upcoming nuptials. Dorcas did not know if he was tempting her to cry off, or adjusting mentally to the fact that he was soon to marry.

"Michael is a paragon. Handsome, witty, kind, pragmatic. One of those people who always knows the right thing to say, the right gesture, though it might not be precisely what etiquette would advise."

"He hugs old ladies?"

"Of course, and when he speaks to children, he kneels down to address them at eye level. My father had the same habit before his knees began bothering him. Michael recalls the dates of other people's bereavements and writes to Papa annually on the anniversary of my mother's passing."

"Then Michael sounds insufferable as a brother, though suited to his calling. Did he never stray as a lad? Never test the limits of propriety?"

"As a lad, of course, but he's no longer a lad. He is truly Papa's pride and joy." Not for anything would Dorcas taint that joy with the truth.

Alasdhair bent a little closer. "You are trying to tell me that I must not expect too much of your time while your brother is underfoot being such a paragon. I must bear up manfully despite a crushing weight of loneliness, secure in the knowledge that my stoicism will be rewarded."

Dorcas resisted the urge to lean against him. "I am trying to tell you not to abandon me when Michael arrives. Papa will expect me to be much in evidence, ready to entertain the callers who will throng the vicarage when Michael is gracing us with his presence. Papa will expect all the best recipes at supper, fresh flowers in the parlor daily. The bishop might be inveigled to dine at our humble table, and the vicarage must show to good advantage without being ostentatious."

"Parade dress, military band, and full honors. Tedious as hell. We could elope."

Alasdhair was in absolute earnest. He was always in absolute earnest, and Dorcas treasured that about him. "Lead me not into temptation, sir."

"A bit late for that, my love." How pleased he sounded, how bashful and delighted.

"We led each other, and it was a consummation, not temptation."

A woman stood under the overhang of a less than pristine awning above the door of what purported to be a dry goods emporium. She watched Alasdhair warily, as the women in jail had watched Dorcas the first time she'd spent the night with them. The lady was young, gaunt, and underdressed for the elements.

"You have that all sorted in your mind?" Alasdhair mused. "Under Scottish law, we'd be considered married by now. We expressed a resolve to wed, then acted on that resolve."

"We are not in Scotland." And that was a blooming pity. "Does that woman know you?"

Alasdhair's gaze followed the direction of Dorcas's nod. "If Aurora Feeney is abroad at this hour, something's amiss. Excuse me."

He slipped his arm from Dorcas's, though she wanted to call after him that he need not spare her sensibilities. She waited, some yards off, studying the neighborhood. The one-legged beggar sat at his usual spot, though today he had a rough blanket over his lap. His usual straight-ahead stare was replaced by blatant interest in Alasdhair's exchange with the fair—shivering—Aurora.

Alasdhair passed the lady his sandwiches and a few coins, then peeled off his gloves and gave her those as well. Another man might have stolen a peek at Aurora's semi-exposed treasures, but Alasdhair's gaze was on her face, and when he spoke to her, he did not touch her.

The conversation was brief. The lady scurried off, already opening the bag of sandwiches.

"She'll pawn your gloves," Dorcas said as she and Alasdhair resumed walking. "That was very kind of you."

"Very stupid of me," Alasdhair replied. "I talked her sister into returning to the village before Christmas, but Aurora refused to go. Some dashing blade promised to set her up, to treat her like a princess. The handsome prince has decamped for the shires, and Aurora has no older sister to look out for her."

"Let me guess," Dorcas said. "The sisters came to London because they sought employment in service, the village having no jobs. They had no characters, no experience, no training, and their speech was as provincial as their mannerisms. They arrived in Town over the summer, when all the best families leave, but when the farming communities are between planting and harvest, and travel is easiest. The jails are full of such women, as are the brothels."

Alasdhair walked along beside Dorcas until they reached the next corner. "I wish you did not know those things. I wish life had shown you a path strewn with rose petals, but because you see clearly, and don't lie to yourself about what's before your eyes, I can trust you to take on the challenge of marriage to such a one as I."

What was she to say to that? "I wanted to give her my scarf, except that this scarf is a gift from you, and had I approached, she would have likely run away. Do-gooders are a plague upon the working women of London."

"By the time I leave for Scotland in spring, I have usually lost all hope of doing anybody any good. Aurora hasn't heard from her sister since I put her on that stage coach in December. Clearly, Aurora's prospects are deteriorating, and if she's lucky, she will perish from cold or starvation before disease can inflict a worse fate upon her."

And that very reasoning—why prolong the suffering of the doomed?—was used to cloak smug indifference behind a façade of pious resignation. Better that these women starve in obscurity than try to make a life through initiative and determination.

"Today," Dorcas said, "Aurora will eat. This week, she will not be turned out from her lodgings. Right now, she has proof that life is not entirely hopeless. Until the good Christians and upright politicians of the realm have a better solution, that is a candle lit against the darkness that would swallow her whole."

"You're thinking of Melanie."

"Of Melanie, of the women in jail, of all the Auroras." *Of myself at a younger age.*

Dorcas would have struck out across the street in a convenient gap in the traffic, but Alasdhair remained on the walkway, gazing down at her.

"As a suitor, I am apparently doomed to awkwardness where you are concerned, but Dorcas Delancey, I love you. I love you for *understanding*. One does not make such declarations on street corners, I know. Bad form and all that. I would kiss you, but Old Man Tingley will report my outrageous conduct to Powell, and Powell might well unleash his sisters upon me. Say something so I will cease babbling."

"I am in a bad mood."

"I'm sorry, I apolo—"

She held up a gloved hand. "I love my brother, but I also resent him bitterly. He renders me not merely drab by comparison, but invisible. I know the times when his charm failed, when his stupidity hurt others and he was never held to account. Men sow wild oats, an occasion for tolerant humor, while women end up like Aurora. Sometimes, Alasdhair, I think if I give vent to my anger, I will end up in Bedlam. Worse yet, that is exactly what society wants me to think, the better to ensure my ire is turned into stitched samplers or dosed with patent remedies."

"Don't you dare take up stitching samplers, Dorcas Delancey. You are right to be angry."

"And that," she said, touching his cheek, "is why I love you. You do not tell me to trust in divine providence or keep to my proper place so men of greater understanding can deal with life's vexing conundrums."

Alasdhair brushed the tail of her scarf back over her shoulder. "Men of greater understanding have been dealing with life's vexing problems for millennia. The result, it seems to me, is much in need of improvement. What can I do to make your brother's visit less bothersome to you?"

Dorcas did not merely love Alasdhair, she *adored* him. "That you ask means much. Simply be patient. Michael must return to his congregation at some point, and a special license is valid for months. I will call upon you when I can and find an occasion to introduce you to Michael."

"Please do," Alasdhair said, taking her hand and starting across the street. "I've never met a paragon before."

"He's not really a paragon."

"They never are. The military boasted its share of paragons, and they invariably proved troublesome."

Dorcas passed the rest of the walk home in silence, trying to put a name to what had transpired between the tea shop and the vicarage. The truth should have appalled her. She had lost her temper *on the street*. Spouted off. Ranted.

Ladies never had such lapses. *Mrs. Alasdhair MacKay* was apparently welcome to have them whenever she pleased. The freedom in that realization was nearly incomprehensible.

As was the comfort of Alasdhair's hand in hers. Dorcas dropped his hand as they approached the vicarage and took up the more decorous arm-in-arm posture. Alasdhair encouraged her candor to a shocking degree, while Papa still expected his daughter to comport herself at all times with appropriate dignity.

Dorcas had time for one other thought—what did she expect *of herself*?—before Alasdhair was bowing over her hand in parting.

~

ISAIAH HAD SPENT the past twenty-four hours putting Thomas Delancey's little show of paternal authority into perspective.

Delancey, with a pathetic lack of both guile and originality, wanted to become a bishop. He wanted the financial security of such a post, the prestige, the respect. Given that deluded hope, Delancey would of course put more emphasis on parading his handsome son around the ecclesiastical race course than he would on practically anything else.

Showing Michael off, all grown up and sporting his collar, would take precedence over announcing a match for St. Mildred's plainest spinster.

Fair enough. But that spinster needed to know exactly what lay in her future, lest she get to thinking of going north with her brother, or—worse yet—accompanying him to some heathen missionary post. If Thomas Delancey were desperate enough for recognition, he might talk his children into just such a display of holy foolishness.

Isaiah was rehearsing his interview with Dorcas as he approached the vicarage, only to see her taking leave of a tall, dark-haired brute before the vicarage's front door. The man presumed to brush his bare fingers over Dorcas's gloved knuckles as he bowed his farewell.

Dorcas ought to have withdrawn her hand in a manner that left no doubt as to the unacceptability of such forwardness. This was not an old man whose flirtations could be considered harmless, nor did the fellow's attire proclaim him to be particularly wealthy. His greatcoat had only one cape, his scarf was *plaid*. He wore no gloves and carried no walking stick.

But then, sometimes the wealthy did not advertise their good fortune.

Still, who the hell did he think he was, this strutting interloper, to embarrass Dorcas at her own front door?

Rather than accost another man on the street, Isaiah waited until Dorcas had ducked into the vicarage, and her escort had jaunted off in the direction of Mayfair. Dorcas's admirer had the bearing of former military, and clearly, London's streets did not intimidate him. He flipped a coin to a crossing sweeper and strolled from view.

Good riddance, whoever he was. Isaiah waited two minutes, then rapped on the door of the vicarage.

The housekeeper greeted him. "Mr. Mornebeth, how do you do? Come in, come in. If you are calling upon Mr. Delancey, I'm afraid he's over at the church meeting with the sextons. The bells don't ring themselves, apparently."

Isaiah passed over his hat, walking stick, and gloves. "I'm here to call upon Miss Delancey, as it happens, and much to my delight, I saw her return to the vicarage not five minutes past."

"Has she come home?" Mrs. Benton did not hang up Isaiah's effects, but rather, placed them on the sideboard. "Let's have your coat off, and I will see if she's receiving. Since we had word of Young Vicar Delancey's impending visit, poor Miss Delancey has been run off her feet."

Mrs. Benton aimed a cheery smile at Isaiah, and he smiled right back. "Please convey to Miss Delancey that my longing for a moment of her company is great."

"I certainly will. Make yourself at home in the guest parlor, and I'm sure she'll be down shortly." She hung Isaiah's coat on a peg and bustled up the steps.

Isaiah thumbed through the stacks of mail in the trays on the sideboard. The outgoing correspondence looked to be intended mostly for other clergy located in various obscure corners of the Home

Counties. Old cronies, doubtless, who must be informed of Michael's royal progress. The incoming mail appeared to be invitations—Thomas Delancey knew a few Honorables—and an occasional merchant's bill.

Not much to be learned there. Isaiah made a quick inspection of the desk in the study and learned only that Thomas was working on some bit of bombast having to do with seed falling on fallow ground, deafness, and blindness. Metaphors to send the congregation into a collective doze, but Isaiah could profitably allude to the parable of the sower when next he and Thomas conversed.

Isaiah was pacing the cozy confines of the guest parlor when Mrs. Benton returned.

"You will have to try your luck another day, Mr. Mornebeth. Miss Delancey is snatching a nap and begs for your understanding. She truly is quite exhausted." And there was that same smile, all pleasant hospitality.

This time, Isaiah did not smile back. "I don't suppose you know what specific errand has reduced Miss Delancey to this state of extreme fatigue? She looked well enough when I glimpsed her at the vicarage's door ten minutes ago."

Mrs. Benton's smile acquired a few more teeth. "In addition to all the preparations for her brother's visit, she is attending to regular church and family duties, Mr. Mornebeth. Spring is a busy time for any vicar's household, and that happy season will soon be upon us. Perhaps you could stop by again tomorrow?"

"I am expected for tea at Lambeth Palace tomorrow." A slight embroidering on the truth. Isaiah would stop around to greet his prospective superior and to burnish his halo as an eager new recruit to the palace. Grandmama had spoken, and Isaiah had seen the wisdom of her suggestion.

"Well then, we'll look for you later this week." Mrs. Benton preceded Isaiah through the parlor door. "Whatever became of that bunch of daffodils you bought at the market?"

He'd taken them to Grandmama. No sense letting good coin go to waste. "Nipped, I'm afraid. The flower girl should have taken better care."

"Nipped? Daffodil buds nipped when the weather has finally shown signs of moderating? Well, that is unfortunate."

Mrs. Benton passed him his coat and other effects, while Isaiah wrestled with the urge to accidentally trip such that Delancey's housekeeper was shoved rather violently against the wall. Her sunny smiles hid too much superiority for a mere domestic, and if she thought Isaiah would be put off by her little games, she was much mistaken.

Mrs. Benton had known Isaiah would not be staying, else she'd have hung up his things and not piled them unceremoniously on the sideboard.

No matter. Dorcas would soon learn that female scheming was doomed where Isaiah was concerned. He'd make that point quite clear to her, and to blazes with Michael Delancey's impending visit.

"YOU HAVE A CALLER," Mrs. Benton said, taking Dorcas's cloak. "You also have flowers. The sweetest little bouquet of forget-me-nots. I put the flowers in your private parlor, and the caller is in the family parlor."

Bother all callers. Dorcas had come from Alasdhair's house, where she'd learned the rudiments of whisky-making. Alasdhair grew animated discussing oak barrels, peat smoke, and the exciseman, his burr deepening to rolled r's and rumbled vowels.

Dorcas could listen to him talk about potatoes and scarecrows—tatties and tattie bogels, to him—and be enthralled.

He'd encouraged her to reminisce about her mother, an indulgence Dorcas generally refrained from around Papa, and about growing up with Michael. Recollections of Mama were sweet. She'd been practical, sunny, and occasionally silly. Michael, who was expected at the vicarage any day, was a more complicated topic.

Mrs. Benton hung up Dorcas's cloak and bonnet. "Your caller is Mr. Mornebeth, miss. I told him you were out, and he announced that he would wait, then saw himself to the family parlor. I can interrupt in ten minutes if you like."

The offer was mildly disconcerting. "You don't trust him for even ten minutes?"

Mrs. Benton eyed the plaid scarf in Dorcas's hands. "I do not. Not very Christian of me, but he's a thrusting sort of man, and I have never cared for such as them."

Isaiah would not cease dropping by the vicarage merely because Dorcas dreaded his visits. "He's calling on me, not Papa?"

"Afraid so."

Well, drat and perdition. "Bring a tea tray. Nothing lavish. Who are the flowers from?"

"I did not peek at the card."

Dorcas longed to wrap the plaid scarf about her neck and shoulders like a magic cloak, but no. That would be eccentric, and Isaiah would notice, and all she wanted was to endure the two cups of tea mandated by good manners and see him on his way. She instead stopped by her private parlor, intent on learning who had sent her flowers only to find Isaiah Mornebeth lounging in Mama's favorite reading chair.

"Mr. Mornebeth, good day." What in blue blazes was he doing in Dorcas's private parlor? "I believe the family parlor will be cozier at this hour."

He rose, and the quality of his smile made Dorcas uneasy. A little too merry, a little too mischievous. "Dorcas dearest. I see the plans for the fellowship meal are all quite in hand."

The dirty blighter was telling her that he'd snooped at her desk. Her unease was joined by annoyance.

"I hope so. The ladies always look very much forward to it." She did not rebuke him for his familiarity, because that would only goad him to worse presumptions.

He took her hand in his. "Your fingers are cold. You've been out.

Where do you go, dearest Dorcas? Do you go to the home of Major MacKay to see young John? Those pretty little posies are from somebody with the first initial A—as in Alasdhair? Is he grateful for your attention to the boy, or does he have another reason to send you flowers?"

Isaiah rubbed his thumb over the back of Dorcas's hand, and the croissants she'd eaten with Alasdhair threatened to make a reappearance. Isaiah had either followed her on several occasions, or he'd had her followed, and he'd made enough inquiries to know exactly what was afoot with John.

She raised her voice, hoping Mrs. Benton lingered near. "I owe you no explanations, Mr. Mornebeth."

His grip on her knuckles became uncomfortable. "I adore your spirit. I am endlessly pleased with your determination and intelligence, but, Dorcas, you must accommodate yourself to a future shared with me. You always knew I would return to London at some point. You declined offers from the hopeful widowers and spotty boys because you were doubtless waiting for me, even if you did not admit that to yourself."

"I was not waiting for you. Never that." She gave a violent twist of her arm—a move the ladies in jail had shown her—and she was free. "You presume much, Mr. Mornebeth, and unless you can comport yourself like a perfect gentleman, I will ask you to leave."

His smile became a grin. "That fire, that lovely, raging fire... You can send me away, for now. Thomas has not yet given me permission to court you, because nothing must be allowed to interfere with Michael's visit. In his usual fashion, Thomas both forbade me to commence courting you and intimated that he'd approve a match between us. Ever the diplomat, that's our Thomas."

Dorcas refused to yield to Isaiah's tactics by edging away. "You will not disrespect my father under his own roof."

"When a man disrespects himself, he invites others to do likewise. Tell me about MacKay. Was he one of the fair Melanie's conquests?"

The door was only half closed, and a sharp rap heralded Mrs. Benton's arrival with the tray. "I did not know you'd removed from the family parlor," she said with every evidence of good cheer. "Shall I build up the fire?"

"A fine idea," Isaiah said, just as Dorcas replied, "That will not be necessary."

Mrs. Benton looked from one to the other.

"Mr. Mornebeth cannot stay long," Dorcas said. "He was inquiring whether we have a more exact date for Michael's arrival."

Mrs. Benton set the tray on the low table near the hearth. "Any day. Vicar's prayers are a constant stream of wishes for Master Michael's safe arrival. Shall I show you out, Mr. Mornebeth?"

Mrs. Benton was trying to be helpful, but her offer resulted in Isaiah resuming his seat. "On a day this chilly, I will always make time for a spot of tea before braving the elements. Dorcas, if you would do the honors, and perhaps Mrs. Benton would build up the fire for us?"

His requests were rude, his willingness to sit uninvited in the presence of a lady was rude, but more significantly, these gestures were *threatening.* They were intended to reduce Dorcas once again to the status of an inexperienced, unworldly girl, who lacked the guile and power to outwit an older, wilier opponent.

Even knowing his strategy for the blatant display it was, Dorcas did not see a means of extricating herself from his company. If she flounced out in high dudgeon, he'd retaliate. If she meekly obeyed, he'd be inspired to intimidate her again at the time and place of his choosing.

I've nonetheless had to make my peace with situations where all of my choices led to sorrow.

Dorcas's own words came back to her. Isaiah Mornebeth excelled at creating such situations, and he'd also managed to ambush her, leaving her no time to plan countermeasures.

That would not happen again.

"The fire is adequate," Dorcas said, taking the second wing chair. "Thank you, Mrs. Benton."

Mrs. Benton gave a brief curtsey and withdrew, leaving the door three-quarters open. All the heat from the hearth would escape, but no matter. Dorcas might need to escape too.

"I like mine strong," Isaiah said, "with plenty of milk and sugar, or cream if you have it. My grandmother likes cream in her tea, being a self-indulgent old dear."

Dorcas poured the tea without checking its strength. She added milk and a dash of sugar—this was not Carlton House, for pity's sake—and passed the cup and saucer to her guest.

He took a sip. "Not as strong as I prefer."

A younger Dorcas would have apologized, taken his cup for herself, and let the pot steep until it suited his tastes.

"Go to blazes, Mr. Mornebeth. You trespassed against my youth and innocence years ago, and I have held my peace about your awful behavior. Disabuse yourself of the fiction that you can continue to rely on my discretion while behaving like a complete dunderwhelp."

He set down his tea cup with alarming calm. "Dorcas, you deliver a very convincing scold, but tell me, who will believe that I played the villain with you on three different occasions? You had every chance to cry foul, to run to Papa and complain of ill treatment, but you acquiesced. *You came to me willingly*, all too happy to taste forbidden fruit. You saw reason then, and you will see reason now. Have some tea to settle your nerves."

"I will not take tea with you."

His smile became pained. "As much as I would enjoy holding this cup to your lips and watching you choose between the ruin of a frock and a simple sip of tea, today is not the day for that little exercise. Let's be logical, shall we? You find my advances abhorrent. They aren't. My advances are as skilled and respectful as any other fellow's, but you have decided to be affronted. Very well."

His gaze fell on the little pot of forget-me-nots, the blue of the flowers the same shade as Alasdhair's eyes.

"Be affronted," he went on. "You are a lady, and your brother's behavior put you in a situation ladies do not expect to deal with. You made the only reasonable choice."

"*You* put me in that situation."

"I gave you a way to preserve your family from serious disgrace, Dorcas, but let's not quibble about the past. The present sees Michael Delancey, son of dear old Tom Delancey, returning to London for a visit, but we all know his real agenda. He's served out his penance in the north, put in a few years before the mast at a drafty rural manse. He served his time marrying lusty couples and baptizing squalling infants. Now he seeks advancement, and thus he's flaunting himself before the church leadership in London."

A moan of grief was building in Dorcas's soul, for she could see exactly where Isaiah's little homily on Michael's ambitions was heading.

"You will tarnish Michael's reputation at precisely the time when he's trying to make a good impression."

"Heavens, you have a lively imagination, Dorcas. I would never willingly interfere with a friend's ambitions. I might, though, express a quiet hope to my superiors at Lambeth that Michael Delancey has seen the error of his youthful ways. I might suggest, out of kindness, that the blandishments of Town ought not to be dangled in Michael's very face, lest he yield to London's many temptations *again*, as he did so woefully in the past."

"You led him into temptation."

Isaiah took a placid sip of his tea. "He will tell you that, Dorcas, and be very convincing, but I assure you, I was trying to dissuade him from his folly at every step along the way. I prayed for him, and I would not abandon him and leave him entirely friendless in unsavory company."

Isaiah shook his head, the picture of regret.

Dorcas wanted to smash the teapot over his head. Two thoughts preserved her from giving in to that impulse. First, Isaiah would delight in her display of temper and gently hint that her spinster status had inclined her to a touch of hysteria. She could not risk handing him that weapon.

Second, he was not bluffing. He could sink Michael's reputation in the course of a day's idle socializing. A word here, a pointed silence there. An intimation in the right ears and a suggestion in the wrong ones. Papa's prospects would suffer by association to the degree Isaiah wanted them to. Dorcas might well be ruined without a word of Isaiah's perfidy toward her being spoken.

Nothing had changed. She was older and wiser, but she was still at the mercy of a man who saw her and her family only as tools with which to advance his own interests.

"You are silent," he said, perusing her. "I have ever admired your common sense, Dorcas. Humility is a virtue, and any woman I take to wife will be a very virtuous woman."

"I cannot marry you."

He sat back and sighed. "We aren't even courting yet, but you need not make a great drama of this. I will be a considerate husband —you already know this. I am not a loutish lover, and I am prepared to limit my intimate demands upon you. Grandmother has decided that we will suit, and thus I will also arrive at the altar with a certain lack of freedom in my choice. I will make the best of the situation. Besides, I am the precise sort of husband you need. I will be kind but firm."

By Lucifer's pitchfork, his arrogance exceeded all bounds. "I am not a lapdog that the likes of you must show me how to go on in company."

He sat forward, his expression eerily earnest. "Dorcas, you struggle. With your temper, with your outspokenness. You could easily fall into the willful, opinionated stubbornness of the confirmed spinster, but I will spare you that. We will have a few children—perfect children, of course—upon whom we will dote. I can offer you a good life, but because we got off on a somewhat unusual foot years ago, you regard my offer with dismay."

He patted her knee, and Dorcas had all she could manage not to shrink away from him.

"Take some time to adjust to the idea," he said, rising. "A highly strung female must be dealt with gently. I'll settle into my post at the palace. We'll enjoy Michael's visit, and perhaps our wedding can serve as his excuse to tarry a few more weeks in the south. Old Tom will like that notion. I will take my leave of you. No need to show me out."

He bent and brushed a kiss to her forehead. Dorcas ignored him and kept her gaze on the fire. She thus did not see him push the pot of forget-me-nots to the floor, but she heard the crash and saw the flowers and dirt scattered all over the carpet.

"My apologies," Isaiah said. "I'll send the housekeeper along to clean up the mess."

"Don't bother."

He bowed and left Dorcas alone to repot the abused little blooms as best she could. The note, now stained and damp, read, *Fondest regards, A.* She was still sweeping dirt off the rug when Mrs. Benton appeared in the doorway a quarter hour later.

"He's here! The prodigal has returned! Master Michael has safely arrived, and you must come on the instant to welcome him! I've already sent the potboy over to the church to fetch your father."

Dorcas dredged up a smile, set the bedraggled flowers on the windowsill, and went to greet her long-lost brother.

CHAPTER FIFTEEN

Dorcas had been indisposed the previous week. She'd handed Alasdhair that confidence, along with her bonnet and scarf, and then blushed as vermillion as a winter sunset. He had hugged her, because she was simply too dear not to hug, and had ordered Henderson to serve up a pot of chamomile tea with ginger biscuits.

Dorcas had hugged him back.

They'd spent two visits merely chatting and admiring John's attempts to crawl. Dorcas still did not hold the boy, but her fondness for him was apparent in the way she watched Alasdhair cuddle him. She'd spoken of the challenges of planning a fellowship meal—church business, always church business—until Alasdhair had prompted her to instead speak of family.

Perhaps her indisposition was more than a passing affliction, or perhaps her brother's visit weighed on her mind, because even as she'd regaled Alasdhair with the tale of that time her mama had confused raspberry cordial with skin tonic, something about Dorcas had been off.

Distracted.

Withdrawn, for all that she listened attentively and asked insightful questions.

She greeted Alasdhair on Tuesday morning, the distracted air more pronounced than ever.

"Michael arrived on Friday," she said, handing over her cloak. "I ought not to stay long, and you probably won't see much of me henceforth."

He hung up her cloak and draped the scarf over it. "Should I attend services at St. Mildred's just to catch a glimpse of you?"

He'd meant the comment to be teasing, but when Dorcas attempted to hang her bonnet on a hat peg, she missed the mark.

"Dorcas? Is something wrong?"

She passed him her hat. "Shall we go upstairs? Don't bother with a tea tray today. I have much to do at the vicarage, and I only slipped away because Papa and Michael are calling on some old friends. I'll just look in on John and be on my way."

Her tone was full of false cheer. Alasdhair touched her arm, and he could see her trying not to flinch. "Upstairs with us, then," he said. "The boy is in good spirits, as usual. He has a new letter."

Dorcas swept up the steps. "A new letter?"

"In addition to *b*, as in baa-baa-buh-bee, he has now mastered the devilishly difficult *f*, feh-fah-fee-fah. A useful letter, in the opinion of many."

Dorcas ought to have proceeded straight to the nursery. She instead paused at Alasdhair's sitting room door. "If you have a moment, I'd like to talk."

That sounded ominous. "I will always have time to talk with you, Dorcas." Alasdhair ushered her into his sitting room, which now sported a pot of primroses on the windowsill and a fern in the corner. Powell's housekeeper had found a lace runner for the mantel and another for the low table and a MacKay plaid blanket of softest merino for the back of the sofa. The draperies were tied back with lacy lavender sachets—another contribution from Powell's housekeeper—and the andirons she'd unearthed resembled wrought-iron terriers.

Foolishness, but pleasant, domestic foolishness.

"How are you and Michael getting on?" Alasdhair asked, closing the door. Surely Michael's visit was behind this odd mood.

"I hardly see him, unless it's at a supper attended by guests. He's put his time in the north to good use, polishing his command of Scripture and acquiring a kind of dignity. He's not the brother who goaded me to try smoking a cheroot."

She gave one of the sachets a squeeze, releasing the fragrance of lavender. Her perambulations took her to the primroses, which she watered from the pitcher on the sideboard.

"Dorcas, are you still indisposed?"

She set the pitcher back on the sideboard. "I am well, thank you, but Alasdhair... Mr. MacKay, I feel it only fair that having reached certain conclusions, I inform you of them in person."

From ominous to dire. Alasdhair had had the experience of facing an enemy army and realizing that the opposing forces were much larger than the scouts had reported. Larger, better arrayed, and better armed. Dorcas's unwillingness to look at him, her restlessness, put the same hollow terror in his belly as those French guns had.

He intercepted her between the sofa and the hearth. "Dorcas, whatever it is, we will weather it. If your father has turned up difficult, if Michael objects to our marriage, if some meddling uncle with a loathing for the Scots has stuck his oar in..." He put a hand on each of her arms, willing her to simply *be honest*. "If you have decided we must elope, we'll elope. If you need more time, I'll wait." *Just don't leave me.* "Tell me what you need."

Her features were composed—when had she ever appeared less than composed?—but her eyes were full of emotion.

"I need *you*," she said. "I need you, and I desire you, and I don't know how to make that stop."

Why would she want it to? Alasdhair could not ask her that, because she'd commenced kissing him. Her passion was a flame to the dry tinder of his longing, and he soon had her up against the door, her skirts hiked to her hips, and her legs around his hips.

"Take me to bed, Alasdhair. Please just take me to bed."

The veteran officer in him protested that her behavior made little sense and wanted more explanation, even while the suitor scooped her off her feet and carried her into the bedroom.

"I've missed you," he said, sitting her on the edge of the bed and going to his knees to unlace her boots. "I've dreamed of you, held entire conversations with you in my head, and cursed your brother for his bad timing."

"I've cursed him too," Dorcas said, her fingers skimming Alasdhair's jaw.

"And have you missed me?" An idiot's question. She'd seen him not four days past.

"Terribly. I want you now, Alasdhair." Her boots were off, but other than that, she was still all buttoned up and braided. She leaned back on her elbows and bunched up her skirts. "Right now."

A man "duchessed" a lady when he made love to her without removing his boots. This was supposedly commemorative of the Duke of Marlborough's reunion with his wife after some ferocious military campaign and protracted separation.

Alasdhair was not a duke, and he did not care for lovemaking that bore too close a resemblance to mindless rutting. And yet, Dorcas offering herself to him like this, eager and insistent, was a powerful temptation.

"Can we not savor one another and cuddle a wee bit first?" Again, he tried for a touch of humor, but Dorcas only sat forward and began unbuttoning his falls.

"We can cuddle later. I have missed you."

This wasn't merely missing. This was something Alasdhair had not encountered in her before. Upset of some sort, frustration perhaps as a result of Michael's arrival. She *needed* Alasdhair desperately, and that was both alarming and enticing.

"Dorcas, settle. You won't have to ask again. Lie back, and let me love you."

Alasdhair eased her onto the mattress and stood between her legs. He kissed her. He nuzzled all the sweet spots she liked to have nuzzled. He stroked her breasts through too many layers of fabric, and the whole time, he had the sense she was humoring him, for all that she remained quiescent and passive.

Somewhere between Dorcas's right ear and her left eyebrow, Alasdhair realized that hesitating because the lady was *too* insistent was nigh ridiculous. They were to be married. They'd endured more than a week of forced celibacy, and he loved her madly.

He sank into her heat on a slow glide, and she sighed as if all the troubles of the world had been lifted from her shoulders. She kissed him with an ardor that combined tenderness and demand, and made a sound of yearning that drove him witless with desire.

He didn't last long, but she didn't need him to. Within a few moments, her yearning had turned to keening and panting, and then she was clinging to him as if he'd rescued her from the pit itself. Alasdhair barely, *barely* managed to satisfy Dorcas before spending in his handkerchief.

He hung over her, his chest heaving and his heart more than a little bewildered. What had they just done? Did this qualify as lovemaking, something more, or something less?

"Talk to me," he said, gathering her close. "Something is afoot, and you think to protect me by keeping it to yourself."

Her hand drifting through his hair paused. "Why do you say that?"

A question where an answer should be. Alasdhair spoke quietly, directly into her ear. "Dorcas, you don't hide the truth from me. What's wrong?"

She applied the lightest pressure to his chest, and he straightened. She was flushed and rosy, her skirts frothed around her waist, and she should have looked like a happily tumbled lady.

"You are crying." She was *crying,* and she'd hidden even that from him.

"I cannot marry you."

Cannot was, by the smallest increment of hope, better than *will not.* Alasdhair clung to that minuscule distinction even as he let the lady go.

"You refuse to be my wife, but I'm adequate for a wimble?"

She pushed her skirts down over her knees and yet remained on her back. "Please don't be difficult."

Alasdhair needed to eat. He'd put off his midmorning snack because he'd wanted to share it with Dorcas if she came by. More than food, though, he needed answers. He offered her his hand to pull her up to a sitting position, then took the place beside her.

"I must know why, Dorcas. If you'd sent me a letter waving me off, if I've given offense somehow... but you come here and all but accost me, doing a very good impersonation of a smitten lady. Now you plan to march back to St. Mildred's without a backward glance?" Curses welled, propelled on a rush of confusion with a violent edge. "If we cannot have a future, might we not at least have the truth between us?"

As anxious and angry as he was, another rotten feeling was crowding out his temper. Had Vicar Delancey and his perfect son pressured Dorcas into considering Mornebeth's suit? She loved her menfolk and would do anything for them, but such a sacrifice was beyond what they deserved from her.

Surely she knew that?

"My cousins were worried for me," Alasdhair said. "They said this courtship was happening too quickly, that I was being incautious. Were they right, Dorcas? Have you found some regrets stashed between committee meetings and calls upon the elderly and infirm?"

She pressed her forehead against his arm. "Don't. Please, Alasdhair. I did not intend for matters to progress as they did this morning. I had a little speech rehearsed, about changing my mind. You said I could change my mind. That the decisions were mine to make. Then you started bragging about John's letters, and I became so angry... I will not know when he masters *p* or *g*. I will not meet your family, I will never learn your complicated Highland tongue, and I will never..."

Tears trickled down her cheeks, and yet, she sounded completely composed. Alasdhair risked an arm around her shoulders.

"I love you. If you bear me any regard at all, Dorcas, please tell me what has brought you to this pass." A relief that, to put aside the anger and focus instead on worry for her.

"I have been a fool."

"Who hasn't? Tell me the rest of it."

DORCAS HAD KNOWN HEARTACHE, when she'd lost her mother, when she'd capitulated to Mornebeth's threats years ago, when she'd parted from Michael. She'd survived the fresh grief by thinking, *I feel awful now, and in an hour, I might still feel awful, but not quite this wretchedly awful.*

She'd known the corrosive pain of living a lie. To be held up as a good example—the vicar's dutiful daughter—while knowing she'd allowed herself to be inveigled into Isaiah Mornebeth's bed, had been excruciating and exhausting.

The sheer effort of maintaining a virtuous façade, that of a lady ignorant of intimate congress and of the depths of her own powerlessness, had worn down her spirit. The lie she would have to live going forward—that of devoted wife—was more monstrous than the lie of the dutiful daughter.

She'd modified her internal litany. *I feel awful now, and in a month, I might still feel awful, but not quite this wretchedly awful. Or possibly in a year. Maybe in a decade.*

"You should hate me," Dorcas said, while Alasdhair sat silently beside her. "I would hate myself, but that's pointless. I will tell you the truth in part because you ask for it and in part because I need to say the words to somebody."

His arm remained around her shoulders, a comforting weight. "I'm listening."

He would always listen, always see, always hear. Alasdhair was the dearest, most honorable man she would ever meet, and she must part from him.

"You know I had relations with Isaiah Mornebeth years ago."

"Passing encounters that I ascribe to youthful folly and curiosity on your part. He is enough your senior that I cannot excuse his taking advantage of you half so easily."

And for that, Dorcas would always love Alasdhair MacKay.

"Neither can I. Mornebeth led my brother astray, sank him in debt, bought up all of Michael's vowels, and gave me a chance to redeem them with my virtue. If I gave Isaiah an hour of my time on three occasions, Michael's debts would be forgiven and his reputation untarnished. If I refused, if I begrudged my family's good name three hours about which nobody would ever know, then Isaiah would inform the bishops that Thomas Delancey's son was a gambler and a disgraceful sot."

Beside her, Alasdhair had gone still. "He extorted sexual favors from you?"

Extortion was a hanging felony. Dorcas mentally could not quite accuse Isaiah of rape—she'd gone to him, after all—but *extortion* was gratifyingly accurate.

"The first time, I had no idea what to expect. The physical act struck me as awkward, but mercifully brief. Not painful so much as undignified. The second time, I approached the occasion with dread. The third time, I dosed myself with the poppy, and the bargain was met. As far as I know, Isaiah has not spoken a word of our dealings to anybody."

"Yet."

Dorcas closed her eyes and gave Alasdhair her weight, the better to memorize the feel and goodness of him. "I was tempted to drink that entire bottle of laudanum and to leave a note: *Mornebeth is to blame.* But the matter would have been kept quiet, and he would have emerged unscathed. I would have been remembered as yet another lovesick, hysterical female. I could not give him that satisfaction."

"So you'll give him the satisfaction of marrying you instead?"

"If I must. He has connections, Alasdhair, and any accusations I made now would have no credibility. I went to him all those years ago —he insisted on that. His grandmother's town house was unoccupied that summer, and I went there at the times of his choosing to disport in the manner of his choosing. I *schemed* to tryst with him, lied to my father about where I was going, and pleaded a headache when I returned home so I could soak in the hottest baths I could stand."

The interludes with Isaiah had been tawdry and brief, but the memories of what had come after... Feeling unclean, brittle, volatile, nervous, forgetful... Dropping things, stumbling, avoiding mirrors, and then peering into them endlessly to practice appearing *normal.*

"You intend to marry a man you hate."

"A man I will never love, but who will not threaten my father or brother as long as I am his wife."

"Perhaps not," Alasdhair said, rising, "but he will continue to threaten *you.* If you are not the perfect wife—and even if you are perfect—he will find ways to make you pay. He can have you committed to an asylum, Dorcas. Have you thought of that?"

Of course she had. "He won't do that if I'm married to him. A man with an insane wife cannot advance in the Church."

Alasdhair knelt by the bed and held out one of her boots. "So the Church will protect you? The Church that would have condemned your father and brother over a handful of stupid gambling markers will suddenly hold Mornebeth accountable for putting away a wife he'll quietly grumble about for years first?" Alasdhair slipped her boots onto her feet, his touch gentle as always. "Though, of course, he'll pray for you without ceasing, to hear him tell it."

Dorcas tucked her hands under her thighs lest she yield to the temptation to touch Alasdhair again. "He won't grumble. That would be unsaintly, and Isaiah has the world convinced he's a saint."

Alasdhair did up the laces, snugly but not too tightly. "I had a commanding officer like him, Dorcas, the rotten blighter I spoke of to you earlier. Dunacre told such bouncers in the officers' mess, and he was so convincing... Mornebeth won't complain about his wife, he'll ask others to keep her in their prayers. He'll admit to being worried about her. He'll pretend he's told you something, then look concerned in front of others when you appear to have no recollection of it."

"Your commanding officer *did that* to you?"

"He did that to all of his direct reports, and we learned not to approach him unless we were in twos and threes. He wasn't as able to claim he'd been misheard, misunderstood, misinterpreted, or ignored when his subordinates stuck together, though he still got away with much." Alasdhair sat back, and yet, he remained on his knees before her. "Don't marry me, Dorcas, and I will somehow live with that sorrow, but for the love of God, don't marry Mornebeth either."

This man... This chivalrous, humble man. Dorcas touched Alasdhair's shoulder. "I know why you stayed under Dunacre's command, Alasdhair. You stayed to protect your men as best you could for as long as you could. You stayed because you knew the havoc he could cause and took every possible measure to mitigate those harms. If I love my family, then I will marry Isaiah."

"*If they love you, you should not have to.*" Alasdhair took her hand and bowed his head. "I transferred to a different unit lest I kill my commanding officer, Dorcas, and I left the men to Powell's care. Please do not marry Mornebeth. I am begging you not to marry him."

A good man was begging on his knees before her, and the moment should have held a little wonderment for Dorcas on those grounds alone. Instead, she was disgusted with herself to have reduced Alasdhair MacKay to begging. She rose from the bed and sidled around him.

"I have some time to accommodate myself to the notion of

marrying Mornebeth. Isaiah understands that upstaging Michael's visit with an engagement would be in poor taste."

Alasdhair stood and braced a hand on the bedpost. "I missed that commandment. Never display poor taste when forcing a woman to marry you."

He did irony bitterly well. "I am not being forced, Alasdhair. Wasn't it you who said I have the latitude to make my own choices? I am choosing to keep my family free of scandal, to make a suitable match, and to—"

"To break my heart, which does not matter, but you put your own wellbeing at risk, Dorcas. I agree with you that Mornebeth is unlikely to stash you away at some walled estate in the north in the near term. He'll want a few children of you first. He will instead tie you in knots, until you believe his lies over the evidence of your own eyes. He already got away with raping you, and because he bound you with ties of familial loyalty rather than physical ropes, you excuse his coercion."

"I don't excuse it, but I admit the degree to which I was complicit."

Alasdhair laid a warm palm to the side of her face. "You were forced," he said gently. "You cannot admit that, because such an admission would mean you were powerless once before and could be again. I understand more clearly than you think I do."

"You are not to hurt him, Alasdhair. That won't solve anything and will see you behind bars."

Alasdhair studied her for a moment, his blue eyes once again growing as chilly and unreadable as they'd been when she'd first brought John to this household.

"You have the authority to make the choices you see fit, Dorcas, but you presume to forbid me the same right?"

"No, but I can implore. Don't hurt him. He'll find a way to hurt you or somebody you love worse."

Alasdhair scrubbed a hand over his face. "Precisely. And thus, the only way to survive an encounter with such as Mornebeth is to care for nobody, not even yourself. You are incapable of surrendering your soul to that degree, Dorcas; hence, he will always best you."

A soldier apparently learned to think like that, in terms of ultimate costs and outcomes. "Don't kill him either, Alasdhair. I won't have that on my conscience." Dorcas did not allow herself to glance at the bed, she simply walked toward the door. That was how a farewell happened, one step at a time.

"You won't look in on John?" Alasdhair asked, ambling at her side.

"I cannot bear to," Dorcas said as they reached the top of the steps. "Isaiah knows John is here, by the way, and exactly who the boy is and who you are. Somebody in your household has probably been treated to a pint at the corner pub, or several pints."

Alasdhair paused, a hand braced on the newel post as if he'd suffered a blow. "Thank you for telling me. Doesn't it bother you that you are marrying a man who has spied on you the better to intimidate you?"

"Yes, it bothers me. It bothers me exceedingly, but I don't see any other way to deal with the threat he poses, Alasdhair. Which murdering general advised keeping friends close and enemies closer? Perhaps he was right. Are you well?"

"Peckish. Heartbroken. A trifle dazed, as if I've suffered a blow to the head in the midst of a classic French ambush." He started down the steps. "Nothing that some biscuits and whisky or twenty years of pining shouldn't put to rights."

"Please try not to hate me." Dorcas trailed after him, half worried that he might stumble and fall.

He reached the foyer and held out her cloak for her. "I could never hate you. Try not to hate yourself, Dorcas, but you have my leave to hate Mornebeth all you please. I certainly hate him." He smoothed her cloak over her shoulders, the touch shading toward a caress.

She did up her own frogs lest Alasdhair's fingers brush her chin. "If you hear anything regarding Melanie, will you send word?"

He gazed past her shoulder. "I doubt I will hear anything, and if you are married to Mornebeth, sending word that your disgraced cousin is alive and well would only give him that much more leverage over you and your family. You are making a mistake, Dorcas."

"I know, but I am trying to make the least costly among several mistakes, and I don't see any other choice, Alasdhair. Isaiah is clever and determined and diabolically patient."

"Diabolical, I'll grant you. You could come to Scotland with me."

"And leave my father and brother sitting in Mornebeth's crosshairs?"

"So instead you will occupy that dubious post yourself." He wrapped the scarf around her neck and ears. "I feel as if I'm watching another blameless woman throw her life away, Dorcas. Please don't do this."

He knew how to strike a blow to the heart without raising a hand. "I am hale and whole. I will manage." She would have offered another platitude or two—*thank you for looking after John, take care, I'll think of you fondly*—but heaping platitudes on heartbreak was beyond her.

"Farewell, Alasdhair MacKay."

"I'm not to walk you home?"

"You need to eat. I need to leave."

"And your intended is likely spying on you, so best not stroll down the boulevard with the besotted Scotsman again."

"Alasdhair?"

"Miss Delancey?"

"There is such a thing as too much honesty. Good day, be well." She would have swept out the door on those parting lines, but Alasdhair stood between her and a grand exit.

"Anytime, Dorcas—three days from now, three years from now—you can send word to me, and I'll come. I will behave with perfect propriety toward you, but I will get you over the border before Mornebeth knows you're gone. I will keep you safe from him if you'll only ask that of me."

"Thank you." She kissed his cheek and waited for him to step aside.

She left, the door closing softly behind her. The day was sunny but cold, with a biting wind. Appropriate, that the weather should promise the appearance of warmth and deliver only a chill. As Dorcas passed the tea shop, she realized what about Alasdhair's parting offer bothered her, among all the many things bothering her:

He gave coach fare from London to any streetwalker who asked him for it. By rejecting Alasdhair's proposal in favor of Isaiah's, Dorcas had reduced herself to the status of a woman no longer safe anywhere in London.

She dredged up her internal litany about feeling awful and tried to refashion it into a source of some comfort, however faint. All that came to her was, *I feel awful now, and in another decade, I will have spent an entire ten years feeling more wretchedly awful yet.*

~

"OFF TO THE TEA SHOP?" Henderson asked as Alasdhair shrugged into his greatcoat.

The butler's good cheer landed on Alasdhair's mood like orders to prepare for another siege. Dorcas Delancey felt she had to marry Isaiah Mornebeth, and Melanie Fairchild had believed it necessary to abandon her son, if not the entire mortal sphere. Alasdhair was tempted to find a compelling reason to start a riot, except that his cousins would be worried when he was taken up for inciting mayhem.

And inciting mayhem invariably resulted in harm to the innocent. "I'm out for a walk. Don't wait lunch for me."

Henderson took up the pile of morning mail waiting in the tray on the sideboard. "You need to eat something, sir. Your cousins have spoken to me very pointedly on that subject on several occasions. You are not to go from breakfast to noon without eating."

I do not care if I ever eat again. I do not care if I ever draw breath again.

Except, if Alasdhair were to leap from the bridge as Melanie had, literally or figuratively, then who would teach John when not to use the letter *f*? Who would explain to him about respect for the ladies and how to hold his drink? Who would put him on his first pony and provide manly reassurances after his first tumble from the saddle?

"Wait here, sir," Henderson said, setting the mail aside. "I'll fetch you some bread and butter. You have that woozy look about you, and you must not go out without eating."

Not woozy, destroyed. "Fetch the tucker, and I'll wait."

Henderson dashed off as Timmens came down the steps, John perched on her hip. "I thought I heard Miss Delancey's voice."

"Miss Delancey has gone, very likely not to return." The words were so simple, the feelings so complicated.

"She's taken you into dislike of a sudden?"

Timmens was a short, plump, unprepossessing creature upon whom John's life depended. She was also a grieving mother, and yet, she'd found a way to move forward after losing her child. She remained on the second step and thus nearly at eye level with Alasdhair.

"I told her I loved her."

Her skeptical gaze turned sympathetic. "Scared her off, then?"

"She's frightened, that much is true. Timmens, have you run across an affable, blond fellow of perhaps thirty-five years down at the pub lately? One whose friendliness shades toward nosy questions about the household?"

"That one." She sneered the words. "Lily-white hands, Mayfair manners, and the eyes of a hungry lizard. Henderson pointed him out to me. Said to keep mum. The fellow had a go at Henderson and got nowhere, so he tried chatting me up. Never you fear, Major. I'm too stupid to know anything more than how to wash a soiled nappy so it doesn't dry stiff."

"And you got a free pint out of it?"

"And some shepherd's pie, though the fellow was also quite friendly with the barmaids and the publican. What will you do about Miss Delancey? She's fair gone on you, and now you say somebody has frightened her off. That woman doesn't frighten easily, sir. Spent nights in jail, she did, and wrote about it for the toffs to read. She went spare on 'em too. Cited holy writ and went on about what we spend on wars and royal fetes while we starve our prisoners and begrudge 'em a single blanket."

Dorcas had a ferocious ally, though she'd likely be surprised to learn of that. "You've had family in jail?"

"Marshalsea. The consumption gets you sooner or later in that place, while Fat George bankrupts the exchequer for his paintings and naughty sculptures. What will you do about your lady, sir?"

"I have been given my marching orders, Timmens. I'm to leave Miss Delancey in peace."

"This ain't the army, Major, and a preacher's daughter is not a general."

John waved a hand in Alasdhair's direction. "Feh-feh-fah-foooo!" He was such a cheerful boy, much as his mother had been cheerful. Until she'd been gone instead of cheerful.

"But a lady is a lady, Timmens, and a gentleman does not argue with, importune, or disregard the clearly expressed wishes of a lady."

"He don't leave her to deal with fawning lizards on her own neither."

Henderson came up the steps, a paper-wrapped packet in his hand. "Sandwiches and shortbread. You'll want gloves today too, sir. It's nippier out than it looks."

"I have acquired a pair of nannies." Who nannied Dorcas? Who had *ever* nannied her? "Timmens tells me the blond toff tried to winkle secrets from you too, Henderson."

Henderson wrinkled his nose. "Thought he was bein' all sly and subtle about it. 'So, you work for Major MacKay? I hear he's taken in an infant. Didn't think MacKay was the charitable sort...'"

"To which you replied?"

"'Sod off, unless you want to wear that ale all over your fancy togs, mate.' He found someplace else to sit, but the next evening, he was back and tried it on with Timmens."

"Fum," John said, patting Timmens's cheek. "Fummmmm."

"How did Mornebeth learn even that much?" Alasdhair asked. "If neither of you told him anything, then where did he learn that John has joined the household?"

Timmens gently extracted a lock of her hair from John's little fingers. "The laundresses, maybe? They are a merry lot and hear all of the talk. Cook avoids the pubs altogether, and the grooms prefer the Ploughman Laddie three streets up."

The situation wanted discussing with Alasdhair's cousins.

But no, the situation was none of his business. Dorcas had made her wishes quite clear, and that was an end to it. London was not Badajoz, and Dorcas had been very clear about what her wishes were.

Alasdhair took out half a sandwich and shoved the rest of the food into a pocket. "Until further notice, I am not at home to anybody save Miss Delancey or my cousins." He touched John's cheek. "Behave, lad. Don't get too carried away with those *f*'s."

"Fum!"

Alasdhair tapped his hat onto his head, his mind full despite his empty heart. The ache of Dorcas's rejection was a dull, hollow sorrow that would worsen as the days and nights went on. The reality of the loss was muted now, but it would bloom into awful splendor when her engagement to Mornebeth was announced.

Alasdhair started down the street, glad for the chill. He ate the half sandwich, because he was a soldier, and soldiers survived to fight again, though nobody told them why that was such a laudable plan when the enemy was doing likewise, and dysentery was always a lethal possibility.

Stumbling from battle to battle was no way to live, and yet, that's also how Dorcas apparently went on.

By the time the sandwiches and shortbread were gone, Alasdhair had wandered to the streets along the river. The Dove's Nest, a humble establishment with a wooden nest fashioned atop its signboard, loomed before him, and the Strand Bridge stretched to the south at his back.

Foot traffic thronged the bridge, and wheeled vehicles crept over its span at an even slower pace. London traffic generally was choked with myriad turnpikes, such that navigating in and out of Town was never efficient. Alasdhair took a seat on an empty bench and idly watched the pedestrians, each intent on some mission, not a one of them knowing or caring that a brokenhearted man observed them pass by.

Dorcas's decision to wed Mornebeth was logical, but also... doomed. Mornebeth would find ways to torment her purely for sport, because he was cut from the same cloth as Dunacre, born with a crippled soul.

Alasdhair was puzzling over the morality of putting Mornebeth on an East Indiaman when a lady dressed in a green cloak hustled past. Her bonnet was adorned with a pheasant feather, and she moved with the energy and purpose of a healthy young woman.

He was too surprised to call out to her, and then he was on his feet, head down, scarf pulled up, and following in her wake.

CHAPTER SIXTEEN

"Is MacKay out when you call," Orion Goddard asked, "or *out*?"

Dylan Powell took his cousin's hat and coat and his walking stick. Goddard was dressing more nattily since marrying Miss Ann Pearson, who was now styled *madame le chef* at The Coventry Club. Goddard had taken over management of the place, a job that he claimed resembled wrangling mules and supplies for the military, but with far better rations and considerably less mud.

At least one cousin was settled, while the other showed signs of having come completely unmoored.

"I have my sources," Powell said, leading the way to his library. "MacKay is honestly from home." Mrs. Lovelace, Powell's housekeeper, claimed receiving even family anywhere but the parlor was a faux pas of monstrous proportions, but a worried man wanted comfortable cushions for his backside and decent brandy for his nerves.

Neither was to be found in the fussy front parlor.

Though the fresh flowers were a nice touch, and the room had the best light of any in the house thanks to Mrs. Lovelace's insistence on lacy drapes instead of musty velvet. The sisters, when they eventually descended, would adore that parlor.

The library, by contrast, had only two windows. Powell told himself the library was snug and quiet because it faced the garden rather than the street. On a winter afternoon, the room was more accurately described as gloomy and stuffy.

"What do your old soldiers tell you?" Goddard asked as Powell led him down the corridor.

"MacKay is out prowling around at all hours. He's chatting up his lady friends, as well as the urchins, drunks, crossing sweepers, night-soil men, lamplighters, linkboys, and even the constables."

"Desperate measures, then. What is all this in aid of?"

"He's looking for the Fairchild woman."

Goddard paused on the threshold. "I thought she jumped from the Strand Bridge."

"Nobody saw her leap, if you'll recall, and MacKay thinks he's seen her since her supposed demise. Brandy?"

"Half a tot to ward off the chill." Goddard eased into a wing chair on a sigh. "Spring is taking its jolly time arriving this year."

Powell poured two drinks and passed one to his guest. "To the arrival of spring and the return of MacKay's wits." He took the second wing chair and sampled very good brandy, which was on his sideboard only because Goddard had family in France, and Powell's sisters—who delighted in warding off chills—were not on the premises.

Yet.

Goddard took a sip, then set his glass aside. "You think MacKay has grown worse?"

"I gather Alasdhair is taking it hard that the Delancey woman tossed him over for some bishop-in-waiting."

Goddard swore softly in French. "He was starting to come back to life, starting to recover his old... I don't know... twinkle in his eye. Quote me on that, and I will thrash you."

"As if you could. The old Alasdhair, the one who drank us under the table as a lad, flirted with anything in skirts, and sang like an Italian, would not recognize himself now."

"Blighted, beastly Badajoz." Goddard, whose household included many children, had taken to limiting his profanity since marrying Ann. "Do you have any idea what happened to him there?"

"Just what you've told me. He was abroad in the worst of the horror." An armed mob wreaking unchecked violence on civilians, prisoners, and officers, destroying all in its path for three straight days. "A more disgusting betrayal of honor could not be imagined this side of opium hellscapes."

"I could not see it," Goddard said. "I was never so tempted to tear off my bandages, but the surgeon assured us we were protected by locked doors and armed guards. When MacKay came by, I heard wildness in his voice, near panic. In the face of massed French cuirassiers, he was the picture of unconcern, but he was nigh unraveled that day."

MacKay had been unraveled ever since. He did not come to London to socialize, he came to hand out money and meals to shivering streetwalkers, to flagellate himself for a day best forgotten.

"I hoped Miss Delancey might ravel him back up." Powell had prayed for that outcome, though he'd never admit to another that he had resorted to importuning heaven. He'd otherwise given up begging the Almighty for anything years ago.

"What happened to the world's fastest courtship?" Goddard murmured. "Miss Delancey is not, by reputation, a woman who dithers or changes her mind."

"Mrs. Lovelace befriended MacKay's staff while she was overseeing the prenuptial cleaning. Seems Miss Delancey did change her mind, as simple as that. MacKay's version is that a more suitable *parti* supplanted his suit."

"Then Miss Delancey is Miss Dunderhead. MacKay is sorely smitten."

"Something untoward is afoot," Powell said. "Alasdhair would never surrender his heart to a fickle female. Now he's wandering all over London at unwise hours. I fear for our cousin. He has been too serious for too long."

"You being the pattern card of jocularity yourself?"

"I can be pleasant company, just as you can."

"Such effusive compliments, Powell, will put me to the blush. I've put away my sword."

Right. Enough about Alasdhair's broken heart and tattered wits, about which they could do nothing but drink and lament and worry.

Powell's sword hung across the library beneath a portrait of Great-Uncle Arwyn, who'd gone to sea as a midshipman at the age of eleven and worked his way up to his own command. He'd had wonderful stories to tell a small boy starved for masculine attention, though Powell suspected most of those stories had been more fairy tale than fact.

"We promised we'd keep our swords in view," Powell said, "lest we forget the horrors of war."

"Ann asked me to take it down. She said I needed no reminding of those horrors when they still haunt my dreams. I occasionally argue with my lady, but not when she's right."

So Goddard had nightmares too. Doubtless Alasdhair did as well, then. "We should send MacKay home. He's miserable here, and winter is almost over. If he's not to court the fair Miss Delancey, then he might as well put distance between himself and the site of his defeated hopes."

"Fine idea. I suggest you be the one to tell him he's banished from Town. I'll start working on your eulogy tonight."

"He's not violent." And yet, MacKay had a powerful temper when roused. Once upon a time, he'd brawled with the best of them. "We need to intervene before he does something he'll regret. He's rambling everywhere, from St. James's to St. Giles, to Southwark, always alone, always on foot."

Goddard took another sip of his drink. "The boys have spotted him along the river, and that is no place for a man alone to linger after dark. I have wondered if what's needed in MacKay's case isn't an eruption of some sort. He's been a monk since Badajoz, barely drinks but for a nip here and there, won't play more than a rare hand of cards, never disports with the ladies… He tends to the family business, passes coin to the streetwalkers, and grows quieter by the year. Whatever happened to him in Badajoz, it still burdens him."

What to say to that? MacKay, being MacKay, would likely take that burden to his grave. Powell was about to renew his argument for Alasdhair's removal to the north when the door opened, sending a gust of chilly air into the library.

MacKay strode in, his open greatcoat flapping with each step. "Two in the afternoon, and my cousins are already hitting the brandy. I'm related to a pair of doddering sots. Don't sit there gawping, lad. Pour a man a drink. I've poked into every coalhole and privy in this wretched town, and I'm parched."

He was also gaunt, rumpled, and in want of a shave. His eyes were ringed with fatigue, and his burr was much in evidence.

"You need to eat," Goddard said, "and don't argue with us, because contrariness is simply more evidence that you've neglected your belly. No brandy until you've eaten something."

MacKay took out his flask and tipped it to his lips. "Keep your frog-water. You'll no' be tellin' me what I need, Goddard. I know what I need, the same thing I always need."

"A sound thrashing?" Powell ventured.

"The truth. I'll also appreciate the use of some beggars and urchins, which is why you find me here when I ought to be keeping watch over the Southwark lodgings of Miss Melanie Fairchild."

Mrs. Lovelace appeared in the doorway with a laden tea tray in her hands. Powell had learned not to attempt to take trays from her, not to hold doors for her, not to in any way demonstrate gentlemanly courtesies where she was concerned.

Had her standards, did Mrs. Lovelace.

"I'll bring up sandwiches in a trice," she said, putting the tray on the sideboard. "Major MacKay can doubtless use a late luncheon, and I will take your coat as well, Major."

She all but whisked MacKay's coat from his shoulders, which he allowed, interestingly, while Goddard's expression had gone bemused.

"A managing woman," MacKay said when Mrs. Lovelace had absconded with his coat. "I used to adore them."

"A pretty woman," Goddard murmured. "Beneath that monstrous cap and all that frosty competence, she's quite pretty. Powell, what have you got yourself into?"

"A clean house, hot meals, and clothing that doesn't come up from the laundry half scorched and all over with stains." More than that, Powell did not dare admit. "You need reconnaissance patrols, MacKay?"

"Aye, and sentries. Melanie Fairchild is alive, and I want to know why she's lied to me, her family, and, by extension, her only begotten son. Deceptions and prevarications might suit the Delanceys and their kin, but for John's sake and my own, I want the truth."

NO AMOUNT of anger or heartache would render Alasdhair capable of keeping eyes on Melanie Fairchild around the clock. He had thus come to Powell to requisition reinforcements and also because he simply could not stand to be under his own roof.

He tossed through the night alone in the bed where he'd made love with Dorcas. He'd had the house spruced up in anticipation of making a home with her there. He'd acquired fripperies and stuffed bears, in part because Dorcas would expect that of him and in part because that was the kind of foolishness a man in love undertook gladly.

And for what? He'd given her his heart, and she'd given him his marching orders so she could martyr herself in marriage to a conniving priest.

Powell's housekeeper had taken one look at Alasdhair. "They're waiting for you in the library," she'd said, "and they are *worried* for you."

Mrs. Lovelace wielded a dust mop and a scold with equally impressive skill.

Alasdhair hadn't bothered passing her his coat, because he would not be staying long. His explanation to his cousins was succinct and to the point.

"You're sure you've seen Melanie Fairchild?" Goddard asked, adding a square of peat to the fire.

"Aye. I know it's her. I've broken bread with the woman, called upon her, watched her cooing at her darling son. I know her by sight quite well."

"Have a nibble," Powell said, taking a plate of shortbread from the tea tray and holding it out to Alasdhair.

"If I eat one more piece of shortbread, I will turn into a pat of butter."

Powell gave him that mournful Welsh stare, the disappointed saint crossed with the chiding nanny. Alasdhair took a piece and popped it into his mouth, lest Goddard and Powell fret even more than they already were.

"I'm raising Melanie's son," Alasdhair said. "I have a right to assurances that she won't come waltzing back from the dead in five years and whisk him off to some godforsaken American slum."

Goddard pushed the fire screen against the hearth and set the poker aside. "Tell us about Miss Delancey."

"Miss Delancey is none of your goddamned business."

Goddard had risen higher in the ranks than either Alasdhair or Powell. They agreed that his good fortune was strictly the result of his paternal English antecedents, though that was not the whole story. Goddard had an air of calm, an unflappable ability to look life squarely in the eye that commanded respect. He neither flinched nor looked away from life's messes and was enviably secure in himself.

Perhaps a brush with blindness did that for a man, or perhaps years of being dogged by scandal had imparted a blessed detachment.

When Alasdhair's rudeness should have earned him a shove, Goddard's expression conveyed only pity.

"You love that woman," he said. "You came back from the dead for her, and now she's tossed you over. That has to hurt."

Alasdhair was hungry, his cousins were right about that, but more than food, he needed to hit somebody, to smash something, to howl at fate, and wreak vengeance on a world that made the wrong kind of sense.

"*She changed her mind,*" Alasdhair said softly. "And if you don't shut your stupid English yap this instant, I will shut it for you."

"Schoolboy taunts," Powell said, taking a sip of his brandy. "A sure sign you have missed lunch and probably gave breakfast a pass as well. Miss Delancey has relieved you of what little sense you brought with you from the Highlands."

Alasdhair curled his hands into fists rather than slap the glass away from Powell's mouth. "And what the hell am I to do about it? Dorcas has the right to refuse my suit. A lady should always have the right to choose, to decide. It's her future, and it's her life that will be put at risk every time she's brought to childbed. She has the absolute right to send me packing, or have you now become an advocate of seizing women and carrying them off against their will, Powell?"

Even Goddard was silent in the face of that tirade.

Mrs. Lovelace, however, was not. How much she'd heard, Alasdhair did not know, but she bustled into the library, carrying a wooden tray piled high with sandwiches.

"Eat something, Major. If you are preparing to thrash your cousins to smithereens, you will need your strength. Wreaking havoc is a hungry business." She set the tray on the sideboard and eyed the three of them. "Will there be anything else?"

Powell shook his head without taking his gaze from Alasdhair. Mrs. Lovelace left, and the tension in the library was thick enough to be cleaved with Powell's cavalry sword.

"I'm sorry," Alasdhair said, sinking into a wing chair. "I know you would never condone rape."

"But," Powell said, "you are nearly so far gone with frustration that you would take a swing at me."

Alasdhair glanced around the tidy little library. "I want to tear down London. Hurl rocks through the windows of every so-called gentlemen's club, raze the churches full of their pious hypocrites, and blow up the bridges so no more young women can take their lives by leaping into the waiting arms of the demon Father Thames."

"A mob of one," Goddard said, rubbing his hip. "But you can't even toss a single insult at Powell without feeling remorse."

The trouble with Goddard was that he knew when to shut his mouth. If he'd launched into a reprimand or a sermon, Alasdhair's dignity might have borne up, but Goddard wasn't half so obliging. He took the second wing chair, sinking into the cushions on a sigh.

"You love her," Powell said. "You love her, and you can't keep her safe, and that drives you mad."

"She doesn't *want* me to keep her safe," Alasdhair replied. "That drives me mad. I am to take her at her word that she's making a choice of her own volition, but I contemplate murdering that slithering disgrace Mornebeth with more joy than I have contemplated anything save marriage to Dorcas."

Alasdhair heard the words come out of his own mouth and knew them to be hyperbole, but only just.

"Is she trying to protect you?" Powell asked, setting his brandy aside and perching on a hassock. "Women do that. They protect their menfolk and their children."

"She's protecting her father and brother," Alasdhair said. "Mornebeth can ruin them. Saint Delancey the Younger was a wild young sprig who gambled indiscriminately and got up to who knows what else. Mornebeth goaded him into it and was on hand to witness the worst of it. He will trot out his recollections at the times of his choosing."

More specific than that, Alasdhair need not be. Not even with his cousins.

Goddard made a face. "But the sprig is a proper vicar now. All he has to do is regret his youthful folly and wait out his penance. He'll acquire a patina of humility—and maybe even some honest compassion for other lost souls—and eventually he'll recover from ruin."

Powell slanted Goddard a look. "You were nearly ruined, Goddard. All it took was persistent talk from an officer or two, and the flames of slander never died down for long. Your business was on the brink of collapse, and you were considering a permanent remove to France. Imagine how much easier targeting a preacher's family would be."

"We can talk the whole business to death," Alasdhair said, "but that doesn't change Miss Delancey's choice of husband. Nothing will change her mind now that it's made up."

"You want to tear down London," Goddard said. "Instead, you ferret out Melanie Fairchild's bolt-hole. Will you confront her?"

I need more food. The thought was peculiar for being so sensible. Alasdhair ambled to the sideboard, retrieved the tray of sandwiches, and offered it to his cousins in turn. When they'd helped themselves, he took a sandwich for himself.

"I will confront her for John's sake," he said, taking a bite of ham, cheddar, mustard, and bread, "and also because Dorcas blames herself for Melanie's ruin and supposed death. At least some of that guilt is misplaced, and that is a situation about which I have freedom to act. I will make a parting gift of the truth to my former intended."

A wedding gift, damn it all to hell.

"You and your insistence on the truth," Powell said. "Maybe Melanie Fairchild has reasons for remaining hidden."

"Maybe she does, and I will respect those reasons when she explains them to me. I will also offer her any assistance I can, but Dorcas loves her cousin. With those who love us, there should be no call for dissembling."

And maybe that, too, was why Alasdhair had come to Powell's doorstep. Here, he could be hungry, angry, bewildered, and rude, and his cousins would offer him food, sympathy, and the best advice they had. Here was friendship, solace, and bodily sustenance.

No stiff upper lip, no battlefield bravado. Just a weary soldier with a broken heart.

Alasdhair demolished two more sandwiches and two cups of tea, while his cousins sorted out which former pickpockets or old soldiers could be dispatched to take the watch at Melanie's door at what hours. The logistics of confronting Melanie, and of arranging for Dorcas to meet with her, wanted some strategy, and Alasdhair was frankly too tired and heartsore to think that through clearly.

That meeting had to happen soon, though, before Dorcas became officially engaged to Mornebeth—before Alasdhair yielded to the impulse to tear down London, or at least whatever corner of Town had the dubious honor of housing Isaiah Mornebeth.

"Please thank Mrs. Lovelace for the sandwiches," Alasdhair said. "And my thanks to both of you for your assistance. I can see myself out."

"A question," Goddard said when Alasdhair would have pushed himself from the seductive embrace of the wing chair and subjected himself again to the chilly, gloomy weather.

"Ask," Alasdhair said. He'd given them Melanie's specific direction and was probably exhausted enough to actually sleep for a few hours. Of course, napping now would mean a sleepless night, but what was one more of those?

"You claim that with those who care for us, we need not dissemble," Goddard said, "so tell us about Badajoz, MacKay. No matter what you did, failed to do, or suspect you might have done, we are still your family, and we always will be. You don't have to carry the burden of memory alone, and we'd really rather you did not. We will tear down London with you rather than see you torn apart by the past."

Cornering an unsuspecting cousin when he wasn't at his best was an ambush, pure and simple, and typical of Goddard's usual lack of fanfare.

Fortunately, long habit pushed the usual platitude into words. "It was just a few bad days, lads. You know how bad."

"So," Powell said, "everybody else is held to a standard of absolute honesty, but you get to fob us off with polite fictions. It was hell, MacKay. It was utter, unimaginable, inhuman hell."

"Then you weren't holed up somewhere waiting for the riot to end?" Alasdhair asked. "I made sure Goddard was minding his orders in the infirmary, but he'd not had word of you. Nobody had."

"Clearly, I weathered the occasion in one piece. Goddard asked you a question."

Actually, he'd issued more of an invitation, and Alasdhair was just tired enough—of London, of heartache, of the past—to part with a morsel of the truth.

"I was looking for you," Alasdhair said. "We'd nearly lost Goddard to the bloody French artillery, and I was desperate to find you. I walked every street and alley, rolled over corpses without number, questioned anybody sober enough to give a coherent answer, and, Powell... I could not find you."

Goddard rose and brought the decanter and three glasses over from the sideboard. "Tell us the rest of it, MacKay. Take your time, and don't think to spare the details."

Part of Alasdhair howled in protest. *Not today, please. Not now, not this too.* To speak the words, of sorrow and rage, bewilderment and regret, would hurt unbearably. Worse yet would be to acknowledge the shame aloud. Worst of all, though, would be to turn aside from the patient concern of the only two people who might understand the horror of that day.

They would not ask again. They would not *invite* again. They would go back to respecting Alasdhair's almighty privacy and guarding his perishing dignity, as they had been for years.

As he had been for years.

Lonely job, guard duty. Hellishing lonely.

"I was desperate to find Powell," Alasdhair said. "Nigh mad with the need to know whether he still drew breath, and he was nowhere to be found. I came across Dunacre, though." Then, more softly, "He was with a woman..."

Haltingly at first, and then in more detail than he should have inflicted on anybody, Alasdhair told them the rest of it.

The silence that followed was thoughtful and sad, but not as ragged as Alasdhair had feared. He'd kept to the facts, neither wallowing in shame nor dressing up a nightmare in euphemisms. He did not feel better, precisely, for recounting that day, but some element of relief had seeped past his fatigue and frustration.

"I'm glad Dunacre is dead," Goddard said. "Spares us having to call him out."

Us. One did not issue challenges as a team, but that wasn't the point. "Your wee Annie would disapprove."

Goddard's smile was sweet. "She'd disapprove of Dunacre a lot more."

"This is why you look after the streetwalkers," Powell said. "You are atoning for Dunacre's bad behavior in Badajoz."

"I'm atoning for my own bad behavior. I did not question when I should have questioned, did not stop to think about the evidence of my own eyes when I should have stopped to think. I had a moment to tarry and intervene, but I could not be bothered."

"So you take those moments now," Goddard said. "Has it occurred to you that Miss Delancey might need you to tarry and intervene?"

"What the hell is that supposed to mean?" Though a quickening in Alasdhair's mental state suggested a wisp of an answer was already within his grasp.

"You found Melanie Fairchild," Goddard said, "because you did not ignore the evidence of your eyes. The evidence you have also suggests Mornebeth is a low-down, manipulative, self-serving wolf in vicar's clothing. What evidence might you uncover about him, if you were to look carefully?"

Was Alasdhair to lurk in the pubs as Mornebeth had? "He's likely a canny wolf. The kind who knows to avoid leaving tracks, else he'd not be frequenting Lambeth Palace."

"You've seen him in Southwark?" Powell asked.

"While keeping an eye on Melanie. Saw him twice." And wanted to kill him both times.

"Think about it," Goddard said. "Inspiration might strike if you'll leave off brooding long enough."

"I'm no' brooding."

"Pouting," Powell said. "Sulking. My sisters have worse names than that for when a man wants to be private with his thoughts."

"When he hasn't a clue how to go on," Alasdhair said. "Where the hell were you, anyway, Powell? While I was interrogating drunken sergeants and generally risking my neck trying to determine your whereabouts, what the hell were you doing?"

Powell abruptly found the flames on the hearth in need of study. "I was charging from one tavern to the next, one infirmary tent to the next, one open grave to the next, desperately looking for you. What else would I have been doing?"

"*Guerre maudite*," Goddard muttered.

Accursed war indeed. "Appears you've found me," Alasdhair said. "Took you long enough."

Powell smacked his arm, and Goddard poured another round, while Alasdhair thought about what honor required of him and what Dorcas needed of him, for they might not be precisely the same things—or were they?

CHAPTER SEVENTEEN

After days of smiling at Michael across the dining room table, smiling at him across a parlor full of guests, and smiling at him as he was whisked out the door to make yet more calls with Papa, Dorcas was out of smiles.

She felt as if she'd been hauled back in time to the weeks following her assignations with Isaiah Mornebeth, when she'd known herself to be forever changed, and had put all of her energy into making sure nobody else could detect her loss of innocence—not the loss of her virginity, but the loss of her innocence.

Smiles in every direction, great good cheer, every day's tasks conscientiously executed no matter how long the list. No need for drama, as Mama would have said. Just get on with the next committee meeting, visit to a new mother, or pleasant supper with Papa and his guests. Heartache eventually fades, shame mutes into guilt.

Though Dorcas did not think the pain of parting from Alasdhair MacKay would ever fade.

"When did you acquire the gift of silence?" Michael asked, strolling at her side.

"When did you? Once upon a time, you would tell me your every adventure and prank." They were making a circuit of the garden, though for once the walls felt confining rather than sheltering. Winter had gone on too long, and yet, Dorcas dreaded the weeks ahead.

"I am a proper vicar now," Michael replied, sounding anything but pleased with his own announcement. "I have no adventures. I pull no pranks. I am frightfully dull and likely to grow yet more boring with the passage of time. You, however, have taken up some interesting causes, sister mine."

"Papa has been complaining?" They'd reached the foot of the garden, and Dorcas did not want to turn back toward the house. "Let's avail ourselves of the churchyard."

"As long as you protect me from dear Mrs. Oldbach," Michael said. "I fear she has a goddaughter all picked out for me."

Dorcas was sick of protecting her menfolk. "Mrs. Oldbach has only the best goddaughters. You could do worse. Papa would delight to see you marry one of them."

"Mrs. Oldbach approves of your reforming adventures," Michael said as they passed through the gate into the alley. "Said Mama was of the same mind. Britain is hell-bent on conquering half the known world, but cannot bother to look after its own burgeoning poor. Charity begins at home and all that."

That Ophelia Oldbach approved of anything—other than her patent remedies and godchildren—was something of a surprise.

"I needed something *real* to do, Michael. Something that mattered more than whether St. Mildred's vestment committee sewed a new altar cloth for Yuletide."

"You are bored?" Michael asked that question as if he and boredom had grown intimately acquainted.

"Bored, yes. Very bad of me." *And I am lonely.* So lonely, and Alasdhair MacKay had made the loneliness go away. "You and Papa were given the option of examining your consciences and deciding whether you had a calling. I was simply born into a family of church*men*, without regard to where my talents might truly lie. I'm doing the best I can."

And making a complete hash of it. They crossed the street and turned down the walkway toward the church.

"Are you happy, Dorcas?"

Utterly miserable. "I have made what peace I can with a life many would envy."

"Couldn't have said it better myself." Michael stood beside her as they waited for traffic to pause. He'd been a handsome youth, and he was a striking man. Tall, dark, and serious. Too handsome to be so holy, to quote Mrs. Prebish.

The younger Michael hadn't been a sober fellow. Now, he was given to carefully modulated speech characterized by tiny pauses before he replied to a question. His polite smiles came with predictable frequency, and his manners had gone from friendly to faultless.

Was that the sum of adulthood's accomplishments? The ability to appear composed and appropriate at all times? Unbidden, the memory of a fallen Alasdhair MacKay came to mind. The sight of him curled on the carpet, overcome with hunger and exhaustion, muttering inanities...

So dear and unexpected, and so lost to her.

"St. Mildred's prospers in your care," Michael said as they reached the gate to the churchyard. St. Mildred's had two gates—one on the street side traditionally used for weddings and christenings and one on the alley side, the lych-gate proper, for funerals.

Michael ushered Dorcas into the churchyard through the wedding gate, though realizing that Dorcas's own wedding might soon take place made that little courtesy discomfiting.

"Papa loves this place," she said while Michael closed the gate behind them. "In fine weather, he comes out here to read by Mama's headstone. I wish he'd remarry."

"As do I, but he's likely waiting to see us settled before he takes that step. Let's pay our regards to Mama."

Michael led Dorcas down a walkway of crushed shells. In warmer months, the churchyard was peaceful and green, with trellised roses along the walls and borders of lavender edging the paths. On a chilly winter day, with the sun disappearing behind slow-moving clouds, the same space was dreary and forlorn.

"I miss her," Dorcas said when they'd reached the modest headstone marking Mama's resting place. A bench in her memory faced the plot where she lay, and Dorcas took a seat there. "And yet, I'm also sometimes glad she's gone. She has not had to see Papa grow old, hasn't had to watch his hopes dim as one colleague after another either retires in comfort or finds advancement."

"Good heavens, that's honest." Michael came down beside her. "But I suppose if you can write about the stench of an overcrowded jail, you can admit to some mixed feelings regarding a departed parent."

Dorcas could not tell if Michael was approving of her writings, disapproving, or simply passing the time. He was her brother, and somewhere along the way, between regular letters and infrequent visits, she'd lost sight of him.

"The financial allotments to the jails for food, blankets, chamber pots, and other necessities aren't increased just because that jail is overcrowded, Michael, and they are all *always* overcrowded. If we took note of that little discrepancy, our jails might not be such cesspits of disease and despair."

"This is where we could have a rousing debate about the necessity for sin to be punished before repentance is possible."

The bench was cold, lichens were encroaching on the pediment of Mama's headstone, and Dorcas was tired of being the perfect sister.

"Shall I quote you Scripture, Michael, about compassion being preferable to making ostentatious displays of piety in the temple? Is it not punishment enough that those women are taken from their children and families, violated by the guards, subject to violence among themselves, starved, and ill? How much more punishment would you inflict on them before you magnanimously forgive them for being so poor, desperate, and determined to survive that they will steal a spoon?"

"I'd let them all go," he said, "save for the truly violent. I'd give them passage to the New World, or the Antipodes if they'd rather, with some means, a packed trunk, and a few good books."

"Many of them cannot read."

"And without books on hand, they will never learn how. You've answered my question. You are not happy."

"I'm tired, Michael. To have you home is wonderful, but winter has been long, and I am weary." Not weary enough to understand why Melanie might have jumped from the Strand Bridge, but weary enough to accept that she'd likely had her reasons.

"I had to come south," Michael said. "Yorkshire winters are a whole series of penances. The cold, the darkness, the overcast that hangs above for weeks, the wind that can blow for days, snow up to your hips... Yorkshiremen are nigh indestructible because they have to be, but I am not made of such stern stuff."

"Then you are seeking a post in the Home Counties? Papa will be delighted." While Dorcas wanted her brother as far from London —and Isaiah—as possible.

"The Home Counties will do, I suppose. I've missed you, Dorcas, but I felt I needed to ruralize until I'd paid off the balance of my debt to Mornebeth. I've finally done that, and now I find he's lurking in Papa's parlor and making sheep's eyes at you."

A different sort of cold passed through Dorcas and settled low in her belly. "What debt to Mornebeth?"

Michael rose and withdrew a handkerchief from an inside pocket. "You know exactly what debt. Mornebeth made the rounds of the clubs and gaming hells with me, showed me around Town when I came down from university. He then kindly bought up the trail of vowels I left all over St. James's. His grandmother sees that he has ample means, and he used his funds to keep me from falling into disgrace."

"Did he?" Dorcas remained on the chilly bench, but inside, she was reeling. "And you repaid him to the penny?"

"With banker's interest, which was arguably quite decent of him. He could have charged me more than five percent."

Dorcas was aware of the bitter breeze toying with Michael's dark locks as he used the handkerchief to wipe at a streak of grime on Mama's headstone. Aware that a man and woman tarried in the shadows of the roofed lych-gate, out of the wind and standing close to each other.

She was aware as well, that she had been an even greater fool than she'd known. How was that possible? Eve dashing from the garden of Eden, cast out over a few bites of fruit and some casual disregard for the rules, could not feel any more foolish or bewildered than Dorcas did at that moment.

"Allowing you to repay debts of honor with interest was *arguably* decent of Mornebeth? What does that mean?"

Michael finished tidying up the marble, folded his handkerchief, and tucked it into a pocket. "Debts of honor are to be repaid quickly. I have taken years to make good on my vowels. Nonetheless, I can't help but wish Mornebeth hadn't been quite so willing to indulge my curiosity in the first place. A night or two on the town for the sake of my education—and humility—is understandable. When I wanted to give it up, he insisted on showing me just one more den of vice."

"And then another and another."

"I should have known better, Dorcas. I should have refused to accompany him when he dropped around yet again offering me supper at his club, as if the company of a goggle-eyed fellow just down from university was such a welcome change from that of his usual associates. He taught me a lesson I will never forget."

"What lesson is that?" Dorcas spoke calmly, though her heart had taken to thumping against her ribs as if the moment had portents beyond the obvious. She'd been stupid, stupid, stupid, and Alasdhair MacKay had been right, right, *right*.

"Don't be so desperate for another's approval that I compromise my honor to win it," Michael said, gaze on the steeple of St. Mildred's. "A man with compromised honor deserves nobody's approval."

"Michael, a man who will lead you into temptation over and over while professing to be your friend deserves your *dis*approval, if not your scorn."

Michael was silent for a time, while Dorcas focused simply on drawing and releasing her breath. She'd surrendered her virtue to Mornebeth three times over, and for *nothing*. Michael's debts had not been forgiven, and now—years later—Mornebeth was exacting interest at far more than five percent as the price of his continued silence.

Dorcas had supposedly paid for that silence in full years ago. But this was exactly how extortion worked—the debt was never paid, the debtor never free.

"And yet," Michael said, resuming his place on the bench, "Mornebeth tells me he hopes to court you and take you to wife. For five years, my objective has been to send him every spare groat until I could look him in the eye again, free of indebtedness. I did that, and now I find him sniffing about your skirts."

Sniffing about her skirts, watching her with a knowing smile from across the parlor, littering his conversations with the clumsy innuendo of a man maneuvering to be perceived as a hopeful suitor.

"I am quite nearly on the shelf," Dorcas said as a raven landed on the headstone. "I should be flattered to have earned Mr. Mornebeth's notice." She had the odd thought that it was the same raven she'd seen with Alasdhair in the back garden of the vicarage. The bird treated her to an unnerving stare, then flew off to perch on the church roof.

"You don't care for Mornebeth in the slightest, Dorcas. I have been gone for five years, but I am still your brother. You are polite to Mornebeth, nothing more than that."

"I am polite to everybody, as you are."

"Mama insisted on manners from me, and if a vicar has one trait, it's mannerliness."

Dorcas's feet were cold, and her heart... Her heart was frozen and breaking and shattered. "Do you know what Mama insisted on from me?"

"Damned near perfection?"

Michael used to swear far more colorfully than that. "As she lay dying, she exhorted me to look after you and Papa. She said to guard your happiness as if it were my greatest treasure. Told me that if I loved her at all, I would honor her memory by dedicating myself to your wellbeing and Papa's."

Michael cocked his head, much as the raven had. "You were fourteen, and she was half delirious with fever. Mama had no right to ask that of you."

"That is *all* she asked of me. All she ever asked of me."

"She was still wrong, Dorcas. She should have been lecturing Papa on the need to spend as much time with his children as he did with his sermons, and warning me not to be such an arrogant dunce. I'm taking a chill." He rose and offered her his hand. "Let's get back to the vicarage and cajole Mrs. Benton into making us some hot chocolate. I learned to love hot chocolate up north."

"No hot chocolate for me," Dorcas said, taking his hand. "Tea will do."

"Mama was wrong," Michael said, leading Dorcas through the wedding gate, "Mornebeth is an ass, and I am done with Yorkshire winters. Are you ready for tomorrow's fellowship meal?"

Dorcas did not give a hearty *Glory Be* for the fellowship meal. She'd known Isaiah was a snake. Michael's revelations only confirmed that knowledge with bitter certainty. She could also accept that she'd given Mama's dying wishes too much weight for too long.

What she did not know was how to find a way forward that freed her and her family from more years of indentured servitude to Isaiah Mornebeth's vile brand of piety.

ALASDHAIR LEFT Powell's house feeling the heavy-limbed weariness of a soldier who'd survived a battle. For some, that was a joyous, celebratory moment. For Alasdhair, an end to battle had brought relief and gratitude and the tearing need to assure himself his cousins yet drew breath.

Then began the aftermath, the hastily dug graves, the visits to the wounded and dying in the infirmary, the letters a commanding officer owed a fallen soldier's family.

Powell and Goddard had clearly been carrying their own memories of the war, though Powell had made a sort of peace with Badajoz. Treat men as if they're expendable for long enough, subject them to enough brutality and abuse, and they become abusive brutes.

For Powell, the barbarity had been a predictable result of Dunacre's brand of leadership, though in no way excusable.

Alasdhair had no stomach for debating a philosophy of war, and yet, he'd been reassured, too, to know that his cousins were as haunted as he was. They had understood the origins of his preoccupation with safeguarding the women on London's streets. Maybe Alasdhair understood it a little better himself for having explained his experiences to Powell and Goddard.

Alasdhair was walking past the tea shop—too many ghosts in that quiet back corner to tempt him inside—when he noticed a woman standing by the tea shop door. She held a bundle tied together at the corners, laundry perhaps.

Not Dorcas. He looked for her everywhere and saw her nowhere, save in his dreams.

Of course, not Dorcas. "Aurora, good day." She wore a decent cloak and had buttoned it up to her chin.

"MacKay. D'ye have a moment?"

No. No, he did not. Alasdhair was out of moments. He needed to go somewhere quiet and think—or weep—or think and weep and drink. He needed sleep. He needed Dorcas, and he could not have her. Worse yet, Mornebeth would yoke himself to her for life, and Dorcas intended to allow that.

"Of course I have a moment. I like the cloak."

"Pawned your gloves. Got a good price for 'em." She dipped her head in an uncharacteristically bashful gesture. "I got a letter, MacKay, from Katie. She sent it to the Drunken Goose, and I haven't been there much."

"You haven't been able to afford their prices." The Goose had a strict policy against loitering, as well as rooms to rent by the hour.

"Mother Goose kept the letter for me. Katie and her Duncan got married before Christmas. Duncan has the chandler's shop now. Has it from his pa, who died of the influenza at Michaelmas. The old man thought he was going to live forever, and he forbade Duncan to marry. Nobody lives forever." She was fiercely pleased to point that out.

"I hope this Duncan is a good sort."

"Katie says he waited for her. He knew the Old Smoke wouldn't hold her for long. She's happy, MacKay. She's happy, and she wants me to come work in the shop with her and Duncan. I can live with them, so I won't have to go back to my pa's house."

Well, thank God for village lads with true hearts and a chandler's skills. "You need coach fare home."

Her chin came up. "I'll pay you back. Katie will too. I mean it."

"You will not," Alasdhair said. "You will come across some other girl whose father has a bad temper, and you will explain to her what really happens to young women abroad in London without means. You will show her the chandler's trade, or help her learn her letters. You will share your good fortune with her as Katie is sharing hers with you."

Alasdhair gave them all the same lecture. That Katie might have heeded him was a small comfort.

"Katie said I was to ask you for coach fare. I don't want to. I don't want to be in any man's debt."

God spare me from female pride. And yet, Aurora had been surviving on the strength of pride alone for months.

"Then pay off the debt by helping another, Aurora. You are clever, determined, tough, and you've learned much here in London. Spare another girl those lessons if you can, and we'll call it even."

She peered at him, the breeze catching the ginger curls framing her pretty face. "The Scots are different. Is this how you do it in Scotland? You hand around a debt until everybody's doing better?"

"Sometimes we hand around a whisky bottle, which does less damage the more widely it's shared. Come along, and Henderson can see to the ticket and some coin for your journey."

He took her bundle, likely everything she owned in the world, and set a slower pace as they started off for home. The afternoon was trying to be sunny, though it was by no means warm. They waited at the corner as a red-wheeled curricle tooled past, matched grays in the traces.

"Somebody's off to drive in the park," Alasdhair muttered. He'd seen that vehicle before, the same natty toff at the ribbons, no tiger behind. He'd been with Dorcas at the time, anticipating an introduction to her father after a delightful stop at the tea shop.

"That's Mornebeth," Aurora said, her tone suggesting the name carried a sulfurous odor. "Whores ain't supposed to tattle, but I'm done bein' a whore. That man likes to pinch and spank—and not in a fun way. Katie called him the pinchin' preacher."

The vehicle bowled around the corner, traveling in the direction of St. Mildred's. "*Isaiah* Mornebeth?"

"If God is merciful, which He sometimes is, there's only the one Mornebeth. Showed up before the holidays and has made a regular pestilence of himself since. Big Nan can handle him, but none of the other girls will go with him anywhere. Has a mean streak. He don't go to the spanking houses because they cost a pretty penny and because they have rules."

A peculiar sensation prickled over Alasdhair's arms and nape.

"You have seen *Isaiah Mornebeth* in Covent Garden doing business with Big Nan?"

"Every Monday, unless it's snowing. She charges him double. Takes him to the Goose because Mother Goose watches the time to the minute, and Papa Goose is better'n fifteen stone in his bare feet."

Dismay was too tame a word for the emotion recoiling through Alasdhair. Dorcas sought to marry herself to *such as that*? Many a man enjoyed recreational sex—many a woman too—but ordained ministers were usually more discreet than to do business with streetwalkers.

But then, Mornebeth couldn't exactly keep a mistress under his bishop's nose, nor would he want to be seen coming and going from a brothel.

"That pinching preacher seeks to marry Miss Dorcas Delancey," Alasdhair murmured. "You will excuse me, Aurora. I need to make straight for the vicarage at St. Mildred's and cast out a demon."

"Dorcas Delancey? Miss Delightful? The pinchin' preacher thinks to marry *Miss Delightful*?"

"He has all but proposed. Why?"

Aurora's mouth thinned, and she drew her cloak up around her neck. "She's a good 'un, MacKay. Big Nan was sick with the flu in the stone jug. Miss Delightful came by with blankets, food, and enough coin to keep the guards on their best behavior for a whole week, not that their best behavior would impress anybody. She brought tea and brandy. She looks after us, same as you do, in her way."

"She looks after everybody."

Aurora peered up at him. "Who looks after her?"

The prickling sensation came again. "*I will.*" Though Alasdhair wasn't entirely sure how when the lady herself was determined to deny him that privilege. "Where can I find Nan?"

"The Goose, usually. MacKay, you can't go killin' a man because he's earned the disgust of a few whores."

"Actually, I can, but I won't." *I hope.*

"MacKay, listen to me," Aurora said, taking his arm. "Katie and I ended up in London because Pa got carried away one too many times. We didn't think. We just bundled up our clothes, put on our best boots, and started walking. You can't march into a vicarage like the wrath of God. If Mornebeth is there, he'll have you tossed out on your ear, if not arrested. He's sly and low-down, and I need my coach fare before you go off half-cocked."

Everything in Alasdhair, every hope and prayer, every conviction and every shred of honor, wanted to storm the vicarage and oust Mornebeth from the post of hopeful suitor. Alasdhair was desperate to achieve that goal, just as he'd been desperate to find Powell all those years ago.

And yet...

Mornebeth could not marry Dorcas without making arrangements, and he'd had no time to do that. Dorcas would insist on the proprieties, as would—Alasdhair hoped—her father and brother.

More significantly, Dorcas was contemplating marriage to Mornebeth precisely because she feared her family's ruin. A half-crazed Scot tossing around sordid accusations without proof would not do.

"Come along," Alasdhair said, offering his arm. "You will have your coach fare, and Mornebeth will face a day of judgment."

Whether Alasdhair ended up with Dorcas was, and always would be, entirely up to her.

~

DORCAS LOOKED FORWARD to the fellowship meal about as eagerly as she would have anticipated a fortnight on bread and water. She nonetheless wanted the church hall to be in good trim for the event and thus made her way to St. Mildred's in the early afternoon.

The parish would gather at sunset, and Dorcas would spend her evening smiling and nodding, admiring other people's babies, and ignoring Isaiah Mornebeth's sly grins. She made sure the flowers had water, made sure at least four buckets of coal sat before both of the hall's hearths. She laid out tablecloths and had begun counting the cutlery when a sound distracted her.

"Mrs. Oldbach, is that you?" Mrs. O, regardless of her other faults, was a willing worker.

A woman in widow's weeds emerged from the corridor into the hall, Alasdhair MacKay at her side. The lady was heavily veiled and her cloak plain.

Dorcas registered those details in an instant, while the rest of her focus remained on Alasdhair. He looked tired, slightly weathered, and so very serious—and dear. The temptation to run to him, to hold him tightly despite the presence of the veiled woman, had Dorcas setting spoon number seventeen carefully in its tray.

"Mr. MacKay. Ma'am. Good day."

"Miss Delancey." He bowed. "Are you expecting anybody to join you?"

That he'd remain across the room, his tone frigidly civil, was both a boon—if he came nearer, Dorcas's dignity might collapse altogether—and a blow.

"I am not. The gathering will not start for hours. Won't you introduce me to your companion, Mr. MacKay?"

"No need for that," he said, the words aimed at the woman beside him. "I will leave you two ladies to speak privately, but I won't go far. I have a few words for you as well, Miss Delancey, though they can wait."

He was angry. Of course he was angry, and Dorcas felt bad about that, but she also felt exasperated. She was beyond furious, and her anger had never made any difference to anybody. Not her anger about the wretched state of women's jails, not about the utterly irresponsible use of government funds, and not about Isaiah Mornebeth.

"I will listen, Mr. MacKay." And then she would send him on his way, again, and mentally don the emotional armor necessary to get through the evening, the week, the month, and her stupid, saintly life.

Alasdhair bowed and stalked off, his military bearing very much in evidence.

"Ma'am," Dorcas said, gesturing to a pair of chairs along the wall. "Shall we sit?"

A vicar's daughter grew accustomed to odd callers with odd problems, but Dorcas could not think of any recent bereavements among St. Mildred's congregants. The widow took one of the proffered seats and pinned back her veil.

Melanie Fairchild sat quite tall on the hard chair. "It's me, Dorie. I'm alive, and MacKay would not allow me to keep you in ignorance. He can be very persuasive, and he's usually right, but I did not know what else to do. I'm sorry. Please say something."

Dorcas sank onto the seat beside her cousin, felled by sheer joy. "I had hoped… I had prayed… I had wondered… You are alive." She seized Melanie in a hug. "I am so glad, Melanie. So very, very glad."

Melanie hugged her back, desperately close. "MacKay said you would be. He said you deserve to know the truth."

"He's a great one for insisting on the truth. I must commend him for that in this case. You look well." Dorcas used the nearest table napkin to dab at her tears and passed another to Melanie.

"I look ghastly in weeds, but that was MacKay's idea too. He's been watching for a chance to find you alone, and I told him you always spend the afternoon before a fellowship meal here at the church."

"I do, but Mrs. Oldbach might come by at any moment, so please explain why you felt it necessary to… do as you did. And, Melanie, I will help you. If you want to move to Ireland, or you need references as a housekeeper, or you—"

Melanie held up a hand. "I'm not fit to be a housekeeper, Dorie. You know that. I'm a pretty bit of fluff who can sew a straight seam and make endless small talk. I've heard from Beauclerk."

Captain Amery Beauclerk had inveigled Melanie into running off with him. "What could *he* possibly want?"

"Me," Melanie said. "He wants me, for his wife. He tried to transfer out of his unit so he wouldn't have to go to Canada. His commanding officers would not allow him to marry, and thus we were at an impasse. He went away to Canada, promising me he'd come back to me or send for me."

"What else could he have said, Melanie? That man ruined you, cost you your family, your good name, your security in life, and that he has the gall to—"

Melanie was smiling and not the darling smile of the bit of fluff she'd called herself. She smiled with the patient wisdom of a woman grown.

"You are so fierce, Dorie, but you must not slander my intended."

"Your *intended*? Melanie, no. Bad enough that I must marry the likes of Isaiah Mornebeth, but for you to trust the word of a man who expects you to leave everything dear and familiar, twice... What about John?"

What about me? Dorcas had missed Melanie sorely. Missed her good humor, missed her mischief. Missed a connection with somebody who had known her before Mornebeth had wrought his damage and before Mama had died.

"It's complicated, Dorie," Melanie said. "Beauclerk and I love each other, and in a simple world, that would be enough. In a world where commanding officers want to make examples of lovestruck subordinates, and where women and babies need to eat..."

"Explain the complications to me, Melanie. Please."

Melanie rose and began a perambulation about the hall. "You were always so good at dealing with the practicalities. I just wanted to be happy, to make everybody happy. I know that's not possible, but Beauclerk... he understands me. He likes me. He says I'm sunshine and laughter and the warmth in his heart."

Oh, Melanie. "He says these things from Canada?"

Melanie shook her head and pushed back the cover from the keys of the piano in the corner. "He has written to me faithfully, but then last year, his letters stopped coming. I despaired, Dorcas. Every warning you ever gave me, every sermon and lecture, came back to me. If MacKay hadn't come across me... but he did. He said I must let my family know I was alive, because family worries about us."

"I did worry. Melanie, I did nothing but worry. I could have stopped you. I could have told Papa or Uncle or somebody and stopped you from running off with Beauclerk. If you were driven to desperate measures, that is my fault. If your reputation is in tatters, that is my fault too."

Melanie ran the nail of her third finger over the keys in an ascending glissando somewhat out of tune. "MacKay said you blamed yourself. I had no intention of giving in to his lectures until he told me that. You are being a gudgeon, Dorcas, and if it's one thing you are not, it's a gudgeon. If I had it all to do over, I would do exactly the same as I did."

"You cannot mean that."

Melanie left the keys uncovered and moved on to the lectern from which Papa would offer a combination welcome grace and Speech from the Throne. His aim would be to bolster flagging spirits as well as flagging contributions to the poor box.

"I love Beauclerk, Dorcas. He loves me. I have known passion, joy, hope, dreams... I found strengths I never knew I had. I escaped from a life that was killing me one proverb and psalm at a time. I have a beautiful son, all because I was—in the eyes of my family—foolish. They attend divine services without fail, but know nothing of what's truly divine about life."

Melanie made an oddly imposing figure behind Papa's lectern. Her false weeds gave her an air of sternness, and her inherent flair for drama added weight to her words.

"But you are *ruined*," Dorcas said, having lost her command of euphemisms. "You are turning your back on that beautiful baby boy. You are trusting the word of a bounder and a cad." And this time, Dorcas could not stop her cousin.

"Beauclerk is neither, Dorie. When his letters ceased, I assumed the worst as well, but he had taken ship for London. The passage was rough, the ship had to put in for repairs in Scotland, and I did not get word that he was making the journey until after he was already in

Britain. By then, I had conceived John, and my life had become quite a muddle."

"I am confused," Dorcas said. "Beauclerk is not John's father?"

"He is not."

Good gracious, and *poor Melanie.* "But Beauclerk... How did he expect you to survive without his pay packets or your family's support?"

"Pay packets go missing in the mail, Dorcas. I was not his wife, so he could not assign me a portion of his pay. I lack much aptitude for profitable sin, as it turns out, but neither could I tell Beauclerk that I'd played him false."

"You did what you had to do to survive," Dorcas said. "I've met entire jails full of women who did much worse than sell their favors for a crust of bread, Mellie."

"But those women are not your cousins."

Maybe not in any legal sense, but the longer Dorcas contemplated marriage to Isaiah Mornebeth, the more she understood their desperate determination.

"You could not tell Beauclerk that you carried another man's child."

"And I could not marry him. He begged me, Dorcas. He pleaded, and when I refused him, he returned to Canada a very hurt and bewildered man. I did the honorable thing by sending him away, and I have never regretted a decision more."

"This is why you've abandoned John? So you can hare off to Canada and be with Beauclerk?"

The question should have been an accusation, but Dorcas could not make it one. She understood the temptation to retreat, to be selfish, to reason away hard truths.

"I'm not haring anywhere, Dorie. I was barely managing. I had to save up to buy paper to write to you, and I was sliding toward debtors' prison anyway. Had John taken sick, had I slipped on the ice and hurt my hands too badly to sew, we'd have been in the poorhouse and from thence to Marshalsea, where my boy would have died before his first birthday. Because I am a fallen woman, I have the legal authority to make provisions for John that a married woman would not. John will thrive in MacKay's care. You know that. John is better off without me."

"Melanie, don't do this. *I* am not better off without you." And that was probably the most selfish and honest thing Dorcas had ever said.

Melanie pushed away from the lectern and took a sniff of the daffodils in the center of the table at the front of the room. "Too late for that, Dorie. I have done it. I will write to you, but if you marry Mornebeth, you will never get my letters."

"Of course I will." Though even as the words left Dorcas's lips, she knew them for a hope rather than a truth.

"You hate that man, Dorie. You would never use those words, but you hold him responsible for leading Michael astray, and I do too. Michael was a lamb to be shorn, and Mornebeth always keeps his clippers sharp. As foolish as you might think me for eloping with Beauclerk, you are *demented* to contemplate marrying Mornebeth."

Increasingly, Dorcas felt demented. "MacKay told you about that?"

"His silences speak volumes. MacKay has offered you his heart, and you turned him aside—for Mornebeth? I can only think Mornebeth has evidence that you've been disporting with a married man or stealing from the poor box."

Dorcas remained silent, though Melanie of all people would not judge her.

"Has Uncle Thomas stolen from the poor box?" Melanie asked, returning to her seat. "I cannot credit that, but I've learned that we all have a price. I never thought I would share my favors for coin, but a body must eat."

"Do you know who John's father is?"

"John Mason, a squire's son visiting an uncle in London. The family hails from outside Aldermaston, their estate is Toftrees, of which Mr. Mason was quite loquaciously proud. I did not inform Mr.

Mason that he has a son. Our arrangement was temporary. Thank God he was a generous and lusty fellow, though overly fond of drink."

Such words in the church hall ought to seem sacrilegious. Dorcas could only marvel at Melanie's pragmatism.

"You look horrified," Melanie went on, while she was clearly amused. "Imagine what life with Mornebeth will be like once the children come along. You can do without reading my letters, Dorie, but what about when Mornebeth decides to send your toddling son off to old Lady Phoebe to be raised? What about when he decides your young daughters should be shipped away to one of those dreary schools where all they teach is Scripture and birchings?"

"Melanie, hush. Mornebeth can ruin my family and ruin me."

Melanie patted Dorcas's arm. "Take it from me, Dorie, ruin has its advantages. I am free to make a good plan for my son. I am free to join a man who loves me in Canada. I am free to slip away from all the judgment and censure polite society turns on such as me. Ruin is vastly preferable to a slow death from excesses of pious hypocrisy."

"My situation isn't that simple, Melanie. I made mistakes—with Mornebeth—and he will use that to his advantage."

"Were you of age?"

"I was seventeen." By law, a girl could consent to intimacies at age twelve, even if she did not entirely grasp what those intimacies entailed, or that conception could result from them. Isaiah was doubtless well versed in those legal niceties.

Melanie wrinkled her nose. "And you think at that age you should have somehow found a way around a man who has been cozening bishops since he went off to university. Mornebeth was a philandering disgrace, Dorcas, and if you do not see him held accountable now, then your children and grandchildren will pay for your decisions, to say nothing of the toll he'll take on you."

Melanie rose and went to the table beside the hearth where dozens of Mrs. Oldbach's hot cross buns were sitting in baskets and swaddled with linen. "MacKay would deal with Mornebeth for you, if you'd let him."

"Isaiah is not Alasdhair's problem." What should have been an assertion of fact felt like a tired and stupid excuse. Strictly speaking, Isaiah had been Michael's problem, and Dorcas had allowed him to become hers as well.

"If you are carrying MacKay's child, and that child ends up as Mornebeth's legal issue, I daresay you will long for widowhood." Melanie helped herself to a sweet bun. "I have missed these. A bit early in the year for them, but they are such a treat."

Oh drat. Oh flaming perdition and hideous hellhounds. "I cannot be carrying Alasdhair MacKay's..."

Melanie passed her a bun. "Keep telling yourself that. The whole world changes when you contemplate motherhood, Dorcas. Life is at once more wonderful and more terrifying. I could never regret John, but I will regret to my dying day leaving him, even leaving him with such a one as MacKay."

Melanie munched her treat in silence, while Dorcas held hers and knew the bitter taste of desolation. "I have been so preoccupied with what Mornebeth could do to Papa and Michael that I did not think of any children."

"You did not think of *yourself* either, Dorie. Get over that. Think of yourself, and if you cannot think of yourself, think of MacKay. Come with me to Canada, and do not allow Isaiah Mornebeth to make you his victim all over again. His bullying and abuse need to end somewhere."

Dorcas took a bite of her bun. "But he's so good at it, so sly and convincing. I am not sly, and nobody will believe me if I told them the truth after all this time."

"I believe you. MacKay believes you. Michael would believe you. More women than you think would believe you."

Every woman Dorcas had met in jail would believe her. Mrs. Oldbach would likely believe her, too, though she'd still be sniffy and prim. Dorcas considered who would believe her and considered

Michael's revelations about having paid Mornebeth back with interest. She considered Melanie's warnings about how vulnerable children could make their mother, and she considered, too, that she loved Alasdhair MacKay.

And always would.

"I take ship next week," Melanie said. "I have the money, thanks to you, MacKay, and my own tragic death. Beauclerk wants to settle in Canada. He says it's beautiful and full of opportunity. I know John will be safe and well cared for, but I will worry about you, Dorcas."

Don't go. Don't leave me. Don't slip away without looking back. "What of John? Is he to be told that you're dead?"

"As if MacKay would countenance that sort of deception on an innocent child. I went to join my officer in the New World, a dangerous place, and though it broke my heart to leave John behind, I entrusted him to the best possible guardian and hope one day to send for him."

"Do you? Hope to send for him?"

Melanie's smile was sad. "It's possible. Beauclerk and I have much to resolve, but we have weathered much already."

"What do I tell our family?"

Melanie dusted her hands and brushed crumbs from her bodice. "Why tell them anything? I am not your problem to solve, just as I cannot push Mornebeth off the Strand Bridge for you, though I'd like to." She hugged Dorcas, a good, fierce embrace. "My money's on you, Dorie, just as you put your money on me when I ran off with Beauclerk and when John came along. MacKay's ready, willing, and able to help, and if I can trust him with my son, you can trust him with some overdue housecleaning. Be happy. For God's sake, let yourself be happy."

She rustled away, calling for MacKay. Dorcas sat, holding half a hot cross bun and trying to wrap her mind around the notion that she had been going about her dealings with Isaiah Mornebeth all wrong.

CHAPTER EIGHTEEN

Alasdhair had paced, and he had not eavesdropped. He'd heard no shouting, no wailing, no loud recriminations, and when Melanie summoned him, he found Dorcas sitting on a straight-backed chair, nibbling on a bun.

"I'll wait for you at the lych-gate," Melanie said. "Try the hot cross buns. They are wonderful." She gave him a shove, and Alasdhair found himself three yards and a world of heartache away from the woman he loved.

Dorcas set aside her bun, rose, and closed the distance between them. "You found her." She wrapped her arms around him. "You found her, she's alive, and she's going to be h-happy."

Alasdhair was helpless not to return Dorcas's embrace. To have her in his arms again was both a torment and the answer to endless prayers.

"I suspect she wanted to be found. She was hoping to catch Timmens on the way to the pub, or to slip a note to Henderson. I gave her a means of listening to her better angels."

"Thank you," Dorcas said. "Thank you from the bottom of my

heart. Thank you for being decent and kind and generous, and I am so glad to see you, I could... I *am* weeping. I hate to cry."

"You have much to cry about."

She gave him one more hearty squeeze, then stepped back. "You were right, Alasdhair. You were right about everything. Mornebeth never forgave Michael's debts. I asked Michael for a few particulars when I'd had a chance to think about it. Isaiah made him sign a promissory note and pay interest. For years, Michael has been scrimping to pay off that debt, and he's free of it now, while I..."

She turned away and crossed the room to close the lid over the piano keys.

"Have you accepted Mornebeth's suit, Dorcas?"

"I have not. He'll wait until Michael has left before he springs that trap. I do not want to marry him, Alasdhair, but I don't see any other way of limiting the threat he poses."

Alasdhair joined her near the piano, though he did not dare touch her again. "Do you trust me?"

"Yes, absolutely, but I do not trust Mornebeth to be anything other than devious, self-serving, and vicious. I don't understand him, Alasdhair. He has been given so much, and yet, he must have more and more. More influence, more authority, more means. He's Lady Phoebe's heir, but even that isn't enough for him."

"What do you suppose he fears most of all?"

Dorcas sat on the piano bench, her expression puzzled. To Alasdhair, the answer was obvious. A thorough public shaming was Mornebeth's worst fear, and the absolute least that justice demanded in his case.

"One hesitates to admit having anything in common with Isaiah Mornebeth," Dorcas said, "but I suspect he fears the same thing I do, the same thing every woman I met in those vile jails fears. Utter powerlessness. Women are dependent on the benevolent offices of men, which is probably why my mother admonished me to be so devoted to Papa's and Michael's happiness."

"*Powerlessness*? Mornebeth is all but attached to the archbishop, who ranks above the entire peerage in precedence. The Mornebeth family has means, and his granny is still quite the force to be reckoned with socially." And yet, Dorcas's assessment had the ring of insight, of truth.

"Isaiah seeks power, Alasdhair. Why do that unless he fears what a life of powerlessness holds for him? His father died too young, much as my mother did. His choice of vocation was all but thrust upon him by his grandmother, while I am consigned to the role of daughter of the vicarage. His grandmother expects him to dance attendance on her, and he relies on her influence, which is considerable. He's another version of the vicarage spinster."

Dorcas fell silent, her gaze fixed on a table of baked goods, though Alasdhair doubt she saw anything of the immediate surrounds.

"I am truly powerless," Dorcas murmured. "I hate that, but that's precisely why Isaiah set his sights on me. I cannot fight back. I have no money, no authority, no influential friends. I am not in jail, but I am not free either. I have spent my life trying to be so good, so proper, and exemplary, hoping that virtue alone would keep me safe from the world's evil, but it doesn't work like that. Melanie was right."

Melanie was a hoyden, at best. "You are not powerless, Dorcas. Far from it."

She peered up at him. "I write my articles. They change nothing. I run this parish, and it might as well be the Sunday pub for all the good we do as a congregation. I look after my father, and he spends hours retranslating Scripture when he ought to be calling on Mrs. Oldbach."

Dorcas was no longer crying, but Alasdhair knew the bitter detachment of heartbreak when he heard it. He sat beside her on the bench and took her hand.

"I ran into Aurora Feeney again."

"The woman to whom you gave your gloves?"

"Aye, and she pawned them, exactly as you predicted. She came upon me in a bad moment, Dorcas. I have missed you sorely, I want to kill Mornebeth, I did not know what was afoot with Melanie, and I am sick to death of the cold and misery of a London winter. I saw Aurora, and I thought, 'I cannot do this anymore. She'll die of the pox, if the gin or the cold doesn't get her first. What the hell am I doing?'"

"You are being kind," Dorcas said. "You are being honorable."

"In that moment, it felt like I was being a fool, pounding my head against a wall of misery so high, wide, and thick that no crack would ever form in that bleak façade. Then Aurora had a wee talk with me."

"What did she say?"

"She said you are not powerless, Dorcas. Neither am I. You are very powerful, and Mornebeth won't know what hits him when your version of the celestial thunderbolt knocks him onto his arse."

Alasdhair wanted to kiss Dorcas. He desired her—he would always desire her—but desire wasn't driving him as he held her hand and searched for the right words. He wanted closeness and accord with her, a shared future, shared dreams. He wanted to kiss the hope back into her, the confidence and courage, as she'd brought those gifts to him.

"Alasdhair, I haven't any thunderbolts."

"Oh, but you do." He did kiss her, gently at first, because he had missed her so and because he still feared to lose her, but Dorcas was apparently not in the mood for gentleness. She got hold of him by the hair and came a-viking into the kiss, until Alasdhair was ready to wrestle her into his lap.

"You've missed me," he said, more than a little pleased.

"Sorely. Desperately, but what does that change?"

He kept his arm around her, lest she go marching off to count the silver. "Everything. Do you know why we sent the Corsican packing?"

"Because twenty years of mutual slaughter were enough?"

"Because he spread his forces too thin, my darling dear. He lost half a million men on that horrific dash to Moscow, and that didn't leave much for the war in Spain. On the Peninsula, Wellington's army was better provisioned, better led, and better trained. A single soldier could not have lasted a moment against the French, but an army got the job done."

"I have no army."

"Neither does Mornebeth, but you have me, and that means you also have—"

"Miss Delancey!" The voice was elderly, female, and imperious. "Miss Delancey, are you here?"

"That is Mrs. Oldbach." Dorcas could not have sounded less pleased. "Away with you, Alasdhair. We will speak more later."

"Don't accept his proposal, Dorcas. Isaiah Mornebeth will try to ambush you, but you must stand fast. Reinforcements are at hand."

He kissed her cheek and withdrew through the door that led directly to the churchyard, while Dorcas remained in the hall, looking disgruntled and weary.

And also as if somebody had just kissed the stuffing out of her.

MRS. OLDBACH, while discoursing confidently on everything from the best polish for everyday silver to the current fashion for shorter hair, had soon put the church hall to rights, which was fortunate.

Dorcas was reeling both with the fact of Melanie's survival and with Alasdhair's parting warning: *Isaiah Mornebeth will try to ambush you, but you must stand fast. Reinforcements are at hand.*

Mornebeth *had* ambushed her, both years ago and with his marital aspirations. He joined the convivial crowd milling about in the church hall, and Dorcas was almost relieved. When Mornebeth was in plain sight, bowing over the hands of the eligible young ladies, she knew where he was. She knew what he was about.

"Did you invite him?" Michael asked, passing Dorcas a glass of punch.

"Certainly not. Perhaps Papa did, but we cannot toss him out on his ear, can we?"

Michael took a sip of his punch. "Mama's recipe?"

"With a few variations. Have you retrieved your promissory note from Mornebeth?"

Michael peered at her over his glass. "That is an odd topic to bring up in this crush, Dorcas."

Dorcas had odder topics than that to discuss with Michael, such as the depths to which she'd stooped in hopes of appeasing Mornebeth. "Please answer the question."

"I called upon him at the Ingleby residence," Michael said. "He danced and dithered and pled forgetfulness and moving quarters and so forth. In the midst of this performance, old Zachariah Ingleby happened into the parlor, supposedly looking for his spectacles. Ingleby noted that Isaiah's worldly goods were all tidily packed and awaiting his remove to Southwark, and any necessary papers ought to be easily retrieved with a few moments' effort. I had my promissory note not five minutes later. I had to remind Mornebeth to initial it 'paid in full.'"

"Mr. Ingleby is friends with Lady Phoebe, if I recall correctly."

"He's like Papa. He gets along with everybody, especially with the old guard. I do believe it's time I reminded Mrs. Oldbach how fond I am of her baking."

"No snitching, and, Michael..."

"Dorcas?"

"I love you, and I respect you, and if I never thanked you for being such a dear older brother, I'm thanking you now."

He studied her, his gaze both puzzled and concerned. "Are you well?"

Isaiah lifted his glass of punch in her direction and kept his gaze upon her while he sipped. That display of besotted devotion felt like a warning slap.

"No, Michael, I am not well. I am so weary I could drop. If Mornebeth doesn't stop making sheep's eyes at me... Oh no. The Prebish twins are threatening to play a duet. Excuse me."

Dorcas hastened to the piano, where two seven-year-olds were trying to push each other off the bench by virtue of excessively undignified wiggling.

"Ladies," Dorcas said, "did I hear that a game of tag is starting up out in the churchyard? Food always tastes better when we've worked up an appetite, don't you agree?"

"Is Charlie Bothey playing?" Beatrice Prebish asked, scrambling off the bench. "He's very fast, but Beulah and I are faster."

"Fetch your coats, and you can go see for yourselves. Let your parents know where you've got off to."

One disaster averted. Dorcas noted Mrs. Matilda Merridew sitting alone, half hidden by the lectern. That would not do, and Michael and Papa were remiss for neglecting her. She was a young widow just out of first mourning, and such a large, loud gathering had to be overwhelming for her.

"You can't spare a greeting for your intended?" Isaiah Mornebeth stepped in front of Dorcas as she crossed the hall. His smile was doting, while his eyes held a challenge.

"You are not my intended." Dorcas kept her voice down and even managed a smile of her own.

"Oh, but I am." He took her hand and not only bowed over it, but pressed his lips to her knuckles.

"Your behavior is unseemly," Dorcas hissed, though she knew better than to try to snatch her hand away. Isaiah would either make his grasp hurt, or create a fuss as she tried to free herself.

How did he always, always manage to put her in situations where she had no good options? No safe choices?

"My behavior is devoted, Dorcas, even besotted."

"You lied to me. You never forgave Michael's debts."

Isaiah's smile became doting. "And I never will. He seems to think a bit of paper with my initials on it will somehow safeguard him from further repercussions. He is *much* mistaken."

Isaiah had no honor, and worse yet, he exploited the honor of his victims. Alasdhair and Melanie had seen that easily. Michael had paid in full, with interest on debts Isaiah had goaded him to incur.

Dorcas had tolerated Mornebeth's advances all three times. What havoc would he wreak on Papa, on Michael, and on Dorcas herself if she again capitulated to his bullying?

Alasdhair would not care that I am ruined. Melanie would not care. None of the women scrapping for their lives on the streets or in jail would care. They'd commiserate with Dorcas and show her again how to drop a man with her knee.

She called upon their generous tutelage, using her left hand to grip Isaiah's smallest finger and bend it back until he released his grasp.

"You, Isaiah, are the one who's much mistaken. Ruin me if you must, ruin Papa and Michael, and spread a few vile rumors about Mrs. Benton while you're at it, but I will not marry you." She did him the very great courtesy of keeping her voice down.

"You will regret this," he retorted. "You will regret it bitterly. You are Grandmama's choice, and by God, I will have you."

Over by the main table, Papa appeared a trifle concerned. Mrs. Benton, guarding the dessert table, looked ready to leap across the room and pin Isaiah's ears back. Ophelia Oldbach and Michael were also watching, and old Mr. Bothey was frankly gawking.

"Excuse me," Dorcas said. "I am needed elsewhere." She wasn't needed anywhere—never had been—but surely she could find someplace else to be useful.

Isaiah grabbed her by the arm. "But, my darling," he said, declaiming as loudly as Mr. Garrick embarking on a Drury Lane soliloquy, "I offer you my heart, my hand, and my fortune, and you turn aside from me. Such cruelty from one so fair!" He sank to one knee, the rotter, Dorcas's hand again trapped in his. "Say you will marry me. Say you will make me the happiest man in all the world."

Mornebeth will try to ambush you, but you must stand fast. Reinforcements are at hand.

Reinforcements were *not* at hand, and the entire congregation was looking on with the sort of smiling indulgence a lovesick swain generally merited. Except that Isaiah Mornebeth was not lovesick, and he was not on his best day any sort of swain.

Dorcas twisted her wrist and extricated herself from Isaiah's grasp. "Do get up, Mr. Mornebeth. We all enjoy the occasional jest at St. Mildred's, but there's no need to make a complete cake of yourself."

His expression became mulish as he popped to his feet. "I am entirely in earnest, Dorcas Delancey. Think carefully before you cast me aside." His words held a thread of venom, and Michael and Papa were elbowing their way through the gawking crowd.

This was precisely how a lady was ruined. She caused talk and speculation. She aired the family's dirty linen in public. She spoke intemperately, and she *caused scenes*. But Dorcas hadn't caused this scene. She had not caused anything.

"If you have any pretensions to gentlemanly manners," she said, "you will apologize for your display and take your leave of this gathering."

"And what about ladylike pretensions?" Isaiah shot back. "What about the decorum and virtue expected of a vicar's daughter? What about temptation wielded like Eve's sharpest weapon upon the unsuspecting?"

Too late, Dorcas realized that Isaiah's ambush had been laid with more cunning than she'd seen. He'd goaded her on purpose, setting the stage for disclosures that would appear to be made in the heat of the moment. When he magnanimously offered for her again, to save the good name he himself had ruined, every member of St. Mildred's congregation would accord him great respect for his forgiving nature.

"Hush," Dorcas said. "You have bothered me for the last time, Isaiah Mornebeth." The urge to slap him, hard, repeatedly blossomed like that temptation he'd mentioned. He had wrought such harm, and with complete impunity.

The mood in the hall had shifted, though, from people good-naturedly enjoying a little romantic foolishness to watchful and alert.

"Marry me," Isaiah said, his tone positively gloating. "Marry me, and be grateful that I'm willing to make the offer."

Dorcas was grateful—for Alasdhair's steadfastness, for Melanie's example, for Michael's warning.

"You may go to perdition, Mr. Mornebeth. You have lied, manipulated, schemed, extorted, and abused my family's trust and good name for years. If your falsehoods and slander ruin me, so be it. I am exercising a lady's power to refuse the servitude you would inflict on me."

Michael winced, Papa looked dumbstruck, while Mrs. Oldbach—had this ever happened in the history of St. Mildred's?—was smiling.

A commotion near the door had heads turning.

"Best slink off quietly, laddie," Alasdhair said. "Miss Delancey was being polite."

At Alasdhair's side were a half-dozen women attired in what was doubtless their best finery.

"Who is he?" Mornebeth sneered. "And what are *those women* doing in a house of God?"

"I am Alasdhair MacKay," said the man himself as the crowd parted to allow him and the ladies to pass. "I am Miss Delancey's devoted servant, and these ladies claim a prior acquaintance with you, Mornebeth. I believe you know Miss Feeney and Miss Winklebleck, as well as Miss Saunders and Miss O'Keefe, for they are *intimately* familiar with you."

"Nan," Dorcas said, addressing the tallest of the women, "you are looking well. It's wonderful to see you again."

Nan winked at her. "Mighty fine to see you too, Miss Delancey. Major MacKay said the pinchin' preacher was getting airs above his station. The ladies and I don't take kindly to that behavior. We don't take kindly to a lot of his behaviors, if you get my drift."

She put her fists on her ample hips and glowered at the good folk of St. Mildred's, who had gone absolutely silent.

"Izzat you, Nanny Winklebleck?" Mr. Bothey called. "I sailed with your pa to the blasted American colonies. You're all grown up, and you have his nose."

"I have his fondness for a good meal too," Nan replied, "but I don't break bread with weasels." She turned that magnificent stare on Isaiah, who began sidling away from Dorcas.

"Neither do I," said Mrs. Oldbach.

"Nor will I," came from the Widow Merridew, who had emerged from behind the lectern.

"Away with you," Dorcas said, making a shooing motion. "You heard my friends. The women of St. Mildred's don't break bread with weasels."

Mornebeth bolted for the door.

Somebody—Alasdhair? Mrs. Oldbach? Michael?—began applauding, until the sound of rejoicing shook St. Mildred's venerable rafters.

"I MIGHT HAVE to marry Mrs. Oldbach," Alasdhair said, "after I marry Dorcas, of course. Those buns are magnificent." Not quite as magnificent as Dorcas delivering a long overdue set-down to the Mornebeth rodent.

"I already proposed to Mrs. O." Michael hefted his end of the table. "Turned me down flat. Said churchmen are a perishing lot of work, but to look her up when I retire." He and Alasdhair walked the table from the center of the hall to a place along the wall. "That's the last of it. Dorcas, am I excused?"

Dorcas had been quiet and busy as the fellowship meal had progressed. She had invited the ladies to stay for supper, and the congregation had risen to the challenge. Mrs. Merridew and Mrs. Oldbach had set the tone, and the rest of the flock had extended a gingerly, curious welcome.

Though Nan and her friends had sat at their own table and had left once their bellies had been filled. That bothered Alasdhair, to see them disappearing into the chilly night, probably returning to business as usual, but Dorcas's quiet bothered him more.

She gazed about the room with a critical eye. At this late hour, with shadows dancing against the vaulted ceiling, the chamber resembled a medieval great hall.

"We should retrieve Papa from his office," she said. "He's not to walk back to the vicarage on his own."

Mr. Delancey senior had retired to his office at the end of the evening with his sexton and curate, to *review a few matters relating to the grounds*.

"I'll fetch him." Alasdhair found the vicar sitting alone in a comfortably stuffy office, beeswax candles burning low, an empty glass in his hand.

"So you will never be a bishop," Alasdhair said. "You also won't have to watch your daughter go slowly mad married to Mornebeth. The hall has been put to rights, and Dorcas doesn't want you walking home alone."

Delancey rose and set his glass on the sideboard. "Her mother used to fuss at me for the same thing. Walking half the length of the street on my own."

"How much of that brandy have you had, sir?"

"Not nearly enough." He used a brass snuffer to douse the candles. "I have questions for you, MacKay."

"I know those ladies because they occasionally come to me for aid. I gather Dorcas met Big Nan in jail, and when I explained what was afoot, the ladies were eager to see justice done. They will swear out affidavits, testify in the church court, or send letters to Lambeth if called upon to do so."

Delancey shuffled from the office and closed the door. "Is that what happened? Justice was done?"

"You will have to take that up with your daughter. I thought she was wonderful."

Delancey's progress down the corridor was slow. "So did I. I always have."

"You might tell her that." More than that, Alasdhair would not say.

Michael Delancey was not simply a son to be proud of, he was spectacularly attractive, with a churchman's gravitas added to dark good looks and a shrewd, nimble intellect. The seriousness and intelligence that gave him depth served only to obscure Dorcas's equally impressive attributes.

She was every bit as smart, formidable, and attractive as her brother, but rather than respect, she reaped committee meetings, a reputation for eccentricity, and an ironic nickname.

Alasdhair was about to point out that particular injustice as the vicar sallied into the hall ahead of him. "Children, do we conclude the evening was a success?"

Alasdhair hung back, sensing that Mr. Delancey's question was an opening salvo of some sort.

"I do," Michael replied. "A good time was had by all, excepting perhaps the man who made my years in the north an exercise in self-imposed penury."

Dorcas occupied herself arranging several chairs before the hearth. "Michael, you need not revisit ancient history."

"Mayhap he does need to," Alasdhair replied from near the door. "Sometimes a fellow needs to unburden himself, and you will still love him dearly when he's had his say. Let's sit, shall we?"

She sent him a brooding, uncertain look. He took her hand and led her to a chair.

Michael ambled over to take a seat before the fire as well. "Come, Papa. You'd best hear this now, because Mornebeth will doubtless put about his own version of events."

The vicar perched on the edge of a chair, looking as if he'd rather be in darkest Peru without a canteen or compass.

"I was foolish," Michael said. "I came down from university too eager to acquire my Town bronze. I let Mornebeth lead me into one gaming hell after another. I lost my shirt, my sense, and my honor. Mornebeth bought up my vowels and kindly offered to hold them for me at five percent interest. He had me sign a promissory note. I did not realize at the time that by signing the note, I arguably converted unenforceable debts of honor into a contractual obligation."

Michael glanced at his father and sister. Neither said a word.

"I further did not realize," he went on, "that by asking me to sign such a note, Mornebeth offered me a grave insult. And finally, until I consulted Papa's solicitors last week, I did not know that a minor's signature on such a document is worthless—unless the minor continues to pay on the obligation into his majority, in which case the transaction can become legally binding. I did not realize much."

"He's why you went north?" the vicar asked. "So far from home and from temptation?"

"Mornebeth did not give me much of a choice," Michael said. "He strongly hinted, he implied, he did not quite threaten, but my options were clear. If I tarried around London, word of my intemperate behavior would become known. The last place I wanted to be was far from my family, but off I went, to where my wages would barely suffice for necessities. Mornebeth knew that would be the case."

Beside Alasdhair, Dorcas was sitting very still, her grip on his hand tight.

"Lady Phoebe alerted me to that parish in Yorkshire," the vicar said. "She allowed as how a newly ordained young man might want to try out his wings away from the paternal eye. She was sending Isaiah north and probably wanted you to serve as her spy."

Michael's brows drew down. "She wrote to me from time to time, always mentioning some sighting of you or Dorcas. I wrote back the usual platitudes. The weather, the church calendar. The Mornebeth apple did not fall far from the tree."

"But what do we do now?" Delancey murmured. "Mornebeth has a post waiting for him at Lambeth. He will not take kindly to having been shamed before an entire congregation, and Lady Phoebe wields considerable influence."

Bugger Mornebeth. Alasdhair silently shouted the words, but held his tongue because clearly, Dorcas had something to say.

"I'm sorry, Papa." She offered this apology, her gaze on the dying fire. "I have ruined your prospects for all time, haven't I?"

That was *not* what Alasdhair had hoped she would contribute to the discussion.

"A bishop's miter, you mean? My dear girl, I would miss St. Mildred's terribly. I thought if I gained a bishop's see..." He hunched forward, the picture of a tired old man. "I wanted you to be proud of me. I wanted your mother to be proud of me. To look down from her celestial perch and think, 'Well done, Tommy, and now you can properly dower our Dorcas.' I suspect she might have very different words for a father who loses track of not one but two children."

Alasdhair passed Dorcas his handkerchief and hoped he was lending her courage as well. *Tell him. Tell them both.*

Not because ancient business needed endless rehashing, but because Dorcas needed to know that she was as lovable to them as ever, perhaps more so, for having blundered in her own eyes out of loyalty to her family.

A silence stretched, and nobody—least of all Alasdhair—moved.

"Mama would not be very proud of me either," Dorcas said. "Mornebeth extorted money from Michael. Led him into debt, then used the debt against him. He told me Michael's debt would be forgiven and forgotten if I parted with something having a different sort of value. I could not see Michael ruined before he'd even taken his first post, and I did not want my papa..."

She fell silent. Michael swore in a most unholy manner.

"Daughter? Are you telling me Mornebeth *interfered* with you?"

"I was willing, Papa, in so far as I could be. I wanted my brother's debts forgiven. I wanted you to be preserved from disgrace. Mornebeth promised me discretion, but what fool trusts a man who'll put that sort of bargain to her?"

Delancey slumped back in his chair. "And all this time...? Merciful, everlasting... And you... And you... He..."

"I am sorry, Papa. I chose to fall in with Mornebeth's scheme. He was wrong to betray Michael's trust, and I made the whole situation worse."

"You most assuredly did not," the vicar retorted. "Mornebeth offered you a choice between trusting a scoundrel or betraying your brother. What sort of devil's bargain is that?"

Thank heavens Delancey grasped the fundamental issue.

"I could call the scoundrel out," Michael muttered. "I'd love to call him out. I grew very familiar with firearms living on the Dales."

"He's hoping you'll do just that," Dorcas said. "He will choose swords and allow you to wound him, then further blacken your name every time somebody asks about his scar. When you think decency or law will stay his hand, he finds a way to turn the moment to his advantage. I am just so sorry I ever... I am sorry. Michael has repaid his debts, and his behavior can be excused as youthful folly. My behavior, though, isn't something polite society will find any excuse for."

"And what of my behavior?" Delancey said. "My children preyed upon by a lying, thieving serpent in holy vestments, and I'm too busy parsing Leviticus to notice? If anybody has apologies to make, I do. You are my children, and if your dear mama left me with one commandment, it was to look after my children. Not the flock, not my prospects, but my children. In this, I have failed, and I humbly beg your pardon."

In Alasdhair's family, this same ground would have been covered with a few shouted oaths, a bout of fisticuffs, and some terse words from Finn or Papa, but the Delanceys weren't the MacKays. All must be earnest and proper, no fisticuffs allowed.

"Come to Scotland," Alasdhair said. "Get a fresh start in new surrounds. My family has plenty of room, and they know everybody."

"Scotland?" Michael put a world of bleakness into one word. "As in even farther north than Yorkshire?"

He made it sound as if Scotland were overrun by polar bears.

"I'll retire," Delancey said. "I'm old enough that nobody will question that decision."

Dorcas was looking considerably less remorseful and downtrodden, and about damned time.

"Miss Delancey," Alasdhair said, "what think you of coming to Scotland?" That solution was not ideal, because it left Isaiah Mornebeth kicking his heels at Lambeth Palace, doubtless hatching up worse schemes yet, but it was a solution Alasdhair could offer.

"That is very generous of you, Mr. MacKay, and yet, I am unwilling to cede the field to such an utter reprobate. I capitulated to Mornebeth's schemes years ago. Michael capitulated, Papa was hoodwinked, and now Mornebeth has breached the palace itself. I hope to see Scotland with you one day soon, but first, I would like the three of you to accompany me on a call tomorrow morning. The whole business wants—"

"Not the newspapers," Delancey moaned. "Please, Daughter, not the newspapers and not the *Charitable Circular*. As you say, Mornebeth will twist the recounting and paint himself the victim."

"He was already trying that tactic on," Michael said. "Implying that he was tempted from the path of virtue by a scheming seductress who barely knew how to put up her hair. Perhaps discretion is the better part of—"

"Hear her out," Alasdhair snapped. "For once in your saintly, gentlemanly lives, show Dorcas the basic manners you show each other and stop interrupting her."

Dorcas smiled at him faintly. "What's wanted is to render Mr. Mornebeth as powerless as he has always feared to become. What's wanted is for him and his family to bear the burden of his bad behavior, rather than me and mine. Be ready to go calling at ten of the clock."

"Hardly a polite hour," Delancey said. "But very well. Michael?"

"Of course I'll come."

"We are not calling at a polite hour," Dorcas replied, "because the reason for our outing wants discretion. Mr. MacKay, you will join us?"

Alasdhair adored seeing her in charge of the situation, assembling her honor guard, taking matters in hand. "I will come around in my town coach on the half hour. Wild unicorns could not stop me."

"Papa and Michael, you can see each other home. Mr. MacKay and I have more to discuss. Don't wait up for me."

Alasdhair expected her to have to shoo them off as she'd shooed off Mornebeth, but her father and brother were learning.

"Good night," Michael said. "MacKay, it's been interesting."

Delancey kissed Dorcas's cheek, nodded to Alasdhair, and fell in beside his son. "Mrs. Oldbach's buns were delicious, but I do believe Mrs. Benton's tarts were better."

"Both were absolutely delightful," Michael said as he closed the door to the corridor behind them.

Alasdhair eased his hand from Dorcas's. "Go on, then, ring a peal over my head. I upset your plans, I meddled, I did not respect your stated intentions. I'm most sorry for that."

"No, you are not. You are not sorry at all."

He waited, ready for her to pronounce him the worst bounder ever to bound from Scotland. "I'm not. Mornebeth was unbearable."

"But you never argue with a lady, Alasdhair. She gets to decide. Those are your eternal marching orders. What changed?"

Alasdhair mustered all of his courage and took the question seriously. What had changed? He'd explained to his cousins why he came to London every winter. They had listened.

He had seen Mornebeth for the sort of menace that could get good men killed and decent families ruined.

He had learned the depths of Mornebeth's hypocrisy and the intimate danger he posed to Dorcas.

"I wanted life to be simple," Alasdhair said slowly. "Follow orders, do my duty, and keep my honor bright, like some boy memorizing his proverbs. I wanted an answer that would always be the right one, in any circumstance, and 'never argue with a lady' fits that description."

"A commandment?"

"Something like that, but proverbs stitched on samplers are meant to hang on the walls of nurseries or be displayed in guest parlors. Life isn't a tidy little cautionary tale that such simple rubrics can always guide us. You told me not to interfere, but in my heart could not bear..."

He fell silent, and at some point, he'd taken Dorcas's hand, to which he now clung fiercely.

"Alasdhair?"

"My heart said to act. My heart said I had to try. If you are angry with me, I am sorry, but I've had the experience of being angry at myself, Dorcas, of being disappointed in myself. I did not go on as I ought in Badajoz. I took no issue with the actions of a superior officer who was behaving abominably. I did not stand up for my own honor or *think for myself.* I despise the man I'd be if I allowed your courage to absolve me of responsibility for that honor."

Alasdhair did not care for this maundering on about complicated, difficult matters either, but Dorcas had found words to explain her past to her father and brother. When the moment had arrived, she had not flinched from the truth. What fool had blathered on at such great lengths about the imperative need for honesty?

"I love you," he said, easing his fingers from her grasp. "I want to be worthy of your love in return. Allowing Mornebeth to force marriage on my beloved when a means of preventing that evil is at hand would make me unworthy. I cannot explain it any better than that. Let's blow out the candles, shall we, and I will walk you home."

He rose and began making a circuit of the room, extinguishing candles until only a single sconce remained lit. He'd known Dorcas would be angry with him, perhaps relieved and angry, but plenty furious enough. Men had been disrespecting her choices and her independence for years.

He'd taken a risk, bringing Big Nan and her friends into the church hall, confronting Mornebeth before the entire congregation. The reward was that Mornebeth had been sent packing, but at what cost?

CHAPTER NINETEEN

Dorcas rose, fatigue making her steps heavy, though the relief—the sparkling, soaring relief—of being free of Mornebeth made her heart light. Alasdhair stood by the lone candle flickering in the drafty hall, shadows dancing about him. He was clearly braced for a tongue-lashing, perhaps even for a rejection.

"Is it like this after a battle?" she asked, joining him in the candlelight. "You are nearly bewildered with gladness to be alive, and also ready to drop from exhaustion?"

Alasdhair took her cloak from a hook and draped it around her shoulders. "For some. But then you read the casualty lists and join the burial details, and the exhaustion wins. For a few moments, though, there's joy in victory, even in plain animal survival."

Dorcas held his coat for him. "We must see your gloves replaced, Mr. MacKay. The night is cold." She took down the plaid scarf and was about to wrap it about her own neck when she changed her mind and tucked it around Alasdhair's.

"My cloak has a decent collar," she said, "and that plaid looks good on you."

"Are you giving me back the only gift you've allowed me to give you?" A Highland winter would have been cozier than the tone of Alasdhair's question.

"I adore that scarf, and you will never get it back. I'm merely lending it to you, seeing to your comfort, as you so often see to mine. Are you hungry again yet?"

One side of his mouth quirked. "Soon. Dorcas, pronounce sentence on me, please. I presumed, I overstepped, I stuck my nose into a situation that was no longer my business."

"You told the truth, Alasdhair. Mornebeth had been presenting himself to the world as a rising ecclesiastical light when, in fact, he's been abusing streetwalkers and at least one vicar's family. His mischief probably encompasses more victims than we'll ever know. What you did was gather witnesses to attest to his wrongdoing."

Alasdhair blew out the last candle, which meant only a few shafts of moonlight illuminated the hall. "I gathered them in the church itself, with every beldame and codger in the congregation looking on. I hadn't meant to do that, but I was concerned..." He stood quite tall. "I was afraid Mornebeth would propose, and then you'd be trapped all over again."

Dorcas led the way to the side door. "Whereas I, once again, could not see that ambush in the making. He did propose, and if I had accepted his proposal, I'd have been doomed. A man who aspires to consign others to doom for his own gain is surely in the grip of evil."

The night was brisk and still, the churchyard quiet.

Alasdhair pulled the door closed. "Do we lock this door?"

Dorcas moved nearer to run her fingers over the lintel. She found the key and passed it to Alasdhair. "Locked in name only." She remained close to Alasdhair in the shadowed doorway while he locked the door and replaced the key. "Alasdhair?"

"My heart?"

She leaned into him and wrapped her arms around his waist. "You followed your heart when you came here this evening. I followed my heart, too, when I decided to accept Mornebeth's devil's bargain. I knew only that I was to protect my family, and I forgot entirely that they are also to protect me.

"I did my best," she went on. "I meant well. I can forgive that bewildered, overwhelmed girl, because she was doing the best she could. She has always done the best she could, and nobody notices that save you. My family loves me, and I love them, and we'll sort out the rest, but for my younger self, trying so hard to be brave and wise when every star was aligned against her, all I have now is compassion."

Alasdhair brushed the end of the scarf over her cheek. "Don't cry. Please, Dorcas. Ye break my heart..." He gathered her close and rested his cheek against her temple.

She did cry, for that wronged young girl, for her family, for the women who'd come to her rescue and then returned to London's cruel streets. She cried for relief and rage, and as Alasdhair held her, she cried as well for joy.

The battle was all but over, and she was in the arms of the man she loved.

"You followed your heart," she said when the tears had run their course. "That takes courage, and without courage, all the virtue in the world is only so many stitched samplers." She slipped an arm around his waist and walked him past the headstones gleaming in the moonlight.

"I am forgiven, Dorcas?"

"There is nothing to forgive, Alasdhair. There's only the man I love, doing the best he can, and a future we will sort out together."

Alasdhair tucked an arm around her shoulders and escorted her through the gate that opened onto the street. They would have parted, for Alasdhair turned one way and Dorcas the other, but she kept hold of his hand.

"My heart? The vicarage is this way."

"True, but our house is this way." She tugged on his hand, and with a low, thoroughly masculine laugh, he let her lead him home.

"THAT IS A KILT." Dorcas sounded both impressed and wary as she regarded Alasdhair standing on the walkway beside his coach.

She'd not been at all wary last night. She'd fed him a midnight snack, then shown him precisely how a couple celebrated their upcoming nuptials. To fall asleep with her in his arms had been sumptuous, to wake up and see her beside him had been the answer to his every prayer.

The words they'd exchanged in the darkened church hall, about compassion, forgiveness, and honor, had been difficult. The loving had been wordless, magnificent, and a new beginning. Alasdhair had walked Dorcas home in the chilly gray dawn a changed man. He was done with marching orders, commandments, and simple answers, except for the simple answer of loving Dorcas.

She, too, seemed to have risen in good spirits.

Not ready to take on the world as a warrior took on the world, perhaps, but ready to be her wonderful self and let the world make of her what it would. For today's outing, she'd dressed in pale blue, which set off the plaid scarf nicely.

"These are the clan colors," Alasdhair said. "They bring out my poetical blue eyes."

She walked a circle around him. "Gracious, Mr. MacKay, you do clean up nicely." She ran a hand over his jacket. "Aren't your knees cold?"

He caught her fingers in a snug grip. "When you touch me, no part of me is cold."

He'd made her smile, though it was the faint, in-public smile rather than the naughty, mister-you-are-in-such-trouble smile he'd won from her at midnight.

Michael and Thomas Delancey came down the vicarage steps, both looking quite sober in their collars.

"MacKay, good day." Delancey touched a finger to his hat brim.

"Dorcas says we're off to call on Lady Phoebe. Shall we be on our way?"

"Good morning, MacKay," Michael said, eyeing Alasdhair up and down. "Battle finery?"

"Those are the MacKay clan colors," Dorcas replied. "And I quite like seeing my intended in his national dress." Her smile acquired a hint of mischief, and Alasdhair knew what she was thinking: *I quite like seeing him in nothing at all too.*

Thank heavens he'd kept that special license.

Dorcas was not smiling when Lady Phoebe's butler ushered the party into an elegant, fussy guest parlor. Their hostess sat in an armchair upholstered in gold brocade, doubtless intended to look like a throne.

Alasdhair was introduced, and though he'd not encountered Lady Phoebe before, he pegged her for a tough old general, despite the luxury of her surroundings. She had the biddy hen's watchful, beady eyes and the casual imperiousness of a woman accustomed to getting her way.

"Miss Delancey, you come with a veritable delegation. Are you here at such an early hour to beg funds for one of your charitable undertakings?"

The question was equal parts pleasant and rude. Dorcas, seated to Alasdhair's right, her brother on her other side, appeared unruffled.

"Why, no, my lady. We are here to discuss your eldest grandson, and as charitable projects go, I'm sure he will soon enough be begging funds of you. More funds."

Lady Phoebe's gaze went cold. "Thomas Delancey, if you permit your daughter to speak to me thus, I must question your fitness to hold the living at St. Mildred's."

That didn't take long.

"Must you really?" Delancey replied, his tone politely ironic. "I suggest you hear my daughter out."

"We come to offer you a solution to a problem caused by your oldest grandson," Dorcas began. "When I was seventeen, he inveigled my brother, who was still a minor himself, into accumulating sizable gambling debts. Isaiah bought up the vowels and agreed to hold them for Michael, provided a promissory note was signed and five percent interest paid."

"Then Thomas Delancey raised a foolish young man," Lady Phoebe retorted, "and because that foolishness has nothing to do with me, I will have my butler show you out." She reached for the bell-pull as Dorcas resumed speaking.

"Your grandson promised me he'd forgive Michael's debts if I allowed Mr. Mornebeth three instances of intimate congress with me. I was innocent, just out of the schoolroom, and determined to protect my family, though—predictably, as it turns out—Mr. Mornebeth did not forgive the debts. Do you contend that the Delanceys are a foolish, profligate, intemperate family much given to vice and self-indulgence and that they victimized your blameless grandson by repaying his loan with interest and bestowing carnal favors upon him at his insistence?"

Lady Phoebe was no longer reaching for the bell-pull.

"Mr. MacKay," Dorcas said, "if you would take up the narrative."

"Cast all the aspersions on the Delanceys you can," Alasdhair said. "False aspersions, of course, and try to blame them for your grandson's schemes if you must. That will not change the fact that Isaiah Mornebeth importunes streetwalkers, mistreats them, and has been seen kicking beggars and urinating on them. He is the nastiest kind of bully, a disgrace to the Church, and worse yet, a disgrace to his family. His behaviors have been witnessed by many, and every one of his victims is prepared to condemn him publicly. I can enumerate their observations, if you like, with dates, time of day, and location."

Powell's old men had supplied those last bits, for which Alasdhair had promised Mornebeth would pay dearly.

"And lest you think we are bluffing," Dorcas added, "Mrs. Ophelia Oldbach was present at St. Mildred's fellowship meal last evening. She heard Mr. Mornebeth referred to as the 'pinching preacher' by no less than four witnesses, while half my father's congregation looked on. Mr. Mornebeth was present. Nobody doubted the testimony against him, and he decamped at a run rather than refute the charges."

Lady Phoebe looked at her hands, which were soft, pale, and sporting a total of five rings, each more valuable than the next. If she struggled with the temptation to defend her grandson, the struggle was brief and silent.

"I sent him north to get him away from London," she said. "I have opened every possible door for him, made sure he wanted for nothing, and this is the thanks I get."

Dorcas rose. "You showed him, over and over again, that he would never be held to account for his many bad deeds. You supported him, you rewarded his vile behavior with opportunity. You are not the victim, my lady. You have other grandchildren, but you chose to make the worst of the lot your heir, a fact he mentions with unfailing regularity. You are complicit in his wrongs, and you will cease that complicity now."

"He's the smartest of the lot," Lady Phoebe said tiredly. "He'd look after the others, for appearances' sake if nothing else."

"He's so smart," Alasdhair said, "that he thinks he can abuse women with nothing left to lose, prey on a vicar's children, and disrespect injured soldiers on the very street, as if those people aren't entitled to basic human dignity. Never was a man such a fool, Lady Phoebe."

She rubbed her fingers across her forehead. "I'll send him away. Back north, perhaps. Find him a little congregation where he can't get into much trouble."

Dorcas resumed her seat. "You think only of him and of the fact that he might well end up in jail for crimes he has committed thus far with impunity. Assault, extortion, blackmail, and worse. I know women who face transportation simply because a shopkeeper accused them of stealing—no proof, no witnesses, just a man's word against theirs—and those women are ripped from home and family to face deprivations without number. You will not inflict your grandson on some unsuspecting rural parish."

"Fine, then I'll warn those in charge of him at Lambeth, and they'll keep a close eye on him."

Dorcas leveled a stare at Lady Phoebe. "He will leave the Church. He will leave the country. He will subsist on an allowance determined by my father and brother and paid by you, and he will receive that money only so long as he maintains good behavior. A breath of scandal, a brush with the law... If he so much as curses at a stray dog, he will be cut off. Are we agreed?"

Lady Phoebe looked honestly bewildered. "He will never agree to those terms."

"He will face a choice," Thomas Delancey said. "He can cling to his lies and to your skirts, in which case he will be held up to generations of aspiring churchmen as the ultimate bad example, or he can for once think of his family's standing. If he's as smart as you believe him to be, he'll quietly put off his collar and discreetly slip away. I'm sure your powers of persuasion are sufficient to help him make the right choice. Shall we be going?"

Michael was on his feet. "Lady Phoebe, good day, and good luck."

"But you cannot... You leave Isaiah no choice at all. He's ruined either way. On remittance in some foreign land or defrocked and disgraced in his homeland."

Alasdhair got to his feet and offered Dorcas his hand. "We could doubtless arrange for both. Public disgrace at the hands of the bishops and transportation to Botany Bay. There's a curious loyalty among the constables to the ladies plying the street trade. Assaulting a streetwalker still qualifies as assault. The charges alone would cause an ocean of talk. I understand false imprisonment might apply, and Miss Delancey is prepared to announce Mornebeth's perfidy toward her to the world."

Dorcas rose. "Indeed, I am, starting with the *Charitable Circular* and moving on to the London papers. I will also make it plain that you knew of Isaiah's crimes against me and my family and sought to protect him by having him marry the woman he'd treated so ill in the past."

Alasdhair had been taught to respect the elderly, but he would have enthusiastically tossed Lady Phoebe out the window in that moment.

"She *knew*?" Alasdhair asked very softly.

Lady Phoebe examined her rings. "I hear much, and Miss Delancey was seen calling several times at my residence when I was away from Town. I know my grandson, and the best I could do was get him out of London for a time. A wife cannot testify against her husband, and Miss Delancey has become formidable. She is a suitable match, up to Isaiah's weight. Isaiah isn't awful, and... it was the best I could do."

"Isaiah," Dorcas replied, "is beyond awful. He's vile and dangerous. He excels at driving others to make impossible choices. You were given a choice between protecting an innocent girl or guarding your family's reputation. You made the wrong choice, given what your grandson is, but you can do something about that now."

Lady Phoebe left off studying her rings long enough to glower at Dorcas. "Begone with you. I will deal with Isaiah, and he will be much improved for some extended travel."

"A decade of extended travel at a minimum," Dorcas said, "because he has been preying on the innocent for at least that long."

Lady Phoebe looked like she wanted to argue the length of the sentence, but the door opened, and Isaiah himself marched into the room, followed by a pink-faced butler.

"I'm sorry, my lady," the butler said. "Mr. Mornebeth refused to wait in the family parlor."

"My lady." Isaiah offered his grandmother a deep bow. "I hope you haven't been listening to the scurrilous accusations from these, these—"

"Hush," Dorcas said. "Your grandmother is changing her will. You will listen to what she has to say, and *you will not interrupt her*."

A brief, complicated look passed between Lady Phoebe and Dorcas.

"Miss Delancey has the right of it," Lady Phoebe said. "I am changing my will, and you, sir, are changing your ways."

Dorcas slipped her hand around Alasdhair's arm. "No need to see us out, my lady. You clearly have family matters to discuss."

Mornebeth drew himself up into the picture of outraged propriety. "You cannot come to my grandmother's house, casting aspersions on the Mornebeth name, making baseless—"

Alasdhair permitted himself a wee display of temper, mostly for show, but not entirely. He grasped Mornebeth by the neckcloth and gave him a gentle, teeth-rattling shake.

"To use words you might comprehend, Mornebeth: *Mene, mene, tekel upharsin.* You cannot bluff, manipulate, slander, lie, or cheat your way out of this. Show some damned dignity for once and listen to your granny."

Dorcas looked at Alasdhair as if he'd just promised her the whole of Scotland as her personal demesne. "The book of Daniel," she said. "Chapter five, Belshazzar's feast."

Mornebeth appeared baffled.

"A slight paraphrase," Michael Delancey said. "Your schemes are at an end, you have been weighed in the balance and found wanting, and your cousins are likely to inherit in your place. Think of them as the Medes and Persians, if you want to get biblical about it."

They left Mornebeth gaping like the fool that he was and proceeded to the tea shop, where Dorcas had both cinnamon and nutmeg with her hot chocolate, and Mr. Delancey pronounced the hot cross buns nearly as good as Ophelia Oldbach's—but not as tasty as Mrs. Benton's tarts.

~

ALASDHAIR'S COUSINS both stood up with him at the wedding, Michael presided, and Papa escorted Dorcas up the aisle of St.

Mildred's. Mrs. Merridew, Mrs. Benton, and Mrs. Oldbach had helped her dress for the occasion and sat in the front pew, smiling as if they each personally had brought the bride and groom together.

Doubtless they were enjoying the sight of Alasdhair in his clan finery almost as much as Dorcas was.

When Michael began the actual wedding service, a heavily veiled woman in lavender—possibly half-mourning?—slipped into the back of the church to sit next to Henderson, Mrs. Lovelace, Timmens, and baby John. For reasons Dorcas did not understand, the bishop of London and Mr. Zachariah Ingleby were present as well, sitting with Papa and gazing benevolently at all and sundry.

The vows were spoken, though to Dorcas, the promise in Alasdhair's eyes was all the assurance she needed to spend the rest of her life with him. The presuming wretch kissed her when Michael pronounced them man and wife, and so Dorcas had to kiss him back.

Michael cleared his throat, the ladies beamed more fiercely, and Dorcas took a somewhat dazed new husband by the hand and escorted him down the aisle.

"You enjoyed that," Alasdhair muttered as they waited on the church steps for the rest of the assembly. "You enjoyed stealing m' wits before your friends."

"You didn't enjoy it?"

The day was unseasonably balmy, or perhaps Dorcas was so thoroughly swaddled in her husband's love that she'd never be cold again.

"Did I enjoy it?" Alasdhair asked, peering at a clump of newly blooming daffodils along the walkway. "I hardly know, Mrs. MacKay. Do it again and help me make up my mind."

"No whispering sweet nothings, Mr. MacKay," Mrs. Oldbach said, coming down the steps. She had Papa by one arm. Mrs. Benton had him by the other. "You are a married man now."

"Correct you are, ma'am," Alasdhair replied. "When I whisper to my lady now, I'm no longer limited to sweet nothings."

Colonel Goddard smacked him on the shoulder for that, and Mrs. Merridew, for perhaps the first time in a year, laughed outright.

The wedding breakfast at the vicarage had been prepared by Ann Goddard and was almost too pretty to eat. Dorcas made Alasdhair eat anyway.

"You are afraid I will swoon?" he asked between bites of fruit quiche.

"You do not swoon," Dorcas replied as Papa began regaling the guests with the story about that time a very young Michael climbed the steeple in an effort to see to America. "You grow a bit lightheaded when you neglect your tummy. I am more concerned that you will need to keep up your strength."

Alasdhair lifted a glass of champagne—Goddard's finest—and winked at her. "As you will, Mrs. MacKay."

How she loved it when he called her that. "I suppose this means I'm no longer Miss Delightful."

"Would you like a new *nom de guerre*? Mrs. Delight*ed*, for example?"

"I heard that," Captain Powell said. "Time for Goddard to start the toasts."

The toasts were by turns sentimental, funny, and sincere, but eventually, the guests were taking their leave, and it was time for Dorcas to bid her father farewell.

"Before you go," Papa said, "take a turn in the garden with me. I must clear my head after all those toasts."

Now Papa wanted to take a turn in the garden with her? Well, perhaps that was the beginning of a new tradition, and Dorcas hadn't the heart to refuse him.

"I'll be a moment," she said as Alasdhair held her chair.

"Take as long as you need," he replied. "As long as *you* need, Dorcas. Not as long as *he* needs." Alasdhair softened that admonition with a wink and was still chatting with his cousins when Dorcas returned from her garden constitutional.

She eventually realized Alasdhair was waiting for her to choose the moment to depart, while she'd been... marveling at the pleasure of becoming his wife. She approached him, wrapped an arm around his waist, and seized on the next lull in the conversation.

"Mr. MacKay, not to be rude, but I believe I'm ready to go home. The day has been long and lovely, and I would have you all to myself."

Colonel Goddard saluted her. "MacKay, you have your orders."

"I have my heart's delight," Alasdhair said. "Come, my dear. We will slip away while Goddard creates a distraction. He's good at that."

Just like that, Dorcas was seated beside Alasdhair in his town coach—a silly indulgence, given the lovely weather—and rolling away from the vicarage.

"You don't want to take one last look?" Alasdhair asked, looping an arm around her shoulders.

"We aren't leaving Town until next week, and Papa will bide at the vicarage for some time to come. He's been offered a post at Lambeth Palace."

"I hear they have a vacancy. When does he start?"

Dorcas settled against her husband and fought the urge to close her eyes. "He doesn't. He turned them down. He wants to see if he can expand my sister-parish scheme, and he said he would miss St. Mildred's if he went to the palace. He allowed as how he would also miss Mrs. Benton rather a lot."

"Spring comes to the vicarage. Do you mind?"

"Alasdhair, I am so relieved... I don't think Papa ever truly wanted to be a bishop. He just wanted Michael and me to be proud of him, and didn't realize we always have been. Never did a family muddle along with as many good intentions and misguided efforts as the Delanceys."

"God be thanked, you are a MacKay now, Mrs. Delighted. Or maybe we should call you Mrs. Magnificent. You should sign your articles that way. That will make me Mr. Magnificent. When we are private, you may refer to me thus, particularly when you behold me as the Creator made me."

"Colonel Goddard's champagne is heady stuff."

"Marriage to you is headier, Dorcas MacKay."

"I like that better," she said, snuggling closer. "Not delightful, delighted, magnificent, or anything fancy. Just plain Mrs. Dorcas MacKay. That is all the magnificent delight I need. You, our John, a home of our own."

Alasdhair pulled down the shades. "Shall I tell the coachman to take a turn in the park on the way home, Mrs. MacKay?"

"I think not. I think we should go straight home, look in on John, then have a nice nap, and enjoy our first marital interlude."

"I am wed to a genius. And then you will wake up, remind me to have a snack, and begin work on your next brilliant article?"

Dorcas ran a hand over the wool of Alasdhair's kilt. "I might put off starting that article until tomorrow. Today strikes me as a day for two marital interludes back to back, or front to front, as it were."

Alasdhair hugged her. "Remind me to keep a supply of Goddard's love potion on hand. Very well. Two marital interludes. I will somehow bear up manfully under the strain."

He *bore up* quite well, and though Dorcas never again had to endure any gratuitous nicknames, married life with Alasdhair MacKay was, indeed, beyond delightful!

Made in the USA
Las Vegas, NV
25 June 2022

50709808R00167